THE STO[illegible]
VEYLIN[illegible]

BOOK 2:
THE PROPHET AND THE WAYZENMOOT

SUE WOOLLEY

SCIMITAR

EDGE

Published by Scimitar Edge

An imprint of Purple Unicorn Media

ISBN 978-1-915692-94-8

Cover design by Allister Nelson

www.scimitaredge.com

Dedication

For David – thank you for your
inspiration,
support and insights.

Author's Note

The following symbols have been used in chapter headings, to indicate the places they are set, or the peoples they concern. Their deeper meaning will become clear in the course of reading.

† Earth
Δ Talamdor
֍ The Commonweal of Veylindré

End Contents

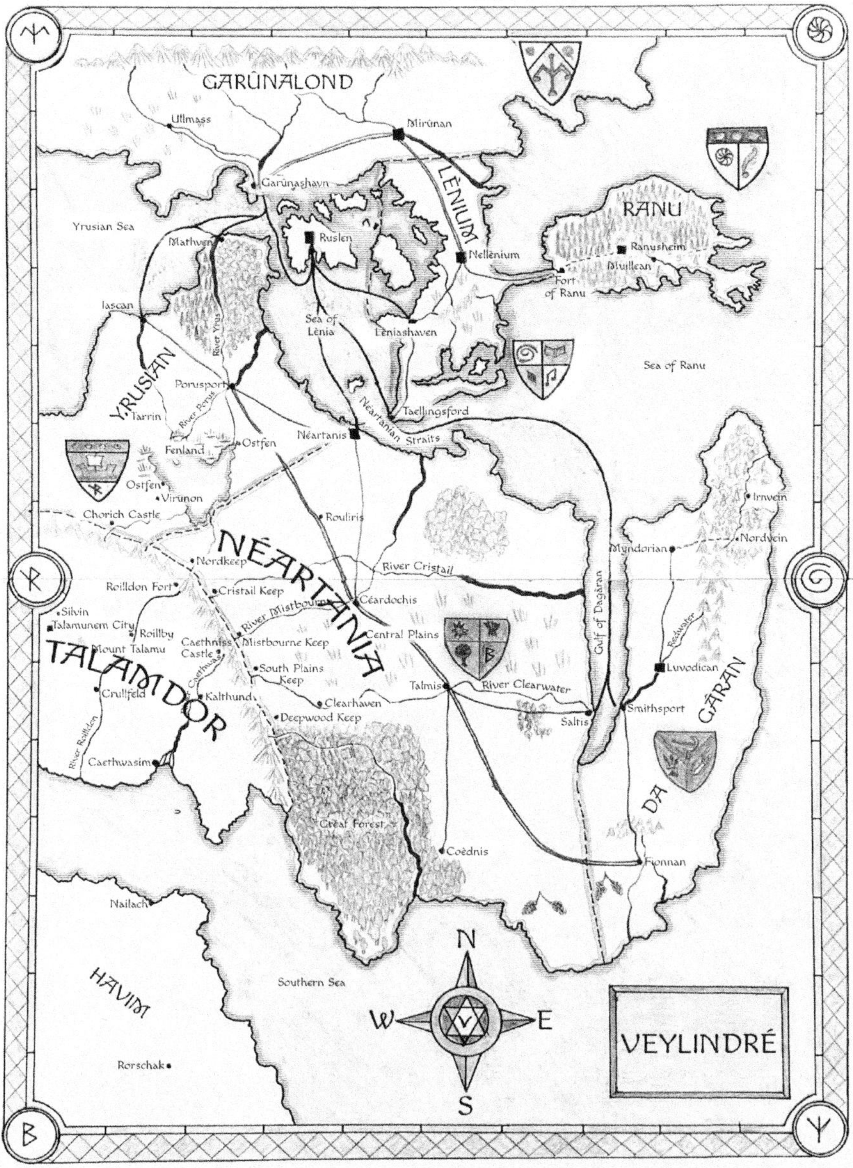
GARÛNALOND
Ullmass
Mirûnan
Garûnashavn
LÊNIUM
RANU
Yrusian Sea
Mathven
Ruslen
Nellenium
Ranusheim
Muillean
Fort of Ranu
Iascan
Sea of Lênia
Lêniashaven
River Yrus
YRUSIAN
Porusport
Sea of Ranu
Tarrin
River Porus
Taellingsford
Néartanian Straits
Néartanis
Fenland
Ostfen
Ostfen
Virunon
Chorich Castle
Rouliris
Irnvein
NÉARTANIA
Nordkeep
Myndorian
Nordvein
River Cristail
Roilldon Fort
Cristail Keep
Céardochis
Silvin
Talamunem City
Roillby
River Mistbourne
Central Plains
Mount Talamu
Caethniss Castle
Mistbourne Keep
Gulf of Dagâran
TALAMDÔR
South Plains Keep
Luvodican
Talmis
River Clearwater
Crullfeld
Kalthund
Clearhaven
Smithsport
Saltis
Deepwood Keep
GÂRAN
River Roilldon
Caethwasim
DA
Great Forest
Coêdnis
Fionnan
Nailach
HAVIM
Southern Sea
N
W
E
S
VEYLINDRÉ
Rorschak

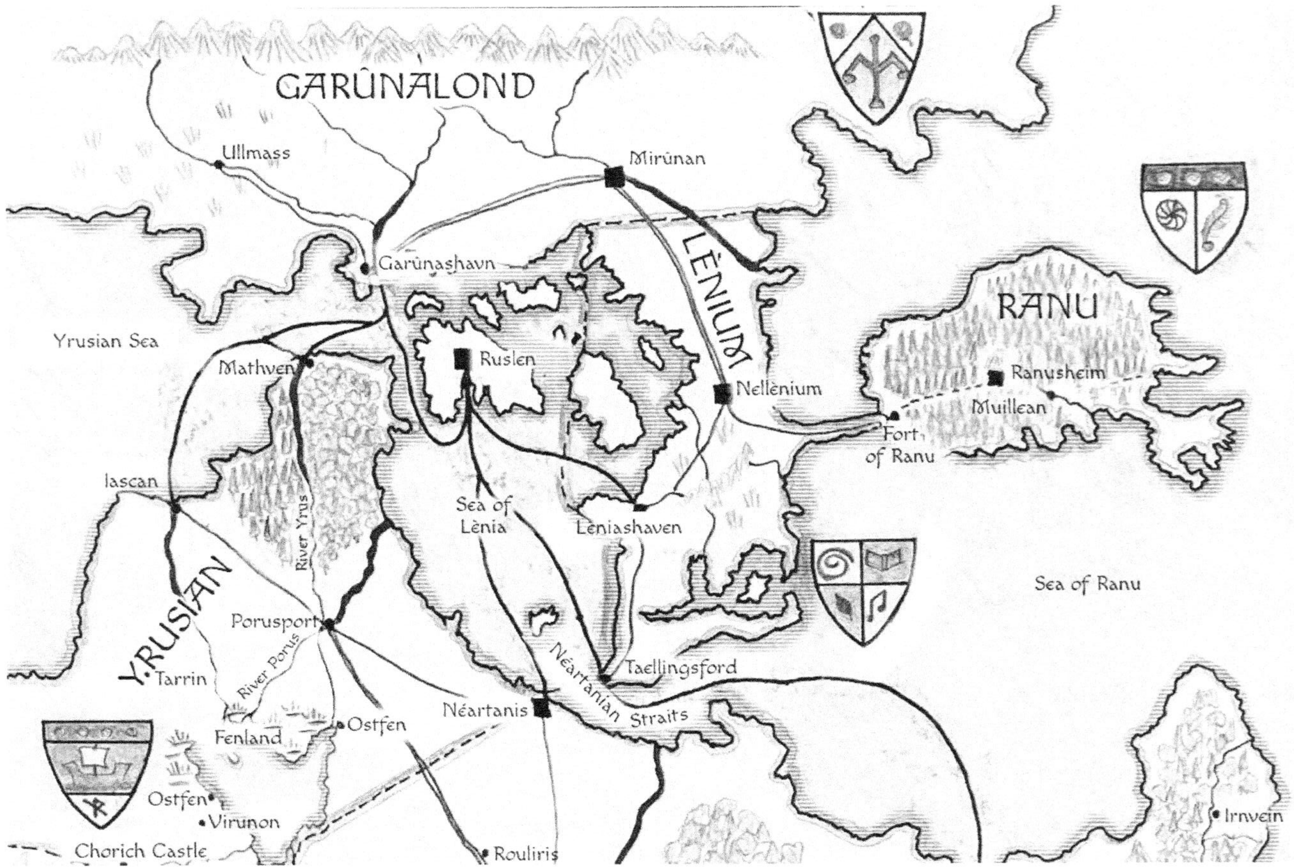
GARÛNALOND
Ullmass
Mirûnan
Garûnashavn
Yrusian Sea
LÈNIUM
RANU
Ruslen
Mathven
Nellènium
Ranusheim
Muillean
Fort of Ranu
Iascan
Sea of Lènia
Lèniashaven
River Yrus
Sea of Ranu
Y.RUSIAN
Porusport
River Porus
Tarrin
Taellingsford
Néartanian Straits
Néartanis
Fenland
Ostfen
Ostfen
Virunon
Chorich Castle
Rouliris
Irnvein

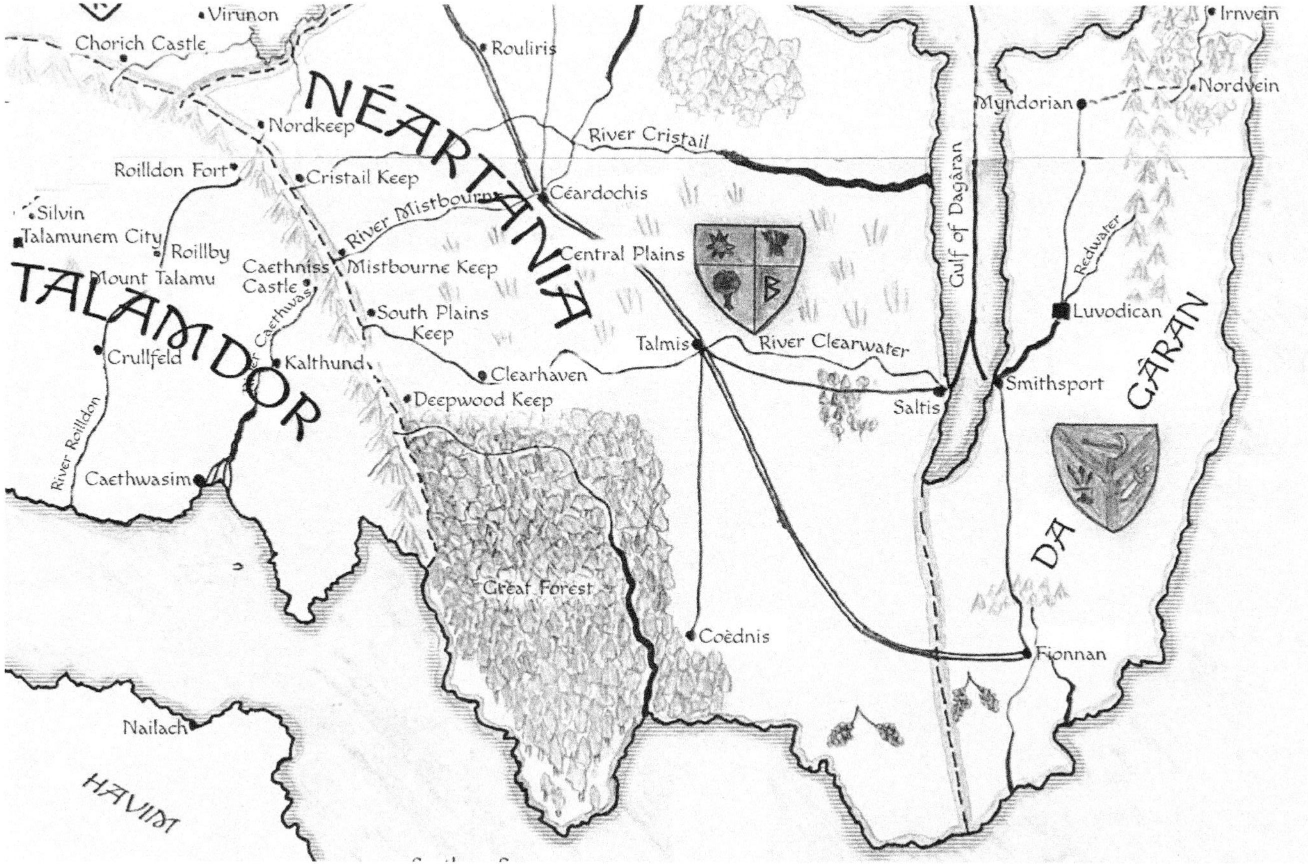

Virunon
Chorich Castle
NÉARTANIA
Rouliris
Irnvein
Nordvein
Myndorian
Nordkeep
River Cristail
Roilldon Fort
Cristail Keep
Céardochis
Silvin
Talamunem City
Roillby
River Mistbourne
Caethniss Castle
Mistbourne Keep
Central Plains
Mount Talamu
TALAMDOR
South Plains Keep
Crullfeld
Kalthunds
Talmis
River Clearwater
Clearhaven
Deepwood Keep
Saltis
Smithsport
Luvodican
Redwater
Gulf of Dagáran
DA GÁRAN
River Roilldon
Caethwasim
Great Forest
Coèdnis
Fionnan
Nailach
HAVIM

The story so far…

In April 1665, Abigail Winters and her family begin a journey to the New World, because her father, Presbyterian pastor Thomas Winters, is being persecuted by the government. On the way, there is a terrific storm, and at its height there is a green flash, and the ship is translated to a new world.

After they land on the east coast of Dagâran, Abigail and her boyfriend, Jacob Wallingford, are sent to seek a source of fresh water. When they return, the rest of the settlers have been massacred by pirates. There are also bodies of three strangers, whom Jacob searches. He finds a triangular, red stone in a red buckskin pouch around the neck of one of them. They burn the bodies of their friends to give what respect they can, then set off through the neighbouring forest to find help.

Two young people from Nordvein, Aidren and Ellyn, come across them and realise Abigail and Jacob are not from Veylindré because they have no Waymark on their foreheads.

Back in Nordvein, they meet the Waymage, Shaunan, who becomes their mentor and guide. They show her the red stone and Shaunan recognises it as a Bloodstone. She warns them to keep it secret. Shaunan decides they need to be taken to Luvodican, the capital city of Dagâran, to be taught about the Way, and Aidren and Ellyn accompany them to gain some experience of the wider world. After some adventures, the five of them arrive in Luvodican and First Waymage Marinden allows them to lodge in the Visitors' Hall of the Temple. Abigail's and Jacob's learning begins – about the lands and peoples of the Commonweal of Veylindré and about the Way – the religious/magic system of this world, which is accessed by using Goldstones. Aidren and Ellyn continue their training as a warrior and a cordwainer respectively.

In the meantime, Portak, an agent of the Prophet of the One, ruler of Talamdor, has been despatched to find out if there were any survivors from the Havimi attack.

Abigail settles down well, apart from grieving for her family, but Jacob finds it harder to accept the Way, which has six goddesses, so different to Christianity. He is apprenticed to Master Kalen, a smith, which helps somewhat. Abigail is mentored by Shaunan, who realises she has special gifts. Shaunan resolves to take Abigail and Jacob to Ranusheim, the spiritual capital of all Veylindré.

At the Festival of Dagârastide, Abigail and Jacob undergo the Ceremony of Assignment and receive their Waymarks. Jacob's is Dagâran, as befits a smith. Abigail's is Ranusian, which means that one day, she could become a Waymage herself.

The five of them visit the rulers of Dagâran and learn that Havimi pirates have been sighted in the Gulf of Dagâran, so they decide to take the overland route to Ranusheim, through Néartania and Lènium. Ylonya, an Yrusian guide, joins the company.

After they have reached Talmis, a town in south-eastern Néartania, Shaunan takes them to the local temple to participate in worship. After the service, Jacob bolts. Aidren follows him and Jacob shares some of his struggles with the Six.

When Aidren leaves Jacob alone for a couple of minutes, he is abducted by Portak.

Abigail is distraught about Jacob's disappearance. When Ylonya fails to find him, Shaunan tells her that the only way to discover where he has gone is to ask the High Waymages at Ranusheim.

Jacob wakes up on a boat on the River Clearwater. His recent memories (since his arrival in Veylindré) have been wiped by Portak, whom he now sees as his only friend. He has even forgotten Abigail, except in dreams.

The company travels to Céardochis, a big trading centre in Néartania, then on to Néartanis, the capital.

Jacob and Portak cross the Talamdorian Mountains using a secret pass. As they continue their journey towards Talamunem City, Jacob learns a little about Talamdor.

Just outside Néartanis, the company is attacked by three strangers and although Ylonya and Aidren win the fight, both are injured.

now read on…

Chapter 1

When Abigail found Ellyn, she was sitting with her back against a tree, her head on her knees, her hands clamped tightly over her face. Abigail sat down carefully beside her, put a hand on one arm.

"Ellyn, my friend, what is grieving you?"

A head shake and the sound of a sob escaping clenched teeth. Abigail sat, waiting in silence for Ellyn to be ready to share whatever was on her heart. It was the only gift she could give her friend.

Eventually, Ellyn raised her head, took her hands away from her face, to reveal it puffy with crying. Abigail put one arm around her shoulders.

"Ellyn, dear one, what is troubling you?"

"Oh, Abi," Ellyn said, horror and loathing filling her voice, "I killed a man – a real person, just like me." She shuddered. "If you'd asked me earlier today whether I could take an axe and drive it into someone's head, I'd have thought you were mad. Yet it turns out I was capable. When I saw that man hurting Aidren, I snatched up that axe and…"

She paused as the tears flowed down her cheeks, biting down savagely on her lower lip. Abigail hugged her close and the younger girl clung to her. Images of an axe cleaving the man's skull were bursting from her. Abigail wasn't trying to use her new gifts, but she had only had to touch Ellyn and could somehow read her mind.

"Ellyn, listen to me," she said, gently but firmly. "You had no choice. If you hadn't – done what you did, Aidren would be dead. And I know that if it had been Jacob, or Shaunan or you, I would have done the same."

Ellyn's head came up off Abigail's shoulder. "Really? You would have done the same? You promise me that's true?"

Abigail took a deep breath before answering. "Yes, I swear it, by the Six and the Way."

"And you're a Ranusian initiate, so you can't lie," Ellyn said, clearly comforted. "Thank you, Abi, that helps."

Abigail hugged her again. "Shaunan will be able to heal Aidren, I'm sure of it," she said.

But her mind was reeling in surprise. 'You're a Ranusian initiate, so you can't lie.' She had never sworn by the Six before, except at the Ceremony of Assignment, and was stunned by how naturally it had come. Maybe she truly belonged in this world now.

After an uneasy night's sleep, Abigail was woken by the light of the morning sun on her face. For a moment, she could not understand why they were sleeping outside, then memory came flooding back. They had been attacked by Talamdorian agents, who were searching for her. Another had already found Jacob. Ylonya and Aidren had been injured. And if Ellyn hadn't killed the man trying to kill Aidren, he would have died. She bolted up out of her blankets and went to find Shaunan.

"You must help me to spy out the land," Shaunan said. "We will take it in turns to keep our minds open along the way."

"How are Ylonya and Aidren?" Abigail asked.

"Ylonya's throat is sore, as you might expect, and I am worried about Aidren's eye. We will need to find shelter in Néartanis, so I can treat it again."

Abigail was more concerned about Ellyn. Her friend had tossed and turned half the night, sometimes crying out in her sleep. But she didn't want to worry Shaunan.

Néartanis was an imposing city, as befitted the capital of all Néartania. Its limestone walls were wide and high, with tall gates of bronze set in them at intervals, to serve the many roads that led there. As Abigail rode through the crowded streets, lined with shops, houses and taverns, she kept her mind wide open. Everyone around her looked so innocent – ordinary citizens on ordinary errands, and swaggering sailors, clad in Yrusian ultramarine blue, with gold glinting in their earlobes and on their fingers. But then again, their attackers had looked like Garûnan Watchmen – she had learned by bitter experience that appearances could be deceptive.

Gulls were wheeling in the air above them, filling it with their strident calls, and among the more familiar smells of beasts and people, she could catch a hint of the clean, salt scent of the sea. Of course. She had forgotten that Néartanis was on the coast.

"What are we going to do next?" Ellyn asked.

"Ylonya will find somewhere safe for us to stay," Shaunan replied in a low voice, "then she and Aidren will go down to the wharf to book a passage on the next ship across the Néartanian Straits tomorrow morning. In the meantime, no-one must go out alone. Keep a good look out all around you and speak to no stranger."

Ylonya glanced up at this, then brought her horse alongside Shaunan's and spoke to her in an undertone. Abigail could sense Shaunan's startled reaction. What was Ylonya saying? Then the Waymage nodded.

"Follow me," Ylonya said. She led them through narrow streets and alleys, taking a convoluted route, doubling back on herself. Surely they wouldn't be followed now? She took them down another narrow street, piled high with refuse. Abigail wrinkled her nose. She hoped Ylonya knew what she was doing. Then the Yrusian halted, swung down off her horse, and gestured to the rest of them to do the same. She led them round the back of a tall house with shuttered windows and a general air of dilapidation. "Leave the horses here but bring your packs."

Aidren and Ellyn looked as mystified as Abigail felt, but Shaunan said, "Do as she says."

Shouldering their packs, they followed Ylonya as she took out her Goldstone, put her other hand on the door and muttered something. It opened silently, but they could see no-one within. "Wait here," she said. "I must speak to Kendris."

The room she had left them in was dark and gloomy, with shuttered windows and a dank smell of disuse. Shaunan held up her Goldstone, murmured, *"Gal lo bynn leumin"* and made light. The warm, yellow glow from her Goldstone lit up a bare space. There was no furniture, and the floorboards were old and poorly set – a cold draught was whistling up through them. The room had two doors, the one they had come in through, and another, through which Ylonya had disappeared. The youngsters clustered round her and she could sense their unease.

"Fear not," she said. "Ylonya has a plan which will allow us to travel to Lènium undetected."

"Who is this Kendris she has gone to see?" Aidren asked.

"I suspect he is the Guild's agent in Néartanis. If she can persuade him to help us, we will be safe."

"But how can we leave here without being seen?" Ellyn said. "Any ship or boat we take will mean going down to the harbour, where anyone might see us."

Shaunan could hear the strain in Ellyn's voice. She was afraid Ylonya's planned route would test the girl's endurance to its limit.

"Do not fret," she said. "You know we can trust Ylonya."

Abigail stepped up and put her arm round the younger girl. "I'm sure it will all work out."

Then Ylonya re-entered the room, followed by a tall, tanned Yrusian with a long, jagged scar on his right cheek. "This is Kendris. He has agreed let us use the secret passage."

"Secret passage?" Aidren repeated. "How will that help us leave Néartanis? And what about the horses?"

"You will see, young man," Kendris said in a gruff voice. "I will care for your mounts. They could not go where you will be going. Bring your packs with you."

Shaunan soothed Aidren's distrust, then said, "Thank you, Kendris. Lead on."

They followed him back through the inner door, then down a long flight of narrow stairs, lit only by her Goldstone and those of Abigail, Ylonya, and Kendris, in the lead. As they descended, the air got colder and damper. Shaunan devoutly hoped this plan would work. They came out into a broad cave, carved out of the bedrock under Néartanis. Its walls glittered with mica. There was a metal door set in one wall, in the centre of which was an engraved Yrusian sigil.

"Where are we?" Ellyn asked.

"Under the harbour," Kendris said, his voice echoing in the space. "This entrance is only known to a few. Do not betray my trust by revealing it to any other."

"We will not," Ylonya said. "My thanks, Kendris. Please let Mistress Margera know where we have gone, and about the attack."

"I will," Kendris said, a crooked smile on his scarred face. "May the Way guard and guide you all."

"Thank you, Kendris," Shaunan said. "The Wayzenmoot is in your debt. May the Way be with you also."

The man nodded at her, then strode across to the door, his Goldstone in his hand, muttering under his breath. It opened and Kendris gestured them through. Then closed the door behind them with a clang.

"Where are we?" Ellyn asked.

"At the beginning of a secret path under the Néartanian Straits," Ylonya said, her voice still hoarse. "It was carved centuries ago, when Yrusian traders wished to avoid certain… obligations, shall we say? Now it is known only to Guild members."

Ylonya raised her Goldstone and Ellyn saw a long, straight track disappearing into the darkness ahead of them as far as the light could reach. The walls and roof of this strange tunnel were irregular in shape, as though its ancient makers had cared only for the smoothness of the path beneath their feet. The darkness around them was immense. It was eerily quiet – no creature lived down here. It felt hard to breathe. Her heart sank. Ever since the nightmares that had followed the deaths of her parents, she had feared being trapped underground, unable to get out. She bit her lip.

"A road under the sea? You mean that the sea is above us, and all around us?" Aidren asked.

Oh, Néarta! What if it breaks in? We will all be drowned. Ellyn fought with her fear, tried to hold on to her faith that Ylonya and Aunt Shaunan would not have brought them this way if it had not been safe.

"Yes, indeed," Ylonya said. "It stretches for twenty miles, across the width of the Straits, and comes up in another safe house in Taellingsford."

Aidren whistled long and low in appreciation. Being underground didn't seem to bother him at all.

"How long will it take us to get there?" Abigail asked.

"About six hours, longer if we stop for a rest."

"Then we had better make a start," Shaunan said.

None of them seemed worried. It was incredible. Ellyn sent up a prayer of silent entreaty, Beloved Néarta, guard and guide me on this path.

Ylonya led the way, the light of her Goldstone shining blue-white, Abigail following her. Ellyn noticed that her friend's Goldstone shed a warmer, yellower light. She must ask Aunt Shaunan why. Then Aidren and Ellyn herself. Aunt Shaunan brought up the rear. Something about this path seemed to encourage silence. The only sounds she could hear were the firm footfalls of her friends and their quiet breathing. The long minutes dragged past, each seeming to last an eternity. She had no idea how long they had been in this… hole, cut off from light and fresh air. The warmth in the tunnel was stifling. Would they ever see daylight again? Clutching the Goldstone around her neck, she started to count her footsteps, hoping to calm herself that way. She got to nearly three thousand before losing count. Doggedly, she began again. Then the fear rose up inside, choking her. She gasped aloud, unable to help herself.

"It is all right, Ellyn," Shaunan said from behind her. "We are quite safe."

Ellyn whirled to face her. "How can you say that?" she demanded. "Nothing on this journey has been 'safe' since Céardochis…" She bit off what she had been going to say, and continued, "What if the sea breaks in? There's nowhere we can escape to."

The others stopped, startled by her outburst. Ylonya came back to join them. "It is safe, Ellyn. We maintain it regularly. And we're nearly half-way through now."

"You mean we still have more than half the distance to go?" Not reassuring. Ellyn fought for self-control. She was a heartbeat from screaming and crying, fleeing from all of them.

A hand reached out, grasped hers. A warm hand, callused from using a sword. Aidren's. She clung to it desperately.

"I am with you," his voice said, reaching through the vortex of her fear. "Walk with me, Ellyn. I will look after you."

The touch of his hand made her fears recede somewhat. "Oh, Aidren. Don't ever leave me." She collapsed against him and burst into tears. His other arm came round her, stroking her hair. So gently.

"I am here, dear one, I am here."

They walked on. Abigail's heart was full of joy for her friend. At last, Ellyn and Aidren were together. She could hear their soft, murmured conversation behind her. Oh, Jacob. Where are you now? A pang of loss, quickly suppressed. Mustn't think about him. Firmly, she directed her thoughts back to her friend. She hadn't realised that Ellyn feared confined spaces so much. Then she remembered the cave on the way to Myndorian. Which seemed like a lifetime ago. In the long seisdags since then, she and Ellyn had become so close.

Up ahead, Ylonya stopped, took off her pack. "I think we could all do with a rest, and something to eat."

Abigail shrugged off her own pack gratefully. Her back and shoulders were aching from the unaccustomed weight. Ylonya and Aidren both looked weary; neither had fully recovered from the fight two days before. She hoped they would be able to purchase horses in Lènium. Soon the five of them were seated in a circle of Goldstone light on the stony path, with blankets from their packs beneath them for comfort, munching on *feolin* and taking sips of water. The darkness around them was vast and Abigail began to understand Ellyn's fear a little better. She and Shaunan took it in turns to eat, so that the light of their Goldstones could be maintained, and to give Ylonya a rest. Abigail felt tired – it was the first time she had used her new powers for any sustained length of time. Then she felt Shaunan's hand on her shoulder blade and new strength flooding through her. Of course, the power of augmentation. Why hadn't she thought to do that herself? She smiled at her mentor.

It is going to take me a while to get used to my new powers.

She heard Shaunan's gentle laugh in her mind. *It was the same for all of us. You are doing well.*

She blushed. *Thank you.*

Soon, all too soon for Abigail, they were on their way again. She sensed a rush of relief from Ellyn and guessed the delay had been hard on her. Aidren had stayed close to her, his one dark eye fixed on her face. The other was hidden by a patch to give it time to heal. Now for the last effort. She raised her Goldstone again, and its golden yellow light flared out through her fingers, warm and reassuring.

By the time they reached the end of the passage, Abigail was so weary that the simple act of putting one foot in front of the other was an effort. She had no idea how much time had passed. Would it still be night outside? The path started to rise gently and they saw another door in front of them.

"Wait here," Ylonya said. "Kendris has taught me the words to let us out of here, but none of you may hear them."

She strode forward, her Goldstone held high, touched the Yrusian sigil at the centre of the door, and murmured something Abigail didn't catch. The door swung open silently. Ylonya stood aside to allow the others to go through, then came through herself and closed it behind her. They were in another cave like the one in Néartanis. Abigail took off her pack and sank to the floor with a weary sigh. She took out her water flask and drained it. Aidren, Ellyn and Shaunan joined her.

"Stay here," Ylonya said. "I must seek the owner of the house and explain our presence to her. Do not stray from this place."

After a short time, she returned with a small, dark woman, her long black hair in braids swung round her head in a coronet.

"This is Genira, an old friend. She will help us. Genira, this is Shaunan, Waymage of Nordvein. Abigail is her initiate. The other two are Aidren, a warrior of Dagâra and Ellyn, a Néartanian cordwainer."

"We are pleased to meet you, Genira," Shaunan said formally, her right hand making the gesture of welcome and friendship. "We would be grateful if you would let us stay here today, then find us some horses to continue our journey."

"Of course, Waymage. It would be my privilege." Her voice was light, musical.

They rose to their feet and followed Ylonya and Genira up the stairs to the house above. It was an effort for Abigail to force her aching knees to bend and straighten.

Genira showed them into three pleasant bedrooms, then said, "Rest, refresh yourselves. I will have a meal ready at sixth hour."

"Thank you, Genira. We are in your debt," Shaunan said.

Once the door had shut behind Genira, Ellyn rushed over to the window of the room she was sharing with Abigail and threw it open. She gulped in the fresh air. Dawn was just breaking, and she drank in the sight of the rooftops of the houses opposite. It was such a relief to be out of that place.

"Take care," Abigail said behind her. "No-one must see us."

For a moment, Ellyn thought of rebelling. She needed to breathe, needed to feel the air on her face. Then her brain caught up with her emotions, and she drew back. Abigail was right, as usual. If an agent of the Prophet saw them now, all the long agony of the fear she had felt for Aidren and of the journey through the tunnel would be wasted.

"I'm sorry," she said, "I just needed to…"

"I know," Abigail said, her voice sympathetic. "You did so well, Ellyn. You made it through."

Ellyn flushed. It didn't seem right that Abigail was praising her. If her friend only knew how close she had been to losing her nerve completely, to running, screaming. If it hadn't been for Aidren, she would have gone mad. Then she remembered. Abigail was Ranusian now. She had probably been reading her thoughts. Ellyn stiffened.

"What is wrong?"

"Have you been reading my mind?" Ellyn asked, fighting to keep the suspicion out of her voice.

"No, of course not. I wouldn't do that to you. But your fear was clear to see on your face. And I could sense it."

Ellyn relaxed. "I don't think I would have made it, if Aidren hadn't been with me," she admitted. "I was so grateful to him. The touch of his hand was what I needed to master my fears."

"I'm so happy for you, my dear friend. I hope the two of you will be as happy together as Jacob and I were."

Abigail's voice was so sad, so wistful. Ellyn felt a pang of sorrow for her. "Oh, Abigail. I'm sure we'll find him. When we get to Ranusheim, the Wayzenmoot will know what to do."

Abigail sighed, a deep sigh that seemed to come from her heart. "I hope so. Every day we are apart, my hope dwindles. Who knows where he may be by now?"

"I'm so sorry," Ellyn said. There seemed to be nothing else she could say. She didn't want to raise her friend's hopes, but surely the Wayzenmoot could do anything they set their minds to.

"Don't worry about me," Abigail said. "Tell me about you and Aidren."

Ellyn felt a surge of joy. "I can't believe he loves me back. He told me he has loved me for a long time, but he thought Aunt Shaunan would never permit him to court me. I don't see why not… do you?"

"I don't really know enough about Veylindréan marriage customs to answer that," Abigail said slowly. "But like you, I don't see why there should be a problem. I think Aidren will have proved his worth sufficiently on this journey to satisfy her. If I know one thing about Shaunan, it is that she is fair."

"Oh, I hope you are right. I love him so much."

"I'm sure I am. Come, let us rest now. I'm so very tired."

The two of them took off their shoes and slipped under the coverlets. As soon as her head hit the pillow, Ellyn was asleep.

Chapter 2

Abigail was woken by Shaunan shaking her shoulder. "Abigail, it is time for lunch."

"Lunch? Where are we?" Then she remembered the events of the night before – the long walk through the under-sea passage and their arrival at Genira's house at dawn. "Goodness! How long have I slept?"

"More than six hours," Shaunan said with a chuckle. "You must have needed it. But come, now."

After they had eaten in Genira's comfortable kitchen, all seated around the table, the copper pans on the dresser winking in the warm light of two oil lamps, the Yrusian woman took a long look at Abigail, making her feel uneasy. "I must say, I agree with Ylonya."

"What do you mean?"

"Your appearance is far too distinctive. Your blonde hair stands out."

Abigail's hand automatically went to her hair. "What are you saying?"

"Your description is known to the agents of the Prophet of the One," Ylonya said. "I think it would be best if you agreed to have it cut shorter and dyed. With your pale skin, we could alter your appearance sufficiently to pass you off as Garûnalonden."

Abigail looked at Shaunan. "Do you agree with them?"

Shaunan nodded. "It would be safer. We still have a long way to travel, and it would be better for you to look less conspicuous."

Abigail's stomach clenched. Was this really happening? "All right, Shaunan, if you think it's necessary," she said, then to Genira, "I am in your hands."

But inside she felt like crying. Jacob loved her long, blonde hair so much. It felt as though another link to him was being severed. Quite literally.

Genira led her to a small room at the back of the house, lined with shelves full of bottles, packets and hanging bunches of herbs, which smelled wonderful, filling the room with their combined scents, reminding her of her mother's kitchen garden in summer. Don't think about that. Below the shelves, a long spotlessly clean wooden table was set against each wall, on one of which stood a set of brass scales and a marble pestle and mortar.

"Please sit," Genira said, gesturing to a chair. "Let me see. I think if we use henna, we can turn you into a redhead. And I'd like to cut your hair to just beneath your shoulders, so you can tie it back in a short ponytail at the nape of your neck."

Abigail looked at her in dismay. "Oh no! Do you really have to cut that much off? It's taken me many years to grow it this long."

Genira's gaze softened. "I know this is hard for you. But reaching Ranusheim unobserved is the most important thing now. Ylonya told me about the attack on the road to Néartanis."

Part of Abigail wanted to rebel, to stand up and walk out of the room. She loved her long, blonde hair. And Jacob… better not think about it. Then she remembered the high price Ylonya and Aidren had already paid to ensure her safety. If disguising herself would prevent another such incident, she had no choice. She met Genira's eyes, saw the sympathy there and knew the woman was right. Steeling herself, she said, "Carry on."

For a while there was silence as Genira plied her scissors. Abigail listened to the soft crunching sound of metal through hair, as the long strands drifted to the floor. She bit her lip, trying not to cry. How stupid, to be so vain. Her father would have been horrified. She distracted herself by looking around the room, moving only her eyes, not her head. She had never seen so many different herbs in one place.

At length, Genira was done. "Now for the dye," she said. She reached up, took a packet off one of the shelves, and measured several large spoonsful of a browny-green powder into a bowl. "I need to mix it with warm water," she said. "I'll be right back."

Abigail took advantage of her absence to stand up and examine the herbs more closely. She recognised some of the names – feverfew, yarrow, sage, comfrey, valerian – but others were unknown to her.

"Here we are," Genira said. "Put this on," holding out a voluminous coverall, "and sit down."

Abigail jumped. She had not heard the woman re-entering the room. "I'm sorry," she said. "These are fascinating."

"I run an apothecary. It is a fine profession, helping to heal others."

"But you're Yrusian. I thought that only people with Ranusian and Lèniumen Waymarks could be healers." She blushed – that sounded rude.

Genira smiled at her. "You are right, but my mother was a healer, and I learned much from her. I do not heal with these herbs. I sell them to healers, so my Waymark is Yrusian. My skill is preparing the herbs to bring out their healing properties."

She put a dark cloth around Abigail's shoulders, then started to apply the dye, working it in with her fingers, until her whole head was covered. It smelled rich, almost grassy and was warm and gloopy in consistency, like thick mud. When she was done, she said, "It has to be left on for two hours. I will wrap another cloth around your head to keep the mixture warm, which will help it to take. In the meantime, let's find you some other clothes to wear. The Prophet's agents will expect you to be wearing Dagâran garb, so different garments will add to your disguise."

She led Abigail to another room, obviously a bedroom, with two large wardrobes against one wall. "If we are trying to pass you off as Garûnalonden," she said, "you had better be wearing blue or green, the colours they favour."

"But what about my Waymark?" Abigail asked. "That shows I am Ranusian, not Garûnalonden."

"That is true," Genira said, with a quizzical glance, "but we are only disguising you from a distance. And there are many Garûnalonden who bear a Ranusian Waymark."

"Oh, of course. I keep forgetting."

"I wonder whether it would be possible to turn you into a boy…" She looked closely at Abigail, who was horrified at this idea. "No, perhaps not. Your figure is too womanly for that and having to bind your breasts flat would be uncomfortable for you."

"Not to mention the fact I would have to share a room with Aidren. I can't do that – I just can't. Ellyn would never forgive me."

"Ah, I had not realised they were together," Genira said, a twinkle in her eye. "Never mind. Fortunately, the women of Garûnalond often wear close-fitting trews for travelling, so let's see what I have here."

She opened the wardrobe door. Abigail was astonished to see an array of clothing of all different colours and styles, breeches, trews, tunics, gowns, shirts and floor-length robes, all hung up neatly, or folded on a wide shelf above.

"Let me see," Genira said. She reached in and brought out two pairs of dark blue trews with straight legs and high waists, a dark brown leather belt and a long-sleeved, high-necked jerkin, also dark blue. "These should do," she said, holding them up against Abigail. "Do you have shirts to go with them?"

Abigail couldn't quite believe this was happening. "Yes," she said faintly, "I do." Then, remembering her manners, "Thank you, Genira." But how she wished it hadn't been necessary.

"You're welcome." She paused, then continued, "Ylonya saved my life when we were on a mission in Garûnalond several years ago. I fell into a fast-moving river and would have drowned, had she not jumped in and saved me. So, anything I can do for you, her companion, helps to repay my debt to her. Would you like to wait in your room until it is time to rinse the dye off?"

"Yes, please. And would you send Ellyn up to keep me company?"

"Surely."

Ellyn found her friend sitting on the edge of her bed, swathed in a coverall, with a cloth wound round her head. She stopped short in the doorway, her hand over her mouth. "What is Genira doing to you?"

Abigail's eyes filled with tears. "She has cut my hair so short – it's not much longer than yours now – and dyed it red. She's trying to turn me into a Garûnalonden."

Ellyn hastened to reassure her. "I'm sure it will look lovely. How long does the dye have to stay on for?"

"She said two hours, and I think about half an hour has passed. Shall we do our Immersion practice?"

"That's a good idea," Ellyn said. "Today has been so topsy-turvy; walking all night, going to bed at dawn and waking up at lunchtime."

The two girls settled in their usual postures on the floor – Abigail on her knees, Ellyn with her legs crossed, and closed their eyes. For the next fifteen minutes, there was no sound in the room except for their gentle breathing as they went through their daily prayer and meditation ritual. This shared practice brought peace to both of them, and they rarely missed it.

"That's better," Abigail said. "I'm going to read the herbal Shaunan lent me. What are you going to do?"

"I'll carry on working on the bag," Ellyn said, walking over to her pack and getting it out.

"It really is a beautiful piece of work. When are you going to give it to Shaunan?"

Ellyn smiled to herself, so pleased her friend had not guessed her secret. "I thought perhaps at Lèniastide. Hopefully we'll be in Ranusheim by then. It will be wonderful to celebrate a festival there."

"Yes, and Lèniastide will be the perfect time. May I have a look?"

Ellyn passed it over. "I've just got the Ranusian sigil to finish now," she said. "I'm planning to stitch it in gold on the top flap."

She watched Abigail examine the bag. She had been working on it for nearly ten seisdags and was pleased at how well it had come together. The rich, brown leather had been burnished until it shone, using beeswax to make it waterproof, and she had incorporated various compartments into the inner lining, using soft, flexible pigskin, to make the contents easy to locate. Two long straps, fastened with buckles of gleaming brass, were for carrying it on the shoulders. It was the most complex piece she had ever crafted. She hoped Master Markhan would find it acceptable as her journeywoman piece. That is, if she ever saw Master Markhan again.

"It really is beautiful," Abigail said. "I'd love to own a healer's bag as fine as that."

Ellyn grinned. "Maybe I'll make another one for you, one day."

Abigail's face lit up. "Oh, Ellyn! That would be marvellous."

A knock on the door. "It is time to have the dye washed out," Genira said, beckoning to Abigail.

Abigail put the herbal back into her pack and stood. "I'm coming."

It took several rinses to wash all the henna out of her hair. Genira gave her a towel to dry it with, and said, "I'll see you downstairs."

"Do you have a reflector?"

"In my bedroom. The third on the right."

Back in her own room, Abigail dried her hair, which seemed to take no time at all, then combed it, and tied it back in a ponytail. Her head felt so light. Then she changed into the Garûnalonden clothing – the dark blue trousers fitted her well, cinched in at the waist by the belt, but she had to turn them up at the bottom. Then she slipped along the corridor to Genira's room. It faced onto the street, so she was careful to keep well away from the window. A beautiful bed dominated the room, covered with a fine embroidered quilt, with a high headboard made of a dark, well-polished wood carved with flowers and leaves. The reflector stood in one corner. Abigail tiptoed towards it, eager to see what she looked like.

She hardly recognised the girl in the reflector. It was amazing the difference the shorter, darker hair made to her face, with the Waymark on her forehead, and the clothes looked so exotic to her, much as the Dagâran riding clothes had when she had first arrived in Veylindré. And she looked taller than she remembered. It had been a long while since she had seen herself in a reflector.

"Now for it," she said to her reflection. "I wonder what the others will think of the new me?"

She walked down the stairs, took a deep breath, then went in. Shaunan, Ellyn, Aidren and Ylonya were sitting round the fire, talking quietly with Genira.

Ylonya glanced up. "Abigail? By the Six, you look so different!"

After that remark, Abigail felt surrounded by eyes. Ellyn jumped up from her chair and rushed over to hug her. "I love it! You look so different, but still so pretty."

"You are a striking young woman in either guise," Shaunan agreed.

Aidren said nothing. He just stared. Abigail felt her cheeks warming.

Genira walked over to her, pressed a sealed packet into her hand. "Here is some more of the henna dye, for when new blonde growth begins to show."

"Thank you, Genira, I am most grateful."

"Now that Abigail's transformation is complete," Shaunan said, "we must be on our way. We leave at first light tomorrow."

It had been so good to stay with Genira. Not only had she sheltered them all and disguised Abigail, but also procured horses for them and given them ample food for the onward journey. And the day's rest, without much conversation, had done wonders for her throat. Ylonya felt a pang of regret as they left, who knew when she would be able to see Genira again… but she had long ago accepted the transience of encounters with friends. It was an inextricable part of her wandering life.

"Which way are we travelling?" Shaunan asked her, as they rode through the winding streets at first light.

Few people were around at this early hour. Their horses' hooves sounded loud in Ylonya's ears, echoing around the empty streets. She hoped they would be able to leave Taellingsford undetected. She would not rest easy until she had delivered them safely to Ranusheim.

"The most straightforward route would be to ride north towards Lèniashaven, then cut through the Vale of Berlysian to the beginning of the Land Bridge."

"I hope we will be able to stop at the Hall of Healing," Shaunan said, "while we are crossing the Vale. I have used many herbs and potions on our journey and would like to stock up."

"I don't see why not," Ylonya said.

"Oh, this is gorgeous," Abigail said behind her. "Why do they paint their houses like this, Ylonya?"

Ylonya answered, "I agree – they do make a colourful display." She glanced around, admiring the brightly coloured houses, which made a wonderful kaleidoscope of soft terracotta reds, pinks, blues, yellows and whites, gleaming in the early morning light. Many had wooden balconies, and most of the houses were decorated with delicate paintings of flowers and herbs, or of scenes from Veylindré's history. "You will find painted houses like these all over Lènium. The Lèniumen like to show their love of the herbs for which they are famous. And Taellingsford is the home of the Hall of Tradition, where all the musicians and storytellers are trained."

"I remember their wonderful costumes, so brightly coloured, when we saw them perform at Luvodican," Ellyn said, her clear voice carrying on the still air. "That was where we heard *The Tale of the Seventh Goddess*."

"Yes, it was marvellous," Abigail said.

"Nevertheless, I will be glad to leave it behind us," Ylonya said, in a low voice, her finger on her lips, "too many eyes and ears." She was not sure even now that the younger girl appreciated the danger they were all in.

"I'm not going to take the main road," she told Shaunan. "We have taken a great deal of trouble to reach Lènium undetected. It would be foolish to draw attention to ourselves again."

"Yours is the knowing. How long will it take us to reach Lèniashaven?"

"Three days if the weather remains fair, longer if not. Then another couple of days to reach the Vale."

"It feels like we have been travelling forever," Ellyn said. "I never knew Veylindré was so large."

Ylonya suppressed a snort of derision. Bless the child, she had no idea. "I expect we will be seeing a great deal more of it before our journey is done."

Once again, Shaunan was grateful for Ylonya's extensive knowledge of the back roads of Veylindré. She took them on a convoluted route, sticking to unpaved, muddy tracks through small villages, avoiding any towns. Yet she always found somewhere for them to stay – her network of contacts seemed endless. Shaunan guessed the Yrusian had stayed in many of these places on her trading journeys as well as on her more clandestine trips. And, so far as Shaunan could detect, they were not being followed. She and Abigail had taken it in turns to open their minds to the surrounding countryside and had not picked up any sense of malevolence. Which was a relief. One such encounter had been more than enough.

The landscape they were riding through was subtly different to Néartania, more hilly and with smaller fields. In other seasons, Shaunan knew the Lèniumen would have every possible patch of land under cultivation, although at this time of year, there were not many crops to be seen – mainly winter-growing root vegetables. It was miserable weather for journeying, cold with a bitter wind and freezing rain, which often turned to sleet. They rode mostly in silence, each wrapped in their own thoughts. At night it took them some time to thaw out before they sought their beds. Lènium was bleaker than Shaunan remembered, although the only times she had visited this land had been first as an adept on her way to Ranusheim, then as a very new Waymage, heading back home to Nordvein, many years before, during the Seasons of Growth and First Fruits respectively. No wonder it looked different.

She was looking forward to visiting the Vale of Berlysian again. She remembered it as a place of beauty and tranquillity, nestled in the Lèniumen Hills. It was there she had done her training as a healer, and it had been a long while since she had re-stocked her healer's bag.

They skirted around Lèniashaven and made for the Hills to the north-east. They made good time, in spite of the weather, and on the fifth day after leaving Taellingsford, they reached the Vale. They rode between the two hills which marked the entrance to it, and the change in the weather was startling. The sky cleared, the sun came out and the very air seemed warmer. Birdsong filled the air around them, a refreshing change from the silence of the past few days.

They followed the path of a small river, which ran down the centre of the Vale. Some miles further on they came to the main settlement, Berlysian itself. Berlysian, home of the Hall of Healing, where she had trained so many years before, and also the main centre for the preparation and sale of the herbs grown all over central Lènium. A collection of compact, two-storeyed wooden buildings set in extensive herb gardens clustered around the Hall of Healing and the Herbarium. Shaunan knew that some of the smaller buildings were home to the herbalists who made their living cultivating and preparing the herbs for which the Vale was famous. Most of the healers lived in the Hall itself. Others were hostels for visiting healers, like her, and for other travellers.

"Here we are," she said. "I will ask at the Hall for accommodation. At this time of year, one of the hostels should have room for us."

She swung off her horse and gave the reins to Ylonya.

The Hall of Healing was even more beautiful than she remembered, and pleasantly warm. Made almost entirely of wood, every surface gleamed gently in the sunlight coming in through the wide windows. She walked up to the reception desk, behind which sat a woman clad in lilac robes.

"My name is Shaunan, Waymage of Nordvein in north-east Dagâran. I am travelling to Ranusheim with four companions. Do you have anywhere we could stay for the night?"

"Good evening, Waymage Shaunan. You are welcome in Berlysian," the woman said with a polite inclination of her head. "I am Danisa, Warden of the Hall of Healing. May I test your Waymark, please?"

"Of course." She sighed inwardly for the changes in the world – she would not have been asked twenty years ago. Even here, it seemed, lessons of caution had been learned.

That done, Danisa asked, "And who are your companions?"

"Abigail, my initiate, Ellyn, my niece, Aidren, a young warrior of Dagâra, and Ylonya, our Yrusian guide. They are waiting outside with our horses."

"Then I will come and meet them. There is room for you all in one of the Herbalist Hostels."

"That was my hope. Thank you."

The hostel Danisa led them to was a broad-fronted two-storeyed building about half a mile from the Hall. "The stables are round the back. I will introduce you to the hostel warden."

Once they had stabled the horses, she led them into the hostel itself. "Tarlen," she said, "I have some visitors for you. Their Waymarks are true. They have travelled far and seek a bed for the night."

The bearded man rose to his feet and walked towards them, his right hand open in friendship. "Welcome to Berlysian. Let me show you to your rooms."

"Thank you, Tarlen," Shaunan said. "Is there somewhere we can eat too?"

Tarlen smiled at her, showing even, white teeth. "Of course. The dining room is through there." He pointed to some double doors, then continued, "Dinner is served at twelfth hour, and breakfast at sixth hour. I will be on duty until sixteenth hour, but there is always someone around, if you have any further questions."

The next morning, feeling well-rested, Abigail and Ellyn did their Immersion practice before going down for breakfast. Abigail had her hand on the doorknob when Ellyn called her back.

"Abigail, I have a gift for you before we visit the Herbarium."

"A gift? For me?"

"Yes. This is for you."

To Abigail's astonishment, Ellyn gave her the beautiful bag she had been working on ever since Luvodican.

"This is for me? Truly? But I thought you were making it for Shaunan…" Abigail flung her arms around her friend. "Thank you so much, Ellyn. It is absolutely beautiful."

Ellyn hugged her back, then a broad smile lit up her face. "Aunt Shaunan asked me to make it for you when she realised that you were going to have a Ranusian Waymark, and to keep it a secret until we got here. Which is why I told you it was for her."

Abigail sat down on her bed and began to examine the bag. It was wonderfully crafted, with many cunning compartments inside, to keep the herbs and potions organised. "It is so special," she said. "I don't know how to thank you enough."

"You're welcome, my friend. I'm so glad you like it."

"Like it? I love it!"

When they reached the dining room, Abigail made a beeline for Shaunan. "Shaunan, how can I thank you? Ellyn has given me the healer's bag, and it's perfect. She told me you asked her to make it for me."

Shaunan smiled at her. "No thanks are needed. Every healer should have their own bag. And it will be a good journeywoman piece for Ellyn, too."

After breakfast, they packed up their belongings and set out for the Herbarium. Abigail was looking forward to seeing it – Shaunan had told her they sold every herb a Healer required. Now that she had her very own healer's bag, she could start to build up her own stock of healing herbs. She was so excited, and so grateful to Ellyn.

The Herbarium complex was fascinating. There were teaching rooms and preparation areas, and gardens and glass houses outside, in which the fresh herbs were grown. But the part they were visiting that day was the shop. As soon as Abigail walked in, the heady scent of the herbs hit her nostrils. She breathed in deeply, savouring it.

"Shaunan, please would you advise me? I don't have very much money and would like to have a selection of the most useful herbs for our journey."

"Of course." Shaunan began to roam around the shelves, picking various herbs as she did. "Let me see… comfrey and calendula, for minor wounds… arnica and witch hazel for muscle aches and pains… peppermint for stomach aches… camomile and lavender for soothing… echinacea for coughs and colds… yarrow for fevers, and coughs and colds…valerian to help sleep… and willow bark as a pain killer. Those should be enough to begin with. Then you will need bandages, a small pair of scissors and some tweezers."

"Tweezers? What do I need those for?"

"They are useful for removing splinters, and for when an insect sting has remained in the wound."

"Oh, I see." Although Abigail had helped her mother prepare herbal remedies back home, she realised she still had so much to learn. She wished she could spend more time here, to learn all she could about healing. She stowed the packets and bottles carefully in her new bag. She felt like a proper healer now, or at least, a proper apprentice healer. She couldn't wait for this journey to be over, when Shaunan would have time to train her properly.

Δ Chapter 3 Δ

As Portak had predicted, it took them another three days of miserable, cold, monotonous riding through the gloomy farmlands of Talamdor to reach Crullfeld. Jacob was rarely warm – a cold wind cut through every layer of his clothing and it took a long time to thaw out when they stopped each evening. Jacob's resentment was growing with every step they took. Why was he doing what this man told him? If he didn't get some answers soon, he was going to… but going to what? He knew no-one here, there was nowhere to run, nowhere to hide. It was as if he were a puppet, and Portak's hands held the strings. He ground his teeth in frustration. He hated having so little control over his life.

Crullfeld was a market town on the west bank of the River Roillon, which marked the western boundary of central Talamdor. Here, Portak told him, the local farmers brought their goods to be sold, and traders from all over Talamdor came to sell their wares. It was a thriving, bustling place. Or so it seemed on first sight. Yet Jacob sensed a frenetic feeling about it, as though everyone was desperate to succeed. As though the consequences of failure would be dire.

"Are red and black your national colours?" Jacob asked, noticing that these were the colours most people wore.

"We favour them above others," Portak said.

"Why do some people have the same red triangle on their foreheads as you, but others wear a silver bangle like mine?"

"Hush. Don't ask so many questions. You will be told in good time."

Jacob relapsed into a sullen silence. But he began to realise that the people with the bangles were of lower status than those with the forehead mark, if the quality of their clothing was anything to go by. What did it mean?

"This way," Portak said, and led him confidently through a maze of narrow back streets. Once they left the main square, Jacob noticed the dwellings becoming smaller, less well-built. He could smell the damp and mould.

He tried again to get an answer out of Portak. "How do you know Crullfeld so well?"

"Not now. There will be time for explanations later."

About halfway down a mean alley, Portak stopped outside a tall, narrow house with shuttered windows. He tied his horse to a hitching post and nodded to Jacob to do the same. Then he knocked on the door; three loud knocks, followed by three soft ones. Jacob could hear footsteps shuffling down the passageway within.

"Who is it?" a quavering voice asked.

"A friend of the Prophet. Let us in immediately."

The sound of bolts being drawn back, a harsh scream of metal on metal. Then the door opened a crack and Jacob could see an old woman's face, hard and suspicious. Then she saw Portak and opened the door wider. "Master Portak! I was not expecting you."

"Tell the boy to see to our horses," Portak said. Then he pushed past her and mounted the stairs at the end of the dim hallway. Jacob shrugged and followed him. At the top of the stairs was a small landing, with three doors opening off it. Portak opened the second one and beckoned Jacob inside. He found himself in a small, bare room with two narrow beds, a table and two chairs. A film of dust lay over everything, and Jacob sneezed as it tickled his nose.

"This is the place I stay when I visit Crullfeld."

"Who is the woman?"

"Nobody," Portak snapped. "I pay her well to maintain this house for me, and to keep her mouth shut. You would be advised to do the same."

Jacob took a step backwards. He had not seen Portak in this mood before. What was going on?

Portak drew a hand across his eyes. "I'm sorry, Jacob. I have much on my mind. We will stay here tonight." He smiled, a smile that did not reach his eyes. "Make yourself at home. We will eat presently."

He busied himself with a tinder box from the mantelpiece and lit the fire. About half an hour later, there was a knock on the door. Portak strode across the room and opened it.

"Here's your supper, Master Portak."

The old woman walked in carrying a laden tray, on which were a tureen, two deep bowls, a couple of plates, table knives and spoons, a loaf of bread and a generous pat of butter. And a jug of ale and two pewter mugs. She laid the tray on the table, bobbed a curtsey and left, closing the door behind her.

Jacob's stomach rumbled – he was more than ready for this. He lifted the lid of the tureen and the savoury scent of mutton stew met his nostrils.

"Help yourself," Portak said.

For a few minutes, silence reigned as they ate their fill. Then Portak dusted off one of the two chairs near the fire now burning merrily in the grate, sat down and gestured to Jacob to join him.

"You asked how I know Crullfeld so well," Portak began. "When I first arrived here, I was fourteen years old, sent to work on a farming collective outside the town, under a Havimi slave master named Tyran Larth. Which is why coming here makes me bad-tempered. It is a reminder of times I would rather forget. But you need to understand." He paused, took a drink, and resumed. "Those were dark days for high-born Talamdorians such as me and my family. The Havimi," and his voice was full of anger and hatred as he spat the name, "had taken over our land and turned us into slaves. We had lost heart, knowing no way to overthrow them. They had eyes and ears everywhere, including some informers among our own people, and any plans for rebellion were swiftly discovered and the perpetrators put to death. My father among them. After that, my mother turned her face away from life and died of a broken heart. My sister had died some years before, so I was all alone."

"You were a slave?" Jacob couldn't believe his ears. "And who are the Havimi? I can't remember what you told me about them."

"Yes, I was a slave... Anyone with a Talamunem Bloodmark," he pointed to the blood-red triangle on his forehead, the fire – or the remembered shame – flushing his normally pale face red, "was considered the lowest of the low, and set to do the most menial, distasteful tasks. If we displeased our masters, we were whipped until the blood ran down our backs. If we refused, we were put to death." He sighed. "I bear the scars still. To answer your other question, the Havimi are a race of pirates and slavers, who live in the land of Havim, across the Southern Sea from Talamdor."

"I see. What happened next?"

"Next," and Portak's voice became warmer, brighter, "the Havimi brought in a new overseer to keep us in line. A tall, thin man, who walked with a limp. He was not Havimi. I don't know where he came from. Not from Talamdor, that much was certain. Yet he bore no Waymark either, so not from Veylindré. Somehow, he had gained their trust, which made me avoid him at first. But after a while we became friends, even though he was so much older than me. Perhaps it was partly because of his limp – a very dear friend of mine, whom I had lost touch with years before, was born with a twisted leg, which left him lame and a little lopsided."

It seemed that Portak had a softer side. Who'd have thought it? Intrigued, Jacob asked, "And then?"

"This overseer," Portak continued, "saw the injustice of our situation and was as kind to us as he dared. Then one day, he killed a guard and escaped. The Havimi sought him everywhere, but with no success. When I was seventeen, inspired by his example, I managed to escape too. I made my way by night to Talamunem City, hoping to connect with former friends. To my astonishment, the first person I met was that overseer, the man who changed my life, who changed all our lives."

"Who was he?"

"His name in the world was George Crutwell, but all now know him as the Prophet of the One. After his escape, he was visited by Holy Talamu Herself and given a sacred quest to free all Talamdor from the tyranny of the Havimi. When you meet him, you will understand why I chose to serve him. He is not as other men – the mark of greatness is on him."

George Crutwell? That sounded like an English name. "So you helped him to free Talamdor?"

"Yes, I knew many trueblood families from before the Havimi conquest and was able to make contact with them. Together we rose up and expelled the Havimi from our land. Talamdor is ours once more."

"When did this happen?"

"About thirty years ago. In the years since then, we have built up our strength, and now we are nearly ready."

"Ready for what?"

"To take our rightful position in this world."

The following morning, back on the road, Jacob mulled over what he had learned the previous evening. Finally, Portak had told him something useful. He had been shocked to learn the man had been a slave, but it explained why he found it so hard to trust anyone. Jacob could not imagine being in that situation.

But this… Prophet. George Crutwell sounded like an English name, and even sounded vaguely familiar. Jacob racked his brains, trying to remember where he had heard it before. It had been back home in England, he was sure of that. George Crutwell… George Crutwell…. Then he had it. A man called George Crutwell had made a name for himself forty or so years earlier, as a witchfinder. His father had told him the story, having long had a fascination for such men. It was rumoured he had taught Matthew Hopkins, the legendary Witchfinder General of the 1640s... But no, it couldn't be the same man. Surely George Crutwell was a common enough name. And in any case, how could anyone from home be here?

The weather continued bitterly cold, although they had left the snow behind. Jacob pulled his cloak tightly around him and endured, although he could scarcely feel his hands and feet. Ahead of them he could see a tall mountain.

"What mountain is that?"

"That is Mount Talamu, our most sacred place, the home of Holy Talamu," Portak replied. "It was on its lower slopes that She appeared to the Prophet and gave him his vocation."

"Your goddess appeared to the Prophet? But surely, things like that don't happen anymore…"

"Maybe not in your world, Jacob. But in our world, Holy Talamu has chosen to appear to the Prophet not once, but twice. He is Her Prophet, which is why we follow him, have faith in him."

"And where is Talamunem City?"

"Not far now. We head straight for Mount Talamu, then skirt around its knees to the west. The City is about twenty miles north-west of the mountain. We should be there in another couple of days, all being well."

"Finally. I am so sick of travelling."

"Our journey is nearly over."

As they rode, Mount Talamu loomed larger and larger in their sight, until it dominated the landscape ahead. Jacob had never seen such a magnificent mountain, rising thousands of feet above them, its peak hidden in clouds. Its shape was unusually regular, almost as though it had been carved by human hands. It was not surprising the Talamdorians believed it was sacred. There had been no mountains near home in England – a few gentle, rolling hills, but nothing like this. It took his breath away.

But he would have exchanged ten Mount Talamus for a sight of home.

On the final day of their journey, they changed direction, and began to ride around the base of the mountain, in a north-westerly direction. There was only one road, paved with a black stone Jacob did not recognise, and obviously well-maintained. They pushed their horses to go faster.

"We should arrive at the gates of the City by nightfall," Portak said. "But if it is after sixteenth hour, we will not be admitted until the morning."

"Where would we stay?" Jacob asked.

"The City has grown in recent years, and there are some houses outside the walls. We will be able to sleep there. I hope we will reach the gates in time."

By mid-afternoon, they could see the City in the distance. It looked more like a fortress than a city to Jacob's eyes.

"Why can we see it from so far off?"

"It is built on a group of hills, with the walls skirting the base. You will see soon enough."

When they reached the gates, it was dark. Portak rode up confidently, Jacob following. The gatehouse was lit by torches and to Jacob's surprise, he could see that the wall was built of bricks made of the same black stone as the paving on the road. It had a forbidding air. He shivered.

"Put your hood up," Portak said. "No-one must see your Waymark until we are admitted to the presence of the Prophet."

Jacob did as he was told. He didn't understand what the mark on his forehead meant, but guessed it was something to do with Veylindré. He still had no idea where or when he had got it.

Portak dismounted, giving Jacob the reins of his horse, and knocked loudly on the gates, using the pommel of his knife. A small hatch opened, and a guard inspected them.

"Who comes to the Holy City of Talamu at this late hour?"

"Portak, trusted lieutenant of the Prophet, with a companion."

"Come into the light and be recognised."

"Come, Yablek, you know me well enough."

The guard's eyes widened. "Master Portak, my apologies. The smoke from the torch was in my eyes."

He shut the hatch. There was the sound of bars being lifted, and the gates were pushed open. "Come within, and welcome," Yablek said. "Who is your companion?"

"That is for me to know and you to wonder about. All you need to know is that I have urgent business with the Prophet."

Yablek blanched but held his ground. "I'm sorry, Master Portak, but it is my business to ask questions as a Guard of the City."

Jacob held his breath. Were they going to get turned away on his account? He pulled his hood further down, so that his face was lost in shadow.

Portak frowned. "Very well," he said testily. "My companion is from Veylindré. I found him lost and alone following a shipwreck and have brought him here for his own safety. I will vouch for him, which should be enough for you."

"Very well, Master Portak. Do you wish me to send the news of your arrival ahead?"

"No. Return to your duty."

"Come," Portak said. "It will take us some time to reach the Great Temple. Keep your hood up."

Jacob followed the man as he led him on a tortuous course through the winding streets, always heading upward. He guessed the Great Temple was at the highest part of the city. As he looked around curiously, he realised most of the houses and other buildings were built from the same black stone as the walls. Or at least, so far as he could judge in the flickering light of the smoky torches placed at intervals in brackets high up on the buildings. He brought his horse alongside Portak's.

"What stone do the city's masons use to build with?"

"It is black basalt, a gift to us from Holy Talamu."

"A gift?"

"In ages past, Mount Talamu was an active volcano. The black stone, which is called basalt, was thrown up from the depths of the world."

"I have never seen anything like it. At home, we use sandstone, or brick for our buildings."

"Keep your voice down!" Portak hissed. "Do you want everyone to know that you are a stranger here?"

Abashed, Jacob shut his mouth and dropped back. He wished they could find a lodging first – he was tired, not ready to meet this famous Prophet, whoever he was.

Eventually, they reached a large, open square, dominated by a massive black building, which looked very like a cathedral to Jacob. He guessed it was the Great Temple. For a moment, he wondered why it did not have seven sides. But why should it? He shook his head, dismissing the question. It was set slightly back from the square, and railings of black iron surrounded it. In the middle of them were two tall gates, intricately crafted of wrought iron. Jacob promised himself a closer look at them in daylight. Behind the gates was a small, wooden gatehouse. Portak once again dismounted and banged on the gates with his knife. A figure came out of the gatehouse and shuffled towards them.

"I'm coming, I'm coming. What do you want?"

Jacob saw a wizened old man, dressed half in nightclothes, but with a sword strapped around his waist and a sputtering torch in his hand.

"Don't you know the Temple is closed until the morning?" he asked in a querulous tone.

"Of course I know," Portak snapped, a vein in his temple throbbing. "Nevertheless, you will admit me and my companion."

"Oh ho, will I indeed?" the gatekeeper said. Then he held up his torch and recognised him. His face went white.

"Master Portak. You're back."

"Let us in, you old fool."

"My humble apologies, Master Portak," the man said, shuffling towards the gates and unlocking them with a great iron key.

"Send word to the Prophet that I have returned," Portak said.

"I am sorry, Master Portak," the man repeated, bowing low, his voice apologetic but resolute. "I won't be able to do that. He has left strict orders that he is not to be disturbed after sixteenth hour. But come within, and I will show you to the Visitors' Hall, where you can stay overnight."

"Don't be ridiculous! I need to see the Prophet tonight."

The old man quailed before Portak's anger. "I am so sorry, Master Portak. The Prophet's orders are clear, and I dare not disobey him."

Portak glared at him, then seemed to realise that further argument would be futile.

"Very well, he said. "But remain at your post. I know where the Visitors' Hall is."

He took the reins of his horse back from Jacob and led him down a narrow passage alongside the Great Temple, and out into a stable yard behind it.

"See that our horses are fed and watered," Portak ordered a gaping stable hand.

"Come," he said to Jacob. "The Visitors' Hall is this way."

For the first time since they had left the Border House near the secret pass, Jacob had a room to himself. It was small and plain, containing a narrow bed made of a dark wood, with a red coverlet, and a chest of drawers of the same wood, on which stood a ewer and basin. There was even an armchair to sit in. The walls were painted dark grey, which made him feel as though they were closing in on him. Hunching his shoulders, he fished the last package of travelling food out of his pack and ate ravenously. Then he washed, undressed down to his shirt and underclothes and got into bed. He was exhausted.

He expected to fall asleep straight away but felt too wound up. The nearer they had come to Talamunem City, the greater respect Portak had been shown by those they had met, and Jacob felt uneasy. What were they doing here? Was he finally going to meet Portak's master, this Prophet of the One,? Why had Portak brought him all this way? There were so many things he didn't understand. He had followed Portak all this time, not because he had wanted to, but because he believed he had no other choice. He knew nobody in this strange land, not even Portak, really. He had never felt so lonely in his life. What was going to happen to him? He hoped he would be able to find work in this great city. Surely they would welcome a talented smith?

All these questions and doubts whirled around Jacob's mind. He tossed and turned, turned and tossed, the sheets tangling beneath him, eventually falling into an uneasy sleep shortly before dawn.

All too soon, he was woken by a knock at the door. "Jacob! It is time to get up."

Portak. Damn the man, he hadn't had enough sleep. "All right, all right. I'll be with you in a few minutes."

"I will wait here."

Throwing back the coverlet, Jacob staggered to his feet and washed his head and neck in the last of the water from the ewer. He got dressed as quickly as he could, shoved the rest of his belongings back into his pack, and strapped it shut. Then opened the door. Portak was waiting outside, an impatient expression on his face.

"Here I am."

"About time too. Come, you must break your fast, then we must wait upon the Prophet. Leave your pack in here. And put your hood up."

Jacob noticed Portak had changed his clothes, that his red hair was neatly brushed, his scraggly beard trimmed to a fine point. He wished he had some finer clothes to wear to meet the Prophet. But he only had the clothes he stood up in, plus one extra shirt. And that had been a gift from Portak. How long would he have to remain dependent?

Portak led him down the winding stairs and into a large room with many tables and chairs. Along one of the long walls was a trestle table, loaded down with food. There were only a few visitors, apart from themselves, all clad in the customary Talamdorian red and black. One man looked up as they entered, met Portak's glare, and swiftly returned his attention to his meal.

"Help yourself," Portak said. "I have already eaten."

Jacob took a tray, and a large plate, and filled it with a fresh loaf of white bread, butter, a small terracotta pot of honey, some slices of cheese and cold meat, and an apple. He was starving. Looking around for something to drink, he saw some pewter mugs filled with an unnamed beverage. He picked one up and sniffed it. A light ale. Perfect. He sat at the table Portak had chosen, well away from the other inhabitants and started to wolf down his meal.

He was so hungry he only gradually became aware that Portak was speaking to him. "… and do not speak unless you are spoken to."

"I'm sorry…what were you saying?"

The man glared at him. "I was saying," he said with heavy emphasis, "that this morning, at fourth hour, which is only a few minutes away, you are going to be privileged to meet the Prophet of the One. He will have many questions for you. Answer him politely, and do not speak unless you are spoken to."

Jacob felt a frisson of fear. Was this Prophet so formidable? But there was nothing for it. This was why he was here, he supposed. He bolted his final slice of bread and honey, wiped his mouth on a napkin and stood up.

"I'm ready when you are."

"That is well."

Portak led him out of the dining room, down several dark corridors and out into a bright courtyard. The sight of the Great Temple in daylight stopped Jacob in his tracks. It was magnificent, a tall, imposing building built of black basalt with columns across the front and twin spires soaring to a great height above them. So like the great cathedrals of home. Portak led him across the courtyard, and in through the wide bronze doors, richly carved with triangular motifs, making a complex pattern.

The interior of the Great Temple was dim and dark, lit only by the light coming in through the tall, narrow windows. Jacob stood for a moment to allow his eyes time to adjust. A double row of basalt columns split the huge space into three – a central nave, and two side aisles. The vaulted ceiling arched high above him. On the walls were huge tapestries, depicting scenes from Talamdorian history, he guessed. His eyes were drawn up the central aisle to a high altar, behind which was a huge painting of a stately woman with pale skin and dark, intense eyes. Was this Talamu? So strange, that the Talamdorians worshipped a goddess, rather than a god.

Meanwhile, Portak was striding up the aisle. He turned and saw Jacob far behind. "Come! We must not be late. The

Prophet is expecting us." His voice was urgent and commanding.

Jacob shrugged. This was it. He was going to see the Prophet. Here, at last, his questions would be answered. He would understand why he was here. He hoped.

Portak led him through a side-door, along a corridor to another door, whose entrance was guarded by two men in red and black livery. Their spears were crossed, denying entrance to any.

"Who seeks audience with the Holy Prophet?" one of them asked.

Jacob waited for the explosion, but it didn't come. Why wasn't Portak angry at being challenged once again? Jacob frowned, then guessed it might be a known ritual, questions asked of any who wanted to see the Prophet.

"Portak, as you know well. The Prophet knows I am coming, together with my companion."

"Leave your weapons here. None may come into the Prophet's presence bearing arms."

Portak undid his sword belt, and gave it to the guard, and nodded to Jacob to give up his knife.

At last, the doors were opened. Jacob's breakfast was lying uneasily in his stomach. He felt sick, and supposed it was fear.

A voice from inside the room, deep, hypnotic, commanding, "Portak, welcome back. Jacob Wallingford, I have waited a long time to meet you."

Chapter 4

Abigail rode away from Berlysian and its Healer Hall with some regret. She would have liked to spend more time there. But she knew Shaunan was anxious to reach Ranusheim as soon as possible. Although she still didn't fully understand why, except for the words Shaunan had said, back in Luvodican – she had never been able to forget them. 'I also believe that your coming to the Commonweal of Veylindré is no accident. I believe you have been given special powers by the Six and will play a central role in the destruction of the Master Bloodstone.'

Abigail shivered – what did she know of special powers and high destinies?

"We should reach the Fort of Ranu in another four days," Ylonya said, as they left the Vale behind them. "It's about forty miles from Berlysian to the beginning of the Land Bridge, and the same again to the Fort."

"What is the Land Bridge?" Abigail asked.

"It is a narrow stretch of land, between three and four miles wide, which connects the mainland of Lènium to the Isle of Ranu. Its only inhabitants live in the hamlet of Olaf, about halfway across, where visitors to the Isle can stay overnight before riding on to the Fort."

"Is it the only entrance to the Isle of Ranu?" Aidren asked. His eye had been tended by the healers in Berlysian and was now well on the way to healing.

"Yes, it is," Ylonya said. "The granite cliffs of the Isle of Ranu rise five hundred feet from the sea below, sheer and forbidding, with jagged rocks all around – none can approach them, let alone scale them. The River Muillean, which rises near Mount Ranu, ends in a precipitous waterfall. No-one can enter the Isle except through the Fort."

"I don't understand. Why is no-one allowed to visit?" Abigail asked.

"People are allowed to visit the Isle," Shaunan replied, "but only if they have business with the Wayzenmoot, the twelve High Waymages who are custodians of the Golden Stone of Ranu, or another legitimate reason. As you know, Ranusheim is the spiritual centre of the whole Commonweal, the place where Waymages go to receive their final training, and from where the lore of Veylindré is disseminated."

"Do they know we are coming?"

Shaunan's amber eyes twinkled as she smiled at her. "I expect they do, by now. They have ways of knowing things which are not shared by the rest of us."

"It will be a new experience for me, visiting the Isle," Ylonya said. "It is the only land in the Commonweal I haven't seen, although I've been as far as the Fort of Ranu, bringing goods from Yrusian for the Wayzenmoot."

"I cannot wait to be there once more," Shaunan said, and Abigail could hear real longing in her voice. "I wonder how much it has changed in the last thirty years."

"Could you tell us about it, if it's not a secret?" Ellyn asked.

"What do you want to know?"

"Everything, I suppose." Ellyn grinned at her aunt.

"'Everything' is much too tall an order," Shaunan said. "But this evening, when we are at rest, I will tell you something of the Isle. Not while we're riding."

"What do you want to know?" Shaunan asked that evening, when they were all sitting together in the common room of the inn Ylonya had found for them. The fire was blazing in the hearth, a welcome change from the freezing weather outside.

"Tell us about your first time here - when you became a Waymage," Ellyn said.

Shaunan sighed. "That was a long time ago. Let me see… I was in my early twenties when I became an adept. I served under Meldar, who was Waymage of Nordvein before me. He taught me much, and I will always be grateful to him. But I wanted to know more. Meldar contacted the Wayzenmoot and they agreed I was ready to travel to Ranusheim for the final stage of my training. I was thrilled to hear the news, but also apprehensive – what if I had bitten off more than I could chew? But it was too late for doubts. So one fine and sunny morning, on a beautiful blue-sky day at the beginning of the Season of Growth, I set off with one companion to make the long journey to the Isle."

"Who was that?" Abigail asked.

"Someone well-known to Ellyn. It was Raimun, who at that time was a journeyman cordwainer. He was travelling to the Hall of Clothiers in Céardochis, to do *his* final training, so we travelled together for some seisdags."

"You travelled with Master Raimun?" Ellyn said. "I never knew he had made a long journey."

"We were both younger then," Shaunan said, "and quite ready for an adventure. It was the first time I had been further than Luvodican and the wider world seemed full of wonders." She smiled at Ellyn. "When we reached Céardochis, I made enquiries and was allowed to accompany a group of Yrusian traders who were heading for the Fort of Ranu to drop off some donations for the Wayzenmoot. I remember travelling through the Vale of Berlysian and being awed by its beauty and serenity. By the time we reached the Fort of Ranu, we were into the Season of First Fruits. At the gates of the Fort, I met Findoran..."

"Was that the same Findoran we met – the Waymage of Myndorian?" Ellyn asked.

"Yes, but at that time she was an adept like me. We took to each other straight away – it was good to have one friend before I reached Ranusheim."

"What is Ranusheim itself like?" Aidren asked.

"Ranusheim is… Ranusheim. It is difficult to describe, because nowhere else compares. It is unlike any other place in the whole of Veylindré. You will see when we get there."

"Is it always necessary for people to travel to the main Guild Hall of their craft to complete their training?" Abigail asked.

"Not always. Sometimes the master or mistress under whom a young person is training is sufficiently skilled to pass on their knowledge to their adept. But I believe training with other adepts is more fruitful, because that way you are learning from more people and your skills will become both broader and deeper."

Aidren nodded. "I can understand that," he said. "I got a taste of it when I trained with the others under Master Sanderon at the Hall of Warriors in Luvodican. Sparring with other people at my level was so good for me. I learned so much in a few short seisdags. Without it, I'm not sure we would have won, back in Néartania. I hope I can go back there when this journey is done."

"I am sure you will," Shaunan said.

As they drew nearer the Isle of Ranu, Aidren's apprehension was growing. He hoped there would be opportunities to train at Ranusheim. Ranusheim – the very name filled him with a nameless fear. He had never dreamed he would be travelling to the forbidden Isle, let alone to the home of the Wayzenmoot. What was he, a simple warrior, doing here? But there was no-one to share his doubts with. Jacob would have understood. But Jacob was gone. He missed his friend. Abigail and the Waymage were both Ranusian, and Aidren was in awe of their powers. He still found Ylonya intimidating, even after the battle they had shared. He was confident he could match her with a blade but would not want to cross swords with her wit or will. And Ellyn… his dear Ellyn. He could not believe she returned his love. Since the crossing under the Néartanian Straits, they had been together. But she was the last person he wanted to share his misgivings with. He couldn't bear the thought of losing her respect.

What would happen after they reached Ranusheim? Their sole aim for the last seisdags had been to reach that goal. But Aidren had no idea what was going to happen after that. Would the Waymage share her news, then they would all return home? Surely not. She could have sent a messenger from Luvodican if that had been the case. Somehow, this was about Abigail. Certainly, those fake Garûnalonden had been after her. From the few hints he had picked up, he knew the Waymage considered Abigail to be special in some way. Perhaps they would all be sent on a sacred quest, like in the tales of the Storytellers.

"A copper bit for your thoughts?" Ellyn asked.

He jumped. He had been so deep in thought he had not noticed her drawing her horse alongside. "Not worth it." He smiled at her, his little love. "I was wondering what was going to happen when we reached Ranusheim."

Ellyn shrugged. "I've got no idea. I'm just enjoying the adventure."

He reached over, touched her hand on the reins. "Thank you, dearling."

They rode past two white posts, each displaying a sign. "Welcome to the Land Bridge. If you do not have business at the Isle of Ranu, turn around here." Abigail felt a thrill of excitement – the end of the journey was getting so close.

"This is the last part of the route known to me," Ylonya said. "Once we have been admitted to the Isle, Shaunan will have to lead us." She kept her voice level, but Abigail felt a twinge of anxiety coming from the Yrusian woman and guessed it was because she hated not knowing where she was.

"I doubt that," Shaunan smiled. "We will be escorted from the Fort of Ranu to Ranusheim. None are permitted to wander freely on the Isle."

"How far is it from the Fort to Ranusheim?" Abigail asked.

"As memory serves, about forty-five miles," Shaunan said. "But there is a guard post about halfway. I expect we will spend the night there."

"We have a way to go before then," Ylonya said. "I've never crossed the Land Bridge in the Season of Dormancy. And even in warmer seasons, there is always a strong wind blowing from the Sea of Ranu."

Abigail could already feel it, blowing against her from her right. The trees which lined the route had been bent by its force, inwards on their right, and outwards on their left. She gripped her reins more tightly, stroking her horse's neck. It was going to be a rough crossing.

They were all glad to reach Olaf as the sun began to set, casting long shadows in front of them. It was a tiny settlement of only half a dozen houses, with a small temple and a large inn. All built of stone, to withstand the fierce weather. Once they had stabled their mounts, they hurried inside gratefully, glad to be out of the wind.

Tremond finally reached the Fort of Ranu on a cold and rainy afternoon half way through the Season of Dormancy. It had been a wet, cold journey from Mirunan and both he and his horse were mud-splattered and weary. All he wanted to do was tend to his horse, get himself clean, and then rest.

He dismounted slowly, then straightened his long limbs, hoping the captain of the garrison would not judge only by appearances. His blue Watchman's uniform was in sore need of a good brushing. But that would have to wait. It was a good job he carried a spare outfit in his pack. He wanted to make a good impression on the High Waymages, so they would listen to what he had to tell.

He was about to knock on the postern gate, when a group of Dagâran soldiers, led by a tall, broad man with a captain's sigil on his shoulders, came out of it.

"Who comes to the Fort of Ranu?"

Tremond stood to attention. "My name is Tremond. I am a Watch Officer from Mirunan and am here to deliver a message from Guildmaster Géorn to the High Waymages of the Wayzenmoot."

"Test his Waymark," the captain snapped.

One of his men came forward and did so. Then stood so that Tremond could test his in return.

"His Waymark is true, captain."

The captain scowled at this, as though he would have preferred to deny Tremond access to the Isle. "Do the Wayzenmoot know of your coming?"

"No," Tremond said with an inward sigh. Patience and diplomacy would be his only friends with such a man. "But as I said, I have been sent by Guildmaster Géorn. The message I bear is of great import."

"Well, give it to me then."

Tremond bowed. "My apologies, captain. It is not only a message. It is vital that I deliver my news to the High Waymages in person."

Another scowl. "Very well. You may enter. But only as far as the Traders' Courtyard. A message will be sent to the Wayzenmoot, to inform them of your arrival."

"My thanks, captain." Tremond bowed once more. "If one of your men would lead me to the stables, I will tend to my tired horse first."

After such a lukewarm reception, he was glad to find the stables clean and airy, well stocked with hay and water troughs. He untacked his horse and rubbed him down. There was another horse there – a splendid black destrier. Who did he belong to? It seemed he was not the only one awaiting the pleasure of the Wayzenmoot.

He stowed his tack in the tack room, taking note of the stranger's horse's fine leather saddle and bridle, then walked back through the arch to the main Traders' courtyard, noting with approval the state of readiness of the Fort's garrison.

A soldier was standing on guard there, so Tremond asked him, "Which is the Lodge of Visitors?"

"That one." The man pointed to a low, brick-built structure to one side of the courtyard. "You will find you are not the only visitor."

"My thanks."

Tremond strode towards the indicated building, tapped on the door, then walked in. As he entered, he saw a young Néartanian with a Dagâran Waymark sitting on one of the narrow beds, sharpening his sword with a whetstone. Such a beautiful sword – long, elegant and sharp. It had some curious runes swirling down it, and Tremond promised himself a closer look at it one day. And the young man's face was oddly familiar – where had he seen him before?

The young man rose to his feet, sword in hand. "I am Ednor of Néartania. Who are you?"

Ednor. The younger son of Lord Éadulf and Lady Aethed of Néartania. What was this scion of the house of Néartania doing here? Tremond walked forward, his right hand outstretched and open. "My name is Tremond. I am a Watch Officer from Mirunan."

Ednor echoed the gesture, then sat back down on his bed. "So you're here to see the Wayzenmoot too?"

"I am indeed." Tremond swung his pack off his shoulder and dumped it on one of the other beds. "Does the Wayzenmoot know you are here?"

Ednor frowned briefly. "Yes. The officious oaf who is in charge here sent to let them know yesterday."

"Then I hope we will be able to go forward to Ranusheim together. I too need to speak with the Wayzenmoot."

Ednor grinned at him. "I expect the Waymages they send will be able to decide that, once they get here."

"Do the seas on either side of the Land Bridge have different names?" Abigail asked, as they set off the next morning. Although she had been told there was sea on either side of them, she could not see it. But she could smell it – the clean, briny scent of the sea was filling her nostrils, and seagulls were wheeling in the air above them.

"Yes," Ylonya replied. "The sea to our right is the Sea of Ranu, and the Sea to our left is the Sea of Garûna, which also borders Lènium."

Before long, Abigail could see the Fort of Ranu, and the high walls on either side of it, ahead of them. It was visible from quite a distance. The walls stretched from shore to shore, and she could guess at the vague shapes of two smaller keeps at either end. It looked as though the Wayzenmoot guarded its isolation well. She shivered, knowing she was one of the reasons they had travelled all this way. She still didn't understand what Shaunan had meant when she had told her she had 'special powers'. She didn't feel powerful at present. She felt apprehensive. She hadn't even known how to defend herself when those men had attacked them. Would Ranusheim be the end of their journey, or the beginning of a new adventure? At the very least, they'd need to rescue Jacob.

The Fort and the walls loomed larger as they approached until, as afternoon faded into evening, they filled the whole of their forward vision,. Now Abigail could dimly see the tiny figures of soldiers patrolling the walls, ever alert for the unexpected, and details of the Fort itself were becoming clearer. It was a massive castle, built of a warm, golden sandstone, gleaming in the light of the setting sun behind her, with a single tower either side of two enormous wooden doors, studded with iron, which were closed against them. Abigail had no doubt their presence had already been noted and reported.

A small postern in the left-hand gate opened, and a party of well-armed warriors marched out, led by a tall man in full armour, with a Ranusian sigil on his breastplate. This looked not like a welcome.

"Who comes to the Fort of Ranu?"

Shaunan rode forward for a few paces, her right hand open in the gesture of friendship. "My name is Shaunan, Waymage of Nordvein," she said with the quiet dignity Abigail so admired. "We have travelled far to consult the High

Waymages of the Wayzenmoot and ask you to grant us admittance."

"What is your business with the Wayzenmoot?"

"I am sorry, but I cannot tell you. It is a matter of great importance. If you would send to the High Temple, perhaps I might speak with someone?"

"Then we cannot admit you. Strangers are not welcome here."

Ylonya said smoothly, "Could you at least admit us to the Traders' Courtyard?"

The man glanced at her Yrusian Waymark and came to a decision.

"Very well. That far, but no further, until we have heard back from the High Waymages. But we will test your Waymarks before you proceed."

The captain signalled to one of his men, who walked up to them. They all dismounted and stood still for their Waymarks to be tested.

"What is the Traders' Courtyard?" Abigail whispered to Ylonya.

"It is where the contributions to the Wayzenmoot are unloaded," Ylonya replied in a low voice. "The rest of the Fort is forbidden to anyone who does not have the goodwill of the Wayzenmoot."

At a signal from the captain, the gates of the Fort swung open just wide enough to admit them, and they remounted and rode in. The crash as they shut behind them sounded ominous in Abigail's ears. She looked around curiously. The Traders' Courtyard was roughly oval, surrounded by high battlements on all sides, with regular guard posts. There were a number of small, single-storey brick buildings hugging the walls. On the opposite side to the gates, two other gates, locked and barred, denied entrance to the rest of the Isle.

"This is as far as I have been," Ylonya told her.

The captain of the soldiers marched up to Shaunan. "I have sent a messenger to the Wayzenmoot," he said. "Until then, you may take shelter in the Lodge of Visitors." He indicated one of the brick buildings. "It is empty at present. Your horses will be taken to our stables."

"My thanks, Captain. Do you know how long we will have to wait?"

"It is some distance to Ranusheim, so the wait will not be short. If there is anything you need, let one of my men know. I respect your Waymark, Waymage Shaunan, but these are troubled times."

"Some food and drink would be welcome," Shaunan said mildly. "We have travelled from Olaf today and are hungry and thirsty."

The captain nodded to one of his men. "Fetch food and drink for them."

"My thanks, Captain." Then to the others, "We might as well make ourselves comfortable. I do not expect an answer until the morning."

The Visitors' Lodge was quite spartan. There was a fireplace and kindling, one large table with eight chairs around it, and eight narrow beds set against the walls, each provided with a thin pillow and equally thin blanket. It was not a place to stay for long. Ylonya strode across to the fireplace and used her Goldstone to start a fire. Abigail chose a bed and dumped her pack down on it. She hoped the promised food and drink would arrive soon.

֍ Chapter 5 ֍

As Shaunan had predicted, they heard nothing until the following morning. The five of them had spent an uncomfortable night on the hard beds and had been brought enough food for a scant breakfast. Abigail could not wait to leave the place.

"They are not exactly hospitable, are they?" she said to Ellyn.

Shaunan overheard her, and said, "What did you expect? We have been given food and shelter. It is not their job to be hospitable. Their job is to guard the entrance to the Isle. Most of their visitors are only here to drop off donations and then return across the Land Bridge. It is rare for people to seek admittance to the Isle itself."

"Was it like this when you and Waymage Findoran arrived?" Ellyn asked.

"No, because our arrival had been pre-arranged. When we got here, someone from the Wayzenmoot was waiting for us, so we were admitted straightaway."

A knock on the door, followed immediately by the entrance of a soldier. "The messenger has returned, with a representative of the Wayzenmoot," she said. "Follow me."

A slim woman in golden-yellow robes with a thick travelling cloak over them was awaiting them. "Waymage Shaunan," she said, smiling. "Welcome back to the Isle of Ranu. It is many years since we have seen you."

Shaunan gazed at her for a moment, then her face lit up. "Joslin! Is it really you?"

"It is good to see you again, my friend. The years have not been unkind to you."

Shaunan turned to the others. "This is my friend, Waymage Joslin. We trained together. And Joslin, these are Abigail, my initiate, Ylonya, our Yrusian guide, Aidren, a young warrior, and Ellyn, my niece."

"You are all welcome to the Isle of Ranu," Joslin said. "If we make haste, we can reach Ranusheim by nightfall. The High Waymages are curious to know what brings you to the Isle. Captain," she turned to him, "please provide me with a fresh mount and bring out those of my friends."

"Yes, Waymage Joslin, at once."

Abigail found the change in the man's attitude amusing. From being stern and reticent, he had become diffident, anxious to please, almost fawning on the Waymage.

The great gates on the far side of the courtyard were opened for them, and they rode out. Joslin set a brisk pace, cantering for a while, then dropping back to a walk to rest the horses, before cantering again. Abigail hung on tight. Her riding skills had improved greatly during the seisdags of their journey, but they had walked most of the time, needing to conserve their horses' energy. This faster pace was exhilarating but scary. The road they were travelling on was bounded on either side by dense forest. When they paused to walk, Abigail could look around and saw tall firs and also some deciduous trees, oak, ash, beech and elm and, of course, Ranus trees, naked at this time of year, but beautiful nonetheless, all illuminated by the pale sunlight ahead of them. She was glad when they stopped for lunch. She sighed deeply, savouring this beautiful place. It seemed to call to a deep and hidden part of her soul.

During the slower portions of their journey, Shaunan and Waymage Joslin talked busily, catching up on three decades-worth of news.

"I had no idea you had stayed on here when we completed our training," Shaunan said.

"The Wayzenmoot captured my heart," Joslin said. "I could not think of any better way to spend my life than in serving them. And you, what did you do after you left?"

"Findoran – you remember Findoran? – and I travelled to the Vale of Berlysian and spent a couple of seasons there to complete our training as healers. Findoran met the love of her life there – a Dagâran warrior from Luvodican, so the three of us travelled to Dagâran together. Findoran became Waymage of Myndorian, and I, Waymage of Nordvein."

"And have you been happy?" Joslin asked.

"Yes," Shaunan said. Then a shadow crossed her face. "Or at least, mostly happy. I lost my husband some years ago."

"I'm so sorry," Joslin said. *What brings you to us now?* Abigail was surprised that she could hear the silent question. Was it an accident, or was Joslin including her on purpose?

Three things. First, I bring news of Havimi raiders in the Sea of Ranu and that they have allied themselves with the Talamdorians. Second, that there is a portal from another world in the Eastern Sea. And third, I have brought my initiate, Abigail, to meet the Wayzenmoot.

Abigail felt Joslin's glance on her. *Welcome to the Isle of Ranu, Abigail.*

Thank you, Waymage Joslin.

We will speak further when we arrive.

They were on the final part of the journey. Abigail's heart was beating fast – she was so excited to be reaching Ranusheim at last. The snow-clad slopes of what she knew was Mount Ranu, the most sacred mountain in the whole of Veylindré, rose ahead of her. The very air she was breathing felt clean and pure. She remembered Shaunan explaining that

Ranusheim lay in Mount Ranu's shadow. Here, at last, her questions would be answered. She would understand why she was here. The mysterious 'purpose' Shaunan had spoken of would be revealed. When she thought back to the girl she had been when she and Jacob had reached Nordvein, she hardly recognised herself. Now she was a Ranusian initiate, about to visit the place of her dreams, the place in which the interpretation of the lore of the Way she served was decided. If only Jacob could have been there to share this with her… where was he now? A pang of sorrow gripped her. She felt an odd mixture of emotions – she was excited, nervous and impatient in turns, longing for the journey to be over. When would she see the city itself?

The road bent to the left and there it was, the holy city of Ranusheim laid out in front of her. Most of it was hidden behind high walls of the same golden stone as the Fort of Ranu, but high above them she could see a seven-sided building of pure ranusfelsen, blushing crimson in the light of the setting sun. That must be it. The High Temple, home of the Wayzenmoot. They were nearly there. Suddenly, she felt sick to her stomach. What was she doing here? Breathe, Abigail, breathe.

The gilded gates swung open and they rode through.

"Stay together," Joslin told them all. "The route to the Wayzenmoot is complex and I do not wish to lose anyone." She smiled at Abigail reassuringly.

The five of them followed her along the wide streets. There were not many people on the streets at that hour, but those who were stared at them curiously. All wore robes or tunic and trews of the same golden-yellow cloth as Joslin's. Of course, everyone here was Ranusian. But who does the menial tasks?

We all share them, came Joslin's voice in her head. *Pure service does not demean those who serve.*

Of course. I'm sorry.

No apology needed, Abigail. We will be there soon. And Abigail heard a laugh in her mind. Joslin must have sensed how impatient she was feeling.

Then a different voice. It sounded like many voices speaking in unison, coming from the heart of the High Temple, or so it seemed. *Welcome, Abigail Winters. We have been expecting you.*

Now she could understand why Shaunan had struggled to describe Ranusheim. It was so different to any other place she had visited in Veylindré. A place set apart from the rest of the Commonweal, centre of the sacred Isle of Ranu, sufficient unto itself. She had never been anywhere as splendid and beautiful, yet the city seemed to welcome her – she felt instantly at home here. As they wound their way up along the wide streets towards the High Temple, she admired the fine buildings on either side, crafted from golden and white stone, so stylish and elegant, fitting homes for the Ranusian elite who made their homes here. And the graceful trees lining the streets, their branches swaying gently in the wind, which made the city feel like an integral part of the whole island. She felt a sense of peace, of belonging, which she had never experienced anywhere else in Veylindré. The air in her lungs was crisp and fresh, and she felt relaxed, yet at the same time, invigorated, full of new energy. At the edges of her hearing, she seemed to hear a subliminal song of serenity and acceptance.

The High Temple itself was beyond her expectations. Built in the traditional fashion with seven sides, but on a different scale altogether, it soared above the rest of the city, its tall spires reaching up to the heavens, the hallowed centre of this sacred city. One day, she might even be able to explore it. She hoped so. Where was Waymage Joslin taking them?

We have been expecting you. What did that mean? A frisson of disquiet seized her. She supposed the High Waymages of the Wayzenmoot had ways of knowing that were beyond her. Perhaps they had "seen" her arrival. Maybe they already comprehended the high purpose that Shaunan had prophesied for her. The thought made her uneasy. What was she, Abigail Winters, an ordinary English girl, doing mixed up in arcane purposes? Yet she was no longer who she had been, all those seisdags ago. She was a Ranusian initiate, and she felt as though she belonged here – more, perhaps, than she had ever belonged anywhere else, even home. It was a strange mix of sensations.

She shrugged her shoulders, left the unease behind. Doubtless she would find out soon enough. She rode on in a dream, suffused with an unfamiliar serenity, allowing the tranquillity of the song to resurge, soothing her mind and heart.

Ranusheim welcomed her.

"Abigail."

Roused from her trance, she started. Shaunan was speaking to her. "Abigail, we are here."

She came back to herself, back to her physical body, and glanced around. They had passed the High Temple and were now… somewhere else. The sight that met her eyes was unexpectedly familiar – she was in a substantial courtyard, surrounded by tall, white buildings with many windows, glinting gold in the light of the setting sun. Each building had a flag flapping in the breeze, with the swirling circle of Ranu in gold on a dark background. In the centre of the courtyard was the largest Ranus tree she had ever seen, its copper-coloured trunk both tall and broad, naked of leaves in this season, yet still beautiful. Then she had it – this was the place that Shaunan had visualised for her, that day in Luvodican when she had discovered that her Waymark would be of Ranu. She was filled with joy to finally see it in reality.

"This is the place you showed me," she said, beaming at Shaunan, "when you tested my powers, back in Luvodican."

Shaunan returned her smile. "That's right. It is as beautiful as I remembered."

Around them, the others were dismounting, going through the processes of arrival. Abigail shook herself, brought her mind back where it belonged, and slid off her mare's back. Then followed Waymage Joslin as she led them all through an arch to the stables behind the courtyard.

Once they had tended to their mounts, the Ranusian Waymage showed them to their rooms. "Get settled in, relax," she said to Abigail and Ellyn, "Supper is at twelfth hour – you will hear the gong. We eat in the dining room on the ground floor."

"Thank you, Waymage Joslin," Abigail said.

Once the woman had left, Ellyn gestured round the room. "This is all so grand," she said. "What am I even doing here?"

Abigail had a good look round, taking in the twin beds with snowy white eiderdowns and plump pillows, the two comfortable chairs, the polished wood of the floor and furniture, the wide window in one wall. She walked over and opened it, leaning out to see what was outside. Their room was in one of the tall buildings surrounding the courtyard. She admired the Ranus tree once more – so graceful, so elegant, so full of life.

Then she turned to Ellyn, "What is wrong, my friend?"

"It's just... Ranusheim. It has always been a place of forbidden mystery to me, to almost everyone I know. Of all the people in Nordvein, only Aunt Shaunan has ever been here. Now we've got here, what is going to happen next? And what use am I going to be? Surely they have no need for an apprentice cordwainer."

So this was why Ellyn was feeling so uncomfortable. She, who had come here from outside, did not share Ellyn's history, had not grown up hearing of Ranusheim as the home of arcane secrets, which only the elect few were permitted to visit. She had only heard of it from Shaunan, who had shared her love for it, her reverence of it. She remembered Ylonya's unease... even the well-travelled Yrusian had never been here. How could she reassure Ellyn?

"We're here because Shaunan has brought us. Once she has shared our news with the Wayzenmoot, we'll have to wait and see what they plan to do about it, and whether we will have any part in that. And," she could feel her lips quivering, "I intend to make sure they search for Jacob. Shaunan promised me."

Ellyn hopped off her bed, hugged her. "Of course they will. The Wayzenmoot can do anything."

"I hope so. I'm not sure I'll be able to stand it, if they can't."

When they heard the gong announcing supper, the two girls retraced their steps down the corridor, then down a wide flight of stairs. They paused at the threshold of the large dining room, to see if they could spot Shaunan and the others. Ylonya waved, and they threaded their way through the groups of diners, all clad in gold or yellow or white. Abigail was reminded of the grand furnishings of the palace at Luvodican –

finely-carved wooden tables with cloths of embroidered white linen over them, dotted around all over the room. Except for one long table which stretched the length of one end on a raised dais. She guessed that must be the one where the High Waymages sat. The people around it certainly looked stern and formidable. Was she catching Ellyn's unease?

"Here you are," Shaunan said. "Is all well?"

"Have some soup," Ylonya said. "It's carrot and coriander, delicious."

"Thank you."

Then Ellyn passed her the basket of rolls and she felt herself beginning to relax again. She smiled at her friend.

"What happens now?" Ylonya asked Shaunan.

"I expect the High Waymages will give us this evening to settle in, then tomorrow we will be summoned to share our story. So let us enjoy our meal, then return to my room to talk about it."

It seemed like good advice. As the soup was followed by roast meats and vegetables with a rich gravy, and then a fruit pie and custard for dessert, Abigail decided to concentrate on the here and now and savour the food in front of her. Tomorrow would come soon enough.

Once they had all made themselves comfortable – Abigail and Ellyn on one of the beds and Ylonya and Aidren in two of the chairs, Shaunan spoke. "Well, my friends. We have made it safely to Ranusheim. Tomorrow, we will speak with the High Waymages of the Wayzenmoot and discover what is to come. Do any of you have questions?"

"I do," Ylonya said. "I still don't understand clearly why we could not have sent a message from Luvodican. Why was it necessary to come all the way here? Not that I'm complaining

– it's the chance of a lifetime to visit Ranusheim – but I am puzzled."

"A good question, my friend," Shaunan replied. "Had it been only the news of the alliance between Havim and Talamdor, we could indeed have sent a message, and saved ourselves much heartache and time. But there are three other reasons why we are here. The first is so the Wayzenmoot can meet Abigail, the second concerns that which she bears, which will be revealed on the morrow. And the third is so we can enlist their aid in finding Jacob."

"I remember you saying," Ylonya said, "that you believed Abigail's coming to Veylindré had some hidden purpose, when we left Luvodican. But I still don't know what that is."

"It is not something I know for sure," Shaunan replied, "but something I deeply sense." She smiled at her initiate, who was looking uncomfortable. "I am sorry, Abigail; it is rude to talk like this in front of you. How are you feeling, now that we are here?"

The girl met her eyes and smiled. "It feels as though I have come home," she said. "I've never been anywhere else in Veylindré which has made me feel that way. But like Ylonya, this talk of a hidden purpose makes me uneasy. I'm not anyone special, I'm just Abigail, a very new Ranusian initiate. All I want to do is learn more about the lore of the Way and find Jacob again."

Shaunan sensed the pang of sorrow that mentioning Jacob's name elicited in Abigail. She hoped the Wayzenmoot would be able to locate him. Otherwise, she was not sure how far the girl would co-operate in what was to come. Time for a change of subject.

"How about you two?" she asked Ellyn and Aidren. "How are you finding being here, in Ranusheim?"

Ellyn gulped once, then said, "I don't know what I'm doing here either, Aunt Shaunan. I'm even less important than Abi – just a simple cordwainer. What use am I going to be to anyone?"

"Don't talk like that, Ellyn," Abigail said. "I'd be far more unhappy if my best friend wasn't here."

"Thank you, Abi." Ellyn reached out and squeezed her friend's hand. "That helps a little."

"What about you, Aidren?" Shaunan asked.

"Like Ellyn, I'm not sure what use I'm going to be," he said. "I am a Warrior of Dagâra. I'm not used to such grandeur. The only thing I know for sure is that I need to have a part in finding Jacob again, and protecting you all, as much as I can, without losing anyone else."

"That is more than enough, Aidren," Shaunan reassured him. "You are a worthy member of our company, as is Ellyn. As are you all."

Her eyes swept around the room, fixing on each of them in turn. Whatever the morrow brought, they would need to believe in themselves, to appreciate that they were going to be an important part of the future quest. Whatever shape that was going to take.

"We had better sleep, now," she said. "I expect the High Waymages will want to see us after breakfast tomorrow."

Ylonya returned to her room, more puzzled than before. Unlike the others, it seemed, her trained mind had caught the second reason for their journey: something Abigail was carrying, which she had apparently kept secret all this time. Her natural curiosity was piqued – what was this about?

She sat down in her comfortable armchair and poured herself a drink of water. Why had she not known of this? Why hadn't Shaunan trusted her? Or the others, come to that? Her agitation was too great for her to remain seated. She stood up, began to prowl around the room, racking her brains to recall any clues. This mysterious whatever the girl was carrying must be something small and easily hidden, otherwise she would have known about it before now. What could it be? She had been with the company ever since Luvodican and had never heard anything of the kind mentioned. She ground her teeth in frustration – she hated not knowing. But she would have to possess her soul in patience – after all, Shaunan had said it would be "revealed on the morrow."

Abigail felt nervous. All this time, during the long seisdags of their journey, the meeting with the High Waymages of the Wayzenmoot had been comfortably in the future. Now it was imminent, this very morning. She dressed with care, anxious to make a good first impression. She hoped Shaunan knew what she was doing.

She and Ellyn trailed downstairs, but she had no appetite for the excellent breakfast laid before them. She picked at her food, her stomach filled with butterflies.

You have nothing to fear, Abigail. We will tell our story to the High Waymages, then they will take counsel with each other as to what needs to be done.

I suppose so. But what if they cannot sense this 'high purpose' you have felt? What if I'm here on false pretences?

I do not fear that. Be at peace, my dear. You have nothing to be afraid of.

And Shaunan's voice left her mind. Somewhat reassured, she finished her breakfast with a better appetite.

Then Waymage Joslin appeared at their table. "The High Waymages are ready to see you, Waymage Shaunan, Abigail, Ylonya."

"What about us?" Ellyn asked.

"Return to your rooms, relax, explore the city. Do what you will."

Ellyn looked hurt and Aidren looked mutinous. Why didn't the Wayzenmoot want to see them too? It didn't seem fair – if it hadn't been for them, she and Jacob would likely have died in the forest near Nordvein.

"I am sorry, my dears," Shaunan said. "We will be back very soon."

The three of them followed the Waymage out of the building and into another, which Abigail had noticed the day before. It was circular in shape, with a pristine golden dome and an arched entrance, behind which was a pair of double doors made of bronze. Joslin laid her hand on one of the doors, which opened silently.

Inside was a large, imposing chamber, with light streaming in through its high windows, and a huge, round, Ranuswood table set in its centre. All twelve of the High Waymages were seated around it, on elaborately carved upright chairs, resplendent in their robes of gold, together with two others, two men Abigail did not recognise at all. One of them looked Garûnalonden, tall, with blonde hair and moustache, and pale blue eyes. The other looked Néartanian, but his Waymark showed he was a Warrior of Dagâra, and he was clad in rich clothing with a fine sword buckled at his waist. There were extra chairs ready for the three of them. She glanced up and saw a beautiful, curved ceiling with glorious images of the Six painted on it. Ceramic stoves were set at intervals around the walls and finely crafted silver wall lamps shed a warm light.

She thought with a pang of sadness how much Jacob would have appreciated them.

One of the High Waymages, a man of middling height, who reminded her of a younger version of Rewald, the Waymage of Talmis, stood and smiled as they entered.

"Welcome to the Audience Chamber of the Wayzenmoot," he said. "I am Gwynmaer, one of the two Néartanian High Waymages. The other is Bryna," and here a jolly-looking woman beamed at them. "Next to her are Onadia and Perran, who represent Dagâran." The two tall, dark-skinned Dagârans nodded gravely, their deep brown eyes fixed on the three of them.

The High Waymage was only speaking softly, but his voice was crystal clear in Abigail's ears. She wondered whether it was Waymagic or some aspect of the room's design. Her father would have loved it.

Gwynmaer continued, "Tarmina and Luciron represent Yrusian, and their intuition and wide knowledge of Veylindré are a great help to us, especially in these troubled times. Next to them are Daefiel and Fenlar of Garûnalond, who liaise on our behalf with the Lord and Ladies of Justice in far Mirunan."

As he introduced each one, Abigail tried to fix them in her memory. The two Yrusians looked as deceptively ordinary as Ylonya could – middle height, with tanned skin, brown hair – but for their brown eyes, which were full of a shrewd intelligence. The two Garûnalonden were a great contrast, being tall, slim of build, and beautiful and handsome respectively, with golden hair and clear blue eyes.

"Finally, there are Shonala and Ianlos, of Lènium," he waved his hand in the direction of two slender Lèniumen, with clear olive skin and dark eyes, "and Valwyn and Vordan, from the Isle. Shonala and Ianlos are our experts in healing and storytelling respectively, and Valwyn and Vordan are that rare phenomenon, natives of Ranu." He smiled at the two Ranusians. "Most of us come here from other parts of the Commonweal."

Abigail looked at the Ranusians with interest – she had not realised that the Isle had natives as well as incomers. But how silly – of course there must be – the Waymages of Ranu were not required to be celibate, after all. And there were two other Guild Halls on the Isle. Both the woman and the man were pale of face, their skin having an almost translucent quality, with light brown hair and spacious, dark grey eyes, which were a striking contrast. They smiled gently at Gwynmaer's remark.

"Also present at our bidding are Tremond of Mirunan and Ednor of Néartanis," he indicated each of them in turn, "who have travelled here with their own questions. This Council is convened that we may discuss the issues and decide on our course of action."

"Please, join us at the table," Gwynmaer said. Led by Shaunan, the three of them took their seats.

"Welcome back to Ranusheim, Waymage Shaunan," Onadia, one of the two Dagârans, said. Had she known Shaunan before she came to Ranusheim?

"Thank you, High Waymage Onadia," Shaunan responded formally. "May I introduce my friends?"

"Please do."

"This is Ylonya, daughter of Guildmaster Brickon and Guildmistress Margera of Yrusian. She has been our guide and helpmeet since Luvodican."

"Welcome, Ylonya," Luciron said. "Your reputation precedes you. We are grateful for your skills in garnering information."

Ylonya nodded. “It has been my privilege, High Waymage Luciron.”

“And this is Abigail, my initiate, our main reason for making this journey.”

“Welcome, Abigail,” Valwyn said, as the rest of the High Waymages affirmed, *You are welcome here, Abigail Winters.*

Shaunan continued, “The other two members of our company, Ellyn, my niece, an apprentice cordwainer, and Aidren, a Warrior of Dagâra, should also be present. Had it not been for them, we should not be here.”

“No slight was intended,” Perran said smoothly, “They will be told what they need to know in due course.”

“Now that we are assembled,” Gwynmaer said, “let the Council begin.”

Chapter 6

Ellyn watched her aunt, Abigail and Ylonya follow Waymage Joslin out of the room. Her heart stung. She felt betrayed.

"I told you they would think we were of no importance," Aidren fumed, once they were back in the privacy of his room. "To be sent to our rooms, as though we were children. It isn't fair."

"What are we going to do now? It seems clear that the High Waymages don't believe we matter. I was looking forward so much to coming to Ranusheim, and now…" A single tear ran down her cheek, and she brushed it away angrily. "I wish we were back home in Nordvein. Or in Luvodican, training with Master Markhan and Master Sanderon."

"Oh, me too. I was learning so much from Master Sanderon."

An idea struck her. "Perhaps we will be allowed to return there, once this council, or whatever it is, is over."

She saw his face brighten. "That would be marvellous. Let's hope we can. But for now, I guess we'd better wait until the others come back and explain what's going on."

"I'm not waiting tamely indoors," Ellyn said. "She said we might explore the city, did she not? Let's go."

They strode out into the courtyard. "Now, where should we go?" Aidren asked her.

"I don't know, I've never been anywhere like this before. Shall we go and look in the High Temple?"

"If you like. Then after that, I'd like to wander the streets, explore the city."

"Fair enough."

It felt so good to be alone with Aidren. There had been precious few opportunities during their journey. Ellyn tried to forget her hurt at being excluded from the meeting with the Wayzenmoot and concentrated on her beloved.

There was so much to see, to puzzle over. They peeped inside the High Temple, but did not dare to enter, not without Aunt Shaunan. So they strolled along the broad streets of Ranusheim, arm in arm. It felt so different to any other city she had experienced on their long journey – it lacked the friendly atmosphere of Luvodican, the noise and commotion of Céardochis and Néartanis. They walked past private homes, which looked light and bright and welcoming, with their wide windows and brightly painted front doors and noticed many other fine buildings, the purpose of which they could not guess. But no shops or taverns. It didn't seem like a regular city at all – every person was going about their business in a calm, unhurried manner. Obviously, something was going on, but it seemed to be at a level she could not discern. There were none of the frenetic qualities she had found so stimulating in other cities.

"I wonder how this place works?" she said to Aidren in a low voice. "It's so much quieter than any other city I've seen. They all appear to be fully occupied, but…" She shook her head, unable to put her finger on what she was finding so strange.

"I know what you mean," Aidren replied. "I miss the bustle of Céardochis."

"That's it. No bustle, no busyness. Like I said, they all seem to be fully occupied, but I can't work out with what. Let's go back to our rooms. I think I'd rather ask Aunt Shaunan about it."

"All right. With any luck, they will have finished their meeting by now."

At which her unease and resentment returned. Why had they been left out? She needed to know.

"Waymage Shaunan, perhaps you would like to speak first," Gwynmaer said courteously.

Abigail was warming to the Néartanian High Waymage. His face was open and kind, like most Néartanians she had encountered.

"Thank you, High Waymage Gwynmaer, although the story is not wholly mine to tell. It started towards the end of the Season of Completion, when Aidren and Ellyn were out riding in the forest south-east of Nordvein, and came across two young UnMarked strangers, Abigail," she nodded towards her, "and Jacob, who is now lost to us. But I will come to that later..."

Abigail sensed the unease of the gathered High Waymages at the mention of UnMarked strangers. She smiled to herself.

As she listened, Shaunan related the salient points of their story – how she had felt Abigail's latent power when she had healed her wrist, how she, Aidren and Ellyn had accompanied the two young strangers to Luvodican, so they could learn enough about Veylindré and the Way to earn their Waymarks, and their journey since then. Abigail watched the High Waymages closely, trying to discern their reactions.

"It was clear to me," Shaunan concluded, having left the unsettling news until last, "that Abigail," and she gestured towards her, "and Jacob had arrived in our world through some kind of magical gateway, somewhere in the Eastern Sea. The two of them were away searching for a source of fresh water, when their settlement was attacked by the Havimi. Their men fought valiantly to defend them, although they fell and failed. Among the dead were three of the attackers, two Havimi pirates and one Talamdorian."

"The Talamdorians have allied themselves with the Havimi?" Fenlar said in dismay, stroking his blonde moustache. Abigail could sense his reluctance to believe Shaunan. "We had heard rumours this might be so but have had no direct corroboration. How can you be sure that the third body was that of a Talamdorian?"

"Because," Abigail put in with a proud lift of her chin, "Jacob searched the bodies of the strangers, and around the neck of the one who was different, he found this."

She delved into the pocket around her waist and produced a cloth-wrapped bundle. She unwrapped it carefully, revealing a red buckskin pouch. Opening the drawstrings of the pouch, she brought forth the triangular-shaped, red stone she had carried for so long, and held it up for all to see.

Pandemonium. Several of the High Waymages blanched, and most cried out. The tranquil atmosphere of the Audience Chamber was disrupted by their fear, anger and dismay. Even the light within the room seemed to change. It was probably only the sun going behind a cloud. At least, she hoped so.

Ylonya said with satisfaction, "Ah, now I understand."

"A Bloodstone. A personal Bloodstone. This is evil news," Vordan said, his grey eyes huge in his pale face. "Yet it explains much. We had feared that the Prophet of the One was growing in power, but this is proof. As you guessed, Waymage Shaunan, that third man must have been his agent, and it seems clear that an alliance has been made between the two erstwhile enemies. Alas for our world."

Abigail felt confused. She had known from Shaunan's initial reaction that the Bloodstone was something dangerous, so she had kept it at the bottom of her pack, out of sight, all this time, only transferring it to her pocket this morning. But their reaction seemed extreme.

"Please, High Waymage Vordan," she said, raising her hand, "would you explain why this stone is such bad news for Veylindré? I don't understand."

"Very well." The Ranusian glanced round at his fellow Waymages and received assenting nods. "Perhaps it is time for this tale to be told openly. You have heard of the ancient war, during which it was believed that the Bloodstone of Talamu had been lost?"

"Yes, High Waymage. We, that is, Ellyn and Aidren, Jacob and I, heard *The Tale of the Seventh Goddess* at Luvodican, during Dagârastide."

"Very good. Thirty or so years ago," Vordan continued, "rumours of a new power in Talamdor first started to circulate in the Commonweal, and we put sources in place," here he nodded at Ylonya, so Abigail guessed he was talking about the Guild of Intelligencers, "to discover more. The Havimi, originally disaffected Talamdorians who had emigrated across the Southern Sea centuries ago to found their own nation, had invaded Talamdor a score of decades previously and enslaved the Talamdorian people. At that time, we reluctantly agreed not to intervene. Then we began to hear tales that a new Prophet of Talamu had arisen in the land and had empowered the Talamdorians to rebel against their dictators and expel them from Talamdor."

"A few years later, we began to notice that the power of the Way was beginning to wane and instigated a search for the cause. High Waymage Daefiel," and here he smiled at his Garûnalonden colleague, whose serene, beautiful face was framed by her pale blonde hair, "had a Truedream, which revealed that the Bloodstone of Talamu had been found, and that this self-styled Prophet of the One was using it to leech power from the Golden Stone of Ranu and from the network of Waystones on which all Veylindréans rely to access the Way through their personal Goldstones. Since when, in spite of our best efforts, the power of the Way has continued to decline, so it is now necessary for all our people to recharge their Goldstones once a year, rather than once a decade, as before."

"But in our darkest nightmares, we had not dreamed that this Prophet had the power to create personal Bloodstones for his agents," the Lèniumen High Waymage, Shonala, put in, consternation in her voice, deep for a woman's. "This is a black day for Veylindré."

"Excuse me, High Waymage Shonala," Ylonya said. "For me, this is the final link in the chain. My Guild has suspected for a long while that there was some connection between the Prophet's recent incursions and the power of the Bloodstone of Talamu. But we had never managed to find any proof. This explains much – why the agents of the Prophet have become so much bolder, and why the Havimi have chosen to ally themselves with their former enemies."

"Your point is well made, Ylonya," Luciron, one of the Yrusian High Waymages, said. "But it does not help us to discern what we must do."

"If I might speak?" The deep, resonant voice belonged to the Garûnalonden Watchman, Tremond. Abigail jumped. She had been focusing so much on the High Waymages, she had forgotten about the two strangers. He was a tall, lean man, clad in the dark blue uniform of the Watch, his long blond hair caught back in a ponytail. His beard and moustache were luxuriant, covering almost half of his face. His pale eyes were fixed on her, which she found disconcerting.

"Of course, Tremond," Vordan said.

"I wonder whether the Academy of the Watch might be able to help," Tremond said, now addressing them all. "The Council is aware that in recent years the Havimi have been raiding our coasts more frequently and are beginning to be a real nuisance to traders, through their presence on our seas. But not all their raids were entirely successful, and some Havimi are being held prisoner in our Watch Houses throughout the lands. I was sent here by Guildmaster Géorn of the Academy of the Watch, to ask what is to be done with them, as it is not our custom to put any to death. Perhaps they might be questioned about their Talamdorian allies?"

"That is a good thought," Fenlar said. "Please do so."

"I have something else to share with you," Tremond said, producing a cloth-wrapped package from the inside pocket of his jerkin. "Although I had not realised it was such an evil until this day. One of the Havimi in captivity also bore a Bloodstone, which we confiscated, although we did not know what it was. I have it here."

Gwynmaer shuddered before taking it, then said, "Thank you, Tremond. Maybe by studying it, we will be able to discern how it has been used."

"I too have ill news to relate," the Néartanian, Ednor, said in a light, tenor voice, strangely at variance with his warrior-like appearance. "I am the younger son of Lord Éadulf and Lady Aethed of Néartania. For the past few years, with my brother, Réothed, I have been in charge of the forces manning the garrisons along the border with Talamdor. In recent months, we have been sending small parties of trusted scouts – loyal people whose word we could count on – over the mountains, to discover what they might about the intentions of the Talamdorians. They have witnessed preparations for war –

companies being drilled in the uses of sword, pike and bow, and much coming and going between the border garrisons on the Talamdorian side and Talamunem City. It is our fear that they intend to invade Veylindré. Réothed has sent a trusted messenger to Mirunan, to alert Veylindré's secular rulers at the Hall of Justice, and I have come to you."

"And if the Talamdorians have allied themselves with the Havimi, as we have heard," Gwynmaer put in, "we may expect further attacks from that quarter also. We will need to contact the Master Mariner at Mathven to discover what our current shipping strength is, and also liaise with all the rulers of the lands."

"But trading ships would be no good in a battle against Havimi warships," Luciron, one of the two Yrusian High Waymages, protested. Perhaps he originally came from one of the Yrusian maritime communities. "It would take many seisdags to re-fit them for that purpose."

"A good point," Gwynmaer said. "How much time do you estimate we have to prepare, Ednor?"

"I am uncertain, High Waymage," Ednor replied.

"Not more than two seasons, and we will need every warrior and sailor we can muster," Daefiel said in a sad voice, which resonated with prophetic certainty. "I have seen it in the Golden Stone."

A moment of silence met this pronouncement. Abigail shivered. But she was becoming impatient with this slow unravelling of the facts. She raised her hand again.

Vordan, the Ranusian High Waymage, looked over at her, his grey eyes flashing. "Yes, Abigail? You have something to contribute?"

It almost sounded as though he was mocking her, but she didn't care. "What about Jacob?" she demanded. "How are you going to rescue him? If it hadn't been for him, you would have no proof at all."

"There are surely more important issues to discuss," the Garûnalonden High Waymage, Fenlar, said dismissively, looking down his long nose at her.

Abigail flushed, not sure whether to feel embarrassed or furious.

Shaunan stood, quick to defend her. "I promised Abigail that when we reached Ranusheim, the Wayzenmoot would search for Jacob. I would not be gainsaid."

Perran, one of the two Dagârans, nodded in acknowledgement. "That seems only fair."

Abigail glanced round at the other High Waymages, sensed when they softened into consent.

"I feel your grief, Abigail," the Ranusian, Valwyn, said, her voice gentle and soft. "Perhaps this is the time for you to share the tale of Jacob's disappearance."

So Abigail explained how Jacob had been snatched from the tavern in Talmis, how Ylonya had failed to trace him, and how Shaunan had persuaded her that the only way of finding him would be to ask the Wayzenmoot. "He could be anywhere by now," she wound up, "and I miss him so much." She bit her lip, determined not to cry in front of these High Waymages.

"We grieve for your loss," Daefiel said softly. "I will attempt to locate him by searching in the heart of the Golden Stone of Ranu."

"Thank you, High Waymage Daefiel," Abigail replied. "I appreciate that his absence may seem a minor issue in light of everything else we have heard, but it means the world to me."

Then she became aware that Shaunan was speaking silently to the assembled High Waymages. *My final reason for making this journey is so you may speak with my initiate privately. I have sensed great power in her and believe she will be central to the quest for the Master Bloodstone.*

That is understood, Waymage Shaunan. We will do so later, when the others are not present.

"We have all learned much," Gwynmaer said aloud. "Perhaps we should reconvene in a few days to consider our course of action." He rose to his feet. "This Council is concluded."

The other High Waymages rose too and processed out of the Audience Chamber. Abigail and the others left by the door they had come in from.

"At last I understand what is going on," Ylonya said as she, Shaunan and Abigail walked back to their rooms. "Why didn't you tell me about the Bloodstone earlier, Shaunan?"

"Forgive me," Shaunan said, "at first, I did not know you, and later on, I almost forgot it as we concentrated on getting here safely."

Ylonya was not convinced by this response but had the sense to let it go. "I felt for Aidren and Ellyn," she said. "They have been staunch companions on our journey. It seemed unfair to exclude them from the meeting."

"I agree," Abigail said. "I couldn't believe it when Waymage Joslin summoned the three of us and not them."

"Yes, I believe it was a mistake," Shaunan said. "We must go to them and share what has happened. Let us hope they are able to forgive us."

Having tried Ellyn's room first, Shaunan knocked on Aidren's. "Who is it?"

"Shaunan. We have come to tell you both about the meeting."

Aidren opened the door. "Come in."

She, Abigail and Ylonya entered the room. Shaunan noticed the traces of past tears on Ellyn's face, the closed expression on Aidren's. Whatever the High Waymages of the Wayzenmoot thought, she must share the truth with them. She owed it to them – without the pair of them, they would not be here, trying to discern how to save the Commonweal.

"Well?" Ellyn said. "What happened? Or aren't you allowed to tell us?"

Shaunan winced at the bitterness in the girl's voice. Automatically, she soothed her.

"Of course we are going to tell you. You are just as much members of the company as we are."

But before she could gather her thoughts, decide on what order to make the revelations, how to break the news gently, Abigail forestalled her. "You didn't miss much. The High Waymages have heard our story, and there were two others there – Ednor, a Dagâran Warrior from Néartania, who told them that the Talamdorians are planning to invade Veylindré, and Tremond, a Garûnalonden Watch Officer, who asked what to do with some Havimi prisoners they have in their Watch Houses. I asked them about rescuing Jacob and the Ranusian High Waymage, Daefiel, promised to search for him. And they all know about the Bloodstone."

"Abigail!" Shaunan cried, as she watched both Aidren's and Ellyn's faces turning grey, felt the fear in both of them. "Gently."

Abigail blushed. "I'm sorry, Shaunan, but they have the right to know."

Yes, but there are ways of sharing such news. None of it is good.

I'm sorry.

"The Talamdorians are preparing to invade Veylindré?" Aidren said, his hand on his sword, as Ellyn whispered, "What Bloodstone?"

"I am sorry, Ellyn, Aidren," Shaunan said. "We know this is hard to hear. But it is as Abigail said." She frowned at her initiate – she would have to learn a little tact. Perhaps she did not yet truly understand the impact of what she had said. She was still young in the ways of Veylindré, after all. "We do not yet know what the Wayzenmoot plan to do – there will be another meeting in a few days."

"But… if the Talamdorians are planning to attack the Commonweal, I need to be there. I am a Warrior of Dagâra," Aidren said.

Ellyn said, dread in her voice, "You said *a* Bloodstone. I thought there was only one, the Bloodstone of Talamu, and that it had been lost centuries ago."

"I fear not," Shaunan said. "It seems as though the Prophet of the One has found it and has discovered a way of using it to make personal Bloodstones for his agents, like our Goldstones. We only know this because of Abigail and Jacob."

"What do they have to do with the Prophet of the One?" Aidren asked, confused.

"Abigail, show them."

So once again, Abigail fished the Bloodstone out of her pocket. "Jacob found this on the body of one of the strangers who slew our people."

Ellyn moved closer to Aidren, a look of horror on her face. He reached out and took her hand.

"What are the Wayzenmoot going to do?"

"I do not know," Shaunan said, "but whatever happens, you will be at the next meeting. But before that, Abigail and I need to speak with them again."

Abigail and Shaunan headed towards the Audience Chamber again the following morning. As they walked, Abigail asked, "Why do they need to meet me again? I've told them all I know."

"They need to test your power," Shaunan said, "to help them to discern what is different about you, why you are so important. I have sensed this but have been unable to penetrate its heart."

Once more, the twelve High Waymages were seated round the Ranuswood Table, waiting for them. Abigail shivered – she was not looking forward to this.

"Come within," Gwynmaer said, "be seated. Waymage Shaunan, perhaps you would share what you have sensed in Abigail."

"As I said yesterday, I have perceived great power in her. And I believe that her origin from outside our world may make her less vulnerable to the evil of the Master Bloodstone."

Gwynmaer nodded. "That may be so. Is there anything else?"

"Yes. While I do not have the Sight," and here Shaunan bowed her head to High Waymage Daefiel, "there have been two occasions when I have divined that her coming to Veylindré at this time is of great import, that she is here to fulfil some high purpose. It felt as though the truth was being revealed to me by Ranu herself."

Daefiel looked intently into Shaunan's eyes. "You have seen clearly," she said. "I too have foreseen the coming of a stranger from another world, to save us all from Talamu."

"I'm sorry," Abigail broke in, "but what has Talamu to do with all this? I thought she had been banished in the ancient war."

The High Waymages glanced at each other, then seemed to come to a decision. “At the end of that war,” Vordan, one of the Ranusian High Waymages, said, “the Six chose to withdraw from direct intervention in Veylindré. They set up magical wards to prevent Talamu from becoming active again. But we fear that since the Prophet found the Master Bloodstone, and started to use it, Talamu has been able to use some of the power leeched from the Goldstones to strengthen herself, and that her long-term plan is to become corporeal once more and to build up enough power to enable her to occupy a human body, and hence become a living goddess.”

Shaunan’s face turned grey. “That is worse than my darkest nightmares. It must not happen.”

“You are right, Waymage Shaunan,” Vordan said. “We believe that the power of the Master Bloodstone is inimical to anyone born of the Six, and that any Veylindréan who attempts to wrest it from the Prophet would sooner or later come under its control. But because Abigail comes from outside our world, she may have the unique strength to resist its power.”

Abigail could feel the colour draining from her face. Was this really why she was here? To attempt something no other could do?

High Waymage Gwynmaer smiled at her. “Fear not, Abigail. If it is the Wayzenmoot’s power, we will do all we can to enable you to fulfil this quest, which is vital for the future of all Veylindré.”

Abigail bowed her head.

“I will work with you,” High Waymage Valwyn said, “to teach you how to attune yourself to the Bloodstone you carry. Say nothing of this to your companions.”

Δ Chapter 7 Δ

Jacob heard the voice, deep, hypnotic, commanding, "Jacob Wallingford, I have waited a long time to meet you."

He walked into the private chamber of the Prophet of the One, his palms clammy, his heart beating fast, entirely unready for this encounter. Black floor, black walls, black statues, polished to a fine black shine, black, floor-length curtains over what he assumed were windows, the space lit only by the pale, wavering light of candles, and by a sooty red glow at the far end. Like the light in the secret pass. He shivered. Portak's sharp finger prodded him in the back, so he moved towards the dark crimson light, his boots loud on the stone floor. The light illuminated a black throne, crafted of either stone or wood, he could not tell, on which sat a tall, imposing figure, so thin he reminded Jacob of a skeleton in black robes, of Death himself.

One lean, white hand beckoned him closer. "Jacob Wallingford. We meet at last."

Behind him, Portak hissed, "Show some respect – bow."

Jacob bent forward in clumsy obeisance. As he straightened up, the Prophet – for this must be the Prophet – said, "You have done well, Portak. I am pleased with you."

"Thank you, my Lord. I am very sorry I did not manage to recover the Bloodstone."

Jacob darted a look at the Prophet's face. The faintest frown between his brows seemed to daunt Portak out of all proportion to its severity.

"Yes, that is a pity," the voice was cold as ice. "Leave us, Portak. I will speak with you later."

"But, my Lord…"

"Leave. Now." The voice cracked out like a whip and Portak cowered.

"Of course, my Lord… My Lord?"

"What is it?" Jacob could hear the irritable impatience, only loosely held in check, in the man's tone.

"When will that be?"

"When I choose."

Portak's face was stricken. "My Lord," he said, bowing deeply. Then he turned on his heel and left.

"Now, Jacob, we may speak in peace. You may sit." The Prophet gestured towards a chair, off in the shadows, and Jacob obediently fetched it and sat, glad for its support.

He risked a longer glance and took in a stern white face, all lines and angles, framed by straight, iron-grey hair, which touched the man's shoulders, and dominated by a pair of fierce dark eyes with the inevitable blood-red triangle on the forehead above them, and a thin-lipped, cruel mouth. The man was sitting bolt upright on his throne, eschewing the comfort of leaning against its back. His only ornament a triangular red jewel, which he wore on a silver chain around his neck. As he breathed, its facets caught the light. Jacob shivered, this was not someone to cross. Why was he here?

"Tell me how you have come here."

Could he read minds too? Jacob noticed his hands were trembling, and clenched them together in his lap, licking dry lips before answering.

"I – I am unsure, my Lord. The first thing I remember is being on board a boat, heading up what I was told was the River Clearwater. Portak told me he had found me wandering, alone and confused, after a shipwreck. And that he was bringing me here for my own safety. But I don't know why."

"You were in a shipwreck? How… unfortunate." The deep voice throbbed in the surrounding silence.

Jacob was instantly sure the sympathy was feigned. He stiffened in his seat.

"What do you remember before that, Jacob?"

"I don't know… there seems to be a gap in my memory. I remember being on board a ship, on the ocean, with some people, but I don't remember who they were or why I was with them."

"What else?" The voice now sounded gentle, encouraging, so Jacob was filled with a desire to say more. He racked his brains, trying to come up with an answer that would satisfy the Prophet's curiosity. Although why the man cared, he had no idea. Better not think about that, perhaps.

"I am from England. My father was a blacksmith and I was his apprentice."

"From England? That is most interesting." The voice was almost purring now. "Then how do you come to be in this world?"

"In God's name," the words burst out of Jacob, "why do you keep asking me? I've told you, I can't remember." Then quailed, expecting to be annihilated by the Prophet's anger.

To his astonishment, the man was leaning back on his throne, a look of satisfaction on his pale face.

"You are telling the truth. No-one from this world would call on the name of God in their extremity. Very good, very good. You interest me greatly, young man."

"Wait, you know who God is?" Jacob was flabbergasted. "I thought everyone here worshipped the goddess Talamu?"

"So we do and so do I," the Prophet said, a curious smile on his face. "But originally, I came from your world, Jacob. Which is a secret known to very few. But I believe I can trust you – after all, we share something that no others do – a common origin."

"You are from England?" The relief was enormous. "Then, can you tell me how to get home?"

"Alas, that is beyond my power. At present. But if you help me in my task, Jacob, we will find the way back in due time. Has Portak told you much about our world?"

The bubble of hope burst with a sad pop. "No, my Lord. Only that the people of Talamdor worship Talamu and the others worship six goddesses and are witches." Jacob shuddered.

"And you know that witches are evil, and need to be rooted out, destroyed, before they influence others with their vile magic? The *Malleus Maleficarum* made it quite clear."

"The Malleus what?"

"You may know it better as *The Hammer of Witches.*"

Jacob nodded. "That book? Of course."

He had never read the book but knew many tales from it. It had been one of the most popular books in all England – after the Bible, obviously. He could remember his father talking about it.

"And we know exactly what we need to do with these devil spawn, these weeds that have found their way into the Garden of Eden, do we not?" Not waiting for Jacob's nod of agreement, the Prophet swept on in a fervent voice, "They must be ripped out, root and stem, purged and set aflame. So that the world may be purified and returned to God's true purpose."

"Yes. That's why I went along with Portak. Because he was saving me from falling into their hands."

"Good. I think I may have a use for you." He clapped his hands once and a door Jacob had not noticed before opened.

"You called, my Lord?" A small man, clad all in black, a silver bangle like his own around his wrist.

"Take him back to his room in the Visitors' Hall." Then to Jacob, "Say nothing of this to any other. We will speak again, very soon."

Portak stomped back down the corridor from the Prophet's apartment, down the aisle of the Great Temple and out into the open air. To be dismissed like that, after all he had done, all he had suffered. It wasn't right. Why was the Prophet so interested in Jacob? He meant to find out, before he was very much older.

Waves of jealousy coursed through him. He had done his level best to fulfil the Prophet's wishes, even if he had failed to find the Bloodstone. He'd expected a little more appreciation. "You have done well, Portak. I am pleased with you." That was all. No questions about his journey, about any information he had garnered along the way, just a peremptory dismissal.

He needed to see Balmak. He hurried through the streets, his blood zinging in his veins at the prospect. It had been so long, so very long. He reached Balmak's apartment and let himself in.

"You're home!" Portak heard the joy in his dear friend's voice and rushed to hug him.

"I've got so much to tell you."

Balmak linked his arm through Portak's, drew him into the living room. "Come, sit down. Do you want anything to eat or drink?"

"No, thank you. The boy and I ate in the Visitors' Hall earlier."

"What boy is this?" Balmak's voice was light, but careful. Portak knew his friend was wary of showing curiosity about his work for the Prophet, because so much of it was confidential. But Portak was in no mood to respect that. He needed to heave his concerns off his heart and he trusted Balmak implicitly.

"I was told to find any survivors of a particular shipwreck. And found one – Jacob. Balmak, he comes from another world."

"Another world? How can that be?"

"There is a portal in the Eastern Sea. The ship came through seisdags ago. The Prophet sent me to find them. I got one – Jacob, but not the other. Not the girl. He's with the Prophet now. I got sent away, like an errant schoolboy. As though the Prophet cared more about the boy than about what I had to tell."

Portak realised his fists were clenched. Balmak's arm came around his shoulders and he forced himself to relax, to breathe deeply.

"Why do you mind so much?"

"It's just so filthily ungrateful. After all I did for him, all the miles I travelled. And I managed to find one of them and bring him all the way back. Then was just dismissed."

"Let it go, my love. I'm sure the Prophet appreciates what you've done for him. But his curiosity about the boy trumped everything else."

Balmak was so wise, so kind. "Do you really think so?"

"I'm sure so. Now tell me all about it."

Portak drew a deep breath and began.

When Portak left his friend, he was feeling a lot calmer, more settled. Balmak had helped him regain perspective. He was so blessed to have him in his life. But his curiosity remained. Where had Jacob come from? Was he from somewhere else, after all? Where had the settlers of that cove come from? And why was the Prophet so interested in them? In Jacob? And how had the Havimi known where to find them? Had the lad been a great warrior, Portak would have understood. But he was only a boy in his late teens with some mundane skill at smithing. It didn't make sense. He knew there was no use asking the Prophet, but perhaps he could get it out of the boy. He would wait in his room.

When the boy walked in, he was looking thoughtful. He started when he saw him.

"What are you doing here?"

"No need for alarm," Portak said in his best reassuring tone, "I was wondering what the Prophet had to say to you."

"That is none of your business. What he said to me was private."

Portak could not believe his ears. He had the quick temper which often went with red hair and felt his face flushing with anger. He fought to keep his expression neutral. Was this how his care was being repaid? He did not deserve this treatment.

"It matters not," he lied. "But you would do well to remain in my favour, Jacob. The friendship of Portak, favoured lieutenant of the Prophet, is not to be discarded lightly, without thought."

The boy had the grace to look ashamed. "I'm sorry, Portak. I didn't mean to slight you. But I've got a lot to think about… would you mind leaving me alone, please?"

Portak bit his tongue. He'd had the boy once, he could have him again. He shrugged, "As you will. Send a servant for me if you change your mind."

Then, holding on to every scrap of dignity at his command, he stood up and left the room.

Jacob watched him leave with relief, mingled with guilt. It did seem ungrateful, after all Portak had done for him, saving him from the witches of Veylindré and bringing him all the way here. But he needed some time alone, time to think about what the Prophet had told him.

He was from England. From Jacob's real world. He remembered his father describing such a man, George… something. The air of cold command, the gaunt, skeletal frame, the fervour against witches and heresy – his father had mentioned all those, they had made a deep impression on him. That George… Crutwell – that had been the name – had been in his forties, thirty years ago, when his father had been a young man. Yet he would swear that this… Prophet was still in his fifth decade. It must be a coincidence. If he had truly been the same person, he would have been in his seventies by now – an old man, not someone in the prime of life.

He sank onto his bed. He still had no clear idea why he was here. The Prophet's final words echoed in his mind, "I think I may have a use for you." He didn't know whether to feel reassured or afraid. And why was Portak so angry with him? If only he had one friend, with whom he could talk about these things. But he had no-one. His previous idea, of finding smith work in the City, seemed laughably naïve, now. It seemed obvious he would not be allowed any freedom of movement. At least, not while the Prophet had a use for him.

Yet he was beginning to understand why Portak spoke of the Prophet with such reverence, such love. After only one meeting, he, too had begun to fall under the spell of the man's charisma. But he needed to know more about him. He'd said he was from England, from Jacob's own world. How had he come here? Why had he stayed? And how had he ever forgotten his God?

What possible use could the Prophet have for him? Jacob's curiosity was piqued. Maybe if he made himself "useful" enough, the Prophet would send him home.

Portak was not summoned to his master's presence until the next day. By which time, he had chewed his fingernails down to the quick.

"Portak," the Prophet said when he walked in, "the young man may be useful."

Portak let out a sigh of relief.

"However," and Portak's stomach clenched, "it is a very great pity you did not capture the girl also, that you failed to recover the Bloodstone."

"My Lord, I'm sorry…"

"Sorry does not suffice. Thanks to your blunder, the Veylindréan witches now know about Gomlak's Bloodstone. Their ignorance was an important part of my strategy."

"Let me try again, my Lord. I know I can find them." He would dare anything, undergo any risk, to regain the Prophet's favour.

"It is too late. The damage has been done. I have sensed it. That is not why I have sent for you. I have another task for you. You are to answer all Jacob's questions about Talamdor and about Holy Talamu."

"But my Lord, how…"

"How is immaterial. Just do it." He paused, frowning. "On second thoughts, I will undertake his religious instruction myself."

"But my Lord, it is no trouble…"

"I *said*, you will leave his religious instruction to *me*."

Portak bowed his head. "Of course, my Lord. I will do my best."

"Do better than that. Do not fail me again.... Now leave."

A knock on the door. "Jacob, it's me."

Portak.

"Come in." Although he wished the man would leave him alone. Even in the short time he had been here, the four walls of this room had become a refuge, a place he could be alone... But at the same time, its' dark grey walls were becoming oppressive, depressing. The only hint of brightness in the room was the red coverlet of the bed. And he was getting sick to death of being stuck indoors with no work to do, not even a piece of wood and a knife to whittle with.

"I thought you might like to have a wander round the City, and I could answer any questions you have."

Jacob had heard this before. When had Portak *ever* truly answered his questions? But he had nothing else to do. Since that first meeting with the Prophet, he had been twiddling his thumbs. The familiar feeling of being trapped filled his mind and heart.

"All right, thank you." He stood up, flung his cloak around his shoulders and followed Portak out of the Hall of Visitors.

As ever, he was glad to be out of doors, even in this freezing cold weather. He remembered to put up the hood of his cloak and was glad of its warmth. He strode along beside Portak, looking around avidly. The tall, dark buildings, the narrow, winding streets. Everyone they passed seemed to be deadly serious – he hadn't seen anyone smiling. Were their lives so bleak? Again he noticed two distinct groups of people – the ones he thought of as upper class, with the red triangular marks on their foreheads like Portak's, and the rest, with silver bangles like his own, who seemed to be disdained, looked down upon by the others. He shivered. This city was so strange, so different from any he had seen in England. Which hadn't been many, to tell the truth. Even Southampton, the port from which they had sailed all those months ago, seemed small and rustic in comparison. Southampton. What did that remind him of? Who had he sailed with? And where were they sailing to? He wished he could remember.

"... and since then, the City has expanded, to shelter the Prophet's closest allies."

"I'm sorry, would you say that again?"

The man frowned. "Aren't you listening to me?"

"Forgive me. My mind wandered for a moment. You were saying the City has expanded in recent years?"

Portak glared at him. "You haven't been listening to a word I've been saying, have you?"

"I was admiring the grandness of this place," Jacob lied. "I've never visited such a fine city before. And I started thinking about the cities I had known back in England..."

"You can forget that, now. You are here and will remain here, in the Prophet's service."

What was he doing here? He wished he were back home. Then he realised Portak was speaking again, in a low tone which only reached his, Jacob's, ears.

"I was *saying*," he said, "that in the thirty or so years since the Prophet came to power in Talamdor, much of the City has been restored to its former glory. Old buildings have been repaired, new ones built, our temples have been restored to the proper worship of Holy Talamu, and the streets repaired and repaved. Come," he said, gesturing towards a flight of steps ahead of them, "let us climb on to the wall, where we will be able to see more."

Jacob obediently followed him up the steps and they came out onto a wide path, bordered on each side by battlements of the same black stone that seemed to be the universal building material here, with guard posts at regular intervals. Portak led him toward the north, judging by the sun, then stopped and pointed.

Following the direction of Portak's finger, Jacob could see what he guessed were hundreds – maybe even thousands – of people, who looked like ants from this height, marching in unison up and down a gigantic square outside the walls, which was surrounded by a sprawling confusion of tents. Further away, others seemed to be practicing swordplay and archery. The pale sun glinted off helmets and weapons. Why did the Prophet need such an army?

"Who are they and what are they doing?"

"They are the forces the Prophet has gathered to himself. They are being trained in the arts of war, so that when the time comes, they will be ready."

Jacob looked at Portak, whose face was full of a grim satisfaction. "Ready for what?"

"Use your brain. What do you think?"

Jacob put two and two together and gaped at him. "You're going to invade Veylindré?"

"Yes, that is the Prophet's plan. Or rather," and here he seemed abashed, "I should say, it is the plan of Holy Talamu. All true Talamdorians believe that everyone should worship none other than Her. The Veylindréan witches and their people are heretics of the worst kind, worshipping six goddesses."

"I see." Jacob had heard about heretics at home. He knew that each faction of Christians believed that they alone followed the true faith of Christ, and that all others were heretics, destined for eternal damnation. But he had never taken much notice – he had attended his parish church dutifully enough each Sunday and was secure in his faith. He was no heretic. Yet who knew what they might think of him, here. He did not worship Talamu, that was for sure. Better keep his mouth shut.

"Could you tell me more about Veylindré?" he asked.

"Why do you want to know?"

"Because the only thing I know about it is that they worship six goddesses instead of one. But the people on the boat didn't seem to be evil."

"In the beginning," Portak began, "Talamdor was part of the Commonweal of Veylindré. But long ages ago, Holy Talamu perceived that the practices of the Six (which is what the Veylindréans call their goddesses) were deeply flawed. So she called people who were loyal to her ideals together, and they waged war on the rest of the Commonweal. That was a sad period in Talamdorian history. The Veylindréans were stronger than us, and Holy Talamu was forced to retreat to the mountain fastnesses of Talamdor. And an earthquake came, which raised the Talamdorian Mountains to separate us from the rest of the Commonweal. Which suited us fine. In the centuries since then, we have been rebuilding our strength. And now," his voice was becoming louder in his enthusiasm, "we are nearly ready to take back what was ours, and to convert all Veylindréans to the worship of Holy Talamu."

Jacob shivered at the fervour in Portak's voice. It seemed he was being caught up in some kind of religious war. On the other hand, if he, Jacob, could play a part in ridding this world of the evil of witches, shouldn't he be proud to play his part?

֍ Chapter 8 ֍

"Shaunan," Abigail said the following morning, as they sat around the table in the dining room, eating breakfast: eggs and rashers of fried bacon, followed by soft white rolls, slathered with butter and honey, "I'd love to know more about Ranusheim."

"You speak for me also," Aidren said. "When Ellyn and I went for a wander around the city yesterday, we both felt as though there were things going on beyond our sight and hearing, and everything seemed so quiet."

"I do not think the High Waymages need us today," Shaunan replied. "Let us go for a walk and I can answer your questions as we go."

They wrapped up well before emerging into the bright sunshine. Abigail once more admired the beauty of the buildings surrounding them – so clean, so spare, so elegant.

"When Aidren and I were walking around yesterday," Ellyn began, "we noticed that everyone had a Ranusian Waymark, apart from the children, of course. How does the city work without Néartanian crafters, Dagâran smiths or Yrusian traders?"

"All the inhabitants of Ranusheim – in fact, all who live on the Isle except for the Dagâran Warriors at the Fort of Ranu, have Ranusian Waymarks. Even the children tend to follow their parents and end up with Ranusian Waymarks too. You know that there are only three settlements on the Isle – the Hall of the Guild of Papermakers at Muillean, the Fort of Ranu at the entrance to the Isle, and Ranusheim itself, which is home to not only the Wayzenmoot, but also to the Guild of Scriveners and Printers. And you may have observed that the city is more compact than others we have visited."

"Yes, we noticed that yesterday, Aidren said. "It seems very small for such an important place."

"Who lives here?" Abigail asked.

"The population is quite select," Shaunan said. "The most important are the twelve High Waymages who make up the Council of the Wayzenmoot, two for each land in the Commonweal. Every adept and Waymage in each land votes for their land's candidates, and elections take place every three years, on a rolling basis, so that six High Waymages are elected every three years, to join the six who were elected three years before that."

"Why are they so important?" Abigail asked.

"Because they are the final arbiters in all matters of the lore of the Way."

"So what do all the rest of the citizens do?" Ellyn asked.

"Many work at the Hall of Scriveners and Printers, which is responsible for formulating, recording and preserving the lore of the Way and sending it out to the rest of the Commonweal. Ranusheim is also the home of the Colaste a'r Teisen, where Ranusian adepts train to become Waymages, and where a select few Waymages undergo further training to become First Waymages, one for each land. So there are also experienced Waymages who act as teachers and mentors. On completion of their training at the Academy, most new Waymages choose to return to own lands, either to their own communities, or to towns or villages without a Waymage. As I did. But some opt to stay on, carrying out research into new methods of accessing the power of the Way. Waymage Joslin is one of those."

Shaunan stopped in front of an imposing building, several storeys tall, built of the same warm, golden stone that seemed to be common here, with a many-columned portico framing double doors. Like all the buildings in Ranusheim, it was spotlessly clean and well-cared for.

"This is the Colaste a'r Teisen," she said.

"What does that mean, Aunt Shaunan?" Ellyn asked.

"Translated from Old Veylindréan, it is the College of the Way, where all Ranusian adepts come for training. This is the administration building. Behind it is the College itself, with many lecture rooms and the halls of residence for Ranusian adepts." She laughed. "I can remember how my knees were knocking, the first time I entered here. Findoran and I knew that from then on, we were committed – there would be no way out but through. Fortunately, we both made the grade."

"What happens to adepts who fail?" Ylonya asked.

"Failure is rare – the senior Waymages of the College make every effort to ensure that their students learn what they need to know. No-one failed to qualify during the time I was there."

"But what happens if they do?" Ylonya persisted.

Shaunan ignored the question. Abigail was disappointed. She wasn't at all sure she would come up to the required standard. If she ever managed to get here. "Could you tell us more about the training?" she asked.

"Perhaps later," Shaunan said. "Much of it is only appropriate for Waymages to know. Most of the College is closed to all except adepts and Waymages."

Abigail was seized by a strong desire to belong here – to be here as an adept, training to become a Waymage. But then, how would she ever find Jacob? She wanted to believe what Daefiel had said, that she would try to find him in the Golden Stone of Ranu, but what if she couldn't? What then? She couldn't bear the thought of never seeing him again. Once more, she pushed the thought away.

As they moved on, Ylonya said, "I'm still a little confused. I understand that serving the lore of the Way is the primary function of the inhabitants of Ranusheim, but people still need to eat, streets and buildings need to be cleaned, and all the other menial services which contribute to the working of a city still need to be carried out. Who does those?"

"A good question, Ylonya," Shaunan said. "The answer is simple. Every inhabitant of Ranusheim over the age of twelve, from the High Waymages to the newest adept, is required to spend one day a seisdag doing some kind of manual labour. They work on their own specialism for a further four days and have one rest day."

"That is so different from all the cities I've known," Ylonya commented. "Everywhere else, only the lowest members of any guild carry out the unskilled work."

"Ranusheim doesn't follow normal rules. Here, serving the lore of the Way is everyone's primary function, and that teaches humility."

"I remember Waymage Joslin saying something about that when we arrived, and I was wondering about this," Abigail said. She wrinkled her forehead, trying to remember Joslin's exact words. "She said, 'We all share them. Pure service does not demean those who serve.' I didn't understand what she meant, then, but I do now."

"I'd like to know what happens to all the food and other goods that are sent to the Isle from the other lands," Ellyn said. "How do the people here manage in the cold seasons?"

"There are deep caves high on Mount Ranu, where surplus meat and vegetables are kept in cold storage and brought out to feed the people when donations of fresh produce dry up," Shaunan said. "Other goods are kept in storage until they are needed. Every Ranusian is entitled to the resources they need to live a plain, modest life. It works reasonably well."

"Where are we going next?" Ellyn asked.

"What do you want to see?" Shaunan said.

"I'd love to see inside the High Temple," Abigail said.

"Very well."

As they walked along the wide streets, down towards the High Temple, Abigail began to see what Aidren had meant about the quiet, serene atmosphere of the place. The purpose of the buildings puzzled her, until she realised they were mainly residential. There seemed to be very few shops or taverns, or other public buildings. In comparison to Céardochis, it seemed so calm, no bustle or excitement. To her surprise, she found that she missed it – the calls of traders, the hubbub of many conversations at once. The white- or gold-clad people they met seemed to be walking with purpose in their strides, but no hurry. The contrast was startling, and a little disquieting.

"How come everyone is so peaceful?" she asked.

Shaunan smiled at her, then answered, "Can you not guess? The practice of Immersion is taken very seriously on the Isle. Not only does everyone do it first thing in the morning, but also last thing at night, and sometimes also during the day. They pause during their daily round to spend time in connection with the power of the Way. Practised purely, it has a calming effect on the mind and heart. It is one of the things I miss about being on the move."

When the High Temple came into view, Abigail caught her breath. It was as beautiful as she remembered, its strong, ranusfelsen walls glittering in the sunlight, its spires reaching up towards the blue sky. She couldn't wait to see inside. To her surprise, although it was not Ranusdag, there was a steady stream of people bound on the same errand. Perhaps they did their Immersion practice in the Temple itself, when they could.

Shaunan led them up the wide, shallow steps, worn in the centre by the passage of many feet over the long years. Two tall door wardens, both lean, with pale, serious faces and dark grey eyes, wearing simple ochre-coloured robes, stood at the top, one on each side of the double doors that led into the Temple. "Leave your troubles without. Embrace the peace within," one of them intoned at regular intervals. The people up ahead of them would bow their heads, sometimes reaching out to touch one of the wardens before slipping inside.

Abigail took a deep breath and followed Shaunan through the doors. The inside of the High Temple surpassed her expectations. It was immense. Arched windows radiant with stained glass were set high in each wall above the six altars, and the sun shining in through them made the space inside seem like she was stepping into a rainbow. The altars themselves were simple blocks of pure, pale gold ranusfelsen, each with six tall candles in silver sconces, which gave off a sweet perfume as they burned. And on a wooden shelf in front of each altar were smaller candles for use by worshippers. Even the benches set in front of the altars shared this sense of purity, being made of a blonde wood she didn't recognise, unmarked by age or use.

Then she noticed a wonderful labyrinth set in the floor at the centre of the Temple. She tried to follow its path with her eyes, but soon got lost. In the centre was what looked like a flower with six round petals, and within each petal was an image of one of the Six. She walked over to take a closer look at it. It was beautiful – it must have taken the people who crafted it long seisdags to bring it to its present perfection.

"I see you are admiring our labyrinth," someone said in her ear.

Abigail jumped. She had not noticed the slim young man in white tunic and trews approaching her. "Yes, it is so beautiful. I would love to walk it one day."

"Why not now?" he asked, smiling at her. She noticed his clear grey eyes, his pale skin. "My name is Ruvyn. I am one of the High Temple guides."

She smiled back at him, unable to help herself. "I'd better ask my mentor," she said. "I'm not sure how long we're staying here."

"As you wish," he said with a slight bow.

She walked back over to Shaunan. "Would it be possible for me to walk the labyrinth now? I've heard of them back home but have never seen one so intricate and beautiful as this."

"Of course," Shaunan said. "Would anyone else like to walk it?"

"I would," Ellyn said.

Aidren and Ylonya both shook their heads. "Then if you two would prefer to carry on wandering round Ranusheim, we will see you back at the Hall of Visitors."

Afterwards, Abigail found it difficult to articulate her experience of walking the labyrinth. She only knew that it had changed her. As she entered the labyrinth, she felt unsure what to do. At first, she was very conscious of Ellyn ahead of her and of others sharing the experience. She began to pray as she walked, first for Jacob, then for each of her companions in turn – Shaunan, Ellyn, Aidren and Ylonya. But before long, as she relaxed into it, and immersed herself in the power of the Way, all consciousness of any others left her. Her father's prayer came into her mind, so she repeated it to herself as she walked, now towards the centre, the next moment being flung back towards the outer circumference. She lost all awareness of time passing, only knowing for certain that she was praying to Someone, whether God or Ranu, and that her prayers were being heard. When she finally reached the centre, she sank to her knees, overwhelmed by the experience. She remained there for a while, breathing softly, her eyes closed, before rising and walking the long path back.

When she finally stepped off the labyrinth, Shaunan and Ellyn were waiting for her, serene expressions on both their faces. She beamed at them, feeling so full of love for them both.

The following Lèniasdag, all five of them were summoned to a meeting with the High Waymages of the Wayzenmoot. When they filed into the Audience Chamber, the twelve High Waymages, plus Ednor and Tremond, were awaiting them as before. Abigail shot a glance at Ellyn, to check how her friend was feeling. She was pulling her tunic straight, smoothing her hair.

"Don't worry," she whispered. "You need not fear them."

And then wondered at her own certainty. Should she have told Ellyn that, when she was far from sure of its truth? She shrugged – the reassurance must have come from somewhere.

"Welcome all," High Waymage Gwynmaer said, "please be seated. Waymage Shaunan, if you would be good enough to introduce your two young companions?"

"These are Aidren, a Warrior of Dagâra, and my niece, Ellyn, a Néartanian cordwainer, both from Nordvein. They have been staunch companions on our journey."

"Greetings, Aidren, Ellyn," Perran, one of the two Dagâran High Waymages said, smiling at both of them. "Although it is long since I have been there, I grew up in Irnvein, just north of

Nordvein. As that part of Dagâran is my second home, may Ranusheim be a second home to you. Welcome."

Aidren nodded in acknowledgement, and Ellyn smiled. Then High Waymage Gwynmaer introduced the rest of the assembled to them.

Abigail felt a different atmosphere in the room today. She could sense that the High Waymages had come to a decision. But she could not discern what it might be and knew better than to use her powers to try and find out.

"We have discussed everything you told us," Gwynmaer said, into the silence, "and have agreed that the Master Bloodstone of Talamu must be found and returned to us to be destroyed. Only here in Ranusheim do we have the power to rid our world of its evil. This quest is essential for the continuing wellbeing of Veylindré. We believe that Abigail's possession of a Bloodstone," and here he smiled at her, "gives us a distinct advantage. We think it may be possible for her to learn to attune herself to it, and through that, be able to discern the location of the Master Bloodstone. If she is willing to take that risk?"

Abigail felt faint. Was this why she was here? Was *this* the high purpose Shaunan had prophesied for her? Her pulse was thundering in her ears, and she hardly heard the High Waymage ask again, "Abigail? Are you willing?"

There was a long moment of expectant silence. Abigail raised her head and saw the eyes of all the High Waymages on her. She realised they were waiting for her response.

"Yes," she whispered. Then she cleared her throat and repeated in a clear voice, "Yes, I am willing. If you really think I can be any use."

"Thank you, Abigail. High Waymage Valwyn will help you to learn the attuning process."

"But what about Jacob?" Surely they hadn't forgotten their promise to try and find him.

High Waymage Daefiel met her gaze. "I have asked the Golden Stone of Ranu about him, and all I could tell was that he is in Talamunem City, very close to the Prophet of the One. But he is alive and well."

Abigail's eyes filled with tears. He was alive and well. "Th-thank you," she said. "Then there is still hope that we may rescue him."

"Perhaps," Daefiel's voice was soft and cool. "I sensed a dark shadow on his heart."

"What do you mean?"

"I could not tell," Daefiel said. "I got no sense that he was being held against his will."

Abigail did not care about the High Waymage's cryptic statements. Whatever happened, she was going to rescue Jacob. Somehow.

"So now we must decide who is to accompany Abigail on her quest," Gwynmaer said. "You cannot march openly on Talamdor, with the rest of the Veylindréan forces, so your numbers must be few, and secret."

"But the Commonweal must be warned of the threat from Talamdor," Ednor said.

"We have already alerted the First Waymages of each land," Vordan said, his voice reassuring. "They will pass on the news to the rulers."

"Then I offer my services to the quest," Ednor said. "I am a warrior. My skills may be useful."

Then Tremond spoke up. "I would also like to be a member of the company," he said. "I have some skill with knife and bow."

"We accept your offers with gratitude, Ednor and Tremond," Gwynmaer said. "As for the others, Waymage Shaunan has indicated her willingness to go along to support Abigail. Ylonya, are you willing to be their guide, as before?"

"Absolutely, High Waymage." Ylonya's eyes were sparkling with excitement. Abigail could not help smiling at her friend's enthusiasm.

"Thank you, Ylonya," Gwynmaer said. "Then the five of you may leave after the festival of Lèniastide."

Abigail could sense the hurt that both Ellyn and Aidren were feeling. "Wait a moment," she said, raising her hand. "I don't want to leave Ellyn and Aidren behind. They have shared many dangers with us. It wouldn't be fair to leave them out."

Aidren stood, and said with dignity, "I am a Warrior of Dagâra. I would be honoured to be included on this high quest."

"And Ellyn's my best friend," Abigail said. "We started this journey together."

Gwynmaer frowned at her. A period of silence followed. Abigail guessed the High Waymages were discussing the matter between themselves. She had already lost Jacob, she wasn't going to lose Aidren and Ellyn too.

"Very well," Gwynmaer said. "They may join you. Abigail, please report to High Waymage Valwyn this afternoon, for training in attuning yourself to the Bloodstone." He stood up. "This Council is concluded."

Ellyn wasn't sure whether to feel excited or terrified. Her heart had sunk when the High Waymage had excluded her and Aidren, but at the same time, she didn't know what use she would be on such an important mission. She slipped her hand through Abigail's arm, as the five of them walked back towards the Hall of Visitors.

"Thank you for standing up for us. I hope I'll be able to help in some way."

"Of course you can," Abigail said in a fierce voice. "You're my best friend, Ellyn. I can't be without you. I-I've already lost…" she gulped, seemingly unable to say Jacob's name, "I couldn't bear to lose you too."

Ellyn hugged her. "We'll find him, you'll see."

"I hope so." Abigail sounded so sad. "I couldn't believe it when Daefiel said she had no sense of him being there against his will. Has he forgotten his life here? His life with me?"

"Surely not. Or perhaps they've made him forget – who knows that magic those Talamdorians can do."

She saw her friend's face lighten at that thought. "Let's hope you're right. But my goodness, what are we letting ourselves in for?"

"I don't know. But I'm so excited. I never dreamed I'd ever go on a quest. It will be like being in a story."

"Don't relax into it too much," Ylonya said from behind them.

Ellyn started; she had not heard the Yrusian coming up behind them. "Why?"

"As I said to you on another occasion, not everyone you meet will be kind, or trustworthy. This is going to be a dangerous journey, for all of us. Talamdor is not a kindly land, not like Veylindré. We will need to be on our guard, all the time. People die in stories, sometimes."

Ellyn hadn't thought of that. "I suppose you're right." Then her irrepressible optimism resurfaced. "But all the same, it is going to be a grand adventure."

Chapter 9

The next morning, at fourth hour, Abigail knocked on the door of the private chambers of High Waymage Valwyn to start learning how to attune herself to the Bloodstone Jacob had found.

Like all the other spaces she had seen at Ranusheim, Valwyn's chambers were clean and simple. Less grand, even, than those of Findoran or Marinden, in far off Dagâran. Here there were no storied tapestries, no decoration at all. A floor-length curtain of some heavy gold material hung across a doorway in one wall, presumably the entrance to the High Waymage's sleeping quarters. But although the furniture was plain, it was of good quality, made of finely polished wood, and the two chairs were covered with soft cushions. There was a personal shrine in an alcove, with a fat yellow candle and a golden stone with the symbol of Ranu carved into it, a meditation bench in front of it.

"Welcome, Abigail," Valwyn said. "Have you done your morning Immersion?"

"Yes, High Waymage."

"In the privacy of these rooms, you may call me Valwyn," the woman smiled. "Let us sit in silence for a while before my shrine, to ask Ranu for success in our endeavours."

She gestured gracefully to the meditation bench, stooped and lit the candle, before seating herself. Obediently, Abigail settled herself next to her. She took her Goldstone out of the pocket around her waist, and gradually sank into the peaceful silence.

A few minutes later, Valwyn closed the session with a brief prayer, "*Belannath Ranu, gal uns treuten im y Teisen. Ganasa mi y peuran ir Abigail trechen. Gan eich Nimen an gan em Sen, than gal et bynn."*

She turned to Abigail as the girl echoed her last words, "*than gal et bynn.*"

"You know the old language?"

"Not very much, but I understood you were asking Ranu to give you the power to do something, and I recognised the last bit, 'by your Name and by the Six, so may it be.' There hasn't been much time for Shaunan to teach me more, because we've been travelling ever since I got my Waymark at Dagârastide."

Valwyn's eyebrows shot up. "I had not appreciated how recently you became Ranusian. I take it that Waymage Shaunan has been teaching you how to attune yourself to your Goldstone?"

"Yes, she has, but as I said, there hasn't been much time. Ever since Dagârastide, we've been travelling here."

"Let us sit in comfort." Valwyn rose and walked across the room to two comfortable chairs. Abigail found this pale-skinned, grey-eyed woman, whose every movement was so dignified, so assured, fascinating. She followed her and sat in the proffered seat.

"Maybe it would be as well for me to review what you have learned so far."

Abigail flushed. It seemed clear this High Waymage thought she was ignorant. She wished Shaunan was here.

"Abigail," Valwyn said in a gentle voice, "this is not a test. I only need to learn what you already know, so that I can decide how best to proceed."

Oh. Abigail blushed. "While she was training me, before Dagârastide, Shaunan showed me how to share a picture in my mind and how to speak together in silence. Let me think… oh, yes. I've had a little practice at healing on our journey – one time Ellyn was attacked by some boys, and I helped heal her broken collarbone, and later on, Ylonya and Aidren fought three enemies, including an agent of the Prophet, and I helped Shaunan with their wounds. But I've only been Ranusian for a few short seisdags, and I know how much I still have to learn."

Valwyn listened, and Abigail could sense her full attention. *Thank you, Abigail. That is very clear. So you have found it relatively easy to attune yourself to your Goldstone?*

Was this another test? *Yes, I think so. I've found that doing my Immersion practice every morning helps, and that if I'm tired, it is harder.*

Valwyn nodded. "Good. Let us try something more difficult. It was most fortunate that Tremond brought that second Bloodstone with him to Ranusheim, otherwise we would not have been able to do this training. But as it is, the purpose of these sessions will be to see if you can attune yourself to the Bloodstone you have carried for so long and use it to attempt to sense the location of the second one."

She paused, then said gravely, "I believe that your origin from outside our world is going to be of crucial importance in this process, as the Master Bloodstone was designed to work against all children of the Six, and you were not born here. Take out the Bloodstone, then close your eyes, please."

Abigail took the buckskin pouch containing the Bloodstone out of her pocket, fished the stone out and held it, shutting her eyes. Nothing. It could have been any old lump of rock. Maybe she wasn't concentrating hard enough. She took a deep breath, tried again, focussing all her thoughts on the triangular stone in her hand. Again, nothing.

She opened her eyes. "It's no use. I cannot gain access to it. Its power is closed to me."

Valwyn frowned, but Abigail sensed she was puzzled, rather than angry. She waited in silence for the High Waymage to speak.

Then started, as the woman rose abruptly to her feet, a look of revulsion on her face.

"Surely not," Valwyn said. "That would be too evil."

"What? What have you discerned?"

Valwyn turned to face her. "It is Bloodmagic," she said. "I'm sensing that it needs blood to work."

Abigail shuddered. "Oh, that's horrible!"

"Are you willing to try?" Valwyn asked.

"I suppose so. What do I have to do?"

Valwyn walked across the room to a large chest of drawers, opened the top drawer and brought out a sewing kit. She selected a sharp needle and held it out to Abigail.

Abigail pricked her finger and warm blood began to ooze out of the wound. She smeared it onto the Bloodstone and felt the difference straight away. Once more, she closed her eyes and concentrated. But it felt so very different to her Goldstone, which welcomed her and linked her to the power of the Way. The Bloodstone felt cold, slippery, as though it was resisting her. Negative thoughts began to fill her mind. *It's no use. You can't do it. You're not good enough.* Each time she sought to dismiss them, to form a link with the stone, they subsided for a moment, then returned in full force. She sighed and opened her eyes.

"I'm sorry, Valwyn," she said, "but it feels as though the Bloodstone itself is resisting my touch. Every time I try to attune myself to it, my mind fills with thoughts of futility and hopelessness."

Valwyn frowned. "Hmm," she said, "I had not realised that would happen. Perhaps I should train you in clearing your mind of negative influences first, before we try again. Put away the Bloodstone for now, and take out your Goldstone, please."

Abigail did as she was told, relieved to lose the disquieting touch of the Bloodstone. She closed her eyes once more and immersed herself in the familiar warmth of her Goldstone, relaxing in its secure embrace, gradually recovering her balance.

"Now, Abigail," she heard Valwyn's voice, "I am going to put some negative thoughts in your mind. Your job is to let them go and return to the power of the Way."

Let it go. You cannot do this. Who do you think you are, someone special? You're nobody, just an ordinary girl. Why even try? And on and on, undermining her self-belief, making her feel worthless. How did the High Waymage know just where she was vulnerable?

Abigail had never attempted anything so arduous. She was reminded of her many arguments with her father, which she had always, always lost. Like him, the High Waymage seemed to have far more power and strong will than she did. It felt like she was trying to push a heavy stone up a steep hill. Sweat sprang out on her forehead and she began to feel dizzy. She fought with everything she had to hang on to her own self-worth, but it was such a challenge.

Then the High Waymage changed tack. *You've lost Jacob. You'll never see him again. You are all alone now.*

Abigail's eyes opened as she sprang to her feet, furious with the woman. "How dare you? How dare you peek into my mind and attack me like this? I'll never give up on Jacob. Never."

She was trembling with the force of her emotion. The High Waymage looked at her for a moment through narrowed eyes, then spoke in a quiet but deadly voice, which was somehow more frightening than shouting.

"You think I am taking a liberty? Foolish girl. Do you truly believe the Prophet would not do the same? He will be able to pick your dearest hopes and dreams from your mind at will, and use them against you, if you do not learn to control yourself, to protect yourself."

Fighting back tears, Abigail sank down into her chair. Of course, the High Waymage was right.

"I'm s-sorry, High Waymage. It's so difficult. What am I doing wrong?"

Valwyn's face softened. She reached out and took Abigail's hand, her touch reassuring. "You are not doing anything wrong, except for trying too hard. The trick of this is to acknowledge the thought, then gently let it go. Imagine you are sitting beside a stream, and you can see fish swimming past you. See each negative thought as a fish, something that is going past you, but with which there is no need to engage. You note its presence, but your emotions do not become entangled with it. Let us try once more."

Sighing, Abigail shut her eyes again. To her surprise, she found that the fish trick helped somewhat, but as time passed, she became tired and so less successful in letting go.

She was brought back to herself by a touch on her arm. "That is enough for today," Valwyn said. "You have made a good start. Return to your chambers for rest and refreshment. I will see you again tomorrow."

"How did your session with the High Waymage go?" Ellyn asked, as Abigail walked into their room. "You look exhausted."

Abigail sank down into the comfortable armchair with a tired sigh. What to tell Ellyn? She didn't want to mention what the High Waymage had said about her coming from outside Veylindré, at least not until she'd thought it through. Nor about her reaction to the woman's suggestions about Jacob. She needed to speak to Shaunan.

"It was so hard – very different to attuning myself to my Goldstone. It felt as though the Bloodstone was resisting me. But Valwyn seemed pleased with my progress. I'm to go there every morning at fourth hour to practice."

"Valwyn? You're calling her by her given name?" Ellyn's voice was shocked, even disapproving.

Abigail hastened to explain, "She said I might, in the privacy of her chambers."

"That is a real honour."

"I suppose it is. I hadn't thought of it in that way." Time to change the subject. "What do you think of Tremond and Ednor? They seem to be very different from each other – Ednor is quite outgoing, but Tremond seems much quieter."

"Tremond scares me a little," Ellyn said. "He looks so serious all the time. I wonder why he so rarely smiles?"

"Perhaps he has some great sadness in his past," Abigail said, "that we don't know about. What about Ednor?"

Ellyn's expression lightened. "I like what I've seen of him, and I know Aidren does too. But I still think it will be weird, travelling with two strangers."

"No more so than when Ylonya joined us," Abigail said, "and we got used to her soon enough."

"That's true. I like Ylonya. I wonder how we'll get on with the other two."

"I'm sure Aidren will be relieved to have some men along for company," Abigail said with a grin, "and Ednor being a

Dagâran Warrior will mean that he has someone to practice his fighting skills with."

"I suppose so."

Shaunan invited Tremond and Ednor to join them for dinner that evening. It was a convivial meal. She was pleased to sense the growing ease between them all as the evening wore on. It was vital that they all bonded with one another, so that when danger came, as she was sure it would, they would be able to work together to overcome it. As subtly as she could, she listened in to the conversations.

"How long have you been a Warrior of Dagâra?" Ednor asked Aidren.

"For nearly eight years. I trained under Swordmaster Sanderon at the Hall of Warriors while we were in Luvodican, before Dagârastide."

Ednor's eyes glowed, his voice warm with enthusiasm. "Sanderon is still Swordmaster? He was my teacher when I was doing my advanced training there. I attained my mastery under his tuition. He showed me how to watch my opponent's body language, so that I could predict their next move. He was the best trainer I ever had."

"Me too," Aidren said, smiling in recognition. "I learned so much from him in a few short seisdags. It was hard to leave. And now I'm growing rusty. I've had no-one to practice with since Talmis, and even then, it wasn't much, because I was the one doing the teaching."

"What happened at Talmis?"

Shaunan saw Aidren shoot an anxious glance at Abigail before answering, in a low voice, "That was when we lost Jacob."

Ednor nodded in comprehension. "I see. You would be welcome to spar with me, if you like, both here and on our journey. I would be happy to pass my skills on to someone already familiar with Master Sanderon's fighting style, and I too need to keep my skills honed."

Aidren's normally serious face lit up in a way Shaunan had rarely seen. "Thank you, Ednor."

Excellent. It would be good for Aidren to have some other men in the company, and Ednor's kindly gesture would help their friendship to develop.

Tremond and Ylonya, at the far side of the table, were deep in conversation. Of course, the two of them were both in the same business in some ways – Ylonya's role in the Guild of Intelligencers and Tremond's as a Watchman both involved digging for information. But she could not hear what they were saying and did not want to abuse their trust by using her powers to eavesdrop.

So she turned her attention to Abigail and Ellyn, who were talking quietly together. She knew that Ellyn's presence on this quest would be essential to Abigail's peace of mind.

"A copper bit for your thoughts," she said.

"I was wondering how long this quest is going to take," Abigail said. "I've no real idea of the distances involved."

"That will depend on the route Ylonya decides to take," Shaunan said. "I would imagine that she will not take the most direct one, but lead us on lesser-known paths, so that we remain undetected by agents of the Prophet for as long as may be."

Abigail sighed. "When we reached here, I was so pleased. I'd hoped we could stay here for a while. But then, we couldn't rescue Jacob."

"At least the weather will be getting better, and warmer," Ellyn said. "We'll be in the Season of Awakening soon."

"How is your training with High Waymage Valwyn going?" Shaunan asked Abigail one fine but chilly morning. They were sitting together in Shaunan's room, in low armchairs in front of the fire, which was blazing merrily.

The girl sighed, stretching out her hands to the flickering flames. "It's difficult to tell. First she taught me how to link with another Goldstone – that was relatively easy. But the first time I tried to attune myself to the Bloodstone, I felt such resistance from it. It was horrible – as though the stone itself was pushing me away, like it didn't want me to touch it, make contact with it."

Shaunan nodded. "I can understand that," she said. "I remember when I held it in my hands, back in Nordvein, and felt an enormous reluctance to touch it, such a sense of malevolent power."

The relief was pouring off the girl in waves. "I'm so glad it's not just me."

"Not at all. I would guess that anyone with a Waymark would have the same problem. So what happened next?"

"She told me to switch to my Goldstone. As I told you, we concentrated on letting negative thoughts go, rather than engaging with them. That was so hard. You know how it is, when someone tells you not to think of a black cat, the first thing that comes into your mind is a black cat."

She laughed ruefully. "And when I had more or less mastered that, we started again with the Bloodstone. I still hate touching it, but in a funny way, it seems to have accepted me."

"Have you told the High Waymage that?"

"Yes, and she said that she thought no-one else could have done it. But I don't understand why…"

"My guess is," Shaunan said slowly, considering her words carefully, "that you have been able to connect with this Bloodstone because you come from outside Veylindré. I believe the Prophet – or Talamu – has made all Bloodstones antithetical to anyone born to the people of the Six. But because you come from a different world, you are protected, at least to some extent, from its power of repulsion. That may be why you are so important, Abigail. You are the only one able to attune yourself to a Bloodstone, and hence track the location of the Master Bloodstone. And perhaps more than that – to remain uncorrupted by its influence. This unique difference of yours gives us our only chance to defeat the Prophet and protect Veylindré."

"Oh, Shaunan, I wish this hadn't happened to me. I wish I could have been an ordinary Ranusian, being trained by you, back in Nordvein, and settling down with Jacob. I miss him so much…"

Tears were standing in her eyes. Shaunan soothed her mentally, before saying, "Whatever happens, Abigail, I will be there to support you. And this quest will also enable us to find Jacob – I am sure that, as High Waymage Daefiel said, he is with the Prophet."

Shaunan leaned down to speak in Abigail's ear as she passed her chair in the dining room the next morning. "Meet me at the North Gate of the city in twenty minutes. I have something to show you."

What was this about? Abigail bolted the rest of her breakfast, scarcely tasting it, made her excuses to the others, and dashed back to her room to fetch her cloak. She had to ask directions to the North Gate and ran most of the way there, arriving breathless and crimson.

Shaunan allowed her time to regain her breath before leading her out of Ranusheim, along a path into the neighbouring woods. The path was clearly in frequent use – the passage of many feet had rendered it smooth.

"What do you want to show me?" she asked her mentor.

"Wait and see."

They carried on walking in silence and came to a sunlit stream, which chuckled to itself as it flowed past them. Abigail began to relax as she took in the beauty around her – the mature, moss-covered trees, dappled sunlight filtering through their leaves, the scent of damp ferns, the ever-present music of the stream. A few minutes later, they came to a beautiful waterfall cascading down a limestone outcrop.

"This is Lower Falls," Shaunan said. "When I was at the Colaste a'r Teisen, I used to come here sometimes, when the pressures of the training became arduous for me."

"It's glorious. Thank you for sharing it with me," Abigail said. "But why have you brought me here now?"

Shaunan stopped walking and turned to face her, her expression serious. "I've brought you here," she said quietly, "because you need to appreciate all the beauty that is at risk if you fail in your quest. And to give you the memory of this place, to aid you in times of trouble."

The quest. Abigail had been trying not to think about it – the idea of walking into Talamdor, the land of Veylindré's enemies, seemed terrifying. She had no idea how she was supposed to recover the Master Bloodstone from the Prophet. The number of things that could go wrong seemed infinite, the likelihood of success small.

"I feel so inadequate," she said. "I've only been an initiate for such a short time, and now the High Waymages are expecting me to – to save the world."

"I know. It is a daunting prospect. But you will not be alone. I will be with you, as will Ylonya and the others. Between us, we should be able to keep you safe from harm, so that there is a good chance of your quest succeeding."

"Oh, Shaunan. I pray you're right."

"All we can do is our best," Shaunan said. "No-one will expect more than that."

Abigail thought about that. It was not as consoling as she hoped.

"Do not think about it anymore," Shaunan said. "There are many miles and seisdags between us and Talamdor. Try to dismiss it from your mind and fix the beauty and serenity of Lower Falls in your heart."

Abigail did as she was told, and began to feel a sense of deep and abiding peace. She would not forget this place.

Abigail's daily sessions with Valwyn continued. By the Néartasdag of the seisdag before Lèniastide, she was managing to let the majority of the negative thoughts pass by, not engaging with them. The High Waymage had also taught her how to link with another Goldstone, and she had become quite adept at finding it with her mind.

"It is time for us to try with the Bloodstone once more," Valwyn said. "Remember what you have learned and hold it in your mind lightly."

Reluctantly, Abigail took the Bloodstone in her hand and shut her eyes. She relaxed into a meditative state, as she had been instructed, and found she was able to ignore most of the negativity. The Bloodstone felt more secure in her grasp and warmer, if that was possible. She opened her eyes again.

"That was better," she said. "It felt quite different to before – less resistant to my touch."

"Then let us attempt to link with the second Bloodstone, which is hidden somewhere in these chambers."

She took a firm hold of the Bloodstone and opened her mind, as Valwyn had taught her. For a moment, she felt a pull to the left, before the negative thoughts poured in and her concentration wavered. By the time she had managed to let them go, the tentative pull had vanished.

"I'm so sorry," she said. "I felt a slight pull, over there," and she pointed to a fine chest of a dark wood, which she had not previously noticed, "then my concentration faltered, and I lost it."

"That was very good for a first attempt," Valwyn said, her voice warm with approval. "If you would wait outside for a moment – leave the Bloodstone here – I will hide the second one in another place."

As the morning wore on, Abigail found that she was getting better at dismissing the stone's resistance and at sensing the location of the second Bloodstone.

"You have done well indeed, Abigail," Valwyn said. "I believe that no-one else could have achieved what you have. We have a full seisdag before Lèniastide, and I believe that by then, you will be able to find it, if not with ease, then at least reliably."

"Thank you, Valwyn. I could not have done it without your aid."

The High Waymage nodded in acknowledgement. "I have aided you, yes," she said, "but your determination and dedication have made the difference. Be very clear, Abigail –

this task is yours and yours alone. Tomorrow, and in the days that follow, I will hide it further and further away, so that we may discover how close you need to be in order to discern its presence. Because I suspect there may be a limit to your ability to find it. For now, go back to your room and relax – you deserve it."

Stumbling a little in her weariness, Abigail left and began the long trek back to her room.

Chapter 10

Abigail was looking forward to celebrating Lèniastide on the Isle of Ranu. It would be fascinating to witness how the Ranusians observed a festival – she guessed it would be very different from Dagârastide in Luvodican.

"Come on," Ellyn said, "Aunt Shaunan asked us to meet her in the courtyard, dressed in our best."

"All of us?" Abigail asked, "or just us two, Aidren and Ylonya?"

"I think she meant Ednor and Tremond as well. She was being very mysterious –something about a 'rare privilege'."

"That sounds exciting. What are you going to wear?"

"I only have my Dagâran riding clothes, but my shirt is clean and pressed. What about you?"

"I think I'll wear my gown, which is from my world. I still feel more comfortable in skirts than trews."

"How strange!" Ellyn laughed. "I much prefer the freedom of trews."

When they were ready, they walked down the wide stairs of the Hall of Visitors and came out into the courtyard, the other five members of their company were already assembled. Aidren and Ednor were standing together and Abigail noticed a new ease between them. Good.

Aidren strode across to join them and gave Ellyn a hug. "You look good enough to eat," he told her, which made her blush.

Tremond was in his Watch uniform and Ednor in full military gear, his breastplate shining. Shaunan, of course, was in her Waymage robes. Even Ylonya had made an effort – her hair was pulled back into a neat bun, and her clothes were clean and pressed. Abigail smoothed down the skirts of her gown with hands that shook a little. What was going to happen?

"Come," Shaunan said, leading them towards a tall, pointed arch Abigail hadn't been through before. "We are honoured to be invited to witness the opening ceremony of Lèniastide in the presence of the Golden Stone of Ranu itself. This is a privilege normally reserved for the twelve High Waymages, or for rulers of the lands. Do not speak unless one of the High Waymages addresses you directly."

When they arrived in the inner courtyard, Abigail had her first sight of the Golden Stone of Ranu. It was taller than any of the Waystones she had seen elsewhere, even the First Waystone of Luvodican, and glowed in the dim light of dusk, seeming to emanate a warm golden light of its own. She stopped dead, almost overwhelmed by the power emanating from it. There was a tall stack of wood in front of it, ready to be lit.

She remembered the lighting of the ceremonial fire at Luvodican, and the awe she had felt when First Waymage Marinden had lit her torch using the power of her Goldstone. She was more used to such things now and wondered how this ceremony would differ. And of course, she had been with Jacob then. Would she ever see him again?

Ellyn grabbed her arm and nodded in the direction of another archway at the far side of the courtyard. The twelve High Waymages processed through it, two by two, in a deep, dignified silence, dressed in gorgeous robes of fine golden brocade, embroidered with subtle patterns in the colours of the Goddess they represented. Each wore a golden circlet in their hair. Like the Waymages at Luvodican, they positioned themselves in a great circle around the Golden Stone and the wood stack, and stretched out their arms, bowing their heads in silent respect. The presence of all twelve High Waymages seemed to deepen the sense of occasion. In Luvodican, the ceremony had been conducted by First Waymage Marinden. Here there were twelve High Waymages, all of equal rank. Who would be lighting the fire?

As if in answer, Ianlos, one of the two Lèniumen High Waymages, stepped forward, and looked up into the darkening sky. Of course, it would be one of the two Lèniumen High Waymages, because it was Lèniastide. They must take it in turns. Abigail followed the direction of his gaze and spotted the Six twinkling high in the sky. The ceremony could begin.

"Holy Lènia, Goddess of Healing, Music and Storytelling, we gather at the end of the Season of Dormancy to honour you. All year long, you have given us your aid, and enabled us to follow the Way of Veylindré with faith and courage. May your Festival be a time of soul healing, and of sharing stories, music and songs."

In unison, the other High Waymages responded, "So may it be," and the company, at a sign from Shaunan, echoed their words a moment later. Then High Waymage Shonala, the other Lèniumen High Waymage, took an unlit torch from a stand behind her, pronounced the words of fire summoning, "*Belannath Lènia, gal lo bynn tanem,*" and the end of the torch burst into flame. She thrust it into the heart of the gathered wood. Like the one in Luvodican, the fire kindled swiftly and was soon sending flames and golden red sparks high into the air.

The Twelve bowed in unison to the Golden Stone of Ranu, and its pulsing light flared out in answer. Had its light always been like this, or had it been stronger, more intense, before the

Prophet had possessed the Master Bloodstone? She'd have to ask Shaunan.

"Now let us light the main ceremonial fire," High Waymage Ianlos said. Turning, he led them all out of the Wayzenmoot building, and down into the heart of Ranusheim, to the wide square in front of the High Temple, with a Waystone at its centre, where all the other inhabitants were waiting for their part in the ritual.

"Why do they do it twice?" Abigail whispered to Shaunan.

"The first ceremony is for the High Waymages themselves, to revitalise them in the purity of their service to Veylindré, the second has the same purpose as the one at Luvodican – to declare the start of the festival."

"Then why were we permitted to be present?"

"I am unsure. I would guess it was because they wished to do us honour, before we start on our quest for the Master Bloodstone."

"What happens now?"

"Once the ceremonial fire has been lit, there will be a feast, as in Luvodican. Most of the festival will be very similar to Dagârastide – except that the ritual of remembrance will be absent, because that belongs to that particular festival. Instead, as this is Lèniastide, there will be more emphasis on music and storytelling. And the Ceremony of Assignment on the final day is different."

"In what way?"

"Wait and see," Shaunan smiled at her. "Hush, now. They are about to begin."

"Let's go and listen to the storytellers," Ellyn said to Abigail and Aidren the following afternoon. "It's my favourite part of any festival."

Aidren put his arm round her. "Good idea. Do you know where they are performing?"

"I'll ask Shaunan," Abigail said and sped off to her mentor's room.

When she returned, ten minutes later, the Waymage was with her. "There is an amphitheatre on the outskirts of the city, furthest away from the gates we entered by. I would like to join you. It is a rare chance for me – I am usually too involved in helping organise a festival to be able to listen to the storytellers."

Ellyn's heart was filled with affection. "It's lovely to have you with us, Aunt Shaunan."

With Shaunan in the lead, the four of them made their way through the streets, noticing that even the calm Ranusians seemed to be more lively and excited than usual. There was a hum of many conversations in the air, and it felt more like any other city. All its' inhabitants were dressed in their finest clothes, gold and white, which they seemed to favour, and there was a holiday atmosphere in the air.

Soon they could hear an even louder rumble of voices. They followed the sound towards the north of the city and joined the crowd of people heading in the same direction. Walking through an elaborately carved archway, depicting meticulously carved scenes from Veylindréan history, they arrived in the amphitheatre itself. It was magnificent. Set in a natural hollow on the lower slopes of Mount Ranu, it seemed large enough to hold the entire population of Ranusheim. Tiers of stone benches rose on all sides of the oval floor, and most of them were full. Above them, the Lèniastide sun shone in a blue sky. The amphitheatre was easily as large as the one in Luvodican, and its superb natural setting took Ellyn's breath away.

She glanced at the large rectangular stage that had been set up in the centre and saw brightly clad figures milling around behind the backdrop at one side. "We'd better find seats quickly. I think they're about to start."

"You're right," Abigail said. "I wonder which story they'll be sharing."

"Let's wait and see," Aidren said.

Then a tall woman, clad in the traditional red and purple striped costume of a story narrator, came forward and raised her arms for silence. "Ladies and gentlemen! Welcome to our show. We are honoured to be performing here, in Ranusheim. The Taellingsford Players are proud to present *The Tale of How the Seven Became Six."*

"In the beginning, Ranu was alone, serene and content, a mote of consciousness amid the stars of the universe." A player clad in golden robes came forward and bowed to the assembled people. "Millennia passed, and Ranu learned much from the spinning celestial spheres. First, she learned of the intricate complexities of life: the cycle of blossoming, plateau, decay, and renewal happening all around her. And from that knowledge she discovered how to create.

"Second, she learned how the heavenly bodies communicated with each other. And it was this star song which gave her an overwhelming desire to share her life with others. She began by singing to the stars herself, in the hope they would return her harmony. But, try as she might, the stars did not respond.

"Next, she tried to impress them by creating a sphere of her own, formed from the dust and minerals ejected from the stars themselves, yet not so large and majestic as to overawe them. And on this planet she established both lands and seas, that would rely on both the sun and herself for their continued existence. The stars gave the world their celestial blessing. And Ranu named her creation Veylindré.

"But this beautiful world, blessed by both Ranu and the stars with glorious mountains, hills, plains, rivers and oceans, still felt empty to her. For she had created this land to share with one and all, but one could not be all. She, the creator, was not yet content with her creation. She realised that the key to her fulfilment would be the creation of other beings who could themselves create.

"Then the Life Force of the Way quickened within her, and she conceived six daughters, each of whom reflected aspects of herself. She apportioned to each of her daughters a land on Veylindré, to cultivate and care for, to realise their own unique potentials. And each of her children formed their lands to their own taste, creating various creatures to live in them."

As the story unfolded, players dressed as each of the goddesses named by the narrator came forward and bowed to the audience. Ellyn remembered this from *The Tale of the Seventh Goddess,* which they had heard at Dagârastide.

"Talamu, the eldest, was a natural leader with a mind apt to power," the narrator continued. "She inherited Ranu's desire for control and an unquenchable will to create, and to hold that which she had created. Ranu gave her the land of Talamdor, in the south-west of the Commonweal. Out of the depths of her passion, Talamu created a land of extremes, with long, cold winters and hot, arid summers. But she made sure to include a fertile portion between the Rivers Caethwas and Roillon, to bring balance to the land.

"Second was Lènia, both studious and creative, who embodied Ranu's desire to heal and her compassion for others. She loved to sing at her work of creation. She was given Lènium, a peninsula abutting south from the northern continent into the sea, where it came to mark the border between the Sea of Lènia and the Sea of Ranu. Lènia fashioned the jewel in its crown, the Vale of Berlysian, a sheltered region in the heart of the land, where she planted flowers of all kinds, including many herbs with diverse healing powers.

"Third was Néarta, who inherited the earthy, practical side of her mother's nature. She was never happier than when her hands were busy. To Néarta, Ranu gave Néartania, and she created a wide land of forests and grasslands, irrigated by three major rivers, located at the heart of the Commonweal, whose clement weather made it perfect for the cultivation of food, and rich in the materials needed for crafting objects for delight and use.

"Fourth was Garûna, caring, diffident and loyal, with a keen eye for details. She inherited her mother's passion for justice and law and the service of others. Ranu gave her Garûnalond in the far north of Veylindré. Its northern portion was made of ice and tundra, where only reindeer lived. But its Southern Plains were suitable for grazing sheep and goats, so Garûna concentrated her powers on the southern third, as she wanted to stay in touch with her sisters.

"Last but one was Yrusia. Lively and witty, with a streak of mischief, she loved to tease her more serious sisters. She had all her mother's curiosity and desire to travel and discover new things. To Yrusia, Ranu gave the land of Yrusian, as its central location in Veylindré was an ideal base for travelling in any direction. And Yrusia created many natural paths and harbours to help with this.

"Dagâra, sixth and last, fierce and dedicated, embodied Ranu's desire to protect others. Which Ranu had not felt until she created Veylindré. Dagâra forged a spartan land from her portion and named it Dagâran. It was high in altitude and strewn with mountains, but beneath the earth were deposits of rich minerals.

"For herself, Ranu kept the forested Isle of Ranu," and the narrator swept her arms wide to indicate their surroundings, "so that she might share this wonderful world with her children. In order to observe them and their lands, she raised the Isle to a commanding height on a seat of granite, rising high out of the Ranusian Sea. But she maintained her connection to the rest of the Commonweal by forming a land bridge, which linked her land with the rest of Veylindré.

"And the hearts of the Seven were glad, all except one. Talamu, the first of Ranu's children, was not satisfied with the division of power among them. She was jealous of the power of her sisters, wanting to be first and greatest in Ranu's heart. Her imperious heart darkened within her. After all, she reasoned, Ranu herself had given her a desire to lead others, which had transformed into a thirst for power which could not be quenched by the rule of one land alone. Resentment began to build in her and she began to plan how she might come to dominate the whole of Veylindré. Her heart grew cold in her breast, and she turned against her mother and her sisters.

"Ranu felt her daughter's unrest from afar and sought to close the distance she could feel growing between them. 'Why has your heart turned against us?' she asked Talamu. 'We still love you as much as ever.'

"Talamu scowled. 'I am the first of your children and want to be first in your mind and heart, first to sit beside you and rule over Veylindré. Yet I am outcast to this one small corner.'

"Ranu's heart was filled with sorrow for her jealous child. 'Can you not see, my beloved daughter, that my heart is big enough for you all?'

"Talamu did not answer, but responded with a question of her own, 'Can *you* not see that you deny us all our birthright? How can we be equals if my sisters and I cannot create creators, as you have?'

"Wise though Ranu was, she did not comprehend the devious mind of her eldest daughter. Anxious to bring all back into harmony, she asked, 'Would that make you happy? If you could create living beings yourself?'

"And Talamu answered, 'Yes, Mother, that is my desire. Let my sisters and I become creators ourselves and work together with the fruits of our creation.'

"Ranu nodded. 'I agree. Each of you should leave a mark on your creation, so that I can truly recognise its author.'

"And so the first human beings were created, and the First Age of our world began. The Seven gave gifts to these first people, so that they themselves could become creators. Ranu gave them brains to store wisdom and lore. Lènia gave them hearts and creative spirits, so that they might feel as great an empathy for others as she did, and a desire to share music and stories. Néarta gave them clever, dexterous hands, so that they could tend the land and become creators in their turn, using the materials around them. Garûna gave them a desire to serve others and a passion for just laws and good order. Yrusia gave them legs and feet and curiosity so that they could travel far and wide and explore their world. And Dagâra gave them strong limbs, and both the power and the desire to protect what was theirs. And all their children were gifted with the ability to access the power of the Way, through which they might channel their gifts.

"But Talamu placed dark emotions in the minds of her people, a fear and mistrust of others and of the unknown, and a strong desire to be controlled by a leader, an omnipotent being who would be able to protect them from these fears. In this way, she sought to enhance her own power, rather than serving the Commonweal as a whole.

"And the people of Veylindré made a binding vow to serve the Seven and the Way, and to work together for the good of the Commonweal. The Seven sealed the vow by placing a Waymark on the forehead of each man and woman, to show their allegiance to the Way. Thereafter, each child was Marked soon after their twelfth birthday.

"At first, all was well. Most of the peoples spread across the lands of Veylindré and worked together for the common good. The years passed and the people were content in their lives. In time, they themselves became parents, passing on their knowledge and wisdom to their children, teaching them to be strong in the Way. And the heart of Ranu was made glad. She gifted the sons and daughters of her daughters with Goldstones, which enabled them to access the power of the Way and to use it wisely and well.

"The only people who did not accept Goldstones were the Talamdorians, because Talamu had corrupted their hearts, so that they believed they were a race apart, superior to the inhabitants of the other lands. Instead, Talamu created Bloodstones in rivalry to her mother's Goldstones, channels for the blood magic with which she planned to conquer the rest of Veylindré. Using them, the Talamdorians were able to leech away the power of the Goldstones gifted to the other peoples by Ranu, and enhance the power of their own Bloodstones.

"Talamu's final act was to fashion a Master Bloodstone, shaped like a five-sided prism, to use against the Six and the other peoples of Veylindré. She launched an overwhelming attack on the rest of the Commonweal, leading a huge army behind her. At first, it seemed as though she would achieve her desire – first scores, then hundreds, then thousands of Veylindréans perished as Talamu's forces inflicted defeat after defeat on them.

"Eventually, the Six pooled their own powers and, guided by the enlightened hand of Ranu, banished Talamu to Talamdor. Talamu did not submit meekly to this banishment and her struggles to break free caused a mighty earthquake, as a result of which the Talamdor Mountains rose up from the earth, forming a border between her land and the rest of the Commonweal. Then the Six gave a choice to the people living in other lands who bore a Talamunem Waymark – to remain within the Commonweal, and have their Waymarks changed to that of Garûna, or to be banished with Talamu to Talamdor. Later on, some chose to take a third way, sailing across the Southern Sea and found their own nation, and thus the country of Havim was created.

"And so the Second Age of our world began. And here my story ends. If my tale has pleased you, give generously on the way out."

The narrator gave a florid bow and the audience burst into applause. Ellyn found she had been holding her breath and let it out all at once. "I've heard that tale many times," she said, "but I've never heard it told as well as that."

"One thing puzzles me," Abigail said, turning to Shaunan. "She said that Talamu created Bloodstones for her people, in rivalry of Goldstones. But when we showed you the Bloodstone Jacob had found, back in Nordvein, you were astonished."

"It was believed that the Six destroyed them all at the end of the war, and that the Master Bloodstone had also been lost. But we know different now, don't we?"

Δ Chapter 11 Δ

In the days that followed, Portak finally made good his promise to answer Jacob's questions and teach him more about Talamdor. No need to tell the boy it was on the Prophet's orders.

"How much do you remember of what I have told you?" he asked Jacob, as they sat at their ease in Jacob's room – Jacob propped up against the headboard of the bed, Portak in the room's single chair. It was a typical Hall of Visitors room – plain but good.

"You haven't told me much," Jacob replied, wrinkling his forehead. "Let me think… Talamdor is known as 'the land of the free', and it's where anyone who wants to avoid the rule of the witches of Veylindré lives. You worship Talamu… It's ruled by the Prophet, who came here about thirty years ago, and helped the people to overthrow the Havimi, who had made all Talamdorians into slaves. And you were one of them…. And, that Havim is to the south of Talamdor, across the sea… And that Talamdor used to be part of the Commonweal, but that Talamu waged war on the other goddesses, so now you're all alone."

Portak nodded. So far, so good. "And what else?"

"Well, I guess I've learned some things about the geography of Talamdor, by travelling from the secret passage to here. Let me see… the most fertile part of Talamdor is between two rivers - I don't remember their names."

"The Caethwas and the Roillon."

"And you're preparing to invade Veylindré." He paused, "I think that's it."

Was that all the boy had retained? For a moment, Portak quailed at the size of the task before him. He was no teacher. But the Prophet had ordered him to educate the boy, so he'd better start.

"All right, then let's start with Talamdor itself, since you have seen some of it already. I have brought a map with me, to show you the full extent of the land."

He brought out a map, which showed the whole of Talamdor, with all its main features – towns, cities, rivers and so on. He stood, then removed the ewer and basin from the top of the chest of drawers and spread the map out on its flat surface.

"Here," and he pointed with his finger, "is the location of the high pass in the mountains which we came through. See if you can trace our journey from there to here."

Jacob joined him and examined the map carefully. "First we went by dog-sled to Kalthund, there," he pointed to it on the eastern side of the River Caethwas, "then across to Crullfeld," he pointed again, "then north-west to here. So mostly across the middle of the country."

"That's right. But as you can see, there is much of Talamdor that you do not know. The south coast, which borders on the Southern Sea, has some important ports, the chief of which is Caethwasim, on the western edge of the Caethwas delta. We do much of our trade with Havim from there." Although why we are trading with them, I really don't know. "You already know that the central part of Talamdor, which you've travelled through, is the most fertile region. And to the north of Talamunem City, there are many mining villages. Talamdor has rich deposits of iron, copper, tin and silver near the Talamdor Mountains."

"Do you have a map of the whole world?" was the next, unexpected question.

"Why?"

"Because I'd like to see how the location of Talamdor relates to Veylindré. At the moment, I've no idea how large or small it is in comparison."

Portak frowned. It wouldn't do for Jacob to become too curious about Veylindré, otherwise some of the names on the map might jog his memory. "I'll see if I can find one. In the meantime, l will tell you about our economy."

"When am I going to be able to go out and about? I'm getting so fed up with being cooped up in here. I need to work with my hands." This last in a despairing wail.

"It is the Prophet's desire that you learn as much as you may about Talamdor," Portak said in a stern voice. "There will be time later for other pursuits."

Jacob scowled at him. What was wrong with the boy? He ought to feel privileged, to be gaining this knowledge. Why did the Prophet think the boy needed to know all this? He meant to find out as soon as possible.

"Very well. I will take you for a walk later."

Portak sighed – this was going to be harder than he had realised.

The next day, at the same time, there was a knock on the door of his room. Portak again, no doubt. Why couldn't the man understand that he really didn't care about learning and information – all he wanted to do was to apprentice himself to a smith somewhere in the City and get on with his life. But it seemed this was not allowed. He shivered – why did the Prophet want him to learn all this… stuff?

"Come in," Jacob said as he opened the door. Like he had a choice. But then, he hadn't had any choices since he had come here. Since waking up on that boat.

"Jacob, today I'm going to tell you about the history of Talamdor."

"Wonderful." For the life of him, Jacob could not help the sarcasm creeping in to his response.

Portak frowned. "You are out of order. You should be grateful."

"I'm sorry," Jacob shrugged. "I've never really been one for book-learning. I'd rather be working with my hands, like I said yesterday."

Portak's normally pale face flushed. "Well, 'want can be your master' as the saying goes," he said. "It is the Prophet's express wish that you have a good working knowledge of Talamdor, and he has told me to give it to you. Your job is to listen and learn. Have I made myself clear?"

Jacob flinched from the anger in Portak's tone and hated himself for flinching. But if it was the Prophet himself who wanted him to learn about Talamdor, then he would do it. Even though he found it hard. He bowed his head. "I'm sorry. Of course, please carry on."

"That is better. As I said, today we are going to cover the history of Talamdor. Our true history began when we broke free from the dominion of the Veylindréan witches and their false goddesses, more than thirteen centuries ago. According to the historians of Talamunem City University, there were some problems in the early years of Talamdor's independence, because all or most of the citizens had a Talamunem Bloodmark." He pointed to his own forehead.

"Why would that be a problem?"

"Because when we were a part of Veylindré, those with the Waymark of Talamu were in positions of power and leadership. So it was difficult to find people to do the more mundane tasks – growing food, crafting goods and doing the services the economy needed to flourish. But over the years, that issue has been resolved. We encouraged our own craftspeople and started to cultivate the land. We now pride ourselves on being self-sufficient, needing little from anywhere else."

"How?"

"How what?"

"You said that issue has been resolved. I was wondering how…"

Portak frowned again. A hint of 'don't ask so many questions'. But he couldn't have it both ways – if the man wanted him to learn about this place, then surely he, Jacob, had the right to ask questions.

Portak sighed. "Very well. Since this has come up, I will answer you. For long centuries, when each young Talamdorian reaches the age of twelve, they have been required to take a Test of Faith. They must present themselves to their local Bloodmage at one of the four festivals that mark our year. The purpose of the test is to see whether they are worthy of receiving a Talamunem Bloodmark. If they are proved faithful, they become a full member of Talamdorian society, with all the privileges that go with that status. The rest are only allowed to do certain jobs and are not allowed to marry trueblood Talamdorians."

"What happens in the Test of Faith?"

"Each young person is handed over to the priest of Holy Talamu in their town or village, blindfolded, then taken to a secret place, known only to the priesthood. They stay there for a seisdag. It is quite an ordeal, but the reward of being chosen to bear a Talamunem Bloodmark," and he pointed to his own forehead, "is worth it."

"An ordeal?" Jacob said. "What kind of ordeal?"

"I don't know why you want to know, since you will not be required to undergo it."

"The Prophet wants me to learn all I can about Talamdor and the Talamdorians."

Portak frowned. "That is true. Very well. It is an ordeal by illusion. The priests are able, by using Bloodmagic, to make the candidate believe that they are being deprived of their senses, or that they cannot trust them. For example, they may feel great hunger, or extreme thirst. Their sight may dim or even stop working altogether. They might hear either intolerable noises or a huge silence. They might feel great pain, or that they cannot feel anything at all. And their noses might smell such a dreadful stench that they ache from it."

Jacob blanched. "What is the purpose behind such a test?"

"The purpose is to test the candidate's sense of self," Portak said. "It is not actual torture, only illusion."

"And it goes on for six whole days?"

"Yes, and they pass very slowly. But if the candidate's faith in Holy Talamu is sufficient, they will come through it stronger than before and will be rewarded by receiving their Bloodmark. If they fail, a bangle of control will be fastened around their right wrist, a permanent mark of their failure."

It was Jacob's turn to frown. "Then everyone without a Bloodmark like yours is looked down on? Seen as a lesser person?"

"That is correct."

"Wait a minute… so that means *I* am one of these second-class citizens?"

To his surprise, Portak smiled at him. "You are a special case, Jacob. You have come to us from outside Talamdor. If you wish to know more, you must ask the Prophet. Now, let us continue with the lesson."

Jacob was all too familiar with this blank wall of deflection. Portak was a master of it. When would the man actually answer all his questions? But he had to suppress his annoyance, because Portak was speaking again.

"About a thousand years ago, a wild, discontented sector of the population in the south of the land, farthest from Talamunem City, decided they no longer wanted to be second class citizens, no longer wanted to be part of Talamdor. So they built themselves some ships in secret, rose up in rebellion, and fled across the Southern Sea to found their own nation. We know them today as the Havimi."

"Are they the same people who ruled Talamdor, not so long ago?"

"Yes. Two hundred and fifty years ago, they invaded our land, and subjugated our people." Portak's voice became harsh and bitter. "For more than two hundred years, we were treated as the lowest of the low, and our land was milked of all its riches. It was intolerable." His voice changed, becoming warm, throbbing with passion. "But then the Prophet came and led us out of slavery into freedom. In the last thirty years, we have rebuilt our land, and restored our people's pride and honour."

"But didn't you say that you now trade with the Havimi? I thought they were your enemies?"

For the first time, Jacob sensed that Portak was stuck for an answer. "I am unsure why," he said slowly, "but the Prophet has decreed that it should be so, and it is not for us to argue with his decisions."

"But you'd rather not?"

"Enough. Let us eat some lunch, then your afternoon is free."

"It's such uphill work," Portak said, flinging himself down in a chair in Balmak's living room. "He knows hardly anything about Talamdor and doesn't seem to want to know."

"That must be hard for you," Balmak said. "Why does the Prophet want him to learn all this?"

"I wish I knew," Portak grumbled. "So far as I can see, there is nothing special about the boy – he's a smith with no unusual gifts. Yet the Prophet wants him to become an expert on Talamdor. He's even undertaking his religious instruction himself. I don't know why he couldn't trust me with it."

"Hmm," Balmak said. "That does seem odd. How are you going to find out?"

How well Balmak knew him. "I'm not sure," he said. "I think I'm going to have to tread carefully with this boy. It seems the Prophet places a particular value on him and I don't know why. And until I know, I'd better go roundabout, answering the boy's questions and adding a few of my own."

"Take care, my love," Balmak said. "How far can you trust this boy?"

"What do you mean?"

"Is he likely to blurt anything you've asked him to the Prophet?"

"Hmm. I hadn't thought of that. Quite likely, I would say. Thank you, Balmak."

Balmak hugged him. "At least," he said, "while you have this task to do, you will be staying in Talamunem City. I've heard the Prophet is preparing for war."

"Yes, but I don't expect I'll be involved. I'm no warrior."

"I have a bad feeling about it," Balmak said. "I fear he may choose to send you with the army."

"By the One! I hope not."

And so, Jacob's education continued. But the Prophet had not summoned him to his presence again. Until today. And he didn't even have Portak with him, for a bit of moral support. At least this time, he was wearing freshly laundered clothes, and looking clean and tidy. He was eager to speak with him once more.

He left the Visitors' Hall and headed for the Great Temple. His spatial memory was good, so he had no trouble finding his way. Once again, he was awed by the sheer scale of the Temple, by its dark grandeur and beauty, and by the painting of Talamu above the high altar. Keeping his eyes on the floor to avoid her penetrating gaze, he ducked through the side door and along the narrow corridor leading to the Prophet's apartments.

He presented himself to the two sentries guarding the door. As before, he was asked the ritual question, "Who seeks audience with the Holy Prophet?"

"Jacob, Jacob Wallingford. The Prophet has sent for me."

"Leave your weapons here. None may come into the Prophet's presence bearing arms."

He obediently handed over his knife, and the spears were raised. He knocked on the door, a gentle peck that no-one who had not been expecting it would have heard.

"Come."

Trembling a little, he opened the door, and walked slowly up the dark room to the Prophet's throne. It still made the hair on the back of his neck stand up – everything black, no natural light. But that was how the Prophet seemed to like it.

"Today we will be starting your instruction."

"Instruction?" So the Prophet was going to teach him himself? Jacob felt a little glow of pride.

"Your religious instruction."

Religious instruction? Alarm bells began to ring in Jacob's mind. Was the Prophet trying to convert him to the worship of Talamu? Never.

"So much resistance – that is a pity." The man's dark eyes bored into his.

Jacob gaped at him. He hadn't said a word. Could the Prophet read his mind?

"I-I'm sorry, my Lord. This is all so strange to me. All my life I have worshipped one God, the three in one. How can I forsake Him?"

"Perhaps it would help if I told you how I – as devout a Christian as you – came to worship Holy Talamu. Yes," he nodded to himself, "I think it may. Listen well, Jacob, listen, and believe. You may sit."

Jacob obediently fetched the same upright chair he had chosen last time and sat.

Then the deep, hypnotic voice began to speak, "When I escaped from the clutches of the Havimi slave master, Tyran Larth, I headed north-west, towards Mount Talamu."

"Portak told me he first met you there, in Crullfeld," Jacob said.

"Larth made the mistake of trusting me," the Prophet continued, ignoring the interruption, "because I had no Bloodmark on my forehead. He knew I did not belong in Talamdor, like him and the rest of the Havimi. So I bided my time, took my chance, killed a guard and made my escape, under cover of night. For six weeks, I was a fugitive, moving mainly by night, starving, my clothing in tatters. My stomach had never been so empty, and I began to understand what our Lord had undergone during his sojourn in the desert. I stayed alive by drinking from mountain streams, and by snaring small animals and eating them raw. It was desperate. But I was determined not to be beaten by these heathen savages. My only goal was to find a way home – back to our world, back to civilisation, where I could freely worship our God. Whatever happened, I was not going to be captured again.

"One night, a high wind rose and, at the end of my endurance, I sought shelter in a small cave in the mountain wall. I stumbled inside, and the shriek of the wind was muffled. I remember it had a dry, sandy floor. I sank to my knees and prayed to God, thanking Him for leading me to that shelter, and asking for strength to continue my journey until I found a way home.

"I knew I must have something to eat before I slept. I had not eaten since the evening of the previous day, and the hunger was making me lightheaded. So I hobbled back outside – I had been crippled in a mining accident some time earlier – and searched for something to pacify the gnawing ache in my stomach. But to no avail. Little grew in that barren land and it was the wrong time of day for the animals to be active. I drank some water from a nearby stream, then re-entered the cave, lay down and fell asleep."

Jacob was listening eagerly, caught up in this tale of endurance and courage. "What happened next?"

The Prophet actually smiled at him – a grim smile, like the grin of a skull, but a smile, nonetheless.

"I was woken from my slumber by a woman's voice, calling my name, 'George, George, wake up. Wake up!' For a moment I believed it was my mother – no-one else called me 'George'. It came again, 'George, George, wake up.' It sounded as though She had been calling me for a long time, and as though She was willing to keep calling me forever. I sat up, rubbing my eyes and looked around me. A bright light was emanating from the darkest corner of the cave. As I watched, the figure of a woman became visible – tall, beautiful beyond my wit to describe, with a pale face and long, black hair. Her robe was a deep, dark blood-red. I could sense her power.

"'Who are you?' I asked. And She replied, 'I am Talamu, and I have chosen you, George Crutwell.'

"I had heard of Her, of course – in Crullfeld, many of my fellow slaves had prayed to Her nightly, begging to be saved, for a prophet to release them from their bondage. But She had never answered them. I, too, had prayed, but had also gone unanswered. I wondered whether my God – our God – was unable to reach into this world. I even tried praying to Talamu. And now, here She was. I pinched myself, sure I was dreaming. It hurt. This was real.

"She repeated, 'I have chosen you, George Crutwell. The plight of my people is abominable in my sight. You must set them free.'

"Then I knew I was in the presence of the Divine – it sounded like God's invocation to Moses, from our Old Testament. I knelt before Her. I knew I had to do whatever She commanded. So I asked Her, 'What must I do?' And She answered, 'I have chosen you, because you do not come from our world. I have read your heart and call you to be my prophet. Set my people free from their subjugation by the Havimi and bring them back to the Way of Power.'

"I questioned Her, as I had not heard of this 'Way of Power'. I will never forget Her answer, 'I am Talamu,' she said, 'the One True Goddess of this world. Set my people free and teach them to follow me as you have followed your God.

You are mine.' And the conviction coursed through me – of course I was. How could I ever have believed otherwise?

"Then She told me what I must do. 'On the far side of the Talamdor Mountains is the Commonweal of Veylindré. Its inhabitants worship six goddesses, and are permitted by them to do magic, using stones of gold. This is an abomination in my sight. They are false goddesses, and their followers are evil. Teach this to my people.'

"Excitement blazed in my heart at these words. They were witches. I would be able to continue my work as a witchfinder."

Jacob shot to his feet. This was too much. "But that's impossible. You cannot be the same George Crutwell my father told me of. That man was in his forties more than thirty years ago, but you do not look much older than that. You cannot be him."

"Much is possible to people of good faith, Jacob. I *am* that man."

"I-I'm sorry, my Lord. This is so hard to believe."

"Believe it, Jacob, because it happened. I swore fealty to Holy Talamu, and She said, 'In order for you to be accepted by my people, I must mark you as one of my own.' Then She reached out with the index finger of Her white hand and touched my forehead. I felt a swift blaze of pain, then it was gone. 'Now you are mine,' She said. Then She waved her hand, and I felt health and strength return to my body – even my damaged leg was healed. My tattered rags were replaced by a good suit of black worsted, with a linen shirt beneath, my worn sandals by sturdy shoes. A miracle.

"'Set my people free,' She repeated. 'Teach them to follow the Way of Power. Go first to Talamunem City, about two days' walk north-west of this place. There you will find aid.' I bowed and said, 'I am yours to command.' Then She vanished."

"What did you do next?"

"I did as She had commanded. I had an important mission. I vowed to serve Her, with all the devotion I had previously given to the Christian God, who had never favoured me with His presence. I was Her prophet – She had chosen me, of all men, to do Her will. I felt exalted by Her favour, as Moses must have done when the Lord spoke to him out of the burning bush. I swore to fulfil the commission She had given me, and to do it with all my might, with all the devotion in my heart. I would free Her people, overthrow the Havimi and preach the One True Way. And here we are."

Jacob sat back, stunned. He had no doubt the Prophet was telling the truth. And he knew, deep in his heart, that if a divine being had visited him, he too would have found it impossible not to obey her.

Truly, the Prophet had been favoured above all men. He, Jacob, needed to learn more about this mysterious… goddess. He was beginning to understand why the Prophet followed her. But he had one more question.

"How did you come here?"

"You said you had heard of me?"

"Yes, my father spoke of you as a Witchfinder General."

The Prophet nodded. "That is correct. Once I had taught young Matthew Hopkins the secrets of witch finding, I decided to leave England and carry on my mission in the New World. I crossed the Atlantic on *The Lyon* in 1632. There was a disagreement."

He paused, as though wondering how much to tell Jacob, then continued, "A disagreement. They put me off the ship in a small boat, with only one flask of water and a little food. A storm blew up and I feared for my life. I began to pray. I had given up all hope of rescue and put myself in the Lord's hands. There was a green flash and it seemed to me that a great grey door appeared, in the middle of the ocean. My little boat was swept through it. Suddenly, the wind died. I opened my eyes and found myself afloat on a calm sea. A miracle, I thought it.

"Then a ship hove into view and I waved my arms to attract its attention. A mistake, as it turned out. It was a Havimi pirate ship. They took me on board, then back to Havim. I was sold as a slave in Caethwasim. And the rest, you know."

Chapter 12

The final day of Lèniastide was similar to Dagârastide, back in Luvodican, yet with some important differences.

"Why aren't the people recharging their Goldstones?" Abigail asked Shaunan, as they walked past the First Waystone in front of the High Temple on the final morning of the festival. It was a cold, dry morning, with a bitter wind. She hugged her cloak more closely around her.

"Because everyone in Ranusheim has a Ranusian Waymark, so they do not need recharging until the end of the Season of First Fruits, at the Festival of Wisdom and Lore, which takes place later this year."

Abigail could feel herself blushing. Why hadn't she thought of that? "Of course. There is still so much I don't know about Veylindré, even though I mostly feel it is my home, now."

"Mostly feel?"

"Yes, most of the time, I do. Then I come up against something like this, which reminds me that in many ways, I'm still a stranger. I don't know things that the smallest child born here does. It makes me feel so stupid."

"You are not stupid – you are just young in our world. You have learned much already. Do not sit in judgement on yourself – it only leads to negative thoughts."

Abigail sighed. "I suppose you're right." Then, changing the subject, "Will the Ceremony of Assignment this afternoon be different too?"

"Yes."

"In what way?"

"Wait and see."

The Ceremony of Assignment was due to take place in the amphitheatre to the north of the city, so Abigail and Ellyn, together with Shaunan and the others, made sure that they found seats in good time. It was still very cold, but the sun had come out, lighting one side of the amphitheatre and leaving the other in shadow. Abigail was grateful to be on the sun-warmed side.

"It's so different this time," she said to Ellyn. "At Dagârastide, I was one of the participants. I don't think I've ever been so apprehensive in my life. I was so nervous that I would not be found worthy, because of being from outside Veylindré."

"But here you are, and with a Ranusian Waymark," Ellyn said.

"You said this one would be different, Shaunan," Abigail said. "In what way?"

"As I said to you this morning, wait and see."

Abigail shrugged her shoulders and turned her attention to the audience. The amphitheatre was packed out – there seemed to be no empty seats. Why were so many people gathered to witness the Waymarking of a few twelve year olds?

Ellyn clutched her arm. "Here come the High Waymages," she whispered. "All of them… I wonder how else this will be different."

"We'll soon find out," Abigail whispered back.

She noticed a large group of young people, probably in their twenties, all seated together in the front three rows of the amphitheatre across from her, and all wearing identical golden-brown robes. "Who are those?"

"Students of the Colaste a'r Teisen," Shaunan replied.

Then a horn rang out, as the twelve High Waymages, resplendent in their festival finery, processed into the amphitheatre. The early afternoon sunshine caught the shot-through colours in their robes – blue, brown, red, orange, green, purple and a deeper gold. The ceremony was about to begin. The High Waymages arranged themselves in a horseshoe formation, the open ends being next to the double doors through which the candidates would come. It was such a relief to be in the audience this time round.

As in Luvodican, the candidates for Assignment were called into the arena, one by one. It seemed as though the High Waymages were taking it in turns to be sponsors for them. Abigail's stomach felt fluttery as she listened to each nervous boy or girl repeat the words of the Vow of Assignment, followed by the Law of the Way. But it must have felt so different for them – they knew in advance what their Waymark would be. Shaunan had told her that all Ranusians had the Waymark of Ranu.

The ceremony seemed to take far less time than she remembered – probably because she was not participating on this occasion.

When the final candidate had received their Waymark and filed out of the arena, Shonala, one of the two Lèniumen High Waymages, stepped forward. "The first part of the Ceremony of Assignment is complete," she said in her musical voice. "It is now time for us to honour those students who have completed their studies at the Colaste a'r Teisen."

"So this is what you meant," Abigail whispered to Shaunan.

"Hush, they are beginning."

To Abigail's surprise, another group of Waymages, clad in plain, ochre-coloured robes, passed through the double doors at the foot of the High Waymage's formation and made another horseshoe in front of them. They must be the tutors of the adepts who had come here to study for their maging. She sat forward on her bench – this would be interesting.

One of the tutors, an elderly man with straggly white hair, and the pale skin and grey eyes of a native Ranusian, stepped forward, leaning on a wooden cane. "I, Reshin, Chief Mentor of the Colaste a'r Teisen, am pleased to announce that six Ranusian adepts have completed their training and are ready to be elevated to the rank of Waymage."

Abigail was surprised. His voice was deep and resonant, at odds with his frail appearance. A pang of longing swept over her – would she ever be a student here?

"Simmond of Néartanis, come forward."

A cheerful looking Néartanian rose from his seat in the front row and took his place in the centre of the double horseshoe.

"Simmond, you have completed your theoretical training in all aspects of becoming a Waymage. Do you wish to be raised to that status?"

"I do."

"Then repeat the Vow of the Waymage after me. I, Simmond of Néartanis…"

"I, Simmond of Néartanis," then the young man started to say the words after Reshin,

> "vow that I will do my utmost,
> to be true to the Power of the Way,
> and to the rank of Waymage.
> I will serve my community faithfully,
> and guide them with kindness and wisdom,
> remembering that all are children of the Six.
> In the name of the Six, in the Power of the Way,
> this is my vow."

"Simmond of Néartanis, you have taken the Vow of Assignment. Are you content to be posted where your gifts will best serve Veylindré and the Way?"

"I am."

Reshin smiled at him and presented him with a small wooden box, and a purse Abigail knew contained money. "Very good. Waymage Simmond, you are assigned to Talmis, in the south-east of Néartania, to shadow Waymage Rewald, in the final years before his retirement. He is an excellent Waymage and will teach you the skills of leading a particular community, that you cannot learn here."

The new Waymage beamed. "Thank you, Mentor Reshin."

"May you follow the Way faithfully and serve the people of Veylindré for the rest of your days."

"I will do my best." Then Simmond bowed to the tutors and the High Waymages and resumed his seat in the front row of the adepts from the Colaste.

"What was in the box the Mentor gave him?" Abigail whispered to Shaunan.

"A golden topaz set in silver, which all of us wear as a mark of our status."

The other five went through a similar ceremony. Cirona, a slight, dark-haired woman, was assigned to the Vale of Berlysian to complete her training at the Healer Hall, before joining a community in northern Lènium. Kimald, a tall, fair young man, sturdily built, was assigned to his home village near Ullmass in Garûnalonden. Shariel, a very beautiful Ranusian girl, was sent to Coednis, to the Hall of Woodworking, and Ferdin, who looked so unremarkable he must be Yrusian, was sent to a village near Iascan. When it was time for the last new Waymage to be assigned, he spoke out before Mentor Reshin could pronounce where he was to be sent.

"Mentor Reshin," he said, "forgive me for speaking out of turn. But it is the desire of my heart to remain in Ranusheim, to assist the Wayzenmoot in any way I can."

"Are you certain of this, Dauran?" Reshin asked, a stern look on his face.

The young man flushed but stood his ground. "Yes, Mentor Reshin, I feel as though I have come home, and I never want to leave here."

"High Waymage Gwynmaer, does the Wayzenmoot require any assistance?"

Gwynmaer nodded. "There is always room for those who wish to dedicate their lives to the furtherance of the work of the Wayzenmoot."

Reshin nodded his thanks, then turned his attention back to Dauran. "Very well, Waymage Dauran. Report to High Waymage Gwynmaer in the morning. He will tell you your duties."

Dauran bowed low and gratefully to High Waymage Gwynmaer, then returned to his seat.

There was a pause as the twelve High Waymages and the rest of the tutors found seats in the auditorium. At length, only Chief Mentor Reshin remained standing. He turned until he was facing the six new Waymages and started to speak. Although he had his back to Abigail, she could hear him quite clearly – the acoustics of the amphitheatre were excellent.

"To be a Waymage is a complex calling. At different times, we have to be leaders, preachers, teachers, pastors, and servants. A tall order.

"There are two possible ways of being a leader – from the front, or as a shepherd figure, from behind and alongside.

Leading from the front can be good, but you have to be wary of losing stragglers. You will need to be in touch with everyone's concerns, so a 'guidance and gathering' approach to leadership is probably wisest. You should always be prepared to adjust the pace of your leadership to the situation, being guided by the needs of your community.

"Your people will also look to you for energy and inspiration. You need to lead unobtrusively, while at the same time being open to ideas from others. You need to be responsible, so that your people can rely on your judgement, and have a good relationship with the secular leaders of your community.

"Perhaps your most visible role will be that of preacher, leading worship each Ranusdag in your temple. Your community will look to you to interpret the Way for them. And to carry out the rituals associated with the various festivals of our year, as well as conferring the Waymark of Protection on new-born infants, and being a mentor to young people, both as their goddess affiliation begins to declare itself, and during the Season of Proving, before they marry. At the end of their lives, your people will look to you to conduct their funeral rites.

"You will also be responsible for gently teaching them how to live most authentically in the Way, with simplicity and integrity, having compassion for others. Your pastoral role will be fulfilled as you get to know all your people as individuals, each with their own joys and concerns, and you will need to be a non-anxious presence within your community – someone to whom they can turn with their doubts, questions and needs. It is a huge privilege to be able to share their lives with them – have a care to respect their confidences and listen well, as you have learned here. If there is no Healer in your community, you will also be required to care for their bodies, when they become sick or injured.

"Finally, you are, through the Way, the servant of your community. You have each vowed to serve your community faithfully, and guide them with kindness and wisdom, remembering that all are children of the Six. Never set yourself up above them, but work alongside them, helping them to fulfil their lives in the Way and in the service of the Six.

"And in all this, you need to be yourself. Communities have many expectations of their Waymages, some of which may be unrealistic. So all that we, the Colaste a'r Teisen and the Wayzenmoot, ask of you, is that you be yourself, doing the best job that you can. And do not be afraid to seek advice – it will always be available to those who ask. May the Way guide you, and may your onward journeys be blessed."

Then Reshin bowed to the new Waymages. They stood and bowed to him in return. Then he led them back through the double doors. The Ceremony was complete.

Abigail sighed and sat back in her seat. "That was marvellous," she told Shaunan, "but I had no idea that the role of Waymage was so…" she searched for the word, "… all-encompassing. I don't think I'll ever be ready to do all that."

Shaunan smiled at her. "Nor did any of us. The training here is a good start, but the real wisdom comes from learning as you grow into the role. I felt like you, once. But now…"

"Now you are all of those things," Ellyn said, "leader, preacher, teacher, pastor and servant."

Shaunan smiled at her niece. "As Mentor Reshin said, I do my best."

Once the Festival of Lèniastide was over, the members of the company prepared for departure. Then a snowstorm came and they were storm-bound on the Isle.

"We need to make the best use of this delay that we can," Shaunan said, as the seven of them sat at the breakfast table. "Abigail, you will have to report once more to High Waymage Valwyn, to hone your skills with the Bloodstone. What do the rest of you plan to do?"

"Aidren and I will continue our daily sword practice," Ednor said, smiling across at the young Dagâran. "He has much promise."

Aidren beamed back at him. His confidence in his own skills was growing. Good.

"It concerns me that Abigail and Ellyn do not know how to defend themselves," Shaunan said. "We may face many dangers on the road, if the Prophet and his agents manage to find us."

"I will teach them," Tremond said in his deep voice. "All Garûnalonden women learn to defend themselves with a knife."

"Why?" Ellyn asked.

"Because the northern part of our land is home to many fearsome animals, which sometimes stray into our human lands."

"Oh, I see. Thank you."

Abigail and Ellyn's disquiet at this prospect was easy to sense. "I hope it will not be necessary," Shaunan said quickly, "but I am grateful for your offer, Tremond, as are the girls."

"But where will we train?" Ellyn asked. "We can't start fighting in the courtyard."

Ednor laughed. "No fear of that," he said. "Aidren and I have been using a room in the main Wayzenmoot building to train in. You can do the same."

"But perhaps at a different time," Tremond put in. "They will need to learn without distraction."

The two men were so different. Ednor was a light-hearted extrovert, secure in his place in society. And why shouldn't he be – he was, after all, the younger son of the rulers of Néartania. Tremond was deeper, more serious, his mind on justice. Shaunan hoped they would work well together.

To Abigail's surprise, Ellyn proved to be a natural fighter, something she would not have expected of her gentle friend.

"You seem to be really good with a knife," she said, as they walked back to the Hall of Visitors, hot and tired after a training session with Tremond. The Garûnalonden was a good teacher, both patient and persistent. It was cold outside, but they didn't feel it after their exercise.

"It shouldn't be that surprising," Ellyn said, "after all, I use one every day for my cordwaining. And," her face took on a determined expression, "if we get into another fight, like the one outside Néartanis, I want to be able to defend you and Aidren and Aunt Shaunan without feeling panicked."

Abigail nodded. That made sense. "What do you think of Tremond now?"

"I like him. I haven't met many Garûnalonden before, but he has been so patient and kind with us. And he seems to have confidence that we will be able to learn to do what he asks of us. I'm glad he will be joining us on our journey."

"I can't decide which I like better, Ednor or Tremond… they are so different."

"Ednor makes me uneasy, somehow," Ellyn said. "He smiles too much."

"Smiles too much? What do you mean?"

"Just that, I suppose. I don't know…" Ellyn's voice trailed off as she tried to find the words to explain her feelings. "I guess it seems like a shield he puts up, so that no-one will know what he's really thinking."

"Hmm. I hadn't thought of that. But I think he's just a confident, outgoing person."

Ellyn shrugged. "Time will tell. How is your training with the High Waymage going?"

"As well as it can, I suppose. But we've discovered there is a limit to how close I need to be to detect the second Bloodstone. If she takes it more than a few hundred yards away, I cannot sense it."

Ellyn shivered. "It's such a dark thing, this BloodMagic. You are so brave, daring to use it to guide us."

"It's not bravery, I think," Abigail answered slowly. "It's as though this is my task, this is what I am here for. I feel that I have no choice in the matter… But I don't want to think about it now… I expect we'll be leaving soon. Would you mind helping me dye my hair later? It's been six seisdags since Genira dyed it and look – you can see the new blonde bits growing through. My hair's always grown fast."

"Of course I will. We can do it now, if you like," Ellyn said, as they arrived at their shared room.

"It doesn't matter so much here, where we're safe," Abigail said, as her friend began to massage the gloopy mixture into her hair, "but once we leave the Isle, I suppose I'll need to be disguised again."

"Yes, and we've used about a third of the powder Genira gave you. I wonder how long this quest is going to take?"

This was a disquieting thought and Abigail paused before answering. "I don't know, because I've got no idea what route we'll be taking. I've left all that to Shaunan and Ylonya and the others."

The storm blew itself out in a few days. On the second Lèniasdag after the festival, the company had their final meeting with the High Waymages in the Audience Chamber. Abigail was feeling so agitated by the imminence of their departure and the gravity of the quest, she scarcely noticed the fine furnishings, the beautiful paintings on the ceiling.

Gwynmaer, once more the spokesman of the High Waymages, addressed them all, "Today, you are setting off on a quest to obtain the Master Bloodstone of Talamu and return it to us here, so that we may destroy it and thus restore balance to the Way. If you succeed, our beloved Commonweal will be stronger and more secure than it has been for a long time. We, the High Waymages of the Wayzenmoot, are grateful for your willingness to undertake this task. We will hold you in our prayers as you set out, and in the future. The blessings of all here are with you, today and in the seisdags and seasons to come.

"We have provided you with warm clothing and travelling food for the journey. Horses you brought with you. They have been well tended and are ready to travel. But once you leave the Isle of Ranu, perils both understood and unforeseen will follow you. Your task is to guide and protect Abigail, using the talents you have between you, so she may use the skills she has learned here to locate the Master Bloodstone. Be on your guard and be chary of trusting anyone outside the Company. Better mistrust unearned, than quest betrayed. Before you leave, is there aught you would ask of us?"

Abigail moistened her lips, her mouth dry with apprehension. "High Waymage Valwyn has taught me to attune myself to the Bloodstone I carry. Surely the agents of the Prophet will be able to do the same, and so be able to find us?"

Gwynmaer looked grave. "I am afraid you may be correct. Which is why I urge you to keep it in your pack, and handle it as little as you may, until your quest nears its completion."

Abigail's hands flew to her cheeks. She could feel the colour draining from her face. "Then I will be hunted, wherever I go? The Bloodstone will draw them to me?"

"It is our hope that you may pass unseen and unremarked for a good while, so long as you do not use it or handle it," Valwyn replied, "and the other members of the Company will be there to protect you. We would not be sending you on this quest, had we believed there was no possibility of success. And the Talamdorians will have other matters to concern them, once our forces begin their defence of Veylindré. It is our hope you will be able to pass unobserved into the heart of Talamdor."

"I have seen no immediate peril in the Golden Stone of Ranu," Daefiel added. "But as the seisdags pass, and you draw nearer to your goal, that may change."

"Our blessings on your quest," Gwynmaer said, standing and bowing to them all. "May the Way guard and guide you all."

Abigail bowed her head. There seemed nothing left to say.

As they rode through the broad streets of Ranusheim, heading towards the main gate of the city and the start of their onward journey, Shaunan gazed around, trying to fix this well-loved place in her memory. She opened her senses, drinking in the sights of the Colaste a'r Teisen and the High Temple, the quiet hum of conversation and the singing of the birds in the Ranus trees. Only Ranu knew whether she would ever be here again. All too soon they were through the gate and on the road to Fort Ranu. She remembered the last time she had ridden this way, with Findoran for company, their hearts and hopes high as they rode towards the Vale of Berlysian to complete their training. Today her heart was full of longing – to stay here, to be at peace. But her path lay ahead, not behind, with Abigail and the rest of the company.

She tried to shake off this negative mood. Then she heard Abigail's voice in her mind.

Shaunan, I've been meaning to tell you. I've learned something else from High Waymage Valwyn.

Shaunan had suspected as much. She had noticed a change in the girl, a new-found confidence, even if the prospect of being hunted by Talamdorian agents still frightened her.

What have you learned?

When Valwyn was doing my attunement training, we discovered that I am one of those Ranusians who can speak mind-to-mind over distance.

Had she not felt the girl's power as soon as she had touched her? But as soon as Abigail told her, she felt a pang of concern, and hoped it was not prophetic. She had grown to love this girl from another world.

Keeping her mental voice level, she replied, *You had already done so in Céardochis, remember? But it is good to hear. It could make a great difference on our journey, being able to contact the Wayzenmoot in case of need.*

I suppose so. Of course, we don't know yet what my range might be, although I've been able to hear her wherever she was in the city. And she said I had a strong voice, whatever that means. She's asked me to speak to her briefly each morning, so that we can test how far away I can contact her.

Take care, Abigail. Although this gift may prove advantageous in some ways, it may be a two-edged sword.

What do you mean?

I… I am unsure. I feel a sense of apprehension when you talk of using it. We do not know what powers the Bloodstones confer on Talamdorians – they may have ways of overhearing such talk, and so pinpoint where you are.

Valwyn didn't say anything about that. Are you sure, Shaunan?

Shaunan could sense the fear in the girl's heart. *No, I am not sure. Just… be on your guard. Do not use this gift lightly.*

Chapter 13

It felt so strange to be riding away from Ranusheim, instead of towards it. It had been their goal for so many seisdags. Abigail wished with all her heart that she had been able to stay there, to join the Colaste a'r Teisen, and become a fully-fledged Waymage. But that was ridiculous – she'd only been an initiate for a short time. It would surely be years before she was ready for the advanced training the College offered... if she lived that long. She shivered – that was not a happy thought.

As they rode along, she noticed that Spring – no, the Season of Awakening – was under way. If she'd been at home, she would have guessed it was early February – the air was still cold, the skies more grey than blue, but the trees on either side of the track were beginning to put forth buds, and in the undergrowth she could see the first shy flowers lifting their heads to the pale sun. She was looking forward to some warmer weather – most of their journey had been in the depths of the Season of Dormancy. As before, the peace of the Isle entered her soul, and she tried to fix the sensation in her memory, so that she could call on it in more perilous places.

But her thoughts kept nagging at her, disturbing her hard-won serenity. What would it be like to travel with two new people? She, Shaunan, Aidren, Ellyn and Ylonya had travelled so far together. They knew they could trust each other entirely, whatever happened. The two newcomers, Ednor and Tremond, were still unknown quantities. She supposed she liked what she had seen of them but liking was a long way from trusting.

Tremond had been kind to her and Ellyn, patiently teaching them to defend themselves, and showing them how to watch their opponent's body, to predict their next move. He was a quiet man on the whole, but when he did speak, his words were measured, considered, and usually full of wisdom. She sensed a passion for justice under his calm exterior. But he would be hard to get to know.

Ednor, on the other hand, was younger and much more outgoing, trading quips gaily with Ylonya. She knew that Aidren liked him, and had learned much from him, which was a point in his favour. But she could not forget that he was a prince of sorts, being a son of the rulers of Néartania. How would he deal with being cold and tired and hungry, if such became their lot?

She shrugged her shoulders. Time would tell. Her mother had always advised her to get to know people before passing judgement on them. How she wished she could speak with her, one more time.

They reached the Fort of Ranu late the following morning, having spent the night in the guard post half way. From this side, it still looked intimidating to Ellyn – she would be glad to be leaving the Isle. Even though the quest they were embarking on would likely be more dangerous than their journey here. She had never settled in the place, being too much in awe of the High Waymages and the quiet Ranusians with their minds on high purposes far beyond her comprehension. She missed meeting ordinary people, people like her.

What use was she going to be on this quest? She was grateful to Tremond for teaching her to defend herself, but apart from maintaining the horses' tack and the Company's riding clothes, she couldn't see a role for herself. Yet she was glad Abigail had insisted on her inclusion. She had grown very close to the older girl, seeing her a something like a sister, and

Aidren was her heart's delight. It would have been too hard to be left behind when everyone she cared about was going off on a great adventure. She resolved to do all she could to support the pair of them.

Ylonya dismounted and knocked on the great gates of the Fort. They were opened at once, and the Company rode in, their horses' hooves clattering on the cobbles of the courtyard. They were met by the same captain of the guard, who bowed deeply.

"Waymage Shaunan, is there anything I can do to assist you, before you set out on your journey?"

Her aunt smiled at him but shook her head. "Thank you, but no. We need to press on – we would like to reach Olaf by dusk."

"Then may the Way guard and guide you on your journey."

"My thanks, Captain."

Such a difference from their former reception. Ellyn guessed that the man had been given orders to receive them graciously. In no time at all, they were riding out through the gate which opened onto the Land Bridge. It clanged shut behind them, an ominous, final sound.

"Waymage Shaunan," Ednor said, "have you taken thought for our route, once we have crossed the Land Bridge?"

"Shaunan will do, Ednor," she replied, "we are going to be travelling far together."

"Thank you."

"To answer your question, it is my intent to travel back through Lènium to Taellingsford and then cross to Néartanis. After that, we will see. Ylonya is our guide and will be able to lead us on the best route to Talamdor."

Oh, Néarta. Would they be taking the secret path under the Néartanian Straits, or crossing by ship? Ellyn's heart sank. She couldn't face that underground tunnel again.

Ednor left the Waymage's side and spurred his horse on until he came alongside Ylonya.

"So you are our guide?"

She turned a level gaze on him. "I am. What of it?"

"Nothing," he said softly, "I was only wondering whether my knowledge of Néartania might assist you. I have spent the last few years on a tour of duty in our forts which border the Talamdor Mountains."

"Then what would you recommend?"

Was she mocking him? Why wouldn't people take him seriously? He was a son of Lord Éadulf after all, even if his father paid him no mind. He cleared his throat.

"I would recommend travelling with all speed to Nordkeep, which borders both Talamdor and Yrusian. Our scouts have found a covert path through the mountains there, which we may be able to use. Then we would be approaching Talamunem City from the north east, which may be least well-defended."

She nodded. "The covert path from Nordkeep may well help us, but our primary requirement is to move in secrecy. If we use the main road from Néartanis to the border, we will be easy to find, perhaps even expected. By the roads I am planning to take, we may hope to remain unobserved by the agents of Talamdor for longer."

He bowed his head, "The knowing is yours."

He'd done his best. They would need his association with Nordkeep, if they wanted a scout to guide them. Until then, he would keep his tongue behind his teeth, and do his best to defend them all. One way or another, he would prove that they needed him.

A bitterly cold wind was blowing across the Land Bridge from their right, and Aidren huddled deep into his cloak, to little avail. The wind's fingers found their way in anyway and, despite his fur-lined gauntlets and sturdy boots, his feet and hands were like blocks of ice. He was glad when the hamlet of Olaf came into sight as the light began to fade. He guessed they would be travelling no further that day.

"Three rooms, and stabling for seven, please," Shaunan said to the innkeeper, a stout Lèniumen with an Yrusian Waymark.

Aidren wondered whom he would be sharing a room with this time around. With the two newcomers now part of the company, he guessed he would not be sleeping alone. He hoped it would be Ednor – he found Tremond quite intimidating. During their seisdags in Ranusheim, his friendship with the younger man had grown through their daily sword practice. But Tremond was old, as old as his father. And he kept himself to himself.

"That will be three guilders for the rooms, plus seven florins for the stabling. There's a fresh-baked ham with potatoes and carrots, and home-brewed ale to go with it," the innkeeper said with a smile. "Will that be satisfactory?"

"It will indeed, my thanks. We will stable our horses. How soon will supper be ready?"

"In about half an hour, Waymage."

Once the horses had been untacked, fed and watered, Shaunan led the way into the inn by the back door. "Ylonya, you are with me, and Abigail and Ellyn will be together as usual. Tremond, Ednor and Aidren may have the largest room. I will see you all presently."

A small boy, whom Aidren guessed was the innkeeper's son, showed them to their rooms.

Four beds," Tremond said. "I will take the one nearest the door, and we can pile our packs on the spare one."

Aidren sat on the bed he had chosen and removed his boots with some relief. Fishing in his pack, he brought out a pair of sandals for the evening. The strap of the left one was beginning to fray – he must ask Ellyn to repair it. Then he set his boots before the open fire, to dry out before the morning.

"You have travelled far with the Waymage?" Ednor asked.

"Yes, we started our journey in Nordvein, on the eastern side of the Dagâran Range. We have been on the road since the beginning of the Season of Completion."

Ednor's eyebrows shot up, and he whistled. "That is a long time."

"Yes, but we spent several seisdags in Luvodican, so that Abigail and Jacob could learn enough about Veylindré to undertake the Ceremony of Assignment."

"Ah, of course. Our stranger from another world."

Aidren shifted his shoulders. He could hear something strange in Ednor's tone – he seemed to be almost mocking Abigail. What was this about? "She is a Ranusian initiate," he said stiffly, "and has proved her worth many times over."

"To be sure," Ednor said. "I intended no disrespect. But we will be travelling together for many seisdags and I would like to know more about her."

"Let us go down for supper," Tremond interrupted, his voice measured and deep. "There will be time for tales later."

They were shown into a side room to eat, around one large oak table. There was a roaring fire in the grate, and the room was wonderfully warm. Abigail guessed Shaunan had asked for privacy. The baked ham was succulent, the servings generous. Tremond cleared his plate in short order and cut more from the joint while she was still halfway through eating, and Ednor and Aidren also pitched in with a will. When they had finished their main course, the innkeeper bustled in and offered apple pie and custard to finish. Both were piping hot and delicious.

When they had eaten their fill, her mentor addressed them all. "We are not going to take the most direct route to Néartanis," she said in a low voice. "Ylonya, will you explain our route to everyone?"

Ylonya settled in her chair, a curious smile on her face. "Surely. Ednor has already give me some advice."

Abigail glanced at the young Néartanian, who looked down, not meeting anyone's eyes. She wondered why. But Ylonya was speaking.

"We are not going to take the same route back to Taellingsford," she said. "Instead, I plan to skirt the south-eastern side of the Vale of Berlysian, as there are fewer settlements there. Then we will work our way back west. All being well, we should arrive in Taellingsford in just over a seisdag. Then we will stay with Genira once more before making our way across to Néartanis."

Abigail met Ellyn's gaze and read the fear in the younger girl's eyes. She knew how hard Ellyn had found it to cross under the Néartanian Straits. Then she saw Aidren take her hand, and felt her friend relax a little. Whatever happened, Aidren would be there to protect her. Oh, Jacob, where are you now?

"If there are fewer settlements, will it not be difficult to find shelter each night?" Tremond asked.

Abigail smiled to herself. He didn't know Ylonya yet. She was confident her Yrusian friend would be able to find somewhere for them to stay, however humble. She was glad of her presence. She wondered what 'advice' Ednor had given her.

When they reached the border of mainland Lènium, the two white posts indicating the end of the Land Bridge, they had a choice of three roads. Ylonya took the left-hand one, heading south on a lane which was probably grassy and pleasant in warmer seasons, but which was now muddy and full of ruts from cart wheels and deep puddles. The sky was full of rainclouds and she knew it would not take long for this track to turn into a positive quagmire. But she would rather risk being mired to the eyebrows than take the main roads. She knew this eastern side of southern Lènium was sparsely inhabited and wished to avoid the Vale of Berlysian this time, as the road through it was the route used most often by traders on their way to the Isle of Ranu.

The young Néartanian was going to be troublesome. It took more than a tour of duty at the forts of Néartania to make a leader. She tried to be charitable – the boy was still young. She guessed he was in his late twenties, so of course he wanted to prove himself. Had she ever been that green?

No matter. So long as Shaunan trusted her leadership, she would continue to guide them on little-used paths, to keep them from harm. She did not relish another encounter with an agent of Talamdor, not after the last one, which had nearly killed her. But now at least they had two more armed men in the company – better odds, perhaps. And the girls had been learning to defend themselves too. It would not be only her and Aidren next time. She was sure there would be a next time. It was up to her to ensure that they were as hard to find as possible.

"Where are we staying tonight?" Ellyn asked. Her face looked pinched and grey – this cold, wet weather did not suit her. Ylonya hoped she would be able to face the secret path under the Straits once more – she had not missed the girl's expression of dread when she had mentioned crossing to Néartanis. But it was far safer than risking being seen at either harbour.

"At the house of a farmer I know," she said. "We will be there soon."

Abigail had almost forgotten, during the seisdags at Ranusheim, how much resolution and resilience were required to keep on travelling day after day, in fair weather and foul. Ylonya had been as good as her word, finding somewhere for them to shelter each night, usually in a farmer's barn, bedding down on straw with their blankets spread over to minimise the prickles. The bodies of the neighbouring beasts lent them a little warmth, but she still awoke each morning feeling stiff and cold. Then a short Immersion practice followed by a scant breakfast of bread and cheese, and a drink of warm milk, fresh from the cow.

This south-eastern corner of Lènium was very different to the lushness of the Vale of Berlysian. The smallholdings were set near the bottom of valleys, under frequent danger of flooding, clinging to the sides of the neighbouring hills, which separated this part of the land from the Vale of Berlysian to the west. She noticed that every inch of possible space between the hills and the Sea of Ranu was under cultivation, growing the herbs for which Lènium was famous. But the land to their left, nearer the coast, was largely uninhabited, and the east wind from the Sea of Ranu blew constantly across their path, making riding a chore rather than a pleasure. She was getting used to freezing cold hands and feet again, in spite of her warm garments. It had been a relief three days ago when their path started to head south-west towards the other coast, with the wind at their backs, before turning south towards Taellingsford the previous morning, re-joining the road they had taken when they had left Genira's house. Which seemed so very long ago.

They must be nearly there now, and she was still able to hear Valwyn's voice clearly, when she checked in with her each morning. It felt odd to be speaking mind-to-mind with someone so many miles away. If only she could reach out to Jacob… but she didn't quite dare try that. Not yet. Maybe when they were closer. And after all, he might not be able to hear her. Or, if he did, he might think her voice was a delusion. She wished she knew what had happened to him… all she had been told was that he was in Talamunem City, the capital of Talamdor. It would be a long while before they were anywhere near there.

"Will we reach Taellingsford tonight?" she asked Ylonya.

"Yes, but I want to wait until it's nearly dark to enter the town. I don't want to risk us being seen by anyone unfriendly."

"Surely that's not likely in Taellingsford?" Ednor said. "I know the town well, and I've rarely heard of anyone being attacked."

Ylonya's mouth set in a straight line. "So long as we are travelling with Abigail, we have to assume that agents of Talamdor will be seeking us, that any stranger is not our friend."

"Ylonya is our expert at moving in secrecy," Shaunan said. "Let us follow her advice."

Remembering the attack outside Néartanis, Abigail agreed with Shaunan. She could do without another incident like that.

They followed the southerly road, lit by the silver radiance of the rising moon, slipping into Taellingsford just before the gates shut for the night and making their way to Genira's house by a circuitous route, as they had done before. Not for the first time, Abigail was filled with wonder at Ylonya's extensive knowledge of the highways and byways of Veylindré. She was looking forward to seeing Genira again, remembering her kindness on their previous visit. As before, Ylonya led them round to the back yard and told them to stable their mounts and bring their packs with them.

Ednor's horse, a splendid black stallion with two white socks and a star in the centre of his forehead, baulked at the entrance. Ednor gentled him in, took his tack off and gave him some hay, as around him, the others did the same.

"I trust we will not be staying here long," he said. "Starfire is used to better."

"He had better get used to it," Ylonya said. "We will be proceeding on foot from here."

"But… I cannot leave him behind," Ednor protested. "He has been mine since he was three years old."

"Come, Ednor," Shaunan said. "You can ask Genira to send a message to the palace in Néartanis to have him collected, then he can wait for you in the stables there."

"I don't understand why we cannot simply take a ship across the Néartanian Straits and bring the horses with us."

"Because if anyone has picked up our trail this side of the Straits, this is a good opportunity to lose them."

"I don't see how…"

"Enough, Ednor," Shaunan said. "Our need for discretion is absolute."

Which silenced him.

Abigail secretly felt a little sorry for him – she sensed he was used to getting his own way and was struggling with not being the leader of their little group. She hoped he would be able to overcome these feelings, as they would need his wholehearted support and his skills with a blade later on.

The hair on the back of her neck stood up. Where had that assurance come from? That they would need his skills with a blade? She did not want to share Shaunan's ability to see into the future, however nebulous a gift it was.

Ylonya led them into the kitchen, then left to seek Genira. The six of them clustered around the pine table, and Abigail admired the dresser with its plates and dishes all neatly displayed, and the copper cooking pans hanging from pegs on the wall, gleaming gently in the light of the oil lamp. They reminded her of home.

"Who does this house belong to?" Tremond asked.

"To a friend of Ylonya's, Genira," Ellyn said. "You'll like her. She is an apothecary."

"But why are we here?"

"You will see. Ylonya will not be long," Shaunan said.

Sure enough, Ylonya returned a few minutes later, followed by Genira. Abigail rushed forward and gave her a hug.

Genira smiled and returned it. "Welcome back, my friends. But I see there are more of you this time."

"Yes, there are now seven of us," Ylonya said. "The ones you don't know are Tremond, an Officer of the Watch from Garûnalonden and Ednor, younger son of Lord Éadulf of Néartania."

Both men bowed.

"This is Genira," Ylonya continued, "an apothecary and an old friend of mine. Genira, can you put us up overnight, then send us on our way?"

"Of course. You have horses?"

"Yes, and one in particular needs to be sent across to the palace at Néartanis, once we have gone. The black stallion. The five you lent us before are yours to do with what you will, but I'm not sure what Tremond wants for his mount."

"If you would care for mine in my absence, Mistress Genira, I would be most grateful," Tremond said with a bow. "I can pay whatever you think fair."

"Then I will do so," Genira replied. "Which horse is yours?"

"He is the dappled grey."

Genira nodded, then, turned to Ylonya, "I guess you want to take the route you did before?"

"Yes, please. But if we could stay the night first, we can start out fresh in the morning."

"Of course. I will show you to your rooms, then make us all supper."

"May Ranu bless you, Genira," Shaunan said, "we are most grateful."

"I can't go back down that tunnel. I simply can't." Ellyn wailed, tears rolling down her cheeks.

"Why do closed in spaces bother you so much?" Abigail asked.

"It started when my parents died, when I was four. There was a cave-in at the mine, and my father didn't get out in time. For seisdags afterwards, I had terrifying nightmares about the roof of the house falling in and burying me, waking up shaking and crying. Then my mother, who was heavily pregnant at the time, lost the baby, before dying herself from childbirth fever. Aunt Shaunan's husband, Donan, was killed alongside my father, so she took me in when my mother died."

"Oh, my dear. I had no idea. I am so very sorry. I know what it means to lose your parents."

Ellyn sat down on her bed and bowed her head. She felt Abigail's arm come round her shoulders and leaned in to the older girl's embrace. Once had been bad enough, and she hadn't known what was to come. This time she knew. The seemingly endless dark miles, lit only by the Goldstones of Abigail, Aunt Shaunan and Ylonya.

"You can do this. You are stronger and braver than you think you are." Abigail's voice was gentle, soothing her fears.

"All right," she said, "I'll do it. But you promise you'll be with me?"

"Every step of the way… and Aidren will be too. I wonder whether either of the other two will mind it."

Ellyn's head came up off Abigail's shoulder. "I hadn't thought of that. Surely not. They're all grown-ups."

"Have you ever had to look after a small child?" was Abigail's next, rather unexpected question.

Ellyn shook her head. "No, I was four when my parents died, and Aunt Shaunan adopted me. I've always wished I had brothers and sisters."

Abigail hugged her, then said, "I was the eldest of five and can remember how Daniel and Faith, my little brother and sister, used to get towards the end of a busy day. They would be tired, their bodies longing for sleep, but they were so afraid of missing out on anything the adults were doing, they would struggle to keep themselves awake. When they were that tired, they would become contradictory and cross – ready to pick a fight with their own shadows."

Abigail smiled at the memory. Such a wistful smile, as though she was remembering what she had lost.

"But what does that have to do with the fear of being trapped underground?" Ellyn asked.

"I learned from my mother that children need boundaries, and that the only way to deal with them when they became fratchety was to be firm but kind. That is what I try to do with my fears. Fear does not become less as we grow older. We just learn to control it better, not to let it be our master. The way I do it is to say to my fear, 'yes, I know how you feel, I do understand, but it's time for us to go now.' But I try to never let it get the upper hand, to control me."

"Does that work?"

"Most of the time. It seems to help, anyway."

"But what are you afraid of? You're one of the bravest people I know."

Abigail laughed, a gentle laugh, which sounded sad in Ellyn's ears. "Thank you. But two things frighten me above all – first, that I'll never see Jacob again, and second, that my fate is to contend with the Prophet of the One."

Ellyn took a deep breath. Compared to those fears, her own anxiety about braving the long dark of the tunnel seemed to dwindle into insignificance. She hugged her friend.

"Thank you. I was being a big baby. I know that so long as Aidren, you and Aunt Shaunan are with me, I'll be fine."

Abigail hugged her back. "That's my brave girl. Now, wash your face and we'll go down for supper."

Δ Chapter 14 Δ

As the weeks – which only lasted six days and which he was learning to call seisdags – passed, Jacob was beginning to find his feet in Talamunem City, even to feel at home here. Most of his mornings were spent with Portak, learning more about Talamdor – about its inhabitants and how its society worked. As his knowledge grew, he began to feel a great respect for the people of this proud land, who had managed to cling to their faith through decades of tyranny and servitude. But he still didn't understand why they traded with the Havimi, who had been their deadliest enemies until thirty or so years before.

Portak – or more likely, the Prophet – had finally heeded his plea to have something to do with his hands, and he was spending every afternoon with Melnok, a master smith in the city. Like Jacob's father, Melnok was a tall, broad man, immensely strong, his face permanently ruddy from his work at the forge. But unlike his father, most of whose life – or at least the portion Jacob could remember – had been spent repairing agricultural implements and shoeing horses, Melnok was more of an armourer than a smith, and spent most of his working hours making swords, maces, spearheads and other weapons. Like Jacob, he wore the silver bangle.

"Why does Talamdor need all these weapons?" Jacob asked one day, as he was helping Melnok, enjoying the heat of the forge as a welcome contrast to the chill air outside. Melnok's workshop reminded him so much of his father's smithy – the racks of instruments hanging neatly on the walls, the iron anvil on its oaken base and the heat coming from the brazier.

"They're for the war, I reckon."

"But why are we going to fight with Veylindré?"

Melnok glanced around quickly before answering, his voice rough and deep, "It is not for the likes of us to question the decisions of the Prophet. Our job is to do as we are told."

Jacob lowered his voice, picking up on the man's unease at such frank speech, "What do you mean, 'the likes of us'?"

"Those who wear the silver bangle. Those of us Holy Talamu found wanting." He swung round and put the spearhead he had been working on back into the fire. Jacob worked the bellows and watched it glow red once more.

"It doesn't seem fair to me, that if you fail that Test of Faith as a child, to be looked down on for the rest of your life."

"Fair?" Melnok's laugh was a deep bark. "It's not about 'fair'. "And it is not for us to question the will of Holy Talamu. If you are wise, you will stop asking these questions. It could get you, and me, into trouble."

"I'm sorry. I'm just trying to understand. Where I come from, all men have a chance to better themselves."

"Aye, I've noticed you bear a Waymark." He spat to one side. "How come you ended up here?"

Jacob's heart sank. That wasn't what he had meant at all. He'd been thinking of home, of England. He had almost forgotten the mysterious mark on his forehead. He hated being judged for something that he didn't understand. And he was desperate to keep Melnok's goodwill. Without that, he would be stuck in the Hall of Visitors all day long.

"Forget it, Melnok. I shouldn't have said anything…. What do you want me to do next?"

Melnok gave him a long look before replying, "We have several more spearheads to work on today. You may start shaping one."

"The teachings of Holy Talamu are like to those of the Lord our God," the Prophet proclaimed.

Jacob shifted uneasily on his hard seat in the dark audience chamber. Once again the Prophet had summoned him, to teach him more about Holy Talamu.

"Did not Moses tell the people the words of the Lord, in the Book of Exodus, 'Thou shalt not suffer a witch to live.'? And again, in the Book of Deuteronomy, did he not name those who used divination, or charms, or enchantments, 'abominations unto the Lord'? And did not Saint Paul, in his Letter to the Galatians, name witchcraft as a work of the flesh? He wrote, 'they which do such things shall not inherit the kingdom of God.' So you see, Jacob, we have a divine cause – to purge the Commonweal of Veylindré of the evils of witchcraft and convert its population to the worship of Holy Talamu."

The normally pale face of the Prophet was alight with religious fervour, his eyes shining as he spoke.

"Yes, my Lord, I see." But wasn't the Bloodmagic of Talamdor the same as witchcraft?

He had forgotten the Prophet's power of reading minds. A black frown came over the man's face, and his voice thrummed with anger. "Do not dare to compare our magic with the wickedness of the witches of Veylindré. It is quite different. Our magic is a gift from Holy Talamu, like the power of our Lord Jesus and his disciples, who were able to do miracles."

Jacob cowered in his seat, wondering what punishment he had earned for his blasphemy. But to his surprise, the man leant back on his throne, and his voice changed to a tone of sorrowful reprimand.

"You are young in our world, so I forgive your doubts. But Jacob, purge them from your heart. Holy Talamu's Way of Power is the one true gospel. If you are unable to overcome these false teachings, you are of no use to me, and I will have to hold you here, under close guard, when our campaign begins."

Jacob's heart sank. He had displeased the Prophet. How could he redeem himself? He blurted, "Please, my Lord, don't do that. Is this Way of Power so all-encompassing, then?"

"It is indeed. It is in our Bloodstones, in our relationship with Holy Talamu, in the way we live. Before Holy Talamu was banished from the Commonweal, Talamdorians had a role to play within it. And that was to lead others. When we came here, at the beginning of the Second Age, Holy Talamu searched Her heart and in the deepest caverns of Mount Talamu, She fashioned a Master Bloodstone, shaped like a prism, to use against the Six and against Veylindré, and gave others to Her people. With its aid, She began to leech the power from the Master Goldstones. But then the rest of the Commonweal rose against us, the Bloodstones of the people were destroyed and it was thought that the Master Bloodstone was lost.

"But it was not so. Nigh on thirty years ago, I was sent a vision by Holy Talamu, the second I had been vouchsafed. She taught me the location of the Master Bloodstone, and I braved many dangers to retrieve it. And She told me how to fashion new Bloodstones, so that my people – those with a Talamunem Bloodmark," and he pointed to his own forehead, to the blood-red triangle there, "could use their power to control others. This we have done, and so Talamdor has arisen from the ashes and is once more a powerful nation. And, like the Jews in the Old Testament, we Talamdorians are the chosen people."

"What happens now?" Jacob asked, trying to sound intelligent.

"You will see. After the end of the Season of Dearth, when we have celebrated Ranusfest, you will see."

"Thank you, my Lord." Thank God. He had been forgiven.

"What's going on?" Jacob asked Portak, as they walked through the marketplace. "It looks as though they're preparing to build bonfires."

The market was his favourite place in Talamunem City, apart from Melnok's forge. Dozens of wooden huts with drop-down flaps at the front displayed all kinds of wares, from fruit and vegetables and spices to household goods and clothing. It reminded him so much of home, of the market in Andover.

"It is nearly the end of the Season of Dearth," Portak replied. "For the last fifteen seisdags, we have endured the cold of that season, and now it is time to celebrate."

"How do you celebrate?"

Portak frowned at him and sighed. Jacob guessed he was getting fed up with answering his questions, but how else was he going to learn about this strange land?

"We celebrate the end of the Season of Dearth with the Festival of Ranusfest."

"But I thought Ranu was one of the goddesses of Veylindré," Jacob said. "Why is there a Talamdorian festival in her honour?"

"It is not in her honour," Portak spat the word. "Ranu has quite a different role, here in Talamdor. She symbolises times of dearth and short commons, so we make an end to her."

"How do you do that?"

"The people build an effigy of wood and straw, then set it on fire, to symbolise that they have overcome another Season of Dearth."

"It sounds like our Guy Fawkes."

"Quietly," Portak cautioned. Then added in a low tone, "who was Guy Fawkes?"

"He was one of a number of conspirators, who tried to blow up our House of Lords, more than sixty years ago. It was called the Gunpowder Plot."

"What is the House of Lords?"

"It's one of the two houses of our government. The other is the House of Commons."

"And why did they want to blow it up?" Portak asked, sounding interested for the first time that day.

"They were trying to kill the king, who was speaking there, because they were Catholics and they wanted to replace him with a Catholic monarch. But Guy Fawkes was caught in the cellars beneath the House of Lords, and the conspirators were all executed. And ever since then, we have celebrated Gunpowder Treason Day by lighting bonfires, and burning effigies of Guy Fawkes on top of them."

"And the king was your ruler, like the Prophet is ours? How did they dare?"

"England is a divided country," Jacob said. "Until Henry VIII's time, we all worshipped God – like your Talamu – in the same way. Then the king made himself head of the Church and we could all read the Bible for ourselves. Later, it became illegal to be a Catholic. But they still believe that their way of worship is the only right one."

"You said they plotted to 'blow up' the House of Lords," Portak said. "How would that be possible?"

"Don't you have gunpowder here?" Jacob asked.

"What is gunpowder?"

"My father once told me it is a mixture of sulphur, charcoal and saltpeter. If you combine it together in the right proportions, it causes an explosion. When the Civil War was going on, he used to help Josiah Welland, the old smith, to make it. They used it to help fire their matchlocks and flintlocks, which my father also helped to make."

"What are matchlocks and flintlocks?"

It was Jacob's turn to feel astonished. "You know, a musket? That fires musket balls at your enemy from a distance?" Jacob mimed the shape and dimensions of each in a way that must have looked like quite a spectacle to passers-by. Portak seemed totally unmoved.

"Forgive me if I don't understand correctly," Portak said more delicately than he ever had before, as if speaking to a very young child. "This… gunpowder helps you make a blowpipe without a need to blow."

"Yes."

"Why not use a blowpipe or better yet a bow?"

"Because the musket ball travels much further and faster."

Portak stared at him blankly for an uncomfortable space of time and Jacob sensed he was thinking deeply. He had never seen him so interested in anything he had ever had to say and he wasn't sure he liked it.

"Would that we had such weapons," Portak said. "We would be invincible."

The Prophet must know, surely? Why hadn't he shared it with his people?

The day of Ranusfest dawned clear and bright. Jacob was woken by a knock at his door.

"Come in," he said, his mind still fogged with sleep.

Portak walked in and shook his shoulder. "Get up, Jacob. There will be a special service at the Great Temple at fourth hour to mark the beginning of Ranusfest. If we do not hurry, we will have to struggle to reach our places."

Jacob gaped at him. He could not imagine the enormous space of the Great Temple being so full that it would be difficult to move through it.

"Come," Portak said. "We must breakfast now and then head over to the Temple."

"Give me ten minutes to have a wash and get dressed."

"Ten minutes. I will wait for you outside."

The Prophet had sent a tailor to him some weeks – no, seisdags – before, so Jacob now had more clothes to choose from. This service sounded important so he selected his outfit with care – a pair of black breeches with a belt of red leather to secure them, a white, linen shirt and black jerkin, and a pair of black, knee-high boots of soft leather. And, of course, a black cloak, with a hood to conceal the mark on his forehead.

The dining room of the Visitors' Hall was full of people, all dressed in their best in robes of black and red, some with fur-lined collars and cuffs, and the hum of conversation was loud and excited. He began to realise that Portak was right. He gulped down his breakfast as fast as he could, then followed his mentor out.

The air outside was cold and crisp as they joined a throng making their way towards the Great Temple. When they got there, the queue of men, women and children, all chattering excitedly among themselves, snaked around the great open space in front of it. Jacob and Portak joined the end of it.

"An hour to go," Portak said. "We should be in time."

Jacob drew his cloak closely around himself and stamped his feet against the cold. The queue moved slowly but steadily and they were admitted into the Temple by a red-robed priest after a wait of forty-five minutes and were each given a small candle. As Portak had foretold, the interior was crowded with people. Not only were all the pews full, but some people stood against the high, black walls. Torches set in brackets illuminated the scene. Their warmth and that of the gathered people made the interior of the Temple feel much less cold than outside. They found their seats and sat down gratefully.

"What happens now?" Jacob asked.

"The service will start at fourth hour. The High Priest will give thanks for the ending of the Season of Dearth and give his blessings for a fruitful Season of Renewal. Later, the Prophet will address the people from the battlements on the northern wall of the City. He will be speaking to both the citizens of our city and to the troops outside our walls. Then the ceremonial fires will be lit."

"It sounds like a full day." Jacob settled himself down to wait. He wondered how a service here would compare with the church services back home. Music, loud and martial, began to play and the assembled people fell silent. Then everyone stood and Jacob swivelled round to see why. Portak poked him in the ribs, hard.

"What was that for?"

"Face the front and stay silent."

A number of priests in red, floor-length robes processed up the central aisle. The one at the front, whom Jacob guessed was the High Priest, had a tall hat like a bishop's mitre on his head and carried a long staff of dark wood, surmounted by a blood-red prism. He took his place on a richly carved chair of the same dark wood to one side of the high altar, and the other priests filed into pews at the other side. As ever, Jacob could not take his eyes off the painting of Holy Talamu, whose eyes seemed to pierce them all. Part of him was beginning to believe she was worthy of worship.

The High Priest was a tall man, his white hair touching the shoulders of his blood-red robes, his face craggy and stern with a strong nose and dark eyes. He rose and lit a large candle in front of the painting, bowed to it, then raised his arms and declaimed, "Holy Talamu, we are gathered here today to celebrate the end of the Season of Dearth. Once more, by Your grace, we have come through this time. We gather to give thanks to You and to ask Your blessings for the Season of Renewal."

He bowed again, then turned and addressed the people, "You may sit."

When all were seated, the High Priest addressed the assembled congregation. "Today is the day of Ranusfest, which marks the end of the Season of Dearth. The cold has begun to lessen and the days are growing longer as our world turns towards the sun. This is a time in which the life of the land begins to stir once more and, by the grace of Holy Talamu, new growth begins to come forth after the long darkness."

One of the lesser priests brought a dark-red candle to the High Priest, and he lit it, saying, "The blessings of Ranusfest to you all. We light our sacred flame, which symbolises the care of Holy Talamu, as She watches over us all. This is a time of rebirth and fertility, as new life begins to stir within the earth, within our people. The Season of Renewal is the time to celebrate the loving nurture of Holy Talamu."

He then placed the candle on the high altar and took up a golden cup. "This wine symbolises the blood of Holy Talamu, who gave of Herself to allow our Bloodmagic to come into being. We drink it in Her honour." He passed it around the other priests, and each took a sip. As they did, he said to each, "May Holy Talamu bless you this season."

Next, he took up a round loaf and broke it in two. "This bread symbolises the body of Holy Talamu, from whom we all came. We eat it in Her honour."

As the High Priest was passing it round the other priests, Jacob watched a number of others walking down the three aisles of the Great Temple, holding large wicker baskets in their arms. Starting at the backmost rows, they offered bread, which he assumed had been blessed by the High Priest, to the congregation, and the loaves were passed along the rows and then forward, each person tearing off a small portion before passing the loaf on. With so many people present, this took some time. When everyone had a morsel of bread, the High Priest addressed them again, saying, "May the love of Holy Talamu nurture you in the seisdags to come."

And the people responded in unison, "May Talamu have mercy upon us," before slowly, reverently eating their bread.

Finally, lit tapers were passed along the rows in the same way, and each person lit their candle. By the time the priests had reached the front row, the whole Temple was illuminated by thousands of tiny, flickering lights. The High Priest said, "May the light of Holy Talamu's flame guide you. May the warm of Holy Talamu's flame nurture you and protect you, today and always."

Then he lifted his own candle off the high altar, turned again to face the painting of Talamu, and said, "Holy Talamu, we are grateful for Your blessings. Be with us as we enter the Season of Renewal. So may it be."

He turned back to the congregation and blew his candle out. Everyone present did the same. After the warmth and light of all those flames, the Temple seemed dark and gloomy to

Jacob. But he did not have time to reflect on it. He and everyone else stood, as the High Priest and the other priests processed back down the central aisle and out of the Great Temple.

The people began to stream out of the Great Temple. Portak turned to Jacob, "We hold special services at the end of each season, to invoke the blessing of Holy Talamu."

"It reminded me of our own Holy Communion services," Jacob said, remembering to keep his voice low. "But the congregation also partake of the wine, which symbolises the blood of Our Lord, which was shed for us. And the bread symbolises his body, broken for us."

"You need to forget about that, now. You are here in Talamdor and must follow Holy Talamu."

Later in the day, Portak led Jacob through the narrow streets of the city towards the northern wall. "The Prophet will address the people at ninth hour," he said.

"Does he do that during each festival?" Jacob asked.

"Always at Talamusfest, which commemorates our ancient liberation from the tyrants of Veylindré and, in recent years, our liberation from the oppression of the Havimi. But not usually at the others. I wonder…"

He fell silent. He could sense the mood of high expectation in the city. Would his master announce that they were finally ready to wage war on Veylindré?

"You wonder what?" Jacob broke into his thoughts.

"Nothing. Let us find a good place to listen."

On the dot of ninth hour, the figure of the Prophet came into view, high above them on the battlements of the northern wall. This place was unusual too… his master generally addressed his people in the central square in front of the Great Temple.

But it seemed as though he was planning to speak to the forces gathered outside the walls too.

A deep silence fell, broken by the cry of a hungry child. It cut off abruptly, as though its mother had put it to her breast.

"How will everyone be able to hear?" Jacob asked.

"Hush. He is about to speak."

"Citizens of Talamunem City, members of our loyal forces, friends," the Prophet began.

Although he did not appear to be shouting, his voice rang clear and powerful in Jacob's ears. Maybe he was using some Bloodmagic to amplify his voice. Jacob put aside the puzzle – he too was eager to hear the Prophet's words.

A sensation of warmth from his silver bangle, which was giving off a gleam of red. He'd noticed it before, when he was in the Prophet's presence. For the first time, he made the connection – did all the silver bangles go red when the Prophet was using Bloodmagic?

"I stand here in the sight of you all, as Holy Talamu's representative in Talamdor, to tell you that the time of waiting is at an end. The omens are good, and we have the blessing of Holy Talamu. We are Her chosen people and we have been exiled for long enough. The hour has come for us to take back our ancient lands."

The crowd roared its approval. The Prophet raised his hands and silence fell once more.

"Each one of you will have a role to play as we take our long-delayed offensive, fighting for what is rightfully ours, which was taken from us long ages ago. We will move across the Talamdorian Mountains and come down on our age-old enemy like wolves. We will fall on them with fire and sword and burn the witches of Veylindré, purging the world of their evil influence. When we light our ceremonial bonfires this evening, burning the effigies of the arch-witch Ranu to symbolise the end of the Season of Dearth, let us pledge ourselves to the renewal of our land. For more than thirteen hundred years, we have been ground down under the Veylindréan heel.

“I know that you will fight to your last breath to retake the lands that should be ours by right. Some of you will have to pay the ultimate price. But I know you will not shrink from doing so, staunch in the knowledge that it will lead to the establishment of a new era, when your children, the children of Talamdor, will no longer live in fear, when we will once more rule in Veylindré, as Holy Talamu intended. Those left behind will mind the hearths and pray for our safe return. I am proud to call you my people. We will triumph on the fields of Veylindré and a new age will begin. We march in four days' time.”

He raised his arms and spread them wide. “The blessing of Holy Talamu upon you all.”

The cheer that arose was deafening. At last, they were going to fight. The days of skulking beyond the mountains were over. Portak could scarcely contain his excitement. The only fly in the ointment was that he would have to leave Balmak again.

Chapter 15

"So where do we go from here?" Tremond asked Ylonya, as they sat around Genira's table, after a delicious meal of delicately poached fish in a flavoursome sauce, with rice and green peas. "I do not understand why we must proceed on foot. Surely our swiftest way onward would be to take a ship across the Néartanian Straits."

Ylonya paused before answering. When she had brought Abigail and the others to the other entrance to the hidden passage, they had been travelling together for some seisdags and had shared experiences which had taught her to trust them. She liked what she had seen of the two men, but it went against the grain to reveal secret information.

However, it could not be helped. If they were to take the secret path under the Straits on the morrow, she would have to trust them, much though it ran counter to her gut feelings. She cleared her throat, tried to ignore the apprehension she was feeling about the risk she was taking. A risk that was not fully hers to take. But the need to protect Abigail and the others from hostile eyes bested her instinct for secrecy. She would have to hope they were trustworthy. But if they betrayed that trust, she would kill them. She glanced at Genira, and received a tiny nod, before answering.

"Before I tell you, I need to exact a promise from you and Ednor that you will not reveal your knowledge of our onward road to any."

"You are asking us to trust you," Tremond said, his deep voice calm, measured, "and demand our secrecy in return. I would like to know a little more before I give you my promise."

Ylonya gritted her teeth. Trust a Watchman to raise an objection. "It is a route known to very few, and I would like to keep it that way."

"Why?" Tremond asked. "You are not evading the Watch's diligence, I trust?"

What to say? "Not exactly. But it is sometimes necessary for members of the Guild to move from place to place unseen by unfriendly eyes."

Tremond thought about that for a minute, then nodded. "Then I give you my word. I will say nothing of this secret road to anyone. This I vow, by the Six and the Way."

"Thank you," she said, bowing her head. "What about you, Ednor? Will you take a vow of secrecy also?"

The younger man's brows came down in a frown. "Does this secret route of yours have a negative impact on Néartania?"

Ylonya scowled at him. How dare he question her? "That is not the question I am asking, Ednor. Will you promise to never reveal your knowledge of our onward road to any? Or will we have to leave you behind?"

Ednor shot to his feet, his face flushed with anger. "I am a son of the rulers of Néartania. I have a right to question anything which might impact on her wellbeing."

"Our quest transcends loyalties to land and ruler," Shaunan said gently. "I give you my word as a Waymage that the inhabitants of Néartania will never come to harm from it. Does that satisfy you?"

Ednor looked from her to Ylonya, who was waiting, her stomach tight with apprehension. Why had Ednor's question wound her up so much more than Tremond's? He had just as much right to ask.

"I know that it is impossible for a Waymage to lie," he said, "so yes, I give you my word that I will never share my knowledge of this road with any other. This I vow, by the Six and by the Way."

Ylonya nodded her head once in acknowledgement. "Good. Then we had better get some rest. We have a long way to walk on the morrow."

Ellyn and Abigail were woken before dawn by a knock on their door. "Breakfast will be ready in twenty minutes," came Genira's voice, "come down as soon as you may."

She and Abigail piled out of bed, got washed and dressed as quickly as they could, and did a brief, ten-minute Immersion practice. Then they picked up their packs and walked downstairs. She was not looking forward to this journey.

After they had breakfasted, Genira led them down the steep stone steps towards the entrance to the secret path, Ellyn's stomach began to roil with anxiety. Her hands were cold and clammy and it felt as though she couldn't pull enough air into her lungs. She put her left hand up to her throat to clutch her Goldstone in its leather pouch, and rested her right hand on the wooden handrail, fixing her eyes on the warm golden light of Aunt Shaunan's Goldstone ahead of her.

They reached the bottom. She moved to stand next to Aidren as Ylonya and Genira walked over to the tunnel's entrance to open it. What had Abigail said? Oh yes, something about talking to her fear, not letting it control her. Might as well give it a try. And in her head, she said, All right, my friend Fear, I know you're here, but I'm going to walk through that tunnel and come out safe at the other end. Aidren and Abi and Aunt Shaunan are with me, so there is nothing to be afraid of. I'm stronger than you think I am. Let's go.

As she and Aidren came up to the entrance, she stepped up and hugged Genira. "Thank you for all you have done for us. I hope I'll see you again, when all this is over."

Genira looked both surprised and pleased. She hugged her back and was then hugged by Abigail and Shaunan as well. Then Ylonya embraced her friend, and said, "All debts between us have been repaid, Genira. Hold us in your prayers."

"Of course I will. The blessings of the Six be on your journey. May the Way guard and guide you all, today and always."

As the heavy door closed behind them, Ylonya, Shaunan and Abigail held up their Goldstones to light the way ahead, and Ellyn heard the words of power, *Gal lo bynn leumin,* spoken in unison. Two golden yellow lights and one white-blue one shone forth from their hands.

Tremond was gazing down the long passageway which vanished into the distance ahead of them, at its rough sides and roof, with pieces of mica glittering in the light of the Goldstones, its smooth surface underfoot. He whistled, loud and long, and the sound echoed around the tunnel. "So this passage goes all the way to Néartanis?"

"It does. It is something over twenty miles," Ylonya said. "We had better get going."

Once again, they set off through the long dark of the tunnel. As before, the silence was immense, broken only by the sounds of their footfalls and soft breathing. Aidren was beside her all the way, and she took comfort in his warm presence, in the touch of his hand surrounding her own. When they stopped halfway through for a brief meal and a breather, she felt less panicked. For whatever reason, the journey seemed to take less time, this way, but she was glad when it was over. Shaunan and Abigail looked tired – it must have been quite an effort to keep their Goldstones constantly alight for so long. When Ylonya led them through the exit at the Néartanis end, she gave a sigh of relief.

"How was it this time?" Abigail asked.

"So different! I took your advice and gave my fear a good talking-to, and it really worked. Thank you, Abi." She gave her a big hug.

"I'm so proud of you."

"Thank you. I still didn't like it, but I wasn't terrified this time. But I'm so glad it's behind us."

"We'll be out in the fresh air soon."

"What happens next?"

"That will be up to Ylonya. I expect she and Kendris will put their heads together and come up with a safe route for us."

Ylonya sped up the stairs and knocked on the door of Kendris's living room. The door swung open and her old friend was standing there, a poker in his hand. When he saw it was her, the poker was lowered, but no smile lit his face.

"Ylonya! What are you doing here?"

"We have just crossed the Straits from Taellingsford and ask for your hospitality for a night."

"The same five as last time?"

"No, we have added two others to our company – Ednor, the son of Lord Éadulf and Lady Aethed, and Tremond, a Watch officer from Garûnalonden."

Kendris's eyebrows shot up. "I know nothing of the Garûnalonden, but how could you trust that puppy Ednor with knowledge of the secret path?"

She had been afraid of this. Keeping her voice even, she answered, "I made both of them vow by the Six and the Way not to reveal its existence to anyone outside the company. He was reluctant at first but accepted the Waymage's assurance that it would not harm Néartania. I'm sorry, Kendris, I had no choice. This quest we are on is vital for the continued wellbeing of the Commonweal, and it was essential that we crossed from Lènium to Néartania unobserved."

"Hmph. I suppose I must trust your judgement," he said. "Where are they now?"

"Waiting in the cave below, for me to speak to you. Will you put us up tonight?"

"I suppose I must. But have an eye to that Néartanian princeling."

"What do you have against him?"

"Nothing specific. But he sets my teeth on edge, with his air of being Néarta's gift to Néartania."

She could not help laughing. "Oh, I know what you mean. But I believe his heart is in the right place. Once we are all here, I would welcome your advice about our onward route."

He huffed, then shrugged his shoulders. "I cannot do that until I know where you are bound."

"I will tell you later, once we are all together again."

"Come, then, let us fetch them." He turned on his heel and preceded her down the stairs.

Abigail was relieved that the long journey under the Straits was behind them. Although she didn't mind the enclosed space like Ellyn did, it had been a long and tiring day. Her back and shoulders were aching from carrying her pack as well as her healer's bag, and climbing the stairs was a real effort. She was also weary from the exertion of keeping her Goldstone lit for so long. She hoped Kendris would be able to put them up for the night, and see them on their way in the morning, with horses. And feed them – she was ravenous.

"Thank you for allowing us to stay here tonight," Shaunan said. "Are the horses we left with you still here?"

"They are." A brusque answer. Abigail winced inwardly – Kendris did not sound pleased to see them.

"But only five," he continued. "If you need two more, that will have to wait until the morning. I know a horse trader who occasionally does me favours."

"Thank you, Kendris, we are most grateful. And we would be happy to pay whatever you think fair for them." Abigail sensed a gentle nudge from her mentor, so was unsurprised when a reluctant smile crept across the Yrusian's scarred face.

"You are welcome, Waymage Shaunan. If you would wait here," and he opened a door into a cosy living room with a fire blazing in the grate, "I will see about supper."

"Thank you, my friend. That is kind of you."

Half an hour later, they were sitting round Kendris's kitchen table, wolfing down bread and cheese and cold meats, washed down with a dark beer. Abigail could not remember eating anything so delicious – hunger was the best savour. Once they had finished, Kendris turned to Ylonya.

"So, where are you heading?"

"To Talamunem City."

His brows came down in a frown. "To Talamdor? For what reason?"

Abigail saw Ylonya glance at her mentor for permission and receive a tiny shake of the head in exchange. "I'm truly sorry, Kendris, but our mission is too secret even to share with you. But you have my word as a Guild member that it is essential to the continued wellbeing of the Commonweal."

Kendris sat back in his chair. Abigail sensed a flicker of hurt at her refusal to trust him. But all he said was, "Then I must take your word for it. How do you intend to pass unseen?"

"This is where we need your advice," Ylonya replied. "I thought it would be best to approach Talamdor from an unexpected direction, from the north."

"So you are planning to go up through Yrusian?"

"Yes."

"I will fetch my maps."

"Why are we going through Yrusian?" Ednor asked, in what he hoped was a tone of sweet reason. "It will take much longer than riding straight through Néartanis."

"Were you not listening to me?" Ylonya replied, with what he considered was unnecessary sarcasm. "Our need for secrecy is far more important than speed."

Ednor shrugged. Yrusians. They always wanted to complicate things.

Kendris re-entered the kitchen carrying a rolled-up map. Without being asked, Abigail and Ellyn began to clear the table, so that there would be space for it to lie flat. How had they known? Then Ednor glanced at the older girl's Waymark and remembered she could probably read minds. He had better learn to think quietly.

In spite of his reservations, he drew closer when the older Yrusian unrolled the map and anchored its corners with spice jars. He had never visited Yrusian and did not know much about its geography.

"You will need to cross the Yrusian border west of here," Kendris began, "then head cross country to the north-eastern tip of the Inland Sea, at Ostfen. The land around the marges of the Inland Sea is mostly fen – you'll need to take great care to follow the paths made by the fen-dwellers, and you'll have to cross three rivers – the Yrus, the Porus and the Iascus." He paused. "Are you sure this is a good idea?"

He spoke for Ednor too. This sounded like a long and complicated diversion, fraught with dangers. But he was a warrior, accustomed to such things.

"Yes," Ylonya replied. "No matter how challenging this route will be, it is still better than approaching Talamdor by a road on which we may be expected."

Kendris grunted, his scarred face giving no hint of his thoughts. "Very well. Once you reach the north-western tip of the Inland Sea," he stabbed the place on the map with his finger, "you'll need to turn south and slightly west to reach Chorich Castle, one of our border forts with Talamdor."

"How far is it?" Ednor asked.

"From here? Just under a hundred miles to Ostfen, another seventy or so around the marge of the Inland Sea, then about sixty from the edge of the Sea to Chorich Castle. About two hundred and thirty miles in all. But the going is rough, so it will take you some seisdags to reach the border."

"By which time the forces of Talamdor may well be halfway into Néartania," Ednor said.

"That is so, my friend," the Waymage put in, "but do you not see? If, as we expect, the Talamdorians are concentrating on invading Néartania as their most direct route to invading the whole Commonweal, we may hope to slip unannounced into Talamdor from the north."

"We will be ready for them," Ednor said. "All the forces at my father's command will be marching towards our border keeps, to reinforce them."

"Let us hope so."

Ednor bit his lip but said nothing more. He did not like the way these people juggled risk for Néartania so lightly.

Abigail and Ellyn were sitting in their little room in Kendris's house, trying to make the most of the time of enforced rest, because he had warned them it would take most of the day to acquire two more horses for Ednor and Tremond without attracting undue attention. Abigail was kneeling on her bed, rearranging the contents of her healer's bag and Ellyn was sitting cross-legged on hers, mending a tear in her riding trousers. A welcome fire was blazing in the grate. Through the window, which backed onto the stable yard, they could hear the swish and clash of swords as Aidren and Ednor practiced their sword-fighting techniques.

"I wonder why Ednor dislikes Kendris so much?" Ellyn said.

"I think it's because he doesn't trust Yrusians," Abigail replied. "Haven't you noticed how wary he is around Ylonya?"

"Aidren likes him."

"I know, and that gives me hope. We are going to need his bright sword and strong arm in the seisdags to come."

"Do you think we will have to fight our way there?"

Abigail sensed the apprehension in the question. But Ellyn deserved to hear the truth. "I think so, yes, particularly as we get nearer to Talamunem City. I would be surprised if the Prophet does not have border patrols. But for now, I'm more concerned about how we are going to travel through the fens around the Inland Sea. At home, there is a large area of fenland in East Anglia and I've heard that travelling through it is arduous, particularly with horses."

"I've never been in Yrusian before – once we've been there, it will mean that the only land I've not visited in the Commonweal will be Garûnalond. I'd never dreamed I would see all the others."

Abigail could not help smiling at Ellyn's enthusiasm. "Yes, we're turning into quite seasoned travellers. But without Ylonya, we would be lost. I'm so glad she's with us."

"Me too." Ellyn looked down at the silver buckle ring on her finger, Ylonya's gift in Céardochis. "When I first met her, I was a little afraid of her – she seemed so self-sufficient. But she's proved herself to be a true friend."

"I think you may have hit on the reason why Ednor is so wary of her. I suspect he's not used to independent women. I think he finds her intimidating."

"I hope he gets over it," Ellyn said, "we're all going to need to have each other's backs on this journey."

As the light began to fade on that cold Yrusdag, Shaunan, Ylonya and Tremond were huddled round the kitchen table, listening to Kendris. He unrolled the map once more.

"As ever, I expect that speed is your first priority?" he said. It was more a statement than a question.

"The longer this journey takes us," Shaunan said, "the more opportunities there are for us to be found by agents of the Prophet. Why?"

Kendris took a deep breath. "In which case, I think you would be better advised to travel through the fens themselves by boat. It would cut about fifty miles off your journey. You could leave your horses with Hamnis, our agent in Ostfen."

"Is Bredor still Lord of the Fen-dwellers?" Ylonya asked.

"I believe so. In any case, his people are the only ones who live permanently in the Fenland and know how to navigate through it without harm. Hamnis can give you a letter of introduction."

"Are the fen-dwellers so independent then?" Tremond asked, his brows drawn together in a frown.

"Although they are nominally subject to Lord Vyncan and Lady Réata," Kendris said, "in reality, the Fenland is so far from Ruslen that they are a law unto themselves."

Shaunan noticed Tremond's lips thin, as though he disliked the thought of anyone being above the law. Which of course he would, being an Officer of the Watch.

"Do they follow the Way?" she asked.

"In their own fashion. To be honest, I think they prefer to rely on their own wits. Their lives are hard. And you should know, there are no Waystones in the fens."

"No Waystones? I had heard that rumour but dismissed it as false. How has that happened?"

"We do not know for certain," Kendris replied, "but we believe that as their independence has grown and as they have become more self-sufficient, they have relied less and less on the Way and the Waystones have been forgotten, and in some cases, cast down."

"Over what area?"

"Something over two hundred square miles," Kendris said. "The distance from Ostfen to Oestfen is about seventy miles, and the fens are more than thirty miles across from south to north."

"Then we too will have to rely on *our* wits, and on our skills with sword and knife," Ylonya said. She did not sound worried, which reassured Shaunan a little.

"Is the goodwill of the Fen-dwellers essential, if we are to travel through their land in safety?" Tremond asked.

"I believe it is," Kendris said. "Given their seclusion, it is hard to say. They do not even allow Yrusian trade caravans in or out of the Fenland. They only trade with us four times a year, at the end of the warmer seasons, out of Ostfen and Oestfen. In fact, it is rare to see a Fen-dweller outside those times. But their knowledge of their land is unparalleled. I think you would be wise to put yourselves in their hands, then pick up fresh horses at Oestfen."

"What do they trade in?" Tremond asked.

"They grow rare herbs, which only thrive in the very damp conditions of the Fenland and are prized by the Healers. And the leaves of the sedge grasses that are so common in the Fenland can be thinned into strips, dried and twisted into strong cordage and ropes, which our fisherfolk use for their nets and in their ships."

"Who is our agent in Oestfen?" Ylonya asked.

"The last I heard, it was Varcin. He has been there since the Guild was set up, more than thirty years ago."

"What do you think, Shaunan?" Ylonya asked.

"Yours is the knowing," she replied. "You and Kendris know more about Yrusian than I do. And I do not think we can afford to lose the time it would take to ride around them. Although it worries me to put our trust in people who do not follow the Way."

"And we may meet perils unforeseen there," Tremond added. "We will have to keep both eyes and ears open."

"Have you decided on our route?" Abigail asked Ylonya, as they headed for the West Gate of Néartanis shortly after dawn the next morning. It was a crisp, bright morning, and the early morning sun cast long shadows in front of them.

"I'll explain once we have left the city," Ylonya said in a low voice.

Abigail opened her mind to her surroundings, but they seemed to be the only people moving at this early hour. She would be glad to leave Néartanis behind. Anywhere there were people, there could be agents of the Prophet. She drew the hood of her cloak more closely around her face.

"To answer your question," Ylonya said a few minutes later, as the West Gate clanged shut behind them, "we will be crossing into Yrusian in a couple of miles, then heading almost directly west towards Ostfen, a large village at the north-eastern tip of the Inland Sea. It is nearly a hundred miles and I'm hoping to reach there by the end of the fifth or sixth day, depending on the weather."

"Why does it depend on the weather?" Ellyn asked.

"Because as usual, we will be avoiding well-travelled roads, and at this time of year, the tracks I'm going to take are likely to be deep in mud."

Abigail looked around her. This part of Yrusian seemed to be fairly similar to the land around Néartanis – well-tended farmland. The brown fields were beginning to show a dusting of green as the new year's crops began to poke their heads up through the soil.

"Then we travel through the fens, is that right?" she asked.

"Yes. Kendris has advised us to leave our horses at Ostfen, with Hamnis, our agent there, and to ask the Fen-dwellers to take us by boat across the fens to Oestfen."

"But that means we will be at their mercy," Ednor put in, a deep frown on his face.

"Yes, but that will be less dangerous than attempting the fens on horseback. Hamnis will be able to give us an introduction to Lord Bredor."

"Who's that?"

"He is lord of the fen-dwellers," Tremond said. "We will need his goodwill to cross the fens in safety."

"How do you know that?" Ednor asked.

Abigail could hear the fear in his voice, which came out as aggression. Sometimes he reminded her of Jacob, who had also taken his fear out in anger. Where was he now?

Almost unconsciously, she reached out and soothed the Néartanian. Then sensed Shaunan's amused approval.

He reminds me of Jacob too.

Abigail smiled, then shrugged, her eyes meeting her mentor's. *I believe he is a good man underneath.*

As do I.

Chapter 16

As they travelled further west, the weather grew colder, with a biting wind, which found its way into their clothing, so that the company were never warm, either on the move or during their brief rest halts. Abigail clenched her teeth together to stop them chattering, wrapped her scarf more closely round her neck and endured.

Shaunan, why is it so much colder here?

Because the prevailing wind comes from the west in this part of the Commonweal and we are riding right into it.

I hope it will be warmer in the Fenland.

I do too, but I know little of it.

You sound worried...

Not worried, exactly, but it concerns me that the Fen-dwellers do not follow the Way. I do not know how we will be received there. Keep your mind open. Can you still hear Valwyn?

Only very faintly now.

Then we will have to hope we do not need her aid, later on.

And Shaunan's voice left her mind. Abigail rode on in silence, chewing over her mentor's concerns – she was beginning to feel worried about this journey into the unknown too. They were putting a lot of faith in Kendris's advice and they didn't really know him. But Ylonya trusted him, and that meant a lot. With an effort, she pushed her doubts to the back of her mind.

Somehow Ylonya managed to find somewhere for them to take shelter each night – there were many smallholdings in this part of Yrusian and Ylonya seemed to know them all. Of course, she was Yrusian – this was home territory. It was a relief to get out of the wind each night, although the thawing-out process was always exquisitely painful as the warmth and feeling returned to their frozen fingers and feet.

"We should reach Ostfen by late this evening," Ylonya said, on the morning of the fifth day out from Néartanis. "I will make us known to Hamnis, our agent there, and he will arrange for our passage through the Fenland."

"What do you know of the Fenland?" Tremond asked.

"Not very much, I'm afraid. I have always tried to avoid it."

"Then how do you know it will be safe for us to travel through?" Ednor put in.

"I do not *know*," Ylonya said with quiet dignity, "but I trust Kendris and know he would not have advised us to take this road unless there was a good chance of getting through the Fenland unscathed."

Ednor smiled, a grim smile, but a smile, nonetheless. "Fair enough. I expect we will be able to defend ourselves should the need arise."

Ylonya was relieved to reach Ostfen. From what she remembered of previous visits, Hamnis's house was on the western edge of the township, so she led the others through the muddy streets.

"What do you know of Hamnis?" Shaunan asked.

"I've met him a couple of times, on trading journeys to this part of Yrusian. He seems to be content to remain here, rather than journeying. Which is unusual for an Yrusian. But he should remember me."

All the same, it felt unsettling to be reliant on someone else for their onward journey. She wished there had been time to ride around the Fenland. But Shaunan had been adamant – every day they journeyed added to the risk of discovery. So she would have to leave her silver mare with Hamnis and put herself and the others in the hands of the Fen-dwellers.

"Here we are," she said. "Wait here – I will see whether Hamnis is at home."

The house was set back from the road, a solid-looking structure of dark brown bricks with a slate roof. Ylonya climbed the steps to his front door and rang the bell. From the other side of the door, she could hear slow, shuffling footsteps walking towards it.

"Who is it?" A thin, reedy voice, not what she remembered.

"A visitor for Master Hamnis."

A peephole in the door opened and she could see one blue eye, nested in wrinkles, peering through it. "Who are you?"

"Tell him it is a wayfarer."

The peephole slammed shut again. This was ridiculous. Who was the old woman?

Again, footsteps, this time firm and regular. To her relief, the door was opened wide, and Hamnis was standing there, looking just as she remembered him – a broad, four-square man, clad in nondescript brown clothing, with deep brown eyes and a ready smile.

"Ylonya! What brings you to this forgotten corner of Yrusian?"

"I'm here with some friends… may we impose on your hospitality?"

"Of course. The stables are round the back – I'll show you."

Shaunan felt uneasy. Once again, they were relying on the goodwill of one of Ylonya's many contacts. So far, they had proved themselves to be true friends to the company. She hoped this time would not be an exception. Hamnis showed them into a wood-panelled room with a welcome fire blazing in the hearth.

"Please, sit," he said. "What brings you to Ostfen?"

How much to tell him? Discretion might be wise at this point.

"We wish to travel through the Fenland, Master Hamnis," she said. "Can you help us?"

His eyes moved over the company. "May I ask why such a mixed group wishes to cross the Fenland?"

"I would rather not say, but our journey is vital for the continued wellbeing of Veylindré."

"Hamnis, you know I would not ask if it was not important," Ylonya put in.

Hamnis gazed into Ylonya's eyes for a moment, and Shaunan gave him a deft mental nudge.

"Very well," he said, "but I hope you'll be able to share the whole tale with me sometime."

"Of course," Ylonya said.

"It may take a while to locate Lord Bredor," Hamnis said, "and you will need his goodwill to make this journey in safety."

"So we have heard," Shaunan said.

"Oh? Who from?"

"From Kendris," Ylonya said.

"That old rascal! How is he? Still in Néartanis?"

Ylonya smiled. "Yes indeed. It was he who recommended that we come to you. Are there any fen-dwellers in Ostfen at present?"

"No, but I could take you to their nearest habitation."

"We were thinking of leaving the horses with you and making the crossing by boat," Shaunan said.

"Ah. In which case I will take Ylonya there, while you wait here. We should be able to return by sundown tomorrow."

Another day lost. But Shaunan supposed there was no help for it. "Thank you, Master Hamnis."

"Have you eaten?"

"No, some supper would be welcome."

"Very well." He bustled out, calling "Ragda? Seven more for supper."

After a long and tedious day of waiting, Ylonya and Hamnis returned, bringing with them two Fen-dwellers, a man and a woman. Both were short, not much taller than Abigail herself, and whip-thin, although the Fen-woman's figure was more subtly rounded. Their skin had an almost greenish cast in some lights and they had bright brown eyes, which shone with intelligence. Both were wearing trews, tunics and hooded jerkins made of cured animal skins, and sturdy boots. Abigail noticed with a start that neither of them bore Waymarks on their foreheads. Or did they? On closer inspection she could see what looked like faded Waymarks. How could that happen?

"These are Modsorn and Modsdara," Hamnis said. "They are willing to guide you through the Fenland, so long as I provide a letter of introduction to Lord Bredor, and we pay in advance."

"For so many people, two boats are needed," the little man, Modsorn, said in a husky voice. "Which is the why of both myself and Modsdara are here."

Modsdara smiled, revealing an even row of ivory-yellow teeth. "Ready to leave when you are, but we need the trust from you."

Abigail probed their minds quickly but could perceive no deceit in them. She sensed Shaunan doing the same.

"Very well, my friends," her mentor said, "we place ourselves in your hands. How long do you think it will take us to travel through the Fenland?"

"At quickest, seven days," Modsorn replied. "But Lord Bredor will wish to offer the welcome at the Homing."

"The Homing? What is that?"

"The place of meeting for Fen People," Modsdara said. "To travel through our land, you need to meet our Lord."

"Very well," Shaunan said. "Let us leave at dawn tomorrow."

"We will be waiting," Modsorn said. The two of them bowed to the company and left.

"Can we trust them?" Tremond asked.

"I think so," Ylonya replied. "But I see no other choice, unless we plan to take an extra seisdag or so, skirting round the Fenland. And they would be insulted if we chose to do that, now."

Abigail could feel a surge of apprehension from Shaunan at the mention of taking extra time.

Why are you so concerned about losing time?

I am unsure, Abigail. But every delay fills me with foreboding. I pray that the Fen-dwellers are true to their word.

I could sense no ill-will in them.

Shaunan sighed. *Nor could I. But they do not follow the Way. I wish I knew why.*

I expect we'll find out, when we meet Lord Bredor.

Shaunan laughed gently. *I expect we will.*

At first light the next day, Hamnis knocked on the door of the room Aidren was sharing with Tremond and Ednor.

"Time to get up. The Fenlanders are waiting."

He rolled out of bed, splashed his hands and face with water from the ewer to wake himself up, and picked up his pack. He wasn't at all sure what he thought of this latest development – they would be entirely at the mercy of these strange Fen-dwellers. According to Ylonya, there was little solid ground in the Fenland, so they wouldn't even be able to escape, if something went wrong.

Less than half an hour later, they had eaten a quick breakfast and were ready to travel. Modsorn and Modsdara were waiting for them outside, apparently immune from the cold. Aidren buttoned up his jerkin and put the hood of his cloak up and his gloves on – he wasn't.

"All here?" Modsorn asked. "Let's go."

The boats were flat-bottomed, with high, curving sides, made of slatted planks. Each had a single mast with a small sail. The sigil on the sail was one Aidren had not seen before – a clump of grasses tied together with a knotted rope. The company divided themselves between the two boats according to their strengths – two warriors and one Ranusian to each boat, and Ellyn with himself, Ednor and Abigail. Aidren was glad to have Ellyn in the same boat with him, so that he could protect her, should anything happen.

As Modsdara and Modsorn began to pole their boats away from the landing stage, Hamnis called after them, "May the Way guard and guide you."

"Thank you," Ylonya called back, "we hope to meet you again at a better time."

Then the reeds closed behind them and they were alone in the Fenland beneath a brooding sky. Aidren looked around. The reeds and sedge grasses seemed to spread in every direction, with narrow channels of dark water in between and beneath them. A mist hovered above the water, obscuring his vision. He felt closed in, almost constricted, by the surrounding vegetation. The silence felt like a weight around them, broken only by the sounds of the wind in the reeds and of the pole being lifted and dropped, lifted and dropped, as Modsdara propelled them along. He noticed Ellyn's hand at the Goldstone around her neck and guessed she was holding it for reassurance. She liked this no more than he did – she hated being confined in a space she could not escape. He reached over and clasped her other hand and she smiled at him gratefully.

"How far are we travelling today?" Abigail asked. Her voice seemed loud in the surrounding silence.

"Some miles," Modsdara answered. "We spend the night at the holding of our father. Then tomorrow to the Homing."

Aidren jumped as a tall white bird exploded out of the reeds ahead of them and took flight, its wings casting a shadow over them, its long, yellow bill holding a fish.

"What bird is that?" Ellyn asked.

"A reed heron," Modsdara said. "Many live in the Fenland. Good eating."

Looking ahead, Aidren could see the other boat, poled by Modsorn, moving out of sight. They mustn't be separated.

"Modsdara," he said, "the other boat."

"Not to worry," she replied, "We know where we are. All together in the evening."

Aidren shot a look at Ednor and saw the older man's hand clenched tight around the pommel of his sword. It would be up to the two of them to take action, should the need arise. Well, he would be ready.

Abigail shifted restlessly on the hard bench seat of the boat – the long hours of sitting in one place were making her feel stiff. Ahead of them the light of the setting sun dazzled her eyes, turning the dark water a rich gold and highlighting the tips of the reeds. She guessed they would soon be there... wherever there was.

With a suddenness which seemed startling, they came out of their narrow reed-lined channel into a wide pool, golden-red in the rays of the setting sun, in the centre of which was the strangest looking dwelling she had ever seen. It was a squat, irregular shape, built of wooden slats, with a roof of rushes dried, then corded together. It was raised high out of the water on a broad platform, supported by sturdy stilts of a dark wood she did not recognise. Perhaps it had been stained that colour by the surrounding waters. Below it was a landing stage, at which Modsorn's boat was already moored.

Modsdara skilfully brought her boat alongside her brother's, leapt out and secured it to an iron ring embedded in the landing stage.

"Here we are," she said, "time to follow."

Nothing loath, Abigail stood up, stretched and followed the others up onto the jetty. Modsdara led them round to the opposite side to the foot of a ladder, which led to the upper level. Abigail forced her stiff knees to bend and straighten and soon came out onto the wide upper platform. And was brought up short by the sight of a man standing at the door of the house. This must be Modsorn's and Modsdara's father.

Unlike his children, he was tall, and broad with it, but shared their greenish skin and bright brown eyes, which were fixed on her. And, also like them, his Waymark seemed to have faded almost into invisibility.

"Come within," he boomed, "be welcome at the house of Mod."

"Thank you, sir," she said, bowing her head in acknowledgement. "We are grateful for your hospitality."

His face split in a wide smile, showing great yellow tusks of teeth. "Well said, girl. Come."

He led them through the entrance hall into a large room, which was dominated by a massive table, made of the same wood as the house itself, with two long benches stretching along either side and one great chair at the far end. The room was dimly lit by rushlights, which gave off almost as much smoke as illumination. Modsorn was already there, with Shaunan, Tremond and Ylonya. Abigail felt something inside her relax – she had not realised how uneasy being parted from Shaunan and Ylonya had made her.

"Sit," Mod said. "Supper comes soon."

He gestured to the benches with one meaty arm. They obediently seated themselves, while he took his place in the chair at the table's head. Before long wooden platters were set in front of each of them, larger ones of pewter being placed along the centre of the table by the women of the house. These were laden with freshly cooked fish, steamed grains and dark green vegetables.

"Help yourselves," Mod said. "Long travelling makes for great hunger."

After a few minutes of silent eating, Mod turned to Shaunan, "What brings you to the house of Mod?"

"We are travelling towards Chorich Castle, in western Yrusian," Shaunan replied, "and speed is of the essence for us, so Master Hamnis of Ostfen advised us to travel through the Fenland to save time."

"Ha! That one has sound head on his shoulders," Mod said. "But you cannot travel far without the good word of Lord Bredor."

"Master Hamnis has given us a letter of introduction for him. We would be grateful if you could tell us something about him, before we continue our journey."

Abigail felt her mentor give the big man a gentle mental nudge, so was not surprised when he leant his elbows on the table and prepared to speak.

"Lord Bredor is chief of Fenland people. We live in small family groups, like mine, but Lord Bredor is our speaker with those from the outside world, such as you. It is he who organises our trading days at Ostfen and Oestfen. He who settles any disputes."

"Have you met him yourself?" Abigail asked.

Mod nodded. "I know him from childhood – as a young man, I was fostered at the Homing, under old Lord Brandor, to learn management of Fenland holding. Bredor and I were friends. Then, when Lord Brandor died, Bredor became Lord of the Fenland. I returned to the holding, here, as my father was growing also old. But we stayed in close friendship for some years."

"I notice, my friend," Shaunan commented with care, "that you speak of your friendship with Lord Bredor as something in the past."

An expression of sadness came over Mod's face. "Yes. It is grief to me. It must have been three-and-twenty years ago that a stranger came to the Homing, asking for refuge. Lord Bredor was pleased to grant it, as is our custom. Since that time, the stranger, whom we know as Gilmak, has become the Lord's most trusted advisor, the chief of his karls."

"What does this Gilmak look like?" Ylonya asked.

"He is pale of face, as this young girl here," and Mod nodded in Abigail's direction, "and has dark brown hair. He is no Fen-dweller, yet he influences our Lord greatly."

Ylonya's eyes widened but she only said, "In what way?"

"He seems more remote, less hospitable to strangers. We Fen-dwellers are independent, mostly, but we come together at the Homing for feasts and storytelling. In the old days of Lord Brandor, he would lead the storytelling. It felt like one big family. But now, though Lord Bredor still attends, he seems separate, less one of us. We see his karls more often, as they travel through the Fenland, to let us know about the next trading day and any changes in the Fen-rule."

"The Fen-rule? What is that?"

His eyebrows rose. "Our law. How we live together – land rights, trading rights. Like that."

"Then you do not follow the Way of Veylindré?" Shaunan asked.

Mod sat upright, the smile leaving his face. "I do not speak of this."

Abigail felt Shaunan soothe the man, as she said, "I did not mean to cause offence. I am merely curious. Is not the Fenland part of Yrusian, which is one of the lands of Veylindré?"

"It is not for me to say," Mod said brusquely. "If you wish to know more, you must ask Lord Bredor."

Abigail could feel him withdrawing, putting up barriers between them. What was it about the Way that made him so uneasy?

"None pass through the Fenland without the goodwill of Lord Bredor," Mod said, standing up. "Now is time for sleeping. Journey on tomorrow."

Chapter 17

Abigail did not sleep well after that unsettling conversation. She gazed at the wooden beams of the ceiling of the little room she was sharing with Ellyn and traced patterns on the cracks in the plaster between them. Nothing made sense. Who was this Gilmak, that he had led the Fen-dwellers from the Way? And if her fears were true, what could they do about it? She tried to lie still, so as not to disturb Ellyn, but it was hard. Eventually, she fell asleep in the small hours of the morning.

"Abigail. Abigail! It's time to get up." Ellyn's voice.

"In a minute. I'm tired."

"We have to get up now. Modsorn and Modsdara are readying the boats and we have to leave in half an hour."

Heaving a deep sigh, Abigail sat up, then swung her legs over the edge of the bed. "How can you be so chirpy?"

The younger girl stared at her. "What's wrong with you?"

"Sorry. I didn't sleep much. I'll be all right in a minute."

Ellyn hugged her. "I'm sorry too. Let's go."

In not much longer than the thirty minutes, the company were ready to leave. Mod's wife had given them breakfast and some food for the day. It was time to go out to the boats.

"Thank you for your hospitality, friend Mod," Shaunan said, "and for lending us Modsorn and Modsdara as guides."

The big man nodded an acknowledgement. "Good journey."

When they had been moving along for a while, through reeds that looked exactly like the previous day's, Abigail asked Modsdara, "Tell us about your life in the Fenland."

"Why?" Modsdara asked, as she once again lifted her sturdy pole, shoved off on the bed of the marsh, and moved them on a few more yards. Somehow, she made the movement look graceful, but Abigail guessed it was harder work than it looked.

"Because I don't know anything about it, and I'm interested."

"What do you want to know?"

"How you spend your days. What the Fen-dwellers trade in. Things like that."

"I am rope maker," Modsdara said, with a proud lift of her chin. "Our family have made ropes for generations."

"What do you make them from?" Ellyn asked.

"From sedge grasses that grow in the Fenland," Modsdara said.

"Like these?" Ellyn pointed to a tall clump of grasses on their left.

"Just like those."

"I'd love to know how you do it," Abigail said.

"Is simple, but hard work. First we gather the grasses, and pound them to separate the fibres. Then we spin the fibres into yarns. But one strand of yarn is not enough – not strong enough."

Abigail noticed that Aidren and Ednor were listening with interest. She was with them – it was easy to take something they used every day for granted, and fascinating to learn how it was made.

"What do you do next?"

"Next is fun part. We twist yarns together to form the strands, then teams of the rope-makers hold opposite ends of the strands and twist them together to make rope. Is important to hold tension right, and to twist the right way."

"I don't understand," Abigail said, "what do you mean – the right way?"

"The twist of the yarn must be opposite to the twist of the strand and the twist of the strand must be opposite to the twist of the rope. It is opposites built up together that make the final rope stable."

"It is like life," Ednor put in. "We bind ourselves into relationships with each other and so are stronger together than apart."

An insightful comment, that Abigail hadn't expected from the self-assured warrior. It sounded as though he was accepting his place in the company. She smiled at him.

"I'd love to see you do it one day," Ellyn said.

"Maybe, if you visit another time."

"Who do you sell it to?" Ednor asked.

"Rope has many uses, depending on thickness. A one inch, three-strand rope made of our sedge grasses is very strong. We sell them to shipbuilders in Yrusian and to builders and traders in Néartania."

"How long do they last?"

"Depends on their use. As long as five years maybe. But always a market for more." She smiled. "Fen-dwellers will always make rope, people will always need it."

Abigail was idly gazing around as the light began to fade, trailing her fingers in the water. Modsorn's boat had once again disappeared out of sight ahead of them when Ellyn shrieked, "Modsdara! Look out!"

As the Fenland girl spun around, a small, pale brown snake with orange horizontal bands lashed out from its place on her pole and bit her on the forearm. As she cried out, slumping to the floor of the boat, Ednor grabbed the pole before it could fall into the water and shook the snake free, a revolted expression on his face.

Shaunan! Modsdara's been bitten by a snake. What do I do?

Is she conscious?

Yes.

Where was she bitten?

On the forearm.

Keep her as still and quiet as possible. Clean the bite with comfrey, then bandage it as tightly as you can. I'll get Modsorn to bring us back to you.

"Clear a space," Abigail said to the others, "I need to treat her."

Then, as Aidren, Ellyn and Ednor scrambled out of the way, she turned to Modsdara, whose arm was beginning to swell and turn red around the site of the snakebite. The Fenland girl was biting her lips to keep from crying out.

"Sit here," Abigail said to her gently. "Modsorn is on his way back to us, and Shaunan is an expert healer. I will do what I can until she arrives."

Modsdara just nodded.

"Pass me my healer's bag, Ellyn."

She rummaged in it for the comfrey lotion she had bought at the Vale of Berlysian and gently cleaned around the puncture marks. Then she bandaged the arm as tightly as she could, before fishing her Goldstone out of its pouch around her neck. She laid the hand not holding the Goldstone over the site of the wound, murmuring, "*Belannath Ranu, Gal ens bynn wellent, gal ens bynn wellent.*"

But for some reason, the words seemed to lack their usual power. Of course, no Waystones in the Fenland. She'd have to rely on Shaunan's healing skills.

"What a foul thing to happen," Ednor said, once Abigail had finished. "Can I do anything to help?"

"You already did, by saving the pole," Abigail replied. "I've done what I can for now. Hopefully Shaunan will have a specific remedy for snakebites in her bag. The important thing now," and she smiled at Modsdara reassuringly, "is for Modsdara to stay as still as she can, to stop the venom spreading."

Ten minutes passed. Then another ten. Where had Modsorn and the others got to? When the other boat came into sight around a corner, Abigail sighed with relief. Modsorn brought it alongside Modsdara's and held it steady while Shaunan clambered across, carrying her healer's bag.

"What ails her?" Modsorn asked urgently, from the other boat.

"She was bitten by a snake," Abigail said, "but the Waymage will heal her."

"What markings did it have?"

"I don't know – it all happened so quickly. Ednor, you saw it, didn't you?"

"Yes, it was about a foot long, pale brown, with orange bands."

Modsorn went pale, his brown eyes wide. "Marsh viper," he said. "Their bite is fatal."

"Shaunan is a skilled healer – if anyone can heal her, she can," Abigail said, trying to reassure him.

"Ednor and Aidren, would you move to the other boat, please?" Shaunan said. "There isn't enough room for all of us."

Not waiting to see whether she was obeyed, she moved to the end of the boat, where Abigail was sitting beside Modsdara. The Fenland girl was looking pale and the beads of sweat lining her hairline and the trickle of blood from her bitten lower lip told their own story of pain, sternly contained.

"What have you done so far?"

"I cleaned her arm with the comfrey lotion, then bandaged it up tightly, as you told me." *But Shaunan, she isn't getting better.* "Then I used my Goldstone to ask Ranu for healing." *I couldn't connect with the Way – not properly.*

No Waystones. I will need your help to augment my healing powers. When I nod, hold your Goldstone and place your other hand on my shoulder and give me your strength.

Abigail did her best to strengthen Shaunan, while the Waymage examined Modsdara.

"It is fortunate we visited the Herbarium not so long ago," Shaunan said. "My bag is well-stocked. And I have this," taking out a small bottle full of a dark purple liquid.

"What is it?" Abigail asked.

"Lènia's Nimbane," Shaunan said. "In liquid form, it is effective against poison. And I have some crushed leaves from the same plant, which I'll make into a poultice to put on the bite. But first, let us get this into her. Do you have a drinking cup handy?"

Abigail searched in her pack and offered her a wooden cup.

"Fill it half full with drinking water."

Abigail did as she was told and Shaunan added three drops of the potion, stirring it with a metal spoon from her bag. Then she held it to Modsdara's lips.

"Drink this – it will make you feel better."

Modsdara took a wary sip, and grimaced. "It tastes horrible."

"That's because it's a powerful remedy for poison," Shaunan replied. "Drink it all, please."

Modsdara held her nose and gulped the potion down, then gave the cup back to Shaunan. "I feel so tired," she said, her eyes sliding closed.

"Yes, you will," Shaunan replied, nodding again to Abigail. "The potion brings sleep to promote swift healing."

Will she be all right?

Yes. You did well.

Shaunan placed her hand over the bandaged wound, as Abigail had done, and again Abigail lent her strength to her mentor. She could feel a flow of healing taking place.

"Is she going to die?" Modsorn asked, a quaver in his voice.

"Not this time," Shaunan said. "Lènia's Nimbane is powerful against all poisons. I reached her in time. She will be weak for perhaps a seisdag and will bear the scar life-long, but her life is not in danger."

"I know not how to thank you," the young man said. "Clan Mod is in your debt."

"It is my calling," Shaunan said. "Now, I guess it is too late for us to reach the Homing before dark. Do you know of anywhere we can take shelter for the night?"

Modsorn frowned. Then his face lightened. "The Roping Hut. Is not far from here."

"Very well," Shaunan said. "Ellyn, move across to the other boat, please. I need to stay here with Modsdara. Ednor, do you think you could pole the boat along?"

Ednor scrambled back to his original boat, pleased to have something to do. If only he had spotted the snake in time – he could have chopped it in half, flung it away. He pulled down the sleeves of his jacket and put on his long, leather gauntlets before taking the pole from Ellyn, who then moved across to the other boat.

"Modsorn, you lead," Shaunan said, "but keep us in sight."

Ednor spread his feet for balance before gripping the pole and lowering it into the water. Then he shoved off, before bringing it back up again. The boat swivelled sideways and he had to push the pole down again, before it righted itself and moved after Modsorn's. This was not as easy as Modsdara had made it look. He would give his next year's pay for a decent rowing boat, with oars.

Modsorn grinned at him. "Stand with feet wide apart, the knees bent. Lift pole out of the water, raising it hand over hand, like this," and he demonstrated, "then put the bottom of the against the outside of boat."

Ednor did as he was told.

"Now drop the pole into the water, letting it slide through the hands. Then bend the knees and start moving the hands to the top of the pole again, hand over hand, like before. Don't let go of the end."

"But how do I steer it?" Ednor asked.

"After pushing off, let the end of pole trail behind the boat. Then drag it left or right through the water. Is needful to turn it under water in the direction you want to go."

Ednor tried that and it seemed to work. "All right," he said, "but don't go too fast."

"I'll watch you," Ellyn said, "and let Modsorn know if you fall behind."

Ednor nodded his thanks and let the pole slide through his hands once more. He hoped the Roping Hut was not far away.

By the time both boats had reached the Roping Hut, it was nearly dark and mists were swirling around them. The hut was raised on sturdy piles, in the centre of another large pool, as Mod's house had been. It loomed over them in the dusk, dark and forbidding. Did anyone live there? Abigail shrugged her shoulders – at least it would be warmer inside, and dry.

Abigail felt a pang of sympathy for Ednor, whose face was red and sweaty.

"Well done," she said. "I'm so glad you were here to help us; I'm sure I wouldn't have been able to do that."

Ednor smiled at her. "It's not nearly as easy as the Fen-dwellers make it look. I think I'm beginning to get the hang of it, but I've got blisters on my hands."

"Abigail will treat them," Shaunan said. "We will need your help again tomorrow. Modsdara will not be able to use that arm for some days."

Ednor's face fell, but all he said was, "As you say. I will do my best."

Modsorn, who had already moored his own boat, hopped across to theirs and took the pole from Ednor.

"You did well, for outlander," he said. "We will turn you into Fen-dweller yet."

Then he led them across the landing stage to a large, rectangular hut, built on piles like the house of Mod. Wearily, the company climbed the ladder. Abigail positioned herself directly behind Modsdara, so that the girl could climb one-handed without fear of falling.

"This way," Modsorn said.

He took a key out of an inner pocket and unlocked the door. Abigail walked into the hut, holding her Goldstone aloft. *Gal lo bynn leumin.* As golden-yellow light flared from her Goldstone, she was relieved that this smaller magic still worked. She looked around curiously. The hut seemed smaller on the inside than it had from the outside. Piles of sedge grass were stacked at one end, and racks of sharp tools lined the walls, with work benches below them. Coils of completed ropes were neatly piled along one wall. To her dismay, there seemed to be nowhere to sit in comfort and a wind was whistling in through cracks in the walls.

Modsorn was gazing at her lit Goldstone in wonder. “How you do that?”

“Through the power of the Way,” she said. “Don’t you follow the Way in the Fenland?”

“We did, long time ago,” he said, “my father told us of it. But not in my years.”

“Never mind that for now,” Shaunan said. “We will have to sleep in our blankets for once. Modsorn, is there any wood here?”

He shrugged. “Some. I will fetch. But not too much – dry wood is of great value here.”

“Nevertheless. I need it to heat water, so that I can treat Modsdara’s arm.”

He nodded, then disappeared back outside and returned with an armful of logs.

“Where would it be safe to make a fire?” Ednor asked.

“There is hearth at this end,” Modsorn said, pointing to it.

Before long, a fire was burning merrily in the grate and the room started to warm up. Shaunan took a small iron pot out of her pack and filled it with water from her water-bottle. Then she brought out a soft leather packet and poured out some leaves from it.

“What are those?” Abigail asked. As always, she was fascinating by watching Shaunan at work.

“The leaves of Lènia’s Nimbane,” Shaunan answered. “I’m going to make them into a poultice for Modsdara’s arm.”

“Is there anything I can do to help?”

“Not at the moment, thank you. If you and the others could prepare a meal for us, that would be good.”

They pooled their rations and made a reasonable meal of *feolin* loaves and dried fruit that Hamnis had given them, washed down with the last of the thin, red wine they had brought with them.

"It is ready now. Come here, please, Abigail. I need you to support Modsdara's arm."

As Abigail watched, Shaunan gently untied the bandage. The arm looked red and swollen, with livid lines radiating out from the bite marks. Shaunan washed it once more with the comfrey lotion, before applying a poultice of the leaves. Then she re-tied the bandage. Modsdara stayed still throughout, but Abigail could sense the girl's pain and wondered at her stoic courage. It seemed that the Fenlanders were hardy folk. In Modsdara's place, she would have been in tears, at the very least.

"We will leave that on overnight," she said, "and renew it before we leave. Now, Modsdara, I think you need another dose of the potion, then you must try to sleep."

"I thank you," Modsdara said. "I thought I would die."

"Put that thought out of your mind," Shaunan said. "You must believe in your healing."

The girl nodded. "I believe."

Shaunan treated Modsdara's arm once more the following morning and was glad to see that the radiating lines were fading and the swelling was beginning to go down. Thank Ranu she had stocked up on Lènia's Nimbane at the Vale. But healing her had been hard work, not having the full power of the Way to draw on. The sooner they were through the Fenland, the better.

Once again, they set off in the little boats, she with Abigail, Ellyn and Modsdara, with Ednor poling.

"How long will it take us to reach the Homing?" he asked Modsdara, who was watching him.

"Two hours, perhaps three," she answered.

Ednor flashed a grin at her. "Or maybe four, the way I pole."

"You do well, for someone unused," Modsdara said.

"Thank you. But in future, I'll leave it to the experts."

"What can you tell us about the Homing?" Shaunan asked the Fen-girl.

"Is where we gather to celebrate turning of the seasons and to be in community together. Lives of Fen-dwellers would be lonely without it."

"Is it a big place?" Abigail asked.

"Yes, largest in the Fenland," Modsdara replied. "Most of us dwell in families, with one or perhaps two buildings in one place. The Homing is like town to us – many buildings all together."

"So who lives there?"

"Lord Bredor and his family, his karls and their families. But there are also barns for storage of ropes and herbs, ready for trading days and hostels for Fen-dwellers who visit."

"And Lord Bredor is the Lord of the Fenland?" Ednor asked.

"He is leader of all the Fenland Clans. His word is law. Our part is to obey the Fen-rule and provide goods for trading. His part is to trade with outsiders for things we need and to be father of us all. We will be there soon," she added, looking around, "and you will see for yourselves."

Δ Chapter 18 Δ

A knock on the door. Jacob answered it, to find one of the Prophet's personal guards outside.

"The Prophet orders you to join him on the battlements above the main gate at fourth hour," he said. "Do not be tardy."

"I'll be there."

The guard clicked his heels in response and left. What was this about? Perhaps the Prophet wanted to watch his army march out of the city. Jacob felt honoured to have been invited to share this special moment.

Ten minutes before fourth hour, he climbed the steep steps up to the battlements. The Prophet was already there.

"Come, Jacob, watch with me."

Jacob obeyed, stepping up to the Prophet's side, overlooking the main gate.

"Do you see it?" the Prophet asked.

"See what, my Lord?"

Jacob gazed out over the battlement wall. A blare of trumpets. He heard the gates below being flung open and saw the first soldiers marching out, behind their leaders, who rode out at the head of the rank and file, on some of Talamdor's rare horses. Was that Portak? It looked like him, but it was difficult to tell from this angle. The standard of the Talamdorian army, a black flag with the blood-red triangle of Talamu at its centre, fluttered bravely in the light breeze. Then the rest of the army began to file out, rank by rank, marching in step, their heads held high. Each man wore a metal breastplate, embossed with the red triangle, a round helmet on each head. He saw a variety of weapons – swords, axes, crossbows and pikes. This was a formidable fighting force.

His ruminations were interrupted by the Prophet's voice. "The beginning."

Jacob's heart lifted. But as he watched the seemingly endless column of men marching out of the high gate, followed by cartloads of supplies, he felt a twinge of anxiety. What if the City was attacked, with so few left to defend it?

"Fear not," the Prophet said, "I have other defences at my command, which I must now put in place. I will not need you for the rest of the day."

"Other defences, my Lord?"

"You do not need to know. Leave me."

Portak was in a state of high excitement. The Prophet's instructions had been explicit: "I am trusting you to keep up morale. Many of our troops are not seasoned warriors and they will need the power of your passion to keep their spirits high and their courage up."

He would not fail him. They would be heading east until they reached the River Roillon, then his force would be turning south-east to march across the fertile farmlands between the two rivers. Caethniss Castle was on the western shore of the River Caethwas. He had never crossed the mountains from there before. With luck, they would reach the castle by the end of the second seisdag. Then they would move through the mountain pass to attack the keeps of Mistbourne and South Plains. The other half of the army would be heading for Roilldon Fort, further north, before crossing the Talamdorian mountains to attack Nordkeep and Cristail Keep on the Veylindréan side.

By the end of the first day, they had marched nearly fifteen miles – not a bad distance for troops as raw as these. He climbed a low hill then looked back – the baggage train that followed the army was still not in sight. This was an impressive force and the men had completed their first day's march in reasonable shape. He knew that their pace would slow as time went on, that they would have to factor in a rest day once a seisdag, so that they could reach their destinations in good heart and ready to fight.

He spotted General Kreldik, who would be leading the southern force into battle, and hastened down to join him.

"We have made good progress, General," he said.

The big man had a more ruddy complexion than most Talamdorians, and sported a magnificent moustache, which partly obscured his mouth. He swung round to face Portak, his chest stiff with medals from the Havimi campaign, thirty or more years before, when they had ousted the usurpers from Talamdor.

"What's that?"

"I was saying, General, that we have made good progress today."

"Humph, I suppose so. I will be surprised if they can maintain this pace, green as they are."

"I am sure they will," Portak replied smoothly, "so long as they get one rest day each seisdag."

Kreldik bristled. "Are you trying to teach me my job? I am in command of this army."

Portak stood to attention. "Of course not, General. I would not presume to do so. I was just going to offer to lend my support in boosting morale."

Kreldik frowned at him. "You are the Prophet's man, are you not?"

"We are all servants of the Prophet." Portak replied.

"Humph, indeed. Then you must do what you need to."

What was he doing here? If only he could have stayed in the city with Balmak. But the Prophet needed him, and he had never been able to refuse his master's commands. He owed him too much.

Jacob would never have guessed in a million years that he would miss Portak. Yet the absence of his first friend in this world made him lonely. And, worse than that, Melnok had marched out with the army, so his enjoyable afternoons spent at the smithy were at an end.

But at least he had his daily visit to the Prophet. Every morning, the Prophet continued his instruction about Talamdor and Talamu. On the third day after the departure of the army, he entered the darkness of the Prophet's apartment on silent feet, to find him not sitting erect, as usual, but slumped down, clutching the red stone around his neck.

"My Lord? Are you well? Can I fetch a healer?"

At the sound of his voice, the Prophet straightened up, a mask coming down over his aquiline features. "I am perfectly well. No healer is required."

"I – I'm sorry, my Lord. You just looked…"

"I am perfectly well," the man repeated with a frown.

Jacob took the hint.

"Now Jacob, I am going to take you into my confidence, share somewhat of the shape of the future, once the Veylindréans have been defeated."

Jacob was confused, yet excited at the same time. He did not know why the Prophet want to share this information with him, of all people. Surely he had Talamdorian advisors, counsellors…

"That, Jacob, is precisely my point."

Jacob flushed. When would he learn to think more quietly in the Prophet's presence?

"Your point, my Lord?"

"Unlike the rest of my advisors," and the Prophet put a sarcastic emphasis on the word, "*you* are not from Talamdor. You do not share Talamdorian values, the Talamdorian way of thinking."

"I'm sorry, my Lord, I don't understand. Surely that would make me less able to help, not more."

The Prophet clicked his tongue.

"My Lord, I'm sorry…"

"My advisors are Talamdorian born and bred. So their memories are full of the recent enslavement of our land by the Havimi. They see the Havimi as their enemies. Whereas you do not have that baggage. You are from my world and can understand that the threat from the Veylindréan witches is far more severe. That we need to ally ourselves with the Havimi against Veylindré. After all, the Havimi were Talamdorian, once."

"Yes, my Lord. My Lord, why did they try to conquer Talamdor?"

"That does not concern you. What is past is past. All that matters now is that we present a united front against our true enemies, the witches of Veylindré."

"What do you want me to do?"

"I want you to listen and to understand. We have wasted enough time already."

By the end of the fifth day since leaving Talamunem City, the Prophet's army had reached the western bank of the River Roillon, still fairly narrow at this point, but gathering breadth and depth on its way down to the Southern Sea. Portak gazed into its fast flowing waters which were clear and cold – with luck, there would be fresh fish for the evening meal.

The inhabitants of Roillby, the village on the eastern bank, had built a sturdy wooden bridge to enable them to farm the land on this side. Hopefully it would be strong enough to support the supply wagons that would be crossing it on the morrow. Here, in a flattish area by the riverbank, not currently under cultivation, they set up camp and rested for a day, on the orders of the two generals, Kreldik and Marnok. Portak, having ridden the whole way, was not too weary, but there were bellows to mend among the foot soldiers. It was a good job they were still in Talamdorian territory, with some time to toughen up before they reached Veylindré.

After a reasonable night's sleep on a camp bed, Portak breakfasted on army rations of salted beef and hard biscuits, washed down with a light ale, then began to visit the many camp fires that were burning between the tents. This would be a good time to boost morale, before the men had to engage the enemy. He strolled towards the nearest one, around which a dozen soldiers were huddling, their blankets around their shoulders, eating their rations out of wooden bowls. All wore the silver bangle.

"Holy Talamu's blessings on you all. May I sit with you awhile?"

One of the soldiers shuffled aside, made room for him. "Thank you, friend."

"Who are you?" one of them said, a broad man with the bent nose and uneven features of a fighter. His voice was belligerent, ready to take offence.

"I am Portak, agent of our Holy Prophet. I am here to tell you that, even if you are feeling some natural apprehension about what lies ahead of us, the Prophet has complete faith in you. Because we have right on our side. More importantly, we have Holy Talamu on our side."

The men were shifting uneasily, glancing at each other, obviously not convinced by his words.

Portak tried again, "You will all have seen dogs fighting in our streets. And sometimes, against all expectations, the smaller dog wins, because he had more determination, more guts, than his adversary. So if you have faith in Holy Talamu, faith in our cause, She will be with us in the battle, lending strength to our arms and the will to conquer to our hearts and minds."

"That is easy for you to say," the bruiser muttered, "but it will not be your blood spilt, your friends killed."

But Portak had excellent hearing. "You are wrong, my friend," he said, keeping his voice even, "I will be fighting alongside you and will be honoured to do so. While we fight together, shoulder to shoulder, we will be strong – strong in our desire to overcome the forces of Veylindré, strong in our hope of putting Talamdor back in its rightful place, at the head of the Commonweal."

He gazed around at the men's faces. Some shone with renewed hope, but others still looked doubtful. He had one card left to play. "My friends, imagine a world in which Talamdor ruled. There will be rich pickings for the victors. The Commonweal is wide – there will be land enough for all. Each of you will have enough for your needs, your children's needs. Think on it."

As he hoped, the prospect of land of their own had convinced the waverers. Best to leave it there. He rose to his feet. "I have faith in you. The Prophet has faith in you. When it comes to the point, you will find your courage, be strengthened by Holy Talamu, and fight the good fight. Farewell."

He walked across to the next fire and started again.

"Our aim in this campaign," the Prophet began, seated bolt upright on his black throne, "is to conquer Veylindré, to overthrow the witches who practice their foul magics to keep their people in subjugation, and to convert the Veylindréan people to the worship of Holy Talamu. When all follow Her Way of Power, as She always intended, I will consider my task complete."

"But…" Jacob began.

"But what?" the Prophet's fierce gaze met his.

"I only thought, my Lord, that when people's faith is under attack, it makes them stronger in it, not weaker. Like in the time of Bloody Mary, when she tried to force all good Protestants to become Catholic again. And look what happened to King Charles."

Jacob watched the man think about this. His frown deepened and his hand crept to the red jewel around his neck, which Jacob had begun to recognise was a sign that he was perturbed.

"I have been away from England for too long. I had forgotten what it was like to be forbidden to worship as your heart bade you. King Charles's tyranny was one reason why I left England."

How long had the man been here? "My Lord, there was a Civil War in England. Before I was born. My father told me that the people would not accept King Charles's belief in the divine right of kings, and that he taxed everyone without Parliament's consent. So the New Model Army, under the leadership of Oliver Cromwell, went to war on behalf of the people and King Charles was captured and his head was cut off."

The Prophet's eyebrows shot up. "They killed a king?"

"Yes, my Lord. And established a Commonwealth, ruled by Parliament under Oliver Cromwell. But when he died, and his son took over, the Royalist forces under Prince Charles, the old king's son, came back and overthrew the Commonwealth. He became King in 1660."

"So you grew up under this Commonwealth?"

"Yes, my Lord. I was thirteen when King Charles returned."

"What happened then?"

"He strengthened the Church of England and many Dissenters were persecuted, along with the Catholics. Three years ago there was a crackdown on Dissenting ministers, and many were thrown out of their livings."

"I see. I will give your point some thought. But you know that witchcraft is evil, whatever faith people follow. Now, Jacob, before you leave..."

"Yes, my Lord?"

"If you are to mix with Talamdorian society, which is my desire, we must do something about that ugly mark on your forehead. It would not do for them to believe you are from Veylindré. Come here."

Obediently, Jacob came closer.

"Stand still. This will not harm you."

That was all the warning Jacob had. The Prophet reached out and pressed the index finger of his right hand on the mark on Jacob's forehead, saying, *"Udulivat sposmetkin."*

An agonising pain shot through Jacob's head. He could not stop himself crying out. But as soon as the Prophet removed his finger, the pain vanished, as though it had never been.

"That is better," the Prophet said. "You no longer bear the mark of our enemies."

"Thank you, my Lord."

"Leave now but return tomorrow. The next stage of your education is about to begin."

Portak took out his Bloodstone and a vial of blood and visualised the face of Tamin, the Prophet's Chief Messenger.

> My Lord, we have reached the west bank of the River Roillon. Our army is resting here for a day, before dividing and marching to Roilldon Fort and Caethniss Castle. I am happy to report that the soldiers are in good heart, and eager to engage the enemy. Generals Kreldik and Marnok are organising our supply lines, so that all things needful for the campaign are ferried through the mountain passes in timely fashion.
>
> I will be in touch again, once we reach Caethniss Castle.
>
> May the blessings of Holy Talamu be with you, and with us all.
>
> Portak
>
> Sent on the third day of the second seisdag of the Season of Renewal.

When Jacob arrived at the Prophet's apartment the next day, the man was holding a piece of parchment in his hand. He flourished it at Jacob.

"A report from Portak."

"My Lord?"

"The army is about to divide into two forces – one will go north-east and attack the Veylindréans from Roilldon Fort, the other will head south-east to Caethniss Castle and attack from there."

"Which part is Portak with?"

"With the south-eastern force. He reports that morale is high and that the soldiers are eager to join battle with the Veylindréan armies."

Jacob heard a note of satisfaction in the Prophet's voice. He hoped he would come to understand the thought behind the Prophet's military policy. These were high matters – he wasn't sure how much help he could be.

"Not much, at present," the Prophet said, answering his thoughts. "But once we have conquered Veylindré, I will need someone who understands the necessity of freeing this world from the evils of witchcraft. You, Jacob, coming from our world, are in a unique position. You have seen the devastation that witches can cause in communities – crops failing, animals being possessed by demons, innocent people suffering from curses. I am convinced our cause is just."

"Convinced, my Lord?" He hasn't seen it for himself?

The Prophet rounded on him, his face distorted by anger, "I do not need to see it for myself. I know only too well what happens when witches are in control. I saw it many times in our world."

"I'm sorry, my Lord." Jacob bowed his head, unable to meet the man's furious eyes. "Of course, you know best."

"I do."

Jacob glanced round the darkened room, wishing with all his heart he was somewhere else. "May… may I ask a question, my Lord?"

A curt nod.

"I was wondering… I know so little of Veylindré. Not even how big it is in comparison with Talamdor."

"And?"

Jacob could feel the man's displeasure. He gulped once, then continued, "I would be able to help you more, perhaps, if I knew more about the lands you are planning to conquer."

"Portak has taught you nothing of Veylindré?"

"No, my Lord, only about Talamdor."

"Very well. I have told you that the Six overcame Holy Talamu at the beginning of the Second Age and that later on, all Talamdorians were banished with her, to Talamdor."

"Yes, my Lord."

"And that thirty years ago, Holy Talamu helped me to find the Master Bloodstone, which was lost long centuries ago, so that I have been able to strengthen Her people and to create personal Bloodstones for my trusted agents?"

"Yes, my Lord."

"What you do not understand, perhaps, is that the secret desire of the Six was to take the power of leadership, which had been Holy Talamu's, to themselves, and to rule the Commonweal in her despite. There are six lands which make up the Commonweal of Veylindré – Garûnalonden, Yrusian, Néartania, Lènium, Dagâran and the Isle of Ranu."

"Dagâran, did you say? I seem to recognise that name."

"It has a border with Néartania, where Portak found you. That is all."

"That must be it. Thank you. Are each of the six lands equally important? Who rules them?"

"Each land is ruled by both secular rulers and by a Veylindréan witch. In this way, the Veylindréans are kept in subjugation to the Way, which is what they call their evil magic."

"And do the witches have as much power as the secular rulers?"

"I'm afraid they do, Jacob. It is like the bad old days in England, when the Catholic Church had far too much power over the King and his court."

"I see. But…"

"But what?"

"I'm sorry, my Lord. Maybe I'm not understanding you right. Your plan is to convert the Veylindréans to the worship of Holy Talamu?"

"It is."

Jacob took a deep breath, "Then isn't that the same as the church influencing the state back home?"

"Not at all, you stupid boy." The force of the Prophet's anger pushed Jacob back in his chair. "The dominion of Holy Talamu is for the benefit of Her people. We will not abuse the power She has given us but use it for the good of all."

"I'm sorry, my Lord. I did not understand."

"Then it is time you did. Leave me. Tomorrow we will meet in the Chamber of Law, next to the Visitors' Hall. It is time I shared some information with the Talamdorian nobility. I want you there."

"Will this be the next stage you spoke of yesterday, my Lord?"

"Correct. Do not be late."

Chapter 19

The sun was high in the sky by the time the company arrived at the Homing. Their arrival had been noticed, and a Fenland official, clad all in black, was striding down the wharf to meet them, his footsteps loud on the wood. And greet them, Ylonya hoped.

Modsorn spoke out on behalf of them all. "Greetings, Karl Erithsorn. I bring visitors to the Homing, from Ostfen." Then he murmured, "Erithsorn is friend of my father. He is good man."

Shaunan nodded. Modsorn continued, "My sister, Modsdara, was bitten by a marsh viper yesterday. We ask for hospitality at the Homing while she heals."

Erithsorn grimaced in acknowledgement. "That is ill news. Who are your companions, Modsorn?"

"Some friends of Master Hamnis, of Ostfen, who are travelling to western Yrusian."

"We do not allow just anyone to enter the Homing. What are their names and what is their business?"

Modsorn looked taken aback by this barely veiled hostility, so Ylonya stood and took over the conversation, her right hand open in the traditional gesture of greeting.

"We are travellers from Néartanis, who have business at Caethniss Castle. I am Ylonya, daughter of Guildmaster Brickon of the Hall of Traders. We mean no harm. We need to travel to Caethniss Castle on urgent business, which is why Master Hamnis recommended that we journey through the Fenland. I have a letter of introduction to Lord Bredor from him."

She passed the letter to the karl, who checked its seal, then returned it to Ylonya.

"Master Hamnis is known to us, but you will need to present this to Lord Bredor. Very well. You may come ashore. Lord Bredor will be informed."

"Thank you, Karl Erithsorn," she said, bowing low.

At this courtesy, his grim expression softened slightly. He nodded to her and said, in a less hostile tone, "Be welcome in the Homing. Modsorn knows where the Place of Healers is. The rest of you may accompany him, then report to Lord Bredor."

Then he turned on his heel and strode off.

"Thank you, Ylonya," Shaunan said.

The Place of Healing was only a few hundred yards away, but by the time they reached it, Shaunan noticed that Modsdara was cradling her hurt arm, biting her lip. The sooner she was lying down, and under the care of a healer, the better.

Modsorn threw open the door, "Healers, we are in need."

A small, round woman of about Shaunan's own age, clad all in green, with light brown hair and tanned skin, bustled out of a side room. "I am Healer Janris. What do you require?"

"My sister, Modsdara, has been bitten by a marsh viper."

"Bring her in – I will see to her."

"Modsorn," Shaunan said in a low voice, "I will need to speak with the Healer about what treatment I have given her so far."

"Healer Janris, this is Shaunan, one of the people Modsdara and I are guiding through the Fenland. She is skilled in healing."

A pair of twinkling blue eyes appraised her and appeared to like what they saw. “Come then, Shaunan. We will examine her together. Modsorn, take the others to the Place of Visitors.”

Shaunan would have liked Abigail to remain but knew better than to compromise her position with the Healer. She nodded to her initiate, *I will let you know what happens.*

Once the rest had left, Janris led Modsdara and Shaunan into a little room, with shelves of healing herbs lining the walls, and a high bed for patients. It reminded Shaunan of her own healing quarters, back in Nordvein and the familiarity reassured her. A fire was burning in the hearth, and she was grateful for the warmth.

“Lie down, Modsdara.”

Janris laid a hand on the girl’s forehead and smelled her breath, before gently untying the bandage on her arm. Shaunan’s poultice was revealed, a little discoloured now, but still damp. As Janris gently sponged if off, Shaunan saw that the arm beneath was still red and swollen, but the red striations had disappeared. Good, she was healing.

“What is this?”

“I used a poultice of the leaves of Lènia’s Nimbane and have also given her a potion distilled from the roots of the same plant to speed the healing.”

Janris’s eyes widened, “Lènia’s Nimbane? How did you come to have *that* to hand?”

“As Modsorn told you,” Shaunan answered in an even tone, “I am a Healer. Our company visited the Vale of Berlysian a few seisdags ago, and I stocked up on everything we were likely to need for our journey.”

“That was fortunate. I know of nothing else that can combat the ill of a marsh viper’s poison.” The healer looked deep into

Shaunan's eyes, then nodded her head, as though coming to a decision.

"You are a Waymage," she said softly. It was a statement, rather than a question.

"I am," Shaunan replied in an equally soft voice. "Is that dangerous here?"

"It could be." The healer's voice was now so low, Shaunan was having to read her lips as the same time. "Karl Gilmak, who is close to Lord Bredor, has spoken out against the Way. But let us heal Modsdara before we speak further."

The two women turned to their patient. "Do you have more Lènia's Nimbane with you?" Janris asked.

Shaunan opened her healer's bag and brought out both potion and leaves. "Here."

"Thank you." Janris hung a metal pot on a hook above the fire to heat some water, then sprinkled a few leaves of Lènia's Nimbane in, checking with Shaunan that the amount was right. Then she poured a glass of water.

"How many drops have you used?"

"Three should suffice. The worst is over, I think."

Janris nodded, then presented the glass to Modsdara, who had been listening to all this with wide eyes. "Drink this."

Modsdara obediently drank, then shuddered. Once more the potion acted swiftly and in a few moments her eyes were closed, her breathing even.

"Now that she is sleeping, we may speak freely," Janris said. "But keep your voice low – there are many ears in this place."

As she spoke, she took the pot off the fire and began to scoop the softened leaves out into a wooden bowl, using a ladle. Then she began to mash them into a poultice, using some of the water she'd used to prepare them.

Janris, can you hear me?

The Healer jumped, her eyes wide as she turned to face Shaunan. *Yes! But how?*

You are a Ranusian adept, are you not?

How could you know?

I could sense it. Many Ranusians can speak mind to mind, as we are. You are not from the Fenland, are you?

No. I was born in a village near Porusport.

How did you come here?

My father, Risdan, was a Waymage, and was called to the Homing when I was ten. So the three of us – he, my mother and I – moved here. Janris sighed deeply. *But the damp climate did not suit my mother; she died within two years. Then, when my Waymark was revealed as Ranusian, my father began to teach me bits and pieces, especially healing skills. It was not a bad life.*

What happened then?

Gilmak happened. Janris's mental tone became full of bitterness. *Three and twenty years ago. I was a Ranusian adept, waiting to be called to Ranusheim, when* he *turned up at the Homing. Old Lord Brandor was still Lord of the Fenland in those days. Bredor and I were very close – we had even spoken of getting married when my training was complete. Then Gilmak came and everything changed.*

Who is Gilmak?

I don't know where he came from. Bredor seemed fascinated by him, like a bird before a snake. They went everywhere together and I was nowhere. A few seisdags after his arrival, Bredor came and showed me Gilmak's gift to him – a broad cuff of silver, intricately engraved. After that, they were inseparable.

And what then?

My father began to sicken, a wasting sickness that was beyond my power to heal. After he died, I was truly alone.

She smoothed the poultice onto Modsdara's arm, then put a new bandage round it.

What does he look like, this Gilmak?

He is taller than most Fenlanders, pale of skin, and dark of eye and hair. His eyes can pierce you.

Is there anything else you can tell me?

Yes. After Gilmak had established himself with old Lord Brandor and with Bredor, he began to undermine the Way, subtly at first. For a while, little changed. Then Lord Brandor died and Bredor became Lord. After that, Gilmak began to work more openly. Always through Bredor, but I knew where the orders were coming from.

What orders?

To cast down the Waystones in the Fenland, not to use our own Goldstones. Gilmak decided we should become independent of the Commonweal, follow our own laws. And Bredor agreed with him. So I kept my head down, learned as much healing as I could. But Shaunan, how could one man change everything?

I suspect he is an agent of the Prophet in Talamdor. But tell me more about how he came to influence Lord Bredor.

I think it has to do with the silver cuff. Bredor is never seen without it. But I don't think it is pure silver – it never tarnishes, and in certain lights, a red gleam comes out of it.

Talamunium, Shaunan breathed. *It must be.*

What is that?

It is a rare metal, only found in Talamdor, which can be combined with silver to form a light but strong alloy. I fear that Gilmak is using Lord Bredor's cuff to subdue his free will, using Bloodmagic.

Bloodmagic?

Have you ever seen Gilmak handle a red stone? It would probably be triangular.

Only once. I came upon him in a place he did not expect to be seen and he was pocketing such a stone. What is it?

The High Waymages have learned that the Prophet has found the lost Master Bloodstone of Talamu and has discovered how to make individual Bloodstones for his agents.

Janris's face drained of all colour. *This is the worst news I have heard in a long time. What can we do?*

Our company is on a quest to do something about it.

Then you must flee this place. If Gilmak realises...

We cannot leave without paying our respects to Lord Bredor. Karl Erithsorn will already have given him news of our arrival. Janris, can I rely on your aid, should matters go awry?

The Healer took a deep breath, then nodded. *Yes. May the Way guard and guide us all.*

"...and so we are in danger," Shaunan finished, "but Healer Janris is an ally."

The company were sitting around an open fire in the Place of Visitors, a large house with two storeys, built on the customary piles. They had been served food and drink by one of the custodians of the Place, and now they were alone. She hoped they could not be overheard.

"Why didn't Hamnis warn us about this Gilmak?" Tremond asked.

"He couldn't have known," Ylonya said. "Or he would have tried to persuade us to travel round the Fenland."

"The sooner we are out of here, the better," Ednor said.

Shaunan sensed their apprehension. "I agree," she said, "but Karl Erithsorn has already taken word of our arrival to Lord Bredor, so I think we will have to meet him, but be prepared to leave as soon as possible afterwards."

"If we are allowed to," Ylonya said darkly. "If this Gilmak doesn't try to detain us."

"We will have to trust in our ability to talk ourselves out of trouble," Shaunan replied, then, turning to Modsorn, who had been listening to the conversation in astonishment, "Modsorn, what is the quickest route out of the Fenland?"

The little man shook his head, "This is all new to me. We know no ill of Lord Bredor. I would not have brought you here, else."

Shaunan smiled at him. "We know that, Modsorn. But now, through no fault of yours, it seems as though we are in danger. Is there a direct route out of the Fenland from here?"

"We could go back same way we came," he said, "but I cannot leave here without Modsdara. The seven of you are too many for one boat. And she is my sister. I am not wishing to leave before she is well again."

Ylonya nodded. "Then we will have to make a plan, to deal with this Gilmak."

The sun was setting, its rays casting a path of gold across the water, by the time they were summoned to Lord Bredor's presence. Abigail hoped they would be allowed to continue on their journey.

Lord Bredor's hall was the most imposing structure in the Homing. It was built of split planks of solid oak, rounded on the outside of the building, flat within and varnished to a high shine. Its roof, unlike the rest of the houses at the Homing, which were thatched using the ubiquitous reeds, was of terracotta coloured tiles, for which the Fenlanders must have traded. Inside, long tables and benches lined the walls, for use when there was a feast. There was a fire pit in the centre of the hall and at the end farthest from the door was a dais, with a wooden chair finely carved enough to be a throne.

A tall, bearded man was seated on it, dressed in richly coloured clothing of linen and fine wool, a broad, silver cuff around his right wrist. He looked up with interest as they arrived and Abigail wondered what he had been told about them. For this must be Lord Bredor. He was not alone on the dais – a group of armed men clad in the black gear that seemed to a uniform of sorts, stood to one side – Abigail recognised Karl Erithsorn among them. Alone, next to the throne, stood a tall, pale man, also wearing black, a deep scowl on his face. Gilmak.

"Welcome to the Homing," Bredor said. His voice was deep and sonorous. "I wonder what brings such a large group of strangers into the Fenland?"

Ylonya stepped forward and bowed low. "Thank you, Lord Bredor. We are a group of Yrusian traders, who have business at Caethniss Castle. Master Hamnis of Ostfen has given us a letter of introduction to you." She held it out to him.

Bredor took it, opened the seal and read it, before passing it to Gilmak. Not a good sign. The Talamdorian, for so he must be, scowled as he gazed at them.

"Yrusian traders, you say? You are a mixed group for… traders," and he spat the word. "I see two Ranusians, two Dagârans, one Néartanian, and a Garûnalonden. You," and he sneered at Ylonya, "appear to be the only Yrusian in your company."

Ylonya ignored him. "If I might explain, Lord Bredor?"

The Fenlander glanced quickly at Gilmak, then nodded. "My counsellor is right," he said. "Your explanation had better be good."

Abigail closed her eyes, clutched her Goldstone and tried to send strength to Ylonya. She couldn't tell whether it had worked.

"Your counsellor sees clearly, Lord Bredor," Ylonya began. "As he has discerned, our business at Caethniss Castle is not purely for trade. These two," and she pointed to Shaunan and Abigail, "are Ranusian. We," and she indicated Aidren, Ellyn, Ednor, Tremond and herself, "have been hired to accompany them to Caethniss Castle, where their healing skills are required."

"Healing skills? Why?" Bredor asked.

"There has been an outbreak of illness, which their healer does not understand," Ylonya said, smoothly inventive. "So he has asked for an experienced healer to come to his aid. And it will be good experience for her apprentice."

Would he believe them? If not, what would happen to them? Gilmak was whispering in Bredor's ear and the Fenland Lord was frowning, stroking his beard as he listened.

"Lord Bredor? If I might speak?"

The voice came from behind them. Abigail looked round and saw a short woman dressed in a green robe, with twinkling blue eyes. She liked her instinctively.

"You may, Janris."

So this was the healer whom Shaunan said was an ally to them.

"My Lord, one of your people was bitten by a marsh viper while ferrying these people to the Homing," Janris said. "Their healer has saved her life. Do we not owe them the courtesy of belief in return?"

"A marsh viper? How could she have healed her? Their bite is fatal," Bredor said.

"Normally, my Lord, it is. But this healer carried with her a rare herb which I have never seen before. A poultice of its leaves combined with a potion distilled from its root has saved Modsdara."

"Modsdara? That would be the daughter of Mod?"

"Yes, my Lord."

Bredor turned to Gilmak. "I think we must let them pass."

"But my Lord," Gilmak protested, "they are unknown to us. How do we know that they are not spies, sent by the Yrusians to ferret out the secrets of the Fenland? If you would allow me to interrogate them, I will soon learn the truth of their tale."

He met Abigail's eyes and she shuddered at the promise of violence in them.

"You have a point, Gilmak," Bredor answered. Then, turning to Ylonya once more, "You Yrusians are known to be inquisitive, poking your noses into everyone's else business. Why should we believe your tale?"

Ylonya bowed her head in pretended submission. Then she met Lord Bredor's eyes once more. "It is true, my Lord, that Yrusians are ever curious about the world around us. But I swear to you, we are only passing through the Fenland in order to reach Caethniss Castle with all speed, so that our healer may save lives."

Bredor's eyes narrowed in thought. Gilmak was looking daggers at Ylonya. Abigail could hardly breathe – what would the Fenland lord decide? She could sense Shaunan giving the gentlest nudge to his mind, making him more receptive, trusting.

"Very well, very well," he said in a testy voice. "You may continue your journey. But do not come here again. We do not like strangers in the Fenland."

"Our grateful thanks, my Lord Bredor. We will leave in the morning." Ylonya bowed low once again, before swinging round and leading the rest of them out of the hall. Abigail hoped that Gilmak would not try to detain them later – he was clearly unhappy with his Lord's decision. They would have to be ready to leave at first light. She hoped Modsdara would be well enough to travel. Whatever happened, it looked as though Ednor would be getting some more poling practice.

Chapter 20

"I do not trust that Gilmak," Tremond said. "I would not put it past him to try to imprison us without Lord Bredor knowing."

"Agreed," Ednor said. "I think we need to plan our escape. And not stay until the morning."

Tremond nodded, his eyes on Ylonya, whose gaze was far away.

Aidren was prowling around the room, clearly restless. Only Shaunan seemed to be relaxed. Modsorn sat in a corner, almost forgotten, it seemed.

"I tend to agree with you," Ylonya said. "Shaunan, I think we should leave tonight."

"But we cannot leave without Modsdara," Modsorn said. "She is my sister. She would be punished for our leaving. And we need her to pole second boat."

Shaunan turned to the Fenlander, warm and reassuring, as always. Tremond had gained much respect for her over the past few seisdags.

"We would not dream of leaving her behind, Modsorn," she said. "Whenever we leave, she will be with us. Tremond, would you have a look outside, please, to see whether the coast is clear?"

Tremond strode across the room and opened the shutter of the window gently, careful not to make a noise. He waited a moment for his eyes to become accustomed to the dark, then had a look round. Two men were standing outside the Place of Visitors, and he could see from their silhouettes that they had spears in their hands and swords at their belts. So Gilmak planned to make it hard for them to leave.

He closed the shutter softly, then said, “There are guards without, two of them, armed with spears and swords.”

Ylonya’s breath was drawn in, in a hiss of displeasure, but all she said was, “Only two? We should be able to manage them between us.”

Shaunan shook her head. “That would be all right if we had only ourselves to think of, but we cannot leave without Modsdara. Ylonya, can you think of a way we could get Modsdara here without alerting the guards?”

“Perhaps there is a rear entrance, which is not guarded. I will check.”

Ylonya left the room. Tremond and the others waited. Just when he had decided to go and look for her, she returned. But not alone. Healer Janris and Modsdara were with her, the girl looking pale still, her face drawn.

“Waymage,” Janris said, “you must leave at once. Gilmak plans to hold you here.”

“Do you know a way out, by which we can remain unseen?”

“I do, and so does Modsorn,” she nodded to him, “but two people will have to fetch the boats and the wharf might be guarded.”

“How can we do that without attracting attention?” Ylonya asked.

Janris bit her lip. “The only way I can think of doing it is if I manage to distract the guards.”

“How would you do that?” Aidren asked.

“Shaunan, do you have anything in your healer’s bag that would make them sleep?”

Shaunan frowned. “I do not use my herbs and potions to harm others.”

"Not harm them," Janris protested, "just send them to sleep, quickly."

"Come, Waymage," Tremond said, "it is necessary to put them out of action, otherwise we will never escape."

He was surprised at himself. Here he was, a Watch Officer, recommending that they break the law. He saw Shaunan's face twist in reluctant agreement.

"Very well," she said, "I have some lethara here, which I use to put people to sleep, to give them some surcease from pain. But use it sparingly – two drops is sufficient to knock out a grown man. And they will not remember who gave it to them."

Janris took the little bottle in her hands with fingers that trembled. "I will return to the Place of Healers and fetch some strong mead," she said, "then mix four drops into it before offering it to the guards."

Without further ado, the healer sped off.

"Now we wait," Tremond said.

"Aidren, go and fetch Abigail and Ellyn," Shaunan said.

The company worked quickly to pack all their belongings. Soon they were ready to leave. Shaunan used the waiting time to examine Modsdara, whom she could sense was still feeling poorly.

"How are you feeling?"

"Better than before, thank you, but I'm not strong enough to pole us any distance."

"Don't worry about that," Ednor said, "I'll pole our boat."

The Fenland girl smiled up at him gratefully. "Thank you."

"But how are we going to reach the boats unseen?" Aidren asked, his brow knitted with worry.

"That will be up to Janris," Shaunan replied. "We must do whatever she tells us to, quickly and silently. Our very lives may depend on it."

Tremond was watching the guards through a crack in the shutters. "Here she comes," he murmured.

Shaunan held her breath. If this didn't work, they were in trouble. She heard Janris's voice as the healer accosted the guards.

"I am come to consult one of the prisoners about Modsdara," she said.

"We cannot allow you to pass – Karl Gilmak's orders," one of them replied.

"Surely he did not mean me," Janris said. "You know I am a healer and one of our own has been bitten by a marsh viper. She wanders now in a high fever and I need to speak with their healer, else I may lose her. And I've brought you some mead left over from the feast – it's a cold night to be standing around."

"Thank you," the second guard said, "but we're not supposed to drink on duty."

"The man who made that rule had no experience of standing in the cold all night, I'll warrant," Janris said, a teasing tone in her voice.

"True," the second guard agreed. "I guess a few mouthfuls of mead won't do us any harm."

"I've brought you two mugs as well," Janris said, and Shaunan heard the gurgle of mead being poured into them. Was this going to work?

"'S ve'y good of you, Janris. No-one cares 'bout…" the guard's voice faded as the drug began to take effect. Moments later, Shaunan heard two heavy thumps as their bodies hit the ground.

Then Janris's voice came at the door. "They are sleeping," she said. "Come, quickly."

They filed out in silence. Ednor and Tremond lifted the inert bodies and put them in the shadow of some bushes. Then all of them followed Janris round the back of the Place of Visitors. She took a convoluted route through the Homing, freezing every so often at the sound of voices. The wharf was in complete darkness when they arrived.

"Wait here," Janris breathed, "I will see whether it is guarded."

Before she could move, they saw the twinkle of a lantern in the darkness and the sound of heavy footsteps.

"Quick!" Janris said in a whisper, pointing to a building nearby. "Hide behind the store house."

They moved behind the low building as silently as possible. What to do now?

Shaunan started as Ednor whispered in her ear, "There is only one guard. We must deal with him."

"How?"

"If the Healer can distract him, I'll get behind him and knock him out. Then we'll have to hide the body."

Shaunan didn't like the sound of this – there were too many things that could go wrong. Then they *would* be in trouble. But she couldn't think of any other plan, so she nodded. "Tell Janris."

Ednor moved over to the healer and put his mouth next to her ear. Her eyes widened, then she nodded. And stepped out into the path of the guard.

"Who goes there?" The guard's reaction was instantaneous and his sword was in his hand.

"Good even, Berlsorn. It's only me, Healer Janris. I'd heard that Modsorn had brought a new consignment of healing herbs with him from Ostfen and I wanted to check what he'd brought."

"At this time of night?" the guard asked, suspicion in his tone.

Shaunan could sense Ednor moving on cat-like feet into position behind him but could not see him, because he was outside the circle of light cast by the lantern. Was this going to work? She held her breath.

Janris continued, "Yes. You may have heard that his sister, Modsdara, has been bitten by a marsh viper. I need to check whether there are any herbs that can help me to treat her."

"Very well," the guard began, then Shaunan heard a dull thunk as the pommel of Ednor's sword connected with the back of his head and he folded at the knees and dropped to the wharf, unconscious.

Tremond stepped out of the shelter of the store house and helped Ednor carry the man into the shadows behind it.

Shaunan moved to speak to Janris. "Here," she said passing her the bottle of lethara again, "If you can trickle a couple of drops down his throat, he will not remember you."

"Thank you." Janris suited action to word, then returned the little bottle to Shaunan once more. "Now go. I do not know when the change of guard is due and the night is waning."

Finally, they were in the boats – Abigail, Ednor, Tremond, Modsdara and Shaunan herself in one, Ylonya, Aidren, Ellyn and Modsorn in the other.

Before they left, Shaunan spoke to Janris. "Do you not wish to come with us? I fear for your safety when our departure is discovered."

"You said the guards would not remember me," Janris replied. "I cannot leave – I am the only decent healer they have and they are now my people."

"You are a brave woman, Janris. I am glad that our paths have crossed. May the Way guard and guide you."

"Go, now. It is nearly dawn."

Ednor and Modsorn began to pole the boats away from the wharf as quickly and quietly as they could. Janris had spoken truly – the light of the new day was beginning to turn the sky a deep, dark blue and Ednor knew they would have to be well on their way before the Fenlanders awoke and discovered their absence. He hoped Modsorn's knowledge of the Fenland channels was as good as he said – they would need to find somewhere to hide up. He was sure they would be followed.

It wasn't long before he heard alarmed voices behind them – someone must have discovered the guard on the wharf. Or perhaps the other two. Ednor saw Modsorn's head go up as he also heard them – he trusted the Fenland man knew somewhere they could take cover.

"When we turn into side channel," Modsorn called in a low voice, which was yet clear enough to carry to the other boat, "you must pull reeds together behind us, so they miss which way we've gone."

"Abigail, Tremond, do as he says," Shaunan said, as Ednor followed Modsorn, poling as best he could, into a narrow channel on their left, which led to a part of the Fenland that appeared completely occupied by reeds. Abigail and Tremond hung precariously over the back of the boat, weaving the reeds back together. Soon they were surrounded by tall, gently waving stalks on all sides. The going was only one boat wide, it seemed, and Ednor was finding it hard not to get his pole tangled up in the surrounding greenery. He noticed Modsdara's eyes on him and hoped he wasn't making too much of a hash of it.

"Try not to dig so fiercely," the Fenland girl said. "That way, boat will steer straighter."

Ednor tried that and found that it worked, much to his relief. He smiled his thanks to her. But once more, his shoulders and back were starting to ache from the unaccustomed movements. Where was Modsorn going?

A few minutes' later, Modsorn stopped. "We can hide here," he said, "until day's end. They will give up after that, if they haven't found us."

Ednor wasn't so sure. But he prayed the Fenlander was right.

Abigail looked around. No solid land in sight. She guessed that was Modsorn's plan, to hide somewhere the Fenlanders would not expect, somewhere without shelter. She strained her ears for the sounds of following boats. Had she and Tremond disguised their passage well enough? If this didn't work, they would be trapped here – there was nowhere to escape to.

Then it started to rain, only a few drops at first, then turning into a steady downpour. Modsdara fished out a heavy skin from her pack and the five of them huddled together under it. But it was not large enough to cover them all completely, being intended for only one person and soon Abigail was feeling wet and miserable, not to mention stifled. The air was close and it was hard to breathe. She hoped Ellyn was bearing up.

To Abigail's surprise, there was a look of satisfaction on Shaunan's face. "This will put them off," she said, "and a little rain won't hurt us."

Then Abigail heard Ylonya's voice from the other boat, "This rain will not last long – an hour at most. Where do we go from here?"

"How you know?" Modsorn's voice was sharp with surprise.

"I have the weather sense," Ylonya replied. "Hush, I hear them."

Straight away, silence fell in the two boats. Abigail hadn't heard a thing, but she trusted Ylonya's instincts. Sure enough, the sound of the pursuing boats came from behind them. She held her breath – would the Fenlanders be deceived?

"How have they got so far ahead of us?" A harsh voice, full of anger. Her stomach knotted as she recognised it for Gilmak's. He was leading the chase himself. She held her breath, praying silently, "Dear God, beloved Ranu, help us to stay hidden and unseen, Amen."

She heard the rumble of another voice, then Gilmak again. "How should I know, you dolt? You are supposed to know every channel in the Fenland."

"I'm sorry, Karl Gilmak," the other man said, "I have seen no signs that they have turned off the main channel. Surely we will catch up with them soon – they only have one competent boatman."

Abigail glanced at Ednor, who scowled as he heard this. She laid a hand on his arm, enjoining silence and stillness.

Then, after what seemed like an eternity, the pursuers moved on. Abigail began to shiver, either in reaction, or from the cold and wet. What could they do now?

Once all sound of the hunters had gone, the company drew cautious breath. They were not out of trouble yet.

"How long must we wait?" Ylonya asked Modsorn.

"It depends which way you want to go," the young Fenlander replied. "They have gone ahead, towards Oestfen, which you told is your journey's end. If you would go that way, we must wait until they have passed again, on their way back to the Homing."

Ylonya thought for a moment. Then she asked him, "Is there another route to Oestfen?"

"There is, but it will take us some miles out of our way."

"How much longer would it take us, than having to wait here?"

"One day, perhaps two."

Ylonya glanced at Shaunan, "What do you say, Waymage?"

The answer was as she expected, "I hate to lose more time, but that seems to be our only solution. Modsorn, won't our pursuers know this other route?"

Modsorn shrugged. "They might, but it is through difficult part of the Fenland, marshy, with areas of quicksand. I only know it because of Mod."

"Why does Mod know it?" Ylonya asked.

"Mod knows all routes in the Fenland," Modsorn said shortly, a closed, almost surly expression on his face.

"I'm sorry, Modsorn," Ylonya said. "I did not mean to doubt your word."

He nodded at her, his face clearing, then turned to Ednor. "You must follow me exactly," he said. "If you pole into patch of quicksand, boat could sink within few minutes."

"I will help," Modsdara said. Ylonya saw Ednor flash her a grateful smile.

"Then let us leave while light is still good."

Abigail remembered little of the following hours – there was little *to* remember. They set off slowly, with Ednor following Modsorn as closely as he dared. She and Tremond continued to weave the reeds behind them – her arms were aching from the unaccustomed exercise. The air seemed close, almost stifling, and the sky overhead was a sullen grey, even when the rain had stopped. And the sky was the only thing she could see apart from the ever-present reeds – she saw no animals and only a few birds, who flew away as they approached. She had no idea how Modsorn knew where he was going. The route he was taking through the reeds seemed convoluted to her, but what did she know? She thought they were travelling north-west, but without the sun to give her a clue, this was only a guess. The main thing was, they were moving away from the area around the Homing and remaining unseen.

As the grey of the sky began to fade towards night, the moon rose. Still Modsorn continued to pole along, apparently without effort. When were they going to stop, to rest? Abigail could see that Ednor was exhausted. Strong warrior though he was, the motions of poling were strange to him and she could sense the aches in the muscles of his arms and back. She and Shaunan would have to tend him when they stopped.

Finally, Modsorn called a halt. Ednor shipped his pole with a sigh of relief and sank to the bottom of the boat.

"I have brought you to northern marge of the Fenland," Modsorn said. "From here, we must head south-west, towards Oestfen. It is not far. We should reach by late evening."

"Thank you, Modsorn," Shaunan said. "You have guided us well and faithfully. We are in your debt."

The young man smiled back at her. "You saved Modsdara's life," he said gruffly, "that is payment enough."

Nobody got much sleep, as they had to stay in the boats, there being no land in sight. So after an early breakfast of stale *feolin,* washed down with the last of the water from their flasks, they set out once more.

I'll be happier once we're back on dry land, Abigail said to Shaunan in silence, as they soothed Ednor's abused muscles. *It's so hard, not being able to see where we're going.*

As for me, her mentor replied, *I am glad to be so well-hidden. Any wide-open space might allow others to see us. We cannot risk Gilmak getting word of our passage.*

You're right, of course. But I feel so helpless, adrift in this boat. If someone does spot us, we cannot escape.

Which is why we have warriors with us. Ednor, Tremond, Aidren and Ylonya between them should be able to deal with any trouble. But I hope we can pass undetected.

As Modsorn had predicted, they did not reach Oestfen while the daylight lasted. Abigail was beginning to wonder whether they would have to pass another night in the boats, when they suddenly came out of the reeds into an open pool, at the far end of which was a jetty, and beyond that, the small township of Oestfen.

Chapter 21

"Wait!" Ylonya said. "I see guards on the jetty. Get us back into the reeds."

Modsorn reacted instantly, poling his boat quickly and neatly back into cover. Ednor did the same, if not so gracefully.

"Now what do we do?" Tremond asked.

Ylonya did not answer. She moved the concealing reeds far enough aside to catch a glimpse of the main channel without revealing their whereabouts, then said, "There is no doubt. Those are Gilmak's guards. They have got here before us."

"What is your plan?" Shaunan asked.

"We cannot enter Oestfen so long as those guards are there," Ylonya said. "Modsorn, is there anywhere else we can leave the Fens on the west side?"

"There is small holding some miles south of here. It is owned by Lem, old friend of my father's. He would not betray us, not to Gilmak. But you would have to continue on foot. Oestfen is only place this side of the Fenland which has horses."

"What do you think, Shaunan?" Ylonya asked.

"All my choices have gone awry," Shaunan sighed. "I wish now we had ridden around the Fenland. I do not see how we can continue without horses."

She turned to Modsorn, "Modsorn, you have served us well and faithfully. Are you willing to take us to the smallholding of Lem?"

"Of course, Waymage. But we must wait until daylight. I do not know route well enough to find my way in dark."

"Very well," Shaunan nodded. "Take us far enough back into the reeds that we will not be in danger of discovery. Then we will rest as we may, before continuing at dawn."

They reached the holding of Lem mid-morning. It was a copy of Mod's on the far side of the Fenland, set in an open pool with the holding high on wooden stilts above the water.

Modsorn tied his boat up at the jetty. "Wait here. I will speak to Lem."

Abigail watched him go, then asked Ylonya, "How far is it to Chorich Castle from here?"

"I am unsure. Perhaps fifty or sixty miles. I have not travelled this road before, only from Oestfen."

"How long is that going to take us?" Aidren asked.

"At least a seisdag," Ylonya said. "Longer, if our pace slows or if we are pursued."

Abigail bit her lip. More delay. She was beginning to share Shaunan's apprehension.

"Perhaps we can get one horse, to carry some of our baggage," Ellyn said, optimistic as always.

"Let's hope so," Ylonya said. "Here is Modsorn."

Modsorn was striding across the jetty towards them. "Come. I have told Lem who you are, that you are pursued by Gilmak."

Abigail stood up and stretched, feeling stiff after so many hours of sitting. She turned to help Shaunan out of the boat. Her mentor's face was pale and set.

Are you feeling all right?

The prospect of walking so far is not a welcome one. Do not worry about me – it is our only choice.

A few minutes later, they had climbed the ladder and were in front of the door of Lem's holding. A tall, skinny man was standing in the doorway, a smile on his face.

"Welcome to Lemshold," he said. "I am Lem. Come away in."

Abigail accepted his invitation with a smile and a nod. "Our thanks, Holder Lem," she said. The rest of them followed her in.

Soon they were seated round an oval table, roughly hewn but solid.

"Fetch them a drink," Lem said to an equally thin woman, who was standing behind him, smoothing down her apron. Abigail guessed she was his wife.

The woman nodded and ducked out of sight, returning a few moments later with a heavy tray full of wooden goblets and a leather wineskin. Aidren jumped up to assist her. Lem nodded his approval.

"You are courteous folk," he said. "Now, Modsorn tells you are fleeing from the Holding, from Karl Gilmak."

"That is so," Ylonya said, "and it is urgent that we reach Chorich Castle as soon as possible."

"I do not want to know why," Lem said. "But Karl Gilmak is an evil in Fenland. If I can hinder him by helping his enemies, I am willing to do so. What do you need?"

"Modsorn tells us there are no horses available, except in Oestfen," Ylonya said. "Do you know any other way of reaching Chorich Castle, except on foot?"

"The River Choris," Lem said, "flows from the mountains of Talamdor near Chorich Castle to the Inland Sea. It is twenty miles south of here. You might be able to persuade a boatman to row you upstream."

Abigail saw Ellyn's face brighten at the prospect.

"I fear we would be sitting ducks for any pursuing us," Ylonya said. "From what I recall, the Choris is not wide. If we were on a boat, it would be easy for them to shoot arrows at us."

"Good point," Tremond said. "But would the danger be more than if we were on foot?"

"We would be freer to fight on foot," Ednor put in.

Tremond and Aidren both nodded their agreement.

"What do you think, Shaunan?" Ylonya asked.

"My vision is clouded," Shaunan said, shaking her head. "But my heart fears this pursuit. I can sense the malice in Gilmak. He will not give up easily."

"Can you remind me what the countryside is like between here and Chorich Castle?" Ylonya said. "I have travelled from Oestfen to the Castle before but have not been this far south for many years."

Abigail was worried about Shaunan. She sensed the older woman was hiding something, something important. *Shaunan, what is wrong?*

I am not as young as I was, Abigail.

Abigail sensed a shaft of pain, quickly suppressed. *Are you feeling ill?*

Do not concern yourself, child. If we rest for the remainder of the day, I will be fine.

Abigail bit her lip, not reassured. She turned her attention back to the conversation and caught the end of Lem's sentence, "…but there are few settlements." What had she missed?

"Holder Lem," Ylonya said, "do you have an animal that could carry our baggage? We would send him back from the Castle once we arrive."

Lem frowned. "I have mule," he said, "but he is quite old and slow. I cannot be without him for long."

"We would pay you well for the loan of him," Ylonya said. "And if matters go awry, apply to Guildmaster Brickon in Porusport and he will replace him for you."

Lem's eyebrows shot up. "Guildmaster Brickon? Of the Hall of Traders? Why should he help me?"

"I am Ylonya, his daughter," Ylonya said.

"Very well, Mistress Ylonya," Lem said. "Your reputation has reached us, even here."

"My thanks, Holder Lem. I swear to you, you will not be the loser in this."

Lem insisted that they share a meal with him before departing. Shaunan was relieved – it would give the pain she would not admit to time to subside. At least they would not have to carry their packs. But the prospect of a sixty mile hike was daunting. She would have to hide her pain from Abigail somehow, or they would never reach the Talamdorian border. And every instinct she possessed was warning her that time was running out.

"Modsorn," Shaunan said, "will you and Modsdara be able to get back home in safety?"

"Fear not, Waymage," Modsdara said. "My brother and I know Fenland well. We will be able to stay out of sight."

"Let me check your wound before we part."

Shaunan unwrapped the bandage from around Modsdara's forearm. The bite was healing well, and the flesh around it was pale and clean.

"Good," she said. "You will bear a scar to the end of your days but have taken no permanent harm."

"I will always be grateful to you," Modsdara said. "Without you and Janris, I would have died."

The rest of them crowded round to thank the young Fenlanders. The mule had been loaded with their packs and was waiting patiently by Aidren, who was holding his guide rope.

"Farewell, Holder Lem," Shaunan said. "You have our gratitude."

"Go well, Waymage," Lem said. "Go well, all of you."

It felt odd, almost wrong, to be leaving Modsorn and Modsdara behind. Abigail had taken to both of them. But they had no part in the company's onward quest. She hoped they would be able to return to Mod's holding in safety.

In spite of the mule, Abigail decided she would carry her healer's bag, reasoning that if the mule bolted, she would still have it safe. The others had likewise chosen to carry a small pack of essentials.

Having started late, they managed only a short distance, covering only half a dozen miles before night fell. When Ylonya called a halt, on the outskirts of a small village, Abigail breathed a sigh of relief.

"I will be glad to rest," she said to Ellyn. "I'm not used to carrying a pack all day."

"Or even for half a day," Ellyn said. "It will be longer tomorrow."

"Don't remind me. I hope Ylonya will be able to find somewhere for us to stay."

"She always does. And we are in Yrusian, after all."

"What difference does that make?" Abigail asked.

"Ylonya is Yrusian – surely her countrymen will give us shelter."

Ellyn was right – Ylonya led them to a small house on the far edge of the village and they were taken in.

The next morning, they set off early. A swirling mist surrounded them, which slowly cleared as the day advanced. The countryside in this part of Yrusian was damp underfoot, almost boggy, so they had to take care where they trod. But Ylonya's steps were confident – she knew in which direction she wished to go. Once more, Abigail was grateful for her friend's skills as a guide.

They had been trudging along for hours, with only a brief halt for lunch, when Tremond stopped.

"Can you hear hoofbeats?"

Abigail closed her eyes and concentrated, pushing her senses out as far as they would go. She sensed Ylonya doing the same. "Yes," she said, "we are being pursued. By five horseman, I think, coming up fast behind us."

"How can you tell?" Tremond asked.

"I am Ranusian."

"Then we must find somewhere defensible," Ednor said, glancing around. "There," he continued, pointing to a small hillock perhaps half a mile away. "That will do."

The company walked as fast as they could, hampered as they were by the mule and their packs.

Abigail scrambled up the hill, then turned around. "They are almost upon us," she said.

"Waymage," Ednor said, "you and Abigail and Ellyn must stay behind us. Aidren, Tremond, Ylonya and I will see off these pursuers."

Shaunan sank to the ground, her face a muddy grey. Her right hand was clutching her riding jacket, over her chest, as though trying to contain some pain.

Shaunan! Are you all right?

I just need to rest.

Regardless of the need to respect Shaunan's privacy, Abigail threw her healing sense into her. A sharp pain in the chest. Why hadn't Shaunan told her about it?

Abigail fumbled in the pouch around her neck for her Goldstone and, clutching it in her left hand, placed her palm on Shaunan's chest. *Belannath Ranu, gal ens bynn wellent, gal ens bynn wellent.*

She sensed a flow of healing moving from her hand into Shaunan, who took a long, shuddering breath, and opened her eyes.

Thank you, Abigail. That has eased the pain somewhat.

Why didn't you tell me you were ill?

I did not want to worry you. The pain is not constant. It only comes when I over-stretch myself.

"Then we must ensure that you do *not* overstretch yourself," Abigail said fiercely, speaking aloud in her agitation. "I need you, Shaunan. I… love you."

"Do not fret, my dear," Shaunan said.

"What is wrong with Aunt Shaunan?" Ellyn asked, crouching down by the pair of them.

Do not tell her. I would not have her worried.

Abigail scowled at her mentor, then nodded. "She is over-tired," she told Ellyn. Which was not a lie, but not the whole truth either.

The five horsemen were drawing near, their horses' hooves kicking up clods of mud. Aidren recognised the distinctive black uniforms of Lord Bredor's Karls. But these also wore breastplates and helmets. He caught the glint of weapons picked up by the sun behind the company. He drew his sword. This time, he was not going to fail. This time, he would not wait. He would defend the women with his life. The three of them – Ellyn, Abigail and the Waymage – were dearer to him than any others.

Beside him, Tremond drew back the string of his bow and shot an arrow. A good shot, which found the gap between one Fenlander's breast plate and his chin guard. He cried aloud before toppling sideways off his horse. One down, four to go.

"That one in the lead – that's Gilmak," Ednor said. "If we can kill him, the others might lose heart."

"Our numbers are even," Tremond said, shooting another arrow, which went wide. "And our position is better – the sun is behind us."

"Do not underestimate this Gilmak," Ylonya said. "We fought another Talamdorian agent outside Néartanis and he put up a fierce fight."

She met Aidren's gaze. "I will be ready," he said.

Then the time for speech and thought was over – the horsemen were on them.

Ednor headed straight for Gilmak. The Talamdorian's lips were drawn back from his teeth in a snarl, his eyes gleaming.

But Aidren had no time to see what happened, for his own foe was upon him, a tall Fenlander who jabbed his spear at Aidren as his horse thundered towards him. Aidren side-stepped neatly and, remembering his and Ylonya's previous battle near Néartanis, slashed across the animal's hamstrings as it went past. With a scream, the horse foundered.

The Fenlander, not expecting this, fell with it. Aidren rushed forward to finish him, but the man was back on his feet with unbelievable speed, his sword ready in his hand. By the Six! The man was quick. Aidren was hard pressed to defend himself – the Fenlander's speed and strength were almost too much to handle. He would have made a good sparring partner but was a formidable opponent. His moves were sly, and though not as technically proficient as Aidren himself, he made up for it with a trickiness not taught to a Dagâran warrior. Every parry was met with the butt of the Karl's sword heading for his nose, with a knee to the belly or a kick to the shin. Half of Aidren's energy and a great deal of his focus was spent on avoiding these. Nevertheless, he was aware of the fighting around him – the metallic clash of sword on sword, the grunts and gasps of the other fighters, the screams of the horses. But he dared not glance aside to see how the others were doing.

"Concentrate on the chest – that will tell you your opponent's next move." The advice of Master Sanderon came back to him and an inner calm came over him as he refined his focus. Fight fire with fire. Yet again the Fenlander took a giant swing to make Aidren parry once more. But Aidren ignored him. Instead he spun and swung in one motion, both shifting his body away from the weapon's downward trajectory and also bringing his sword across in a sharp, swift stroke at the Fenlander's neck.

The man had good reflexes, but not quite good enough. As he leaned to his right and tilted his head back, Aidren sliced through both bushy beard and the cartilage beneath. A jet of crimson spurted from the man's mouth as he tumbled to the ground.

Aidren looked down to ensure this wasn't just another cunning trick. When he saw both the man's hands cradled around his neck without a weapon to be seen, he knew he was done.

Suddenly he heard a cry, not of anger but of pain and the voice was unmistakable. Ellyn!

"No!" he screamed and plunged towards the women, every bit of caution thrown to the wind.

Ylonya was getting sick and tired of the Fenland. She was a quintessential Yrusian, a born trader and loved exploring every corner of Veylindré. But for the first time in her life, she realised some places simply weren't worth the effort. They had just been through one and were on the way to another.

Before the previous fight, outside Néartanis, she had launched herself into the thick of the action, believing she and Aidren were the only ones even vaguely capable of defending the others. Thankfully, Ellyn had proven herself that day or they all would have been lost. Today was different: they had two trained warriors on their side. Or at least, one trained warrior and one very competent Watchman.

So Ylonya found herself in a supporting role. She had driven a grey-bearded Fenlander onto the edge of Ednor's blade and was now herding the four remaining horses for later use by the company. If there was another wave behind these riders they might well need them. In any case, she did not intend to walk all the way to Chorich Castle.

As she returned she saw Aidren running straight across the mêlée, his sword held low. He was paying no attention whatsoever to the danger he was in. She wanted to shout out but supposed he knew what he was doing.

Then she saw a karl crashing through the undergrowth, a gleam of malice in his eyes as he raised his blade to cut Aidren down.

"Aidren!" she screamed.

But Aidren didn't even look. He ploughed on with gay abandon. Right at the crucial moment as the karl was about to strike, a whoosh came past Ylonya's ear and a feather stung her forehead as an arrow shot past her. It sailed across the clearing and pierced the Karl's cheek, taking him out for the moment.

Without stopping, without even looking, Aidren sprinted past the prone figure and swiped his sword under the plate across his gullet. The Karl's intestines sprang from his belly like snakes escaping a basket.

Ylonya tracked Aidren as he went out of view. Then she turned. Tremond looked at her and winked, already loosing another arrow.

Across from him, Ednor was trading sword strokes with Gilmak. The Talamdorian was a skilled fighter, she would give him that. But he had little chance of beating Ednor, who had been trained to fight from his cradle. As she watched, a tricky twist of Ednor's wrist forced the other to drop his sword. Ednor plunged his own into the man's chest and it was over.

Where had Aidren gone?

Abigail continued to work on Shaunan. She took a couple of the packs from the pile behind them and gently moved the woman so that she could lean against them.

"That is better," Shaunan said. "I can breathe more easily sitting up."

Do not try to talk. Save your breath.

"Is Aunt Shaunan going to be all right?" Ellyn asked.

"She needs to rest," Abigail said. "The sooner we reach Chorich Castle, the better." If we get that far. She didn't like the sound of Shaunan's breathing at all – every breath seemed a ragged effort.

Behind them, the fight had begun. Abigail tried to block out the sounds, ignoring the fighting behind her. She trusted the men to keep them safe and concentrated on checking

Shaunan's vital signs, putting a light blanket over her and offering her a water bottle.

Then she felt an intense surge of anxiety from Ellyn. Before she could turn to see what was happening, she heard the swish of an arrow and, immediately after, Ellyn crying out in pain.. As Abigail spun around, she was just in time to catch her friend, who had sunk to her knees, an arrow deep in her chest.

"Ellyn!"

Abigail lowered Ellyn gently to the ground. How could this have happened? She began to strip off Ellyn's jacket, but her friend raised a hand to stop her.

"No good," Ellyn whispered. "I had to do it… I had to save you. Tell Aidren I…"

"Hush, now. I'm the healer. Let me see your…"

Then to her horror, there was a gush of blood from Ellyn's mouth and her body became slack, then still.

No, no, no! Abigail's heart was racing, her vision growing dark. This couldn't be happening. Ellyn couldn't be dead. Tears pouring down her face, Abigail tore her friend's shirt open, tried to find a heartbeat. Ellyn could not be dead. Could not.

"Abigail! What has happened to Ellyn?"

Shaunan's voice. What to tell her?

"I – she – she took an arrow in the chest."

Shaunan slumped back against the packs, her face greyer than ever, tears leaking from her eyes.

Then Aidren came charging up. "What's wrong with Ellyn? I heard her cry out."

"Aidren," Abigail said, taking his hand, trying to contain her own pain, "I'm so very sorry. She – she dodged in front of an arrow fired at me."

But she might as well have saved her breath. With a great cry Aidren tore free from her grasp and slumped to the ground beside Ellyn's body, taking her in his arms. He rocked backwards and forwards, cradling his dead love. And as he rocked, he keened, a sharp wail of grief that pierced the air.

The others came running.

Δ Chapter 22

Portak's heart lifted as the grey stone battlements of Caethniss Castle began to fill his horizon. It had taken them seven long days to march from Roillby, including one rest day, which General Kreldik had insisted on. It could only have been seventy miles – Portak was grinding his teeth in frustration. But the old man had been right – the slow pace had meant the foot soldiers were arriving in fairly good shape, ready to tackle the mountain pass the next day.

With luck, they would catch the Néartanians unawares.

"Portak, come with me," Kreldik said.

Portak started – he had not heard the general approaching. "Where are you going?"

"Into the castle, to receive reports. You come with me, then report back to His Holiness."

Portak followed Kreldik over the drawbridge towards the main gate of the castle, which was flanked by two towers, dark and forbidding. Caethniss Castle had been built in the foothills of the Talamdorian Mountains long centuries ago, on the northern bank of the River Caethwas. Its purpose was to guard the fertile region of central Talamdor against possible invasion from the east. Over the years a small town had grown up around it, which was a centre for trade between central and southern Talamdor.

Portak looked up at the sturdy towers of grey stone, with narrow slits of windows set at intervals for shooting arrows from. The Castle was a formidable defensive structure. He knew that the high battlements continued all the way round it, and that the gate in the north-eastern portion of the walls was most tirelessly guarded, as it led directly to the mountain pass on the other side of the River Caethwas, the route to Néartania.

Kreldik banged on the door of the sally port. "Open up!"

A small shutter was opened and a guard looked through. "Who goes there?"

"General Kreldik, leader of the Prophet's army. Open up!"

Portak watched the guard's eyes widen as he took in the general's uniform.

"Right away, General, sir."

The man opened the sally port and gestured them in. Then he saluted Kreldik. "My apologies, General Kreldik. We were not expecting you today."

"Obviously." Kreldik brushed past the man and Portak followed him.

They came out into a sunny courtyard as busy as a hive of bees struck with a stick.

General Kreldik seized a passing soldier by the arm. "Take us to Major Turnik."

Portak was amused by the soldier's reaction – first annoyance then, as he took in Kreldik's rank, shock.

"Yes, General. Right away, General."

Major Turnik was a stout, middle-aged man with ruddy features, his Bloodmark barely visible against his skin. Portak and Kreldik entered his office, the main feature of which was a massive wooden desk piled high with papers. When Turnik saw the general, he struggled to his feet and saluted.

"General Kreldik, sir!" he barked.

"At ease, Major," Kreldik said. "This is Portak, agent of the Prophet. Your report, please."

Turnik sat back down and gestured to two wooden chairs with padded seats opposite his desk. Portak sank into one of them – it was a welcome change from his horse's saddle.

"The news is not good," Turnik began. "By some witch's trick, the Veylindréans have got wind of our plans. The element of surprise has been lost."

"Why didn't you send us this news straight away?" Portak asked.

"I'm sorry, sir. Our scouts only returned a couple of days ago so I thought it best to wait until you arrived. They report that a sizeable army has reached the border forts of both Mistbourne Keep and South Plains Keep."

"I want numbers, man," Kreldik snapped, "not vague generalities."

"Yes, General. I mean, no, General." The portly major cowered back in his chair.

"Well?"

"We – we do not have exact numbers," he said, shuffling the papers on his desk, as though reluctant to meet Kreldik's eyes. "But my scouts estimate several thousand at each Keep, in good order and well-armed."

"How long have they been there?"

"My scouts think about a seisdag, General, sir."

"And the conditions through the mountain pass?"

"Not bad, General, sir. But they may have spies…" The major's voice tailed off as he saw the anger in Kreldik's face.

"It's a bit of a shambles, isn't it, Turnik?"

The major hung his head.

Kreldik stood up, turned on his heel and marched out of the room. Portak shrugged, then followed him.

Once they were out of the castle, Kreldik said, "You had better report to His Holiness. I will meet my staff to formulate a plan of attack."

"I would like to be present," Portak said, "so that I can send a full report to our Master."

Kreldik frowned, then said, "As you will."

Jacob made his way to the Chamber of Law the next morning and knocked on the door. He felt both apprehensive and excited – the Prophet had promised that today would see the next stage in his education. Whatever that meant.

"Come."

Jacob walked in and looked around. It was an impressive room, large and square, with framed paintings showing scenes from what he guessed was Talamdorian history on the walls. In the centre was a massive, three-sided table with a marble top of black and red. Ornately carved wooden chairs were set around it, with one larger one at the triangle's apex. That must be the Prophet's. So this was the place he ruled from. On the high ceiling was a painting of Talamu, who seemed to be gazing directly into his soul. Jacob hunched his shoulders as the Prophet beckoned him forward.

"Good, Jacob. You are on time. This morning I will be meeting representatives of Talamdor's first families and of Holy Talamu's church. I want you to sit here," and the Prophet indicated a chair on his left. "You are to listen and learn."

"Is there anything special you want me to listen for, my Lord?"

"I will be telling the nobles something of my – I should say, Holy Talamu's – plans for the future. Your task is to watch their reactions to what I say and report back to me afterwards."

The first nobles began to arrive a few minutes later. Well-dressed men in the customary Talamdorian black and red, often with fur trimmings, and a few Talamunem priests in their long, red vestments. All seemed surprised by Jacob's presence and soon his cheeks were burning. He wished he could leave.

But the Prophet wanted him to be there, so that was all there was to it.

When all were seated, the Prophet glanced around the table and silence fell.

"My Lords," he began, "I have invited you here to report on the progress of the war and to share Holy Talamu's plans for the future… Yes, Lord Domlok?"

An older noble with a mane of iron grey hair and dark eyes had raised one finger. "Who is the young man by your side, my Lord?" he said. "Surely this is a confidential meeting, for truebloods and the priesthood only."

The Prophet glowered at him. "This is Jacob, a young protégé of mine. He is here to listen and to learn."

"But my Lord," the old man began.

"Enough, Domlok. It is my wish that he should be present. That should suffice."

Lord Domlok flushed and sat back, shooting Jacob a hate-filled glare. "As you say, my Lord."

"So I should think," the Prophet snapped. "Now, if you are all ready to listen, I will tell you what is happening."

Jacob watched and listened as the Prophet alternately cajoled and soothed his nobles and priests into complacency. He was an impressive speaker – none who heard him failed to fall under the spell of his voice. Even these proud Talamdorian nobles and Talamunem priests were not exempt.

At the end of the meeting, Jacob watched them rise, bow to the Prophet and file out. He sat back in his chair and sighed.

"Well, Jacob? What have you learned?"

Jacob's mind raced. He had not been playing close attention to what the Prophet had said to all these people, being far more diverted by the ways he had handled them.

"I have learned something about Talamdorian society, my Lord."

"Such as?"

"That – that there are three different ranks of nobility – lords, earls and princes, and that they differ both in the purity of their bloodlines and in the amount of land they own. And that they are paying for the war."

"Very good. What else?"

"That the Talamdorian armies have reached the borders of Talamdor."

"And what did you notice about how they took the news?"

"Some seemed uneasy at first, but by the end, I think they were all happy. My Lord, what am I doing here?"

"Listening and learning."

"But I am no courtier," Jacob said. "Why do I need to learn how you deal with your subjects?"

"They are not my subjects. They are Holy Talamu's subjects. I am Her mouthpiece, that is all."

Which was no answer at all. Jacob tried again. "If you would explain what you want of me, perhaps I could serve you better."

The Prophet swung round to face him. "Do you not understand even yet?"

"My Lord, I'm sorry… "

"Listen carefully. Then you will understand. I am growing old, Jacob, although I do not look it. In our world I would be in my eighth decade. Talamu gave me the strength and power to lead Talamdor out of slavery and to build Her land anew. But my task is not complete – and will not be complete until the people of Talamdor rule the entire Commonweal."

"Then it is nearly complete, surely?"

The Prophet scowled at him. "You have no experience of war and its aftermath. You do not understand that fighting is but the first step on the road to subjugation. It will take us years to establish the new order over the whole of Veylindré. And I need someone with the youth and strength to carry on, should my own strength fail me."

Jacob felt the sweat break out on his forehead, his stomach clench as he took this in. The Prophet was preparing him to be his successor. This was a terrible idea. He must be mad.

"No, Jacob, I am not mad. You are the only one for the task, because you come from our world and understand how evil the Veylindréan witches are. Put aside your yearnings to be a smith. I offer you an empire to rule."

"But my Lord… "

"No buts, Jacob," the Prophet said, with a downward cut of his hand. "This is my will and the will of Holy Talamu. You *will* listen and you *will* learn."

Jacob bowed his head. "Yes, my Lord."

"What you do *not* know," the Prophet continued, "because I have not shared it with the nobles, is that the Veylindréans have learned of our plans and have already reached the border keeps on their side of the mountains."

"How do you know that?" The words came out before Jacob had time to censor them.

"I have received a report from Portak. Pay attention. Listen and learn."

"I'm sorry, my Lord," Jacob said, flushing. "Where is our army now?"

"Here."

The Prophet pointed to an unrolled map of the borderlands spread out on a side table, with candle holders to anchor the corners. Fascinated, Jacob leaned forward to see better.

"They divided at the River Roillon." The Prophet's pale finger jabbed at the place on the map. "Half have gone north-east," another jab, "to Roilldon Fort, to attack the northern forts of Nordkeep and Cristail Keep, the other half south east to Caethniss Castle," a third jab, "to assail Mistbourne Keep and South Plains Keep."

"Which half is Portak with?"

Jacob realised he actually cared about the man, who had been his first friend in Talamdor.

"I told you before, with the southern army. They will be heading through the mountain pass tomorrow and engage the enemy the following day. Those Veylindréans are going to need all the weaponry Dagâran can produce to beat our troops."

Dagâran. That name again. It was familiar to him for some reason. But before Jacob could trace the memory back to its source, the Prophet was speaking again.

"Did you notice that some of our Talamdorian worthies were not convinced by our strategy?"

"I noticed they weren't very happy about my presence."

"That is irrelevant," the Prophet snapped. "What else did you notice?"

Jacob thought. "Lord Domlok seemed to think we should be fighting the Havimi."

"Good," the Prophet said. "And he is a prominent member of the nobility, head of one of the oldest trueblood families. He will bear watching, Jacob."

"Yes, my Lord."

After a final rest day at Caethniss Castle, the Talamdorian army marched out through the north-eastern gate, then crossed the River Caethwas over a narrow stone bridge and began to head for the pass through the mountains. They turned left into a narrow defile a few miles south-east of Caethniss Castle, which would bring them out between the Mistbourne and South Plains Keeps.

"This is the most perilous part," Kreldik told Portak. "Only four can ride or march abreast and there is little space to fight, or to bring up reinforcements. If the Veylindréans are planning to ambush us, this would be the best place to do it."

"What do our scouts say?"

Kreldik scowled at him. "They have not yet returned. The Prophet's orders are to march today."

"When were they sent out?"

"Yesterday morning, after we arrived."

"Then surely… "

"Do not tell me how to do my job, Portak." The general's face was flushed with anger. "You may be His Holiness's agent, but that does not give you the right to question my judgement."

"My apologies, General. I meant no offence."

So he was expecting an ambush. Portak dropped back and loosened his sword in its scabbard.

Thereafter, Jacob attended all the meetings between the Prophet and the Talamdorian nobility. At first, he watched and listened only, but slowly, as he began to understand more about the campaign and about the Prophet's plans for the conquest of Veylindré, he became more confident, and began to make the occasional comment.

One morning, he was eating breakfast in the dining room of the Visitors' Hall, when he became conscious of someone looming over him. He looked up.

"Good morning, Lord Domlok."

"There's nothing good about it, young man," Domlok said, seating himself opposite Jacob without invitation.

"I don't understand," Jacob said. "What is the problem?"

"The problem," Domlok said, leaning heavily on the word, "is this scheme of His Holiness's to conquer Veylindré."

Jacob raised his eyebrows in polite enquiry, a trick he had watched the Prophet do on several occasions. It seemed to work.

"What you may not understand," Domlok continued, "is that the enemy of Talamdor is not Veylindré. It is Havim."

"Havim, my Lord?"

"Havim. They are the ones who took over our land. They are the ones who forced true blooded Talamdorians into slavery. They are the ones who should be put down."

Domlok's face was turning red and his voice was getting louder and angrier as he tried to elicit a response from Jacob. People were beginning to look their way.

"Softly, Lord Domlok," Jacob said. "People can hear you."

Domlok's mouth snapped shut. Then he leaned forward across the table and said, "You seem to have His Holiness's ear, although I cannot discover why. You must persuade him to abandon this campaign, recall the troops."

What to do? What to say? Jacob fought to keep his face impassive. Then the right words came to him.

"My Lord Domlok, the Prophet has told me that the invasion of Veylindré is at the command of Holy Talamu. Would you go against Her wishes?"

The Talamdorian sat back, disappointment etched all over his face. "Then you refuse to help us? You will not use your influence to aid us?"

"Us, my Lord?"

Domlok stood, slammed the chair back into the table. "I will not forget this, young man," he said. "The day you lose the Prophet's favour – and I will find a way to make that happen – I will be waiting for you."

Great. Now he had made another enemy.

The vanguard of the army reached the head of the pass without incident. The rest of it was strung out in a long line stretching miles back to the base of the pass. Portak could sense the tension in the troops as they prepared to engage the enemy for the first time. But they had been trained well and it did not show on their faces. The only tell was the constant checking of equipment. They ate their noonday meal as they marched because Kreldik aimed to have the crossing of the mountains behind them by the time dusk fell.

A further hour passed. Then without warning, the enemy was upon them. Arrows fell amongst the leading men and Portak glimpsed shadowy figures above them. The Veylindréans had set their ambush well – the vanguard was in a narrow place with no room to spread out and there were archers above them.

Kreldik was shouting orders and most of the soldiers lifted their shields above their heads and started to run. Others began to climb the steep sides of the path to take the fight to the enemy.

Portak had his hands full keeping his horse from bolting. There was nowhere to bolt to. Was this where he was going to meet his end? Surely not.

And he was right. The Veylindréans seemed to be unprepared for the ferocity of the Talamdorian counterattack. He was proud of them. Even at a disadvantage, they fought fiercely and more and more Veylindréans fell to their thirsty swords.

Forty minutes later, it was all over. The last Veylindréans withdrew and a roar of victory came from many Talamdorian throats.

Portak was exultant. They had won their first skirmish with comparatively little loss of life. His master would be pleased. He took out his Bloodstone and a vial of blood and sent his report.

Chapter 23

Ylonya stood stock still. Ellyn was dead. All that lovely innocence, all that life-affirming joy, gone. Wasted. Why hadn't she stayed near them to protect them? She bowed her head, struggling to contain her feelings of grief and guilt.

The quest was in ruins. Aidren continued to keen, oblivious of all else. And what was wrong with Shaunan?

"Abigail. What has happened?" Ylonya asked.

"She – she took an arrow meant for me," Abigail said, her voice low, desolate, her face streaked with tears. "I – I was tending Shaunan, with my back to the fighting. She died to save me."

"You must not blame yourself," Ylonya said, feeling compassion for the girl. "What is wrong with Shaunan?"

"I think it is her heart. We need to get her somewhere safe, so she can rest. I've done my best, but I need to speak with Valwyn, find out what to do."

"Valwyn?" Ylonya had to think for a moment. "Oh, the High Waymage at Ranusheim. But how?"

"When we were there, they found that I could speak over distance, but I'm not sure I can reach that far."

Ylonya could perceive the girl's confusion, knew she had to do something to bolster her sense of herself. "We have horses," she said. "Can the Waymage ride, do you think?"

"Yes, I think so, so long as one of us is close to watch over her."

Ylonya swung round to speak with Tremond and Ednor, who were standing behind her, spattered with mud and other people's blood, as shocked as she was by this aspect of sudden and unexpected death.

"I've tied their horses up back down there. Go and fetch them. Then we can decide what to do next."

The two men headed back down the hill.

"Abigail," Ylonya said. "Tell me what I can do to help."

Abigail met her gaze. "Can you speak to Aidren? I don't know what to do, what to say… "

Ylonya squared her shoulders. "I'll do my best."

Tremond was stunned by the loss of Ellyn. Over the seisdags they had travelled together, he had come to admire her fierce desire to protect the people she loved. It chimed well with his own passion to protect and serve. And if Marlees had lived, she would have been just about Ellyn's age.

Tears stung his eyes. He had not thought of Marlees for some time.

Ednor was looking at him, a question in his eyes. Tremond dashed his hand across his eyes, trying to regain his customary dispassion.

"What is wrong, my friend?" Ednor asked.

"It's just – if my daughter had lived, she would have been around Ellyn's age. It hits home."

Ednor clasped his arm. "I'm sorry," he said, "I didn't know."

"Very few people do. She and her mother were taken from me ten years ago, when a devastating illness swept across Garûnalond. It was brought by the Havimi," and Tremond had to fight to control the wave of hatred that was sweeping over him. "Our healers did their best, but many died."

"I'm so sorry," Ednor repeated.

"It is ancient history now," Tremond said. "But sometimes, something happens which brings it all back. She was such a shining girl, so full of life."

"Ellyn? Yes, she was. I don't know how badly this will affect Aidren."

Aidren. Yes. The young man would be devastated.

"You're right," Tremond said, pulling himself together. "Let's go and find those horses. The others will need us."

Aidren cradled his dead love in his arms. He had lost her. He had lost her. His little love.

Gradually, he became conscious that someone was speaking to him. Ylonya.

"Aidren. I am so very sorry. She was a wonderful girl."

"And now she's dead," he said, hunching over her body. "Leave me alone."

"The Waymage is sick. We need to find a place of shelter for her."

"Then go and find it."

A small part of his mind knew he was being unfair to Ylonya, but he had no room for anything but his grief at losing Ellyn.

"Aidren, we must leave this place. We need to find a village, somewhere to care for Shaunan, somewhere to…" and here Ylonya's voice broke, "… to bury Ellyn."

Automatically, his arms tightened around Ellyn. How could he consign her to a foreign grave? It would mean leaving her behind.

"I can't…" he said.

"You must," she said and the words fell like a hammer to his heart. "I'm so sorry. But we need you with us. The success of the quest may depend on it."

"What do I care about quests?" The tears were choking him. "If we hadn't found Abigail and Jacob in the woods near Nordvein, Ellyn would still be alive."

Ylonya reached out, touched his shoulder. "I know. But we need to go now, or Ellyn's sacrifice would have been in vain."

He froze. How could she talk about Ellyn in that way? But something in her words reached him, reminded him that he was a Warrior of Dagâra.

"All right. I'll come."

"What are we going to do about the bodies of the Fenlanders?" Ednor said, as he and Tremond led the horses back towards the others. "We can't just leave them lying in plain sight."

"I agree. But we have no tools to bury them."

"Then we'll have to hide them somewhere."

Ednor cast his eyes over the landscape around them, damp and uninviting. There were no convenient outcrops of stone, which they could have used to build a cairn. And in any case, he did not wish to do his enemies that much honour. "Look," he said, pointing to a small copse of trees in the middle distance, "we could leave them in there."

"Good idea," Tremond nodded. "They will be found eventually, but we can hope that we will be long gone by then."

The two men tied the horses to a nearby tree and went to speak to Ylonya. She was kneeling beside Aidren, but when she heard them coming she rose to her feet, a finger on her lips and walked to meet them.

"What news?" she asked.

"We have brought the four uninjured horses back with us," Tremond said in a low voice, "but there are six of us. So we'll have to stick to a walking pace. How is Aidren?"

"Grief stricken," Ylonya said, "but I think I've managed to persuade him to bring her to the nearest village, for burial."

"And the Waymage?" Ednor put in. "How is she?"

"Abigail says it is her heart. We need to find shelter for her and someone with healing skills."

"Do you know this part of Yrusian?" Ednor asked.

Ylonya gave him a faint smile. "I do," she said. "There is a village a few miles west of here. I was planning to stop there tonight."

"That is good news," Ednor said. He was beginning to respect this Yrusian woman.

"You two had better dispose of the bodies somehow," Ylonya said, "and I'll get the others ready for departure. It's getting late."

"We thought to hide them there," Ednor said, pointing to the stand of trees.

"Good idea."

So he and Tremond walked back down the hill to the bodies of their slain enemies. One by one, they carried them to the shelter of the trees, hid them in the undergrowth and left them.

The light was beginning to fade as they set off and a fine but persistent rain was falling, adding to the general misery. Ylonya led the way on one of the horses and Aidren followed her on another, Ellyn's slight body cradled in his arms. Abigail could sense his overwhelming grief – but how to deal with it? She shared it herself.

She and Shaunan were on the two remaining horses. Ednor was walking on the other side of the Waymage, leading her horse, his hand on the hilt of his sword. Which left Tremond, who brought up the rear, leading the mule.

Abigail prayed there would be a competent healer in the village they were heading for. In spite of her new powers, she had not been trained except through watching Shaunan and now it was Shaunan who needed healing.

It was all so awful. Shaunan's collapse had been bad enough, but Ellyn's death and Aidren's distress were too much. She had become used to relying on Shaunan's gentle wisdom to deal with any problems. Now her mentor had withdrawn into herself, oblivious to the rain, oblivious to everything, it seemed. Abigail couldn't tell whether she was concentrating on staying on the horse or in a stupor of grief. Perhaps both. Shaunan had closed the doors of her mind and Abigail could not reach her. Which hurt. Although she was sure Shaunan wasn't doing it on purpose.

It was nearly dark by the time they reached the small village of Virunon – a score of wattle and daub houses, a stone built inn and a simple temple, all clustered around a Waystone. Abigail was relieved to see the Waystone – she had missed them in the Fenland.

Ylonya dismounted in front of the temple, strode up and banged on the door.

"Open up! We need a healer!"

The door was opened by a middle-aged, dark haired man wearing the ochre trousers and tunic of a Waymage. Thank goodness! Now, if only he was a healer too…

Ylonya held her right hand ahead and open, in the traditional gesture of friendship.

The man returned the gesture and said in a deep, firm voice, "I am Waymage Tabor. Who needs healing?"

"Look after Shaunan," Abigail said to Ednor.

She slipped off her horse and walked towards the Waymage, her hand outstretched.

"Waymage Tabor, I am Abigail, initiate of Waymage Shaunan of Nordvein." She pointed back towards Shaunan, who was sitting slumped on her horse. "She collapsed earlier today. Are you a healer?"

"Welcome, Abigail. Yes, I am. Bring her within."

We are also in sore need of your hospitality and aid, she added in silence. *We have lost one of our own and are in grief for her.*

That is understood. We will speak of this later.

Then he called over his shoulder, "Yesta! We have guests. Show them to the inn."

"Our thanks, Waymage Tabor," Ylonya said. "We ask a further boon – to lay our friend to rest within the temple's graveyard."

She nodded her head in the direction of Aidren, still carrying Ellyn in his arms.

Tabor's eyes widened. "I am sorry for your loss," he said. Then to Aidren, "Bring her in to the temple, young man, and lay her in front of Néarta's altar."

Abigail walked over to Aidren, put her hand on his knee. "Come, Aidren. Let us bring Ellyn in."

He met her gaze and she winced at the deep misery in his eyes. "How can I leave her here?" he said.

"Bring her within," Abigail repeated. "We will do the right thing by her tomorrow."

Ednor strode forward. "Give her to me, Aidren," he said, a surprising gentleness in his voice, "while you dismount. Then we will take her in together."

Abigail felt something inside Aidren break. Numbly, he passed Ellyn's body to Ednor and dismounted. His grief nearly brought her to her knees in shared empathy.

She had never witnessed a Veylindréan funeral, had no idea what was involved. But she hoped it would give Aidren some peace.

Ylonya stood with Tremond and Yesta, waiting for Ednor and Aidren to reappear. Abigail and Shaunan had disappeared into the temple with the Waymage. Ylonya hoped and prayed he would be able to heal Shaunan.

Aidren walked out slowly, propelled by Ednor's hand on his shoulder. He seemed to be in a daze.

"Come," Yesta said, "I will lead you to the inn."

Numbly, Ylonya mounted up and followed her and felt the others falling in behind, Tremond and Ednor now astride the other two horses, Tremond still leading the mule. Yesta led them down the village's only street to a low stone building, with the sign of a bear waving in the night breeze.

"Wait here," she said. "I will tell Dakin you are here."

She went inside and returned with a short, jolly-looking man, who said, "Good evening, masters and mistress! You'll be wanting beds for the night, and dinner?"

"Yes, please, Master Dakin," Ylonya said. "And stabling for the horses."

"Very good, very good. This way, please."

He led them round the back of the inn into a stable yard and they dismounted gratefully.

"You'll not mind tending them yourselves, I hope?" Dakin said. "Our stableboy has run off to fight in the war."

"The war?" Ednor said, urgent for information.

"Where have you been that you haven't heard?" Dakin asked, pleased to be the one to share the news. "Word came from Ruslen, from Lord Vyncan and Lady Réata, must be oh, three seisdags ago, telling that we were to send anyone we could spare, to fight against the Talamdorians. We have lost ten men from the village, and a couple of older boys, including my stable lad."

"We have been in the Fenland," Ylonya said.

"The Fenland?" Dakin said. "What business did you have there?"

"Private business," Ylonya said.

"Very well, Mistress, no offence. I'll see you within later."

And he left them to untack their horses and the mule, rub them down and make sure each had a hay net and fresh water. Then they headed for the rear door of the inn, standing invitingly open.

It seemed no time at all before they were sitting around a table with a mug of beer apiece, and a fine meal laid out in front of them – a joint of lamb, mashed potatoes, carrots and a rich gravy.

But Ylonya had little appetite and noticed that the others too were eating slowly, picking at their food. And there was none of the usual conversation – each of them was lost in their own thoughts.

Then she noticed Aidren had not even started to eat. "Aren't you hungry?" she asked.

He looked up. "No. I don't deserve it."

"Of course you do," Ylonya said. "Come, Aidren, eat. You'll need your strength for the rest of the journey."

"No, I don't," he snapped. "First Jacob, now Ellyn. I've failed them both. I wish we had never set out on this journey, never found Abigail and Jacob in the forest. Then Ellyn would be back home in Nordvein, whole and well."

Ylonya's heart sank. She was the only one here who could understand how he was feeling. Tremond and Ednor had not been around when they had lost Jacob. She shared his feelings of guilt. But he mustn't know. Instinctively she knew he needed something else from her.

Aidren continued, "She forgave me for losing Jacob – who will forgive me now?"

"Ellyn's death was not your fault, Aidren. She was a girl who loved life and lived it to the full. And she loved Abigail and Shaunan, which was why she didn't hesitate when the chance came to protect them."

She paused, then continued gently, "I loved her too. And I know she would not want you to spend the rest of your life grieving. She would want you to carry on, to see the quest done."

Aidren pushed aside his plate, folded his arms on the table and rested his forehead on them. His voice was muffled. "All right. I'll try."

Ylonya patted his shoulder. She wished Shaunan were here. Or even Abigail. Both of them knew Aidren better than she did.

Abigail guided Shaunan as Tabor led them into a room behind the temple, which Abigail guessed were his private quarters. A wooden bed with a bright patchwork quilt stood in one corner and most of the rest of the space was filled with a large table, piled high with books, more books lining one wall. The other walls also had shelves, filled with herbs and potions. A warm fire was burning in the hearth. Thank God he was a healer. She caught herself. No, thank Ranu.

Shaunan went where she was led, seemingly indifferent.

"Abigail, plump up the pillows, so that they support her," Tabor said, nodding to the bed. Abigail rushed to do what he asked.

"Lie down here, Waymage Shaunan," Tabor said, "so that I may examine you."

"Thank you, Waymage Tabor," Abigail said. "I'm so worried about her. I've only been an initiate for a few seisdags and all the healing I've done has been under Shaunan's direction."

"What are her symptoms?"

"I think it is her heart. She had pains in her chest and couldn't breathe. I did what I could, but I know it's not enough. Then Ellyn died..."

Abigail's voice broke. She couldn't bear it. Her darling Ellyn, gone. Tears began to roll down her face and she had to bite her lip before she could continue. "Ellyn – Ellyn was Shaunan's niece."

Comprehension dawned in Tabor's face. "I see. I will do what I can for her."

He turned to Shaunan. "How do you feel, Waymage?"

"So tired," Shaunan said in a husky voice. "Why are the young taken, and the old linger, grieving?"

"I am sorry for your loss, my friend," Tabor said gently. "It is up to us who remain to make meaningful the sacrifices of the dead. Now," and his voice became brisk and practical, "where do you feel pain?"

Shaunan placed her hand on her chest. "Here, she whispered, "and it is so hard to breathe."

Tabor examined her, using hands, eyes and nose. Then he turned to Abigail.

"On the third shelf down, over there," he nodded towards the wall filled with medicines, "you will find a purple bag. Bring it here."

Abigail did as she was told. Tabor unknotted the bag and she saw the crushed leaves of a herb. "What is that?"

"It is dried foxglove," he said. "a sovereign remedy for problems of the heart. I will prepare a potion for her. It is strong medicine and should be taken sparingly. When she is feeling a little better, I will prepare another potion for her to take, to prevent a reoccurrence."

Abigail watched, fascinated, as Tabor put the leaves to steep in a small pot over the fire.

"Keep an eye on it for me," he told her. "When the mixture begins to bubble, take it off the fire, using this," and he passed her a thick leather glove, "then set it to cool."

She moved forward to the hearth, glad to have something to do.

Then Tabor took out his Goldstone and moved back to Shaunan, examining her once more, muttering under his breath, while Abigail divided her attention between him and the water in the pot. When it was bubbling, she took it off the fire and set it on the hearth, as she had been told.

Tabor raised Shaunan gently to a sitting position. A few minutes later, he fetched the cooled potion from the hearth and decanted it into a wooden bowl. He measured out a tablespoonful and put it to her lips.

Shaunan moved her head aside, trying to avoid taking it.

"Waymage," Tabor said, "you must drink this. It will ease the pain in your chest."

Tears began to trickle down Shaunan's cheeks. "My little Ellyn," she said.

But she took the potion. Tabor eased her back down onto the bed and motioned to Abigail to leave.

"She will sleep now. Let us see what the morrow brings. Remember to bring Ellyn's pack with you, when you return."

"Why?" Abigail asked in surprise.

"Because we will need it to prepare her for burial. I must go to her now, before the stiffness that follows death makes it impossible to lay her out in a seemly manner."

After leaving the temple, Abigail returned to the inn. It was a luxury to rest in a proper bed, but the absence of Ellyn in the next bed kept her awake.

She joined the others the next morning, feeling bone tired. They were sitting round a circular table in the inn's taproom, picking desultorily at the bread, cheese and cold meats Dakin had provided for their breakfast. A heavy silence lay over them.

"Ellyn's funeral will be today," she said, taking the only vacant seat.

"Surely the temple will be in use for Ranusdag worship," Tremond said.

"Yes, but the funeral will be after that. It will give Shaunan another few hours to rest and recover. I must go to Tabor now, to check on Shaunan and to help him prepare" she gritted her teeth to stop her voice from breaking, "– prepare Ellyn's body for burial."

"I will come with you." Aidren said.

Abigail looked to Ylonya, not sure what to say. She had no idea whether it was usual for friends and family to take part. Not for the first time, she wished Shaunan was here.

"Better not," Ylonya said. "You know it is the job of a Waymage to do this."

"Please," Aidren said.

Abigail looked at the deep misery in his eyes and could not refuse him.

"Come, then," she said. "But then you must leave us to do what we must. Ylonya, will you come with us to bring Aidren back?"

"Of course."

The three of them walked the short distance to the Temple in silence. Abigail knocked gently on the door, which was opened straight away by Tabor.

"I have brought Aidren to say farewell to Ellyn," she said. *He needs to do this.*

Tabor nodded. "Very well. Come with me."

He led them through to a small, bare room behind the temple. Ellyn's body was lying on a stone slab, covered up to the neck with a fine linen sheet, her hands crossed over her breast, her eyes closed.

Aidren kissed the top hand, then her forehead. "I will never forget you," he said. "I loved you like a flower loves the sun. My life will be empty without you. Be at peace, my dear love."

After a few moments of respectful silence, Ylonya touched his arm. "Come, Aidren. We must leave now."

Abigail watched them both go, wishing she could go with them. What did she know about Veylindréan burial customs? Then she squared her shoulders. With Shaunan out of action, she must do what had to be done.

"Have you prepared a body for burial before?" Tabor said, as though he could sense her hesitation.

"No, I'm a fairly new initiate."

Tabor's eyebrows shot up, but he said only, "First, we must wash her body – I removed her clothes last night – and dress her in her best clothes. You have brought her pack?"

"Yes, it's here."

The door opened silently and Shaunan walked in, looking exhausted. Her face was still an unhealthy colour – an undertone of grey beneath the brown.

"Shaunan! How are you?" Abigail said.

"Better than I was, physically, but in other ways..." She looked sadly at Ellyn. Abigail could sense the depths of her grief.

"You should be resting, Waymage," Tabor said.

"No," Shaunan said, "I must be here for Ellyn."

"Very well," Tabor said. "Sit down and watch. Let your initiate and I do what is needful."

Shaunan bowed her head in acquiescence.

Abigail shot her an anxious look. *I had hoped to spare you this.*

Thank you, but I must be here.

Together, Abigail and Tabor washed Ellyn reverently, then, with some difficulty, dressed her stiff body in her best clothes, which Abigail found in her pack. She worked with tears standing in her eyes – the last time she had seen Ellyn in these clothes had been at Ranusheim, on the first evening of Lèniastide.

"What else do we have to do?" Abigail asked.

"Now we wind a shroud of linen around her," Tabor said. "Then you must choose the tools she will be buried with, to aid her in the afterlife."

Abigail once more delved into Ellyn's pack to find her leather-working tools – a set of awls and a pack containing needles of various sizes. The last object these tools had made had been her own healer's bag, which would be doubly precious now. She could hardly bear to think about it. Then she slipped the silver ring Ylonya had given Ellyn from her friend's finger and put it in her pocket to give to Aidren later.

"These," she said. "Ellyn was a cordwainer."

"Thank you," Tabor said. "I will produce them at the proper time. Now, you need to return to the inn and rest. The funeral will be at seventh hour."

Abigail did a swift calculation in her head. One o'clock.

"And you, Waymage," Tabor said, "must return to your bed, else you will not be fit to attend the funeral."

Once more, Shaunan bowed her head. Then she walked over to Abigail and stood in front of her, her arms by her side, her head bowed. Abigail gave her a gentle hug and was shocked by how frail the woman felt in her arms.

"Thank you." Shaunan said.

"I loved her too."

Half an hour before seventh hour, the reduced company left the inn for the temple. Abigail walked by Aidren, hoping to give him some comfort by the simple fact of her presence. But he seemed unconscious of anything, anyone.

The five of them found Tabor at the front of the temple, waiting for them, with Shaunan by his side. Her colour was a little better than it had been.

"Come," Tabor said, and led them round to the back of the temple, where a small graveyard lay. A new hole had already been dug and Ellyn's shrouded body was on a trestle table beside it, with wide strips of linen around it. A basket of her leather-working tools stood beside it.

When they were all in position, Abigail between Shaunan and Aidren, Tabor began to speak.

"Friends, we meet here today to mourn the death, and pay tribute to the life of Ellyn. Death draws us together, in the deep-felt emotions of the heart. It reminds us of the essential community of humankind that lies beneath all the ups and downs of our everyday lives.

"We share our sorrows on this occasion. Each of us feels a sense of loss, of separation, of emptiness. How could it be otherwise? There is nothing in human life which brings greater sorrow than the loss of someone we love, whose absence will leave a painful gap in our lives. There is no reason why we should conceal our sadness and grief. It is the purest, and most natural expression of our common humanity.

"But sadness is not by any means our only emotion at this time. It is sweetened and tempered by our fond memories of Ellyn and by our gratitude for her love and affection, for her warmth and kindness, and for the example which she set us.

"A life well lived is a fit offering to the goddesses, to Mother Ranu and to Néarta. Ellyn lived with honour, loved well, trod gently on the earth. She followed the Way as best she could, creating laughter, joy and meaning in her life."

How had Tabor managed to find out so much about Ellyn? He must have spoken with Shaunan.

"And yet, humankind is diminished by her loss. She was taken too early, her life cut short. We who are left behind weep for her, and she will sail across the ocean of our tears.

"The season of grief is needful for the soul's healing. And so we weep, and so we weep, for all that is lost, for all that we left unsaid, for the beloved dead."

Abigail put her arm around Shaunan, who was shaking with grief, the tears tracking down her face. She too was weeping – would there ever be a day when she did not miss Ellyn – her adventurous spirit, her sense of fun, her innate kindness? She could sense Aidren's vast grief and guilt but had no idea how to comfort him.

Tabor continued, "Blessed Mother Ranu, we are called this day to gather round the darkening flame of sadness and death. We come with confused and confusing feelings, remembrances and regrets, as we look back upon the life of Ellyn, which has now ended.

"Lend us the strength, we pray, to accept and embrace the whole of Ellyn's life and memory, to rediscover the startling light of her in our hearts safely stored, and to allow that light to shine into the dark corners of this funeral day.

"As we call her to mind and speak her memory to one another, may the words, the feelings, and the remembrances we share this day strengthen us each in our grief, and all in our support one for another."

Tabor fell silent. Abigail's hot tears fell faster as she remembered all the times Ellyn had been a staunch friend to her. She did not know how she would be able to continue without her.

Tabor began to speak once more, "Now we have come to the moment in our ceremony when we must say goodbye to the body of Ellyn. We commit her body to the earth which sustained and nourished her during her brief time among us, and which regenerates all life. She will return to Mother Ranu and find rest and peace.

"In committing the body of Ellyn to this special ground we do so with deep reverence for that body was the temple during life of a unique and much loved personality. Here under the wide open sky Ellyn will now rest in peace."

Then Aidren lifted her leather-working tools out of the basket and placed them gently on top of her, tears pouring down his face. Tremond and Ednor stepped forward to each side of the trestle. They lifted Ellyn's body by the strips of linen and gently lowered her into her grave.

As they did so, Tabor said, "Go now from us, Ellyn. Go with a wealth of love and affection, as you leave us with such wealth of remembrance. Go with this tribute of thanks and pride that we were those who knew your days. Go in the deep peace of the love of these gathered here to take their leave of you."

Then he spoke to the rest of them, his hands raised in blessing, "May the love and friendship that you felt for Ellyn, be among you now and go with you into your onward lives, giving comfort in these sorrows, delight in all the joys still to come, drawing life and vitality from the Way which sustains us all. May peace be with you, now and always. May it be so."

It was over. It was done. Somehow they would have to carry on without her, leave her behind them. Abigail scrubbed at her sore eyes with her fists and met Shaunan's gaze.

Help Aidren. Shaunan said in the silence. He is going to need your friendship in the seisdags to come.

I'll do my best.

Chapter 24

"D'you want to help groom the horses?" Ednor asked.

Aidren shrugged. He didn't know what he wanted. He was drowning in a sea of grief and loss. Each night, he dreamed of Ellyn – of her smile, her warmth, her joy in life – and each morning he experienced his loss anew.

"Come on," Ednor said. "It can't be doing you any good, sitting up here all alone."

"I suppose."

He followed Ednor down to the stables, patted his gelding, twisted some straw into a loop and started to groom him. The quiet rhythm of the work, the familiar scent of the horses helped, at least a little. In silence, he listened to the conversation between Ednor and Tremond.

"I can't wait to reach Chorich Castle," Ednor said.

"Because Shaunan will be able to get proper treatment?" Tremond said.

"Well, yes, but mainly because we'll be able to get some up to date news about how the war is going."

"I hope the warning we sent arrived in time," Tremond said soberly. "We are not a warlike people."

"Speak for yourself. I wish I could be with our armies."

"We need you with us, if we are to have any chance of reaching Talamunem City we will need your bright sword and fighting skills."

"I know, but all the same, I wish…"

Aidren was with Ednor. Tremond was such an old woman sometimes. The only thing keeping him going now was the thought of revenging himself on the Prophet, who was behind the abduction of Jacob, the death of Ellyn. If he could only strike a blow for them, without risking losing anyone else he cared about. One thing was certain – he was not going to allow Shaunan or Abigail to be in danger. Whatever happened, he would protect them – with his life if necessary.

In the meantime, he went where he was told, did what he was told. There was no room in his mind for curiosity, no room for hope. Only grief and guilt and the fierce heat of his desire for revenge. Now he could understand how Abigail must have felt when Jacob was abducted. But at least she had some hope of seeing him again, of rescuing him from the Prophet's clutches.

He, on the other hand, could not hope. His little love, his Ellyn, was dead and buried. He would never see her, never hear her laugh, never hold her, ever again. He could not bear it.

Food and drink held little attraction, talking even less. A small part of his mind appreciated Abigail's and Ylonya's attempts to offer comfort, but mostly he was simply angry. His only solace was to sit by Ellyn's grave and now they were trying to persuade him to leave her behind. He was only continuing with the quest because of his strong sense of duty. He no longer cared whether he lived or died.

He had no-one to live for.

Abigail was sitting in a small private room in Virunon's inn, near the open hearth in which a fire was blazing merrily, its light reflected in the brass fire-irons. Yet she could take little comfort from it. Her mind was in turmoil, her chest aching with grief. The quest was in ruins. She did not see how they could continue, with Shaunan sick and Ellyn… gone. One by one, all the people she loved were being taken from her. How much more could she bear?

Ylonya's voice broke into her thoughts, "How is Shaunan?"

"We need to stay here for at least another three days," Abigail said. "She has to have the chance to regain her strength."

Tremond and Ednor were out trying to find two more horses for them to ride. With the four they already had, the mule was now superfluous, and they had sent him back to Lem, as Ylonya had promised.

"I suppose you're right," Ylonya said, holding out her hands to the flickering flames. The firelight made the gemstones in her rings flash like tiny stars. "But I don't like it. The longer we stay in one place, the greater the chance of Gilmak's agents finding us."

Gilmak. The name filled Abigail with a complex mixture of anger, sorrow and dread. Anger and sorrow about his hand in the untimely death of Ellyn, dread that they would lose more people, before this quest was over. In her worst nightmares, she had not foreseen the death of her best friend.

It felt so wrong to be continuing the quest for the Master Bloodstone, when Ellyn would be left here, no longer a part of the company. She and Aidren had found Abigail and Jacob wandering in the forest south-east of Nordvein. The two of them had been Abigail's introduction to Veylindré, to Veylindréans. Tears filled her eyes as she remembered Ellyn's infectious smile, her bubbly enthusiasm, her warm and generous friendship.

But Abigail knew Ylonya was right. They had to continue, to find the Prophet, to wrest the Master Bloodstone from him and, most important to her, to rescue Jacob. She remembered what Tabor had said the previous evening, "It is up to us who remain to make meaningful the sacrifices of the dead." If they gave up now, Ellyn would have forfeited her life for nothing.

She had died to protect Abigail and Shaunan. That sacrifice had to have meaning.

"How is Aidren?" Ylonya asked, breaking into her thoughts.

"I don't know," Abigail sighed. "I've hardly seen him since the funeral. I think he is by – by Ellyn. I've no idea how to bring him back to us, or even if I should. You and I feel badly enough about losing her, goodness knows how he is feeling."

"He should be taken away from here," Ylonya said, "to give him a chance to come to terms with it."

"But if he is unwilling?"

"Hmm," Ylonya said, "I don't know. But bluntly, we need him with us. Do you want me to go and find him, let him know we'll be leaving in three days?"

"Yes, please. But be gentle with him."

"Trust me. I loved her too."

Abigail nodded. "Then I will go to the temple to speak with Shaunan and Tabor. She will listen to him more than she listens to me."

"You should remain here, to rest and recover your strength," Tabor told Shaunan, as he examined her once more, his fingers on the pulse of her wrist.

Shaunan knew his advice was good. But she could not bear to stay behind with only her grief for company, when the rest of them continued with the quest.

"I feel much better than I did, thanks to you," she said. "I will rest for another couple of days, then we must leave."

"What is the urgency?" Tabor asked.

"A charge has been laid upon us," Shaunan said, "by the High Waymages of the Wayzenmoot. I am sorry, Tabor, but I may not reveal its import, even to you."

"I hazard it is something to do with the Bloodstone of Talamu."

Her heart began to beat faster. How had he guessed? Surely no-one in the company would have mentioned it.

"How do you know about that?"

"You forget how near we are to the border of Talamdor, here. Many rumours come to my ears."

Shaunan took a deep breath. "I am sorry, Tabor. I cannot tell you more."

"Of course," Tabor said, nodding his head in acquiescence. "Then I must not stand in your way."

"Thank you, my friend. When Ednor and Tremond have found us a couple more horses, we will leave on the third day from today."

"Only if I am sure you are well enough, and I've had a chance to distil enough potion for you to take with you."

Shaunan nodded. "I am grateful," she said, touching his hand, "for that and for your many kindnesses."

In the end, they did not leave Virunon until the Dagârsdag morning, four days after Ellyn's funeral. Abigail was glad they had stayed the extra day – Shaunan was looking so much better for the rest, and it had given Tabor the time to brew sufficient potion to prevent a reoccurrence of her malady. But Abigail would be keeping a sharp eye on her, just the same.

They ate a final hasty breakfast of bacon, eggs and mushrooms, paid Dakin for his hospitality, packed their belongings onto the six horses. Then waited in the inn's yard for Shaunan, who was still at the temple.

The air was fresh and invigorating and it promised to be a fine day. Abigail was losing track of her seisdags, but it felt like late March. At any rate, the flowers she associated with early Spring – primroses, violets and celandines – were pushing their way up in between the cracks between the paving in the yard. Dakin even had a tub of daffodils, their bright colour lifting her mood. Even so, her grief for Ellyn lay like a heavy weight in her chest.

She was glad to be on the move once more. And relieved that the horse Tremond and Ednor had found for her seemed to be fairly placid. She was still not a confident rider.

Even Aidren was there, although Ylonya had to pry him away from Ellyn's grave. He seemed to have aged five years in a few days. Grief had chiselled deep, downward lines on his face. Abigail grieved to see them. She must speak to Shaunan about what to do about him. Then she remembered – maybe there was something she could do, now, while they were waiting. She slipped down off her horse and walked over to him.

"Aidren," she said, "I have something for you."

He looked down, met her gaze without interest.

"Here," she said, holding out her hand. "Ellyn's ring, which Ylonya bought her in Céardochis. I thought you might like to wear it in her memory."

Tears filled Aidren's eyes. "Thank you," he said, taking it and putting it on the little finger of his left hand. "I will treasure it."

Abigail returned to her horse, satisfied.

Shaunan and Tabor appeared at the door of the temple. Shaunan was looking almost like her old self, except for the deep sadness in her eyes. The loss of Ellyn was affecting them all. Maybe she'd better not share her worries about Aidren.

"Hold my horse, Ylonya," Abigail said. "I must pay my respects to Waymage Tabor before we leave."

She went to meet the two Waymages, her hand outstretched.

"Thank you, Waymage Tabor, for all your help," she said. "I don't know how we would have managed without you."

"You are welcome, Abigail," he said. Then, raising his voice so they could all hear, "May the Way guard and guide you all."

Shaunan clasped Tabor's hands between hers. "Thank you, my friend. We are in your debt."

"You are welcome," he said. "Maybe one day, when all this is over, you will return here and tell me the whole story."

"I hope so," Shaunan said. "May the Way be with you also."

Then she led the way back to the waiting horses, mounted up and gestured to Ylonya to lead on.

Are you really all right? Abigail asked her mentor.

Yes. I just need to remember that I am no longer as young as I was and husband my strength.

I'll see that you do.

The fierceness in her tone made Shaunan smile, a sad smile, but a smile, nevertheless. "I will be sensible, I promise."

It was a good forty miles from Virunon to Chorich Castle. They were riding through what Abigail would have called moorland back at home, over peaty ground with many deep brown pools, so they had to be careful to stay on the track. It took them three days because it soon became clear, first to her, then to them all, that Shaunan was not as well as she had pretended. At the end of the first day's ride, through the wild scenery of this corner of Yrusian, she had dismounted unsteadily from her horse in the yard of the lonely croft Ylonya had chosen to stay in, her hand once more clutching her chest.

"Shaunan! Your lips – they're blue!" Abigail said. "Come within."

She put her arm around Shaunan and followed Ylonya to the door. Ylonya produced her Guild token.

The crofter's wife, who had answered the door, nodded at Ylonya, then clucked sympathetically. "Come away in, Waymage. A good night's rest is what you need."

"Take her inside," Abigail told her friend.

Abigail darted back to her horse, rummaged in her pack for the potion bottle Tabor had given her, then rushed back in. She heard Tabor's voice in her mind, *I have made it strong, to last longer. Give her three drops in a glass of water, morning and evening.*

"May I have a glass of water, please?" she asked the woman.

"Of course, Waymage."

"I'm not –" Abigail began, but the woman had already left the room.

"Let it lie," Ylonya said. "She respects your Waymark."

In what seemed like the twinkling of an eye, the woman came back with a jug of water. "We have our own well," she said, "the finest water in this corner of Yrusian."

Abigail tasted it cautiously. It was clean and fresh. Quickly, she added three drops of the potion then held it to Shaunan's lips. She drank it down without protest and after a few minutes, her breathing eased, her skin colour returned to something like its normal dark brown and the bluish colour left her lips.

"I am sorry," Shaunan said. "Just need to rest."

Abigail turned to the woman. "Do you have extra pillows, so she may sleep propped up?"

"I'll find something, Waymage, don't worry. This way."

She led Abigail and Shaunan up a short flight of stairs to a small bedroom, bare and neat, with a single bed and a small rug on the floor. "It's my son's, but he won't be back until late tonight. He can sleep by the fire for once."

Between them, they got Shaunan settled in a semi-recumbent position, her breathing easier.

"Come down when you're ready, Waymage," the woman said.

"Thank you for your kindness," Abigail said.

Once they were alone, Shaunan said, "I am so sorry, Abigail. I have let you all down."

"Nonsense," Abigail said. "It's my fault for not looking after you well enough. When we reach Chorich Castle, I'll ask a Healer to look you over properly. Do you want anything to eat, or had you better just rest?"

A tiny smile curved Shaunan's lips. "A Waymage indeed," she said.

"How is she?" Ylonya asked in a low voice, when Abigail re-joined them in the farmhouse kitchen, warm and welcoming on this chilly evening. The crofter's wife was bustling around in the background, preparing the evening meal, and appetising scents were beginning to fill the room.

"Her breathing has eased, and she is resting quietly."

"That is good to hear," Tremond said. "Will she be fit to travel tomorrow?"

"I – I'm not sure," Abigail said. "If she sleeps well and wakes up refreshed, then yes. Otherwise…"

"We cannot stay here," Ednor put in. "The Waymage would be better off at Chorich Castle, where there is an experienced Healer."

Abigail winced a little at that. It was clear that Ednor had doubts about her healing skills. But she could not blame him – so did she. The sooner they reached the castle, the better.

"I agree," she said. "How far away are we now, Ylonya?"

"About twenty five miles, I guess," Ylonya said. "But we will have to take it slowly, for Shaunan's sake."

"So another two days on the road?" Tremond said.

Ylonya nodded. "I think so. And when we reach Chorich Castle, we'll get a Healer to examine her. It might be," she said, looking at Abigail, "that we should leave her there."

Abigail caught her breath. How would she cope without Shaunan's gentle guidance? But she saw the sense in what Ylonya said. In her present condition, the Waymage was not fit to travel, let alone to fight.

"Let's see how she is when we reach there," she said.

Ylonya was relieved when the strong towers and battlements of Chorich Castle came into view over a rise in the land. A couple more miles and they would be safe. She and Abigail were leading the way, with Shaunan just behind them, lost in her thoughts. Hopefully the Waymage would see the wisdom in staying behind.

"You must persuade Shaunan to stay at the Castle," she told Abigail quietly. "She is not fit enough for the onward journey. We may need to run or fight – we cannot risk her collapsing at the wrong moment. And I do not know Talamdor but, from what I have heard, the land is bleak and inhospitable."

Abigail frowned. Ylonya could sense how reluctant the girl was to take this advice.

"I know your words are wise," Abigail said. "But can we make it without her?"

"I don't see why not," Ylonya said. "Four of the remaining five of us are able to fight. And your own powers have not yet been tested. We will protect you."

"How did it all go so wrong?" Abigail sighed. "First Ellyn, now Shaunan. At this rate none of us will reach Talamunem City."

It was Ylonya's turn to frown. "Keep that to yourself," she said sharply. "Don't you trust me to get us there?"

"Of course I do," Abigail said, her lips quivering, "and I know you're right. But it's going to be so hard, leaving Shaunan behind."

"This quest is more important than any one of us," Ylonya said. "If we give up now, Ellyn's sacrifice will have been for nothing."

Abigail flushed. "I know," she said softly. "I'll do my best to persuade the Waymage."

"You have the best chance of all of us."

Abigail's chin came up. Ylonya could sense her new resolution. Good. She would need it all in the days to come.

Soon the castle was looming ever larger in their forward vision, its grey, granite walls dominating the horizon. They were nearly there. Abigail was relieved – she hoped there would be a skilled Healer there.

The sun was beginning to set by the time they reached the drawbridge, which was down. Their horses' hooves clattered on it and she saw a sally port in the sturdy gates open.

Three men in guard's uniforms with the Yrusian sigil on their breasts came out. The leading one strode forward, his hand held out, signalling them to stop. His other hand held a drawn sword.

"Name yourselves and your purpose."

Ylonya dismounted and gave her horse's reins to Abigail. She walked forward a few paces, then stopped a short distance away from the guard.

"My name is Ylonya," she said. "I am daughter of Guildmaster Brickon and Guildmistress Margera of the Guild of Traders. We are here on important business."

The guard's eyes widened in recognition of the names. "Mistress Ylonya!" he said. "You are welcome here. But," he added, "I still need to test your Waymark."

"Of course." Ylonya walked forward, allowed her Waymark to be tested, then tested his in return.

"Will you vouch for these others?" the guard asked.

"I will," Ylonya said.

Then over her shoulder, she said, "Dismount, then come forward."

The five of them did as they were told and Ylonya introduced them one at a time.

"These are Ednor of Néartania, Tremond of Garûnalond, Waymage Shaunan of Nordvein in Dagâran, Aidren, also of Nordvein, and Abigail, initiate of the Waymage."

Each of them suffered their Waymarks to be tested.

Then Abigail said, "Do you have a Healer? The Waymage is ill."

"Yes, Waymage," the man said respectfully. "Come."

Then he strode back through the sally port, shouting as he went, "Here are friends. Open the gates!"

To be continued in Volume 3 *The Bloodstone of Talamu*

The Stones of Veylindré – Glossary

Bangles of Control – Bangles made of talamunium, used to control all lower status Talamdorians.

Ceremony of Assignment – Takes place at each of the six Festivals, during which Waymarks are assigned to young people who have completed the Time of Testing.

Dagârastide, Festival of All Souls – Marks the end of the Season of Completion.

Dagârsdag – Fourth day of the Veylindréan seisdag.

Feolin – A loaf baked with meat and bread combined. Used as travelling food.

Garûnastide, Festival of Dedication – Marks the end of the Season of Awakening.

Goldstones – Tools used by Veylindréans to work the magic of the Way.

Golden Stone of Ranu – The master ranusfelsen stone, located in Ranusheim.

Lènia's Bruagan – A herb that can help restore lost memory.

Lènia's Nimbane – A herb which can counteract poison.

Lèniastide, Festival of Music and Storytelling – Marks the end of the Season of Dormancy.

Lethara – A drug used by healers to induce unconsciousness.

Néartastide, Festival of Thanksgiving – Marks the end of the Season of Thanksgiving.

Ranusfelsen – The mineral out of which Goldstones are made, and all Veylindréan temples built. It looks like a pale sandstone, but in the sunlight, hints of gold, green, red, orange, purple, blue and brown show through.

Ranustide, Festival of Wisdom and Lore – Marks the end of the Season of First Fruits.

Season of Awakening – Equivalent to early spring.

Season of Completion – Equivalent to late autumn.

Season of Dormancy – Equivalent to deep winter.

Season of Growth – Equivalent to late spring.

Season of First Fruits – Equivalent to summer.

Season of Thanksgiving – Equivalent to early autumn.

Season / Cycle of Proving – Time spent by a couple waiting to marry, to prove their commitment.

Seisdag – A period of six days, equivalent to our week.

Talamunium – A metal found only in Talamdor. Used as an alloy of silver, to overpower the will of any who wear the bracelet.

Temple of the Six – Seven-sided building which is a place of worship.

Test of Faith – Undertaken by all Talamdorians at the age of 12, to see whether they are worthy of becoming truebloods.

Time of Testing – A time of learning and testing undertaken at puberty by each person in Veylindré, to discern their goddess affiliation.

Truebloods – Talamdorians who have passed the Test of Faith, and are the ruling class of Talamdorian society.

Way of Veylindré – The magical / religious system of Veylindré.

Waymage – Local wise person / priest/ess of the Way. One in each community.

Waymarks – A special mark on the forehead of all Veylindréans, which shows their goddess affiliation.

Waystones – Pillars of ranusfelsen – one in each community. They help the inhabitants to access the power of the Way.

Wayzenmoot, The – Council of the Way. Located in Ranusheim.

Yrusiastide, Festival of Journeying – Marks the end of the Season of Growth.

The Stones of Veylindré: Characters

Characters from 17th century England:

George Crutwell – Witchfinder. Prophet of the One in Talamdor for 30+ years.

Richard Forster – A friend of Abigail's.

Mercy Paignton – Abigail's best friend.

Squire Petty – The gentry from Abigail's and Jacob's village.

Elder Sanderson – Presbyterian Elder. Pastor Winters' second in command

Matthew Sanderson – Son of Elder Sanderson. Pastor Winters sees him as a prospective husband for Abigail.

Thomas Winters – Presbyterian Pastor. Abigail's father and instigator of pilgrimage to the New World.

Mary Winters – Wife to Thomas, and mother to Abigail, **Isaac, Daniel** and **Faith**.

Captain Wood – Captain of the *Sweet Sarah.*

Characters in Veylindré:

Abigail Winters (Abi) – The heroine, from 17th century England. 17 years old.

Aidren – A young Warrior of Dagâra. Skilled with the sword. From Nordvein. Member of the Company.

Alaine – a weaver, wife of Rodis of Néartania.

Baldis – Agent of the Guild of Intelligencers in Céardochis.

Balmak – Portak's lifelong friend and lover.

Balon – A warrior who led the forces of Veylindré against the Talamdorians in ages past.

Barlan – An innkeeper in a village south of Myndorian.

Bélia, Lady – The ruler of Dagâran. Lives in Luvodican.

Bodan – A member of the Council of Nordvein.

Brann – A member of the Council of Nordvein.

Brickon – Guildmaster of the Hall of Traders. Ylonya's father.

Brunan – A servant at the Temple of Myndorian.

Donan – The former husband of Shaunan, now dead.

Ellyn – A young apprentice cordwainer, from Nordvein. Niece of Shaunan. Member of the Company.

Findoran – Waymage of Myndorian.

Gadaria – Dagâran silversmith, living & trading in Céardochis.

Gildon – Master Warrior of the Hall of the Warriors of Dagâra. Lives in Luvodican.

Gomlak – An agent of the Prophet, killed at the cove.

Grunen – A man of Nordvein.

Haldor – A young man of Luvodican, handfasted at Dagârastide in Luvodican.

Havimi – A race of pirates, living in Havim to the south of Veylindré.

Hedwin – Adept of Ranu, trained by Findoran, sent to Nordvein to cover for Shaunan's absence.

Jacob Wallingford – Abigail's boyfriend, from 17th century England. A talented smith.

Janissan – A young woman of Myndorian, handfasted at Dagârastide in Luvodican.

Jaradol – Messenger from Smithsport, to Lord Lesym and Lady Bélia.

Jordis – Son of Rodis, Néartanian farmer.

Kalen – A smith, living in Luvodican. Old friend of Shaunan's who takes Jacob on as his apprentice.

Kormak – Garûnalonden Watch officer (Portak in disguise).

Lesym, Lord – The ruler of Dagâran. Lives in Luvodican.

Lyma – A member of the Council of Nordvein.

Lymon – A boy at Ceremony of Assignment in Luvodican. From Myndorian.

Mardal – Yrusian trader and agent of the Guild of Intelligencers. Lives in Porusport.

Margera – Guildmistress of the Hall of Traders, and Head of the Guild of Intelligencers. Ylonya's mother.

Marinden – First Waymage of Dagâran. Lives in Luvodican.

Markhan – Master Cordwainer in Luvodican.

Mekin – Son of Mardal, has a withered arm. Encountered in Céardochis.

Meldar – Waymage of Nordvein before Shaunan.

Norin – A stable hand in village south of Myndorian.

Oltan – A guard of the East Gate of Myndorian.

Petan – The husband of Waymage Findoran.

Portak – Agent of the Prophet of the One. Uses the alias Kormak while in Veylindré.

Prophet of the One – The principal antagonist, ruler of Talamdor.

Raimun – Master Cordwainer of Nordvein.

Rewald – Waymage of Talmis.

Rodis – A Néartanian farmer on the road to Talmis, with whom the Company take shelter.

Sanderon – Sword Master at the Hall of Warriors in Luvodican.

Shaunan – Waymage of Nordvein. Abigail's mentor and member of the Company.

Shula – A girl at the Ceremony of Assignment at Luvodican. From Myndorian.

Tamin – Chief Messenger of the Prophet, responsible for sending and receiving messages from agents in the field.

Torlin – Trade Master at Smithsport.

Ylonya – An Yrusian guide and intelligence gatherer. Member of the Company.

The Stones of Veylindré – Places

Avarin – A mining village in northern Talamdor.

Berlysian – A settlement in the Vale of Berlysian, Lènium. Home of the Healer Hall and the Hall of Apothecaries.

Caethniss Castle – A border fort of Talamdor.

Caethwasim – A slave port of Talamdor.

Céardochis – The commercial centre for the many craft items made by the Néartanians. Home of the Hall of Clothiers and the Builders' Hall.

Chorich Castle – A border fort in Yrusian.

Claymont – A village in western Dagâran, on the River Redwater.

Coèdnis – Located in Néartania, on the edge of the Great Forest. Home of the Woodworkers' Hall.

Colaste a'r Teisen – The training school for Ranusian adepts, to turn them into Waymages. In Ranusheim.

Commonweal of Veylindré – A federation of six Lands: Dagâran, Garûnalond, Isle of Ranu, Lènium, Néartania, and Yrusian.

Cristail Keep – A border fort in Néartania.

Crullfeld – The location of a farming collective in Talamdor.

Dagâran – One of the six Lands of the Commonweal of Veylindré.

Deepwoods Keep – A border fort in Néartania.

Fenland – A substantial area of marsh and fen, which skirts the Inland Sea of Yrusian, to the north and west.

Fionnan – Centre of the wine-growing region in Dagâran. End of the Great South Caravan Route.

Fort of Ranu – The only entrance to the Isle of Ranu.

Garûnalond – One of the six Lands of the Commonweal of Veylindré.

Garûnashavn – The principal port of Garûnalond. Home of the Hall of Messengers.

Havim – Country of pirates and slave traders. Loose alliance with Talamdor.

Homing, The – The central settlement of the Fenland.

Iascan – The main centre of the fishing industry in Yrusian. Home of the Fisherfolks' Hall.

Inland Sea – A large inland sea in Yrusian, the southern part of which forms the border with Néartania.

Irnvein – A mining village to the north of Nordvein in Dagâran.

Isle of Ranu – One of the six Lands of the Commonweal of Veylindré.

Lèniashaven – The principal port of Lènium, where the shipbuilding industry of Lènium is based.

Lènium – One of the six Lands of the Commonweal of Veylindré.

Luvodican – The capital city of Dagâran. Home of the Hall of Weaponcraft and the Warriors of Dagâra.

Mathven – Located in Yrusian, a port at the mouth of the River Yrus. Home of the Hall of Mariners and Shipbuilders.

Mirunan – The capital city of Garûnalond. Home of the Hall of Justice and the Academy of the Watch.

Mistbourne Keep – A border fort in Néartania.

Mount Talamu – In Talamdor, mountain sacred to Talamu.

Muilléan – Located at the mouth of the Ranu River. Home of the Hall of Papermakers.

Myndorian – A town to the West of the Dagâran Range. Commercial centre for the mining industries of Dagâra. Home of the Hall of Metalworking.

Myner's Gap – A pass through the Dagâran Range between Nordvein and Myndorian.

Nailach – The northern port in Havim.

Néartania – One of the six Lands of the Commonweal of Veylindré.

Néartanis – The capital city of Néartania and its main port. Home of the Hall of Plenty.

Nellènium – The capital city of Lènium. End of the Great North Caravan Route.

Nordkeep – A border fort in Néartania.

Nordvein – A village to the east of the Dagâran Range.

Northern Range – A range of high mountains which divide the habitable parts of Garûnalond from the Northern Wastes beyond.

Plavin – A village in Lènium, home of Raewe.

Porusport – An inland port at the confluence of the Rivers Porus and Yrus. Start of the Great South Caravan Route. Home of the Hall of Traders.

Ranusheim – The capital city of the Isle of Ranu. Home of the Wayzenmoot and the Hall of Scriveners and Printers.

River Caethwas – Located in Talamdor.

River Choris – Located in Yrusian.

River Clearwater – Located in Néartania.

River Cristail – Located in Néartania.

River Elvan – Located in Garûnalond.

River Iascus – Located in Yrusian.

River Mistbourne – Located in Néartania.

River Porus – Located in Yrusian.

River Ranu – Located in Isle of Ranu.

River Redwater – Located in Dagâran.

River Roillon – Located in Talamdor.

River Yrus – Located in Yrusian.

Roillby – A village on the eastern bank of the River Roilldon in Talamdor, due east from Talamunem City.

Roilldon Fort – A border fort of Talamdor.

Rorschak – The location of a copper mine in Havim.

Rouliris – A town on the Great South Caravan Route in Néartania, north-west of Céardochis.

Ruslen – The capital city of Yrusian.

Silvin – A village in northern Talamdor.

South Plains Keep – A border fort in Néartania.

Taellingsford – Located at the southern tip of Lènium. Home of the Hall of Tradition.

Talamdor – The country of the enemy, ruled by the Prophet of the One.

Talamunem City – The capital city of Talamdor.

Tarrin – A village in western Yrusian.

Talmis – Centre of the agricultural region of Néartania. It hosts an annual Cattle Fair.

Ullmass – Site of the annual Wool Fair in Garûnalond. Beginning of the Great North Caravan Route.

Vale of Berlysian, The – Fertile area in the centre of Lènium.

Virunon – A village in south-west Yrusian.

Yrusian – One of the six Lands of the Commonweal of Veylindré.

Acknowledgements

I would like to thank my son, David, for suggesting, one day in October 2019, that I might enjoy writing a fantasy novel, for his many helpful suggestions and for his warm support throughout the process; Mike Richards for his encouragement and excellent advice; early readers Yvonne Aburrow, Stephanie Bisby, and Sue Jacznik; the members of Northampton Writers Group for their encouragement along the way; and Jon Davies for his efficient editing. And last, but not least, Maz, David and Becky Woolley, for being the best family in the world.

Printed in Great Britain
by Amazon

44205763R00198